WHO SHOT
THE
SCHOOL BOARD?

WHO SHOT
THE
SCHOOL BOARD?
LUST, GREED AND GLUTTONY
a Novel

JOHN J. DUNN
WITH MARYLYN R. DUNN

Oliver Press ⓞ
New York

WHO SHOT THE SCHOOL BOARD?
LUST, GREED AND GLUTTONY
by John J. Dunn
www.johnjdunnauthor.com

Published by Oliver Press ❶, New York

Names: John J. Dunn, author, with Marylyn R. Dunn
Title: WHO SHOT THE SCHOOL BOARD? LUST, GREED AND GLUTTONY
a novel / John J. Dunn
Description: New York: Oliver Press ❶, 2018
Identifiers: ISBN 978-1-7327085-0-1 (softcover) ISBN 978-1-7327085-1-8 (ebook)
Subjects: BISAC: Fiction/murder, school board, education, sex, crimes, corruption

Book and Cover Design: Ghislain Viau of Creative Publishing Book Design
Cover Art: Bogdan Maksimovic

To my sister, Dorothy, for stepping up to the plate.

ACKNOWLEDGMENTS

It is important to have friends who are smarter than you and I am lucky enough to have no better friends than Artie Perkins and Philip Bartlett.

Thank you to my brilliant first readers Hope Ross, Marilyn Patterson, Phyllis Brown and Rita Gallo.

Special thanks to Phil Bartlett for his tireless efforts in helping edit this book and for his encouragement throughout the writing process. Without Phil's help, this book may not have happened.

Thanks to Jim Ingoglia who gives an educated and helpful response every time he is asked. Thanks to Jen Reilly.

Many thanks to go John Hanc, professor at NYIT. Kudos go to Mateo Alarcon, a social media genius.

Gratitude to Ghislain Viau for the superb cover. Thanks to Ali at SHAH-TECH and to Andre for the photos.

CHAPTER 1

TOM FOSTER CHARGED INTO A WORLD FILLED WITH LESS charm than a rectal thermometer.

This cold December night was the first time Tom had been back to John Bogart High School since graduating six years ago. He was there to write his last report for his Master's Degree in Education. Tom cringed at spending an evening in a room filled with sanctimonious parents and school personnel. He hoped to be in and out of this boring school board meeting in a few hours. He'd go home, finish the report on school politics and mail it to his professor.

When he arrived tonight, Tom Foster knew nothing about school politics or the rumor his neighbor, Bunny Krouse, serviced her five kids' principals at the beginning of each school year. His ignorance would change dramatically within minutes.

Looking around the auditorium Tom felt uncomfortable, a little creeped out. People sat and stood in clusters and spoke in loud voices. Eyes flashed, heads shook, faces wore vile, scheming expressions.

As Tom walked to the back of the auditorium, he heard glass breaking ten feet above him. Instinctively, he put his hands over his head. A woman a few feet away screamed as shards of glass rained down. Someone screamed, "It's that Dragon Gang at it again." Across the room, a guy yelled, "Somebody better do something about them, and quick."

Tom Foster had no clue by the end of this frigid evening his life would change forever.

§

Luis Gomez, head of the Dragon Gang, came from El Salvador four years ago. Gomez's small frame belied his strength of purpose, and his piercing brown eyes scared the shit out of anyone with half a brain.

Rumor had it Luis Gomez had killed twenty people. Four killings occurred during his journey from Central America to the United States. The first death happened in his front yard in El Salvador.

Throughout El Salvador, gangs demanded protection money from locals in every town. The gangs called it 'rent.' Families lived in constant fear. Luis Gomez's father couldn't pay the 'rent' one week, so a local gang member dragged Luis's mother out of her house. In front of Luis, his two sisters and his father, the gang member put a bullet in her head. Luis watched in disbelief. Slowly, he walked into the house and found his father's gun. He came out of the house with the gun hidden behind his back, carefully approaching the gunman. The murderer scowled at the young boy.

Luis walked within six feet of his mother's killer and quickly pulled the gun from behind his back. Before the gunman raised his arm to shoot, Luis shot his mother's killer right between the eyes, then pumped four more bullets into his face, neck, chest, and crotch.

Fifty neighbors gathered in the yard and five quickly picked up the gunman's body and threw it under a low-lying bush. One neighbor collected money from the crowd, including Luis' grandmother's life savings of three hundred dollars. Luis' father placed all the money in a leather wallet with the boy's Salvadorian passport and said to his son, "Luis, you must leave immediately."

Young Luis knew this meant he must go to the United States. He had heard hundreds of stories of people escaping gang violence by immigrating to the United States. Usually, more planning occurred before such a trip, but today there was no time. Word of what happened would bring local gang members to Luis' house seeking vengeance.

Within an hour, Luis was packed and on the road. His father gave a hug so strong, so loving, it carried young Luis through Mexico, over the border to El Paso and then to New York City.

The trip through Mexico took four months. Along the route, Luis took three more lives. The first happened as soon as he got into Mexico. Luis was walking along a dark road when a man appeared from the bushes and demanded money. Luis reasoned, "If I give the thief my money, I won't eat today, but at least I will live."

Luis handed over his leather wallet, the one his father gave him before he left El Salvador. The thief smiled. "Now, take off your clothes."

Luis responded, "Please, I'll have nothing to wear."

The thief grinned, "You can have your clothes back after we finish."

At first, Luis didn't understand. As the thief came toward him, the young boy realized what was about to happen. Luis slipped a knife out of his pant's pocket. He let the thief come right up to him and in the darkness he plunged the knife deep into his attacker's neck.

The man fell onto the dirt road. Luis reached down, took his wallet from the molester's hand and ran as fast as his legs would go. Luis didn't stop running until he reached a small bodega a mile up the road. He purchased a piece of candy, and the owner of the bodega immediately knew this young kid's destination was the United States. The owner saw two or three young people like Luis pass through his store each week, but he sensed this boy was different, less worldly, softer, and gentler.

"What's your name?"

"Luis."

"Listen carefully, Luisito. There will be people on the bus trying to pick your pocket. Keep any money in your shoe. After you get off this bus, you'll have to take another bus to the border." The old man gave young Luis a medal of Our Lady of Guadalupe. "Keep this near your heart for protection." The store owner rubbed Luis' head and wished him well.

The bus arrived ten minutes early, and Luis hurried aboard. He had the exact amount in his fist to avoid showing his wallet. He saw an empty seat next to a woman; she tried to pick his back pocket as soon as he turned to sit down. Luis quickly moved to another seat. The bus ride took four days and stopped countless times. Luis exited the bus only to go to the bathroom and buy snacks. When he reached the end of the bus line, Luis was unsure what to do next. He was sore and stiff from sitting for so many hours.

A young woman selling bus tickets informed Luis where to find the bus which would take him to within five miles of the US-Mexican border. "The bus isn't scheduled to leave for six hours."

The bus stopped in a small business district right in town. Luis bought two tamales and a bottle of soda; then, headed for the shade of a big tree to wait for the bus. Luis finished his meal, leaned back against the tree trunk ready for a short nap when the sound of gunshots rang loudly in the scorching sun. Luis jumped to his feet and hid behind some nearby bushes.

A family of four ran in his direction blocking his vision. Mother, father, and two young children ran frantically toward him. As the family reached Luis, they yelled, "Follow us." Luis ran with them for another mile.

The father stopped and pointed to a farmhouse two hundred meters away. "We live there."

Luis followed closely, and when they finally slowed down, the father explained to Luis the shooting in town was a massive robbery of all the stores by a local gang. The gang had kidnapped four young children and some old people to hold for ransom.

The mother told Luis, "Stay for a few days until the dust settles, then venture back into town and continue your journey."

Luis accepted the generous offer which included food, shelter, and safety. Days passed, and Luis felt the best he had since leaving El Salvador. Days turned to weeks, and Luis remained. He helped with farm chores, content in his new surroundings. The family treated him like he belonged.

One late afternoon while repairing a fence at the end of the property, Luis heard gunshots coming from the house. As he reached the beginning of the corral, he saw all four members of his new family kneeling on the ground, two men with pistols standing over them.

The first man shot a bullet in the father's head. The mother was next. When Luis saw the second gunman shoot the two children, he fell to the ground, his legs unable to support him. Luckily, the grass was high enough to obscure Luis from view.

When Luis heard the men drive away, he tried to get up, but his legs were too weak. He lay in the grass until dark. The fresh night air gave the young boy the strength to stand and walk toward the house. He cried as he came closer to the bodies of his new family. He ventured within ten feet of the people he had recently come to love, knelt on the ground and whispered prayers his mother had taught him.

After ten minutes, Luis rose and went into the house. He took a leather bag off the hook in the kitchen, threw fruit and bread into it and headed for the root cellar in the back of the house. Luis wasn't looking for food. He wanted the two pistols his new father had hidden under burlap bags at the far corner of the root cellar.

Luis put the larger pistol in the leather pouch, partially crushing the fruit; the other gun he stuck in his pocket. He quickly hurried out of the cellar and ran across the field to the road, never looking back. It would have been too painful. About five miles up the road, Luis spotted the two men who several hours ago had destroyed his new world. They sat on the hood of their car drinking and laughing.

Luis approached the Chevy as quietly as a soft rain falls on grass. When he was ten feet from the two monsters, he took the gun from his leather bag, aimed the gun at their backs and pulled the trigger twice. The two fell off the car hood onto the ground. Luis ran to the front of the car. The men were still alive. Luis looked each man in the eye and shot two more bullets into their groins. He stood over them and watched the two die painfully.

Hours later Luis remembered how he enjoyed watching the monsters suffer. He felt good, and this feeling became stronger during the next few years. Luis didn't run from the two dead bodies. Instead, he calmly took the food out from his bag, picked up the monsters' guns and placed them in his bag, along with numerous rounds of ammunition he took from the back seat of the car. He sat in the front seat and stuffed his mouth with food, then took off. Luis glanced at the guns in the pouch. "Now, I'll have no problem finding food." The security of knowing he'd have food made the thought of his trip to New York bearable.

Luis' fifth killing occurred after he successfully crossed the U.S. border in El Paso. Luis was out of money but armed to the teeth. The young boy's empty stomach growled. He hadn't eaten in twenty-four hours.

On the dark, lonely road, Luis tripped over the body of an old man. He bent down and saw the man was dead. Holding his breath, Luis riffled through the old man's pockets and pulled out a wad of dollars.

Luis stood up realizing he wasn't alone. A boy about eighteen stood ten feet away with a big smile on his face. Luis recognized the colors on the boy's shirt as those of a famous gang in El Salvador. "Thank you for finding my money," chuckled the older boy pulling out a ten-inch knife from his pants' pocket.

Luis shook with fear, but slowly slipped his hand into his pouch and gripped one of his guns. The older boy moved closer to Luis and demanded, "Now, throw the money over here."

Suddenly, Luis lost all sense of fear. Recollections of the man who killed his mother in their front yard, the man who wanted to rape him, and the two men who killed his new family, flashed through his mind. "No more, no more," Luis cried out in the night air." The older boy looked puzzled by Luis' scream. The older boy's face held a confused expression as Luis pulled out the gun and shot him dead, firing bullet after bullet into his attacker.

Two months later, Luis arrived at the door of his grand-aunt in New York City. She welcomed her grand-nephew with open arms. Luis soon connected with the street people in the neighborhood and his new friends introduced him to the local gang which Luis quickly joined.

§

Tom Foster stood in the auditorium of his *alma mater* and watched the custodian sweep the broken glass off the floor. He listened for more information about the Dragon Gang but heard nothing. Everyone else present was on to something else. The chatter buzzed with anticipation of the meeting about to begin.

The warm auditorium decorated with large evergreen wreaths made Tom reminisce about the fun he had in high school. On stage, a huge artificial Christmas tree stood festooned with colorful ornaments. Next to it, a long rectangular table with metal chairs waited for seven assholes to sit and begin their monthly con.

The place jumped with raucous noise. The packed crowd's babble deafened Tom's ears and ignited the room with electricity. No one came tonight for quiet introspection. These parents hadn't been out at night since last month's meeting, and they hungered for an evening of lively entertainment; some gladiators and a few lions would be a good start.

For the past half hour, Tom needed to use the bathroom. He cursed the cold winter wind and his procrastination for not going before he left home. As a kid, Tom hated using the school bathroom and tonight was no exception. He scanned the area and remembered a bathroom off the hallway. A short creepy guy with terrible skin blocked the entrance. Tom whizzed past him with a polite, "Excuse me." To Tom's surprise, the bathroom urinals didn't smell; all the stalls had doors, the receptacles filled with hand towels and toilet paper. Tom finished his business and headed for the door, steeling himself for a boring night ahead. As he gripped the doorknob, Tom heard two noticeably upset women talking loudly. He put his ear to the wooden door and listened.

"Betty, you idiot, you swore you wouldn't tell anyone. You're my cousin, my best friend. I trusted you."

"I'm sorry, Emily. I didn't tell anyone except Felicia."

"And Felicia Estes told the world. I can't believe it, of all people to tell!"

A loud buzzer signaled the start of the school board meeting. Tom listened to an angry Emily Cusack threaten her cousin. "You'll be sorry for this, Betty Kramer, but that's for later. Now, I have to go on that fucking stage and pretend everything is alright."

"But Emily, I…"

"Tell that bitch, Felicia, I'm informing Bunny Krouse, it was she who told everyone about Bunny blowing all her kids' principals."

"Emily, wait…"

"You wait until your husband wakes up and sees what's happened to his new Corvette."

Betty knew her cousin came in contact with some dangerous people through her school board connections; she knew the threats were real.

Tom waited for the two women to leave and when he heard quiet, he turned the brass doorknob to go, but before he could escape, some loud-mouthed woman yelled, "What did Emily want?"

"Thank God, you're here, Felicia. Emily's furious I told you about Elliot. She threatened to get even with me, and you, too. She threatened to tell Bunny Krouse you were the one who told everyone about the blowjobs."

"Fuck Bunny. Let's go inside and watch the fireworks."

The two women walked off, and Tom darted from the bathroom. This cold night had suddenly turned hot, and now Tom didn't want to miss a minute.

§

Tom Foster came out of the bathroom and paused in the back of the large auditorium looking over the crowd. A chill shot up his spine when it finally dawned on him what was going on: "These people aren't here for their kids. They're here for themselves."

In the front of the auditorium, seven school board members sat behind a blue courtesy curtain donated by the PTA. The parents hoped the table curtain would spare the audience the disturbing sight of certain school board members scratching their genitalia during meetings. "Worth every cent," snickered a PTA president.

Tom looked for an empty seat and heard someone call, "Tommy, Tommy Foster, over here." The cry came from thirty rows down the long center aisle. His neighbor, Bunny Krouse stood on her seat waving frantically, "Come, sit here." Tom felt self-conscious, but Bunny wasn't taking no for an answer. Tom marched down the freshly polished center aisle almost knocking over an old woman handing out fliers for an upcoming blood drive.

"Hi, Mrs. Krouse, some crowd tonight, not an empty seat."

"I saved this seat for a girlfriend, but now she can find her own."

"Thanks, but I almost knocked over an old lady coming down the aisle."

"That's a good friend of mine, Esther Portnoy."

"What's a woman that old doing at a school board meeting?"

"That's a long story. I'll tell you about Esther another time. Let's catch up with you. It's good to see you, Tommy. I can never decide if you look more like Brad Pitt or Robert Redford. Of course, you're taller and younger than both."

Tom blushed.

"What brings you here tonight?"

"I'm home for Christmas. I finish my Master's Degree in Education next month. I've one more report to do and decided to write it on how local school boards make policy."

Bunny laughed, "You'll see how they do it tonight."

"I hope so."

"By the way, do I hear wedding bells anytime soon?"

Before Tom answered, the school piano played *The National Anthem*, and the loud din in the room abruptly stopped. Everyone rose. 'Rockets Red Glare' saved Tom from answering.

After an off-key attempt at singing, two hundred people took their seats and watched a heavy-set man bang a gavel trying to begin the meeting. Talking continued and only stopped when some loud-mouthed man screamed, "Shut the fuck up."

The man with the gavel welcomed everyone, "I'm Lou Marinara, chairman of this school board. I want to remind you we have monthly school board meetings to give the community a chance to see what's happening in our schools."

Bunny turned to Tom, her foot-long ponytail almost smacking him in the face. "The bastard makes me puke."

Bunny's smooth, creamy complexion, blue eyes, perfect nose, light brown hair and petite shape were a pleasant sight. Tom tried not to think of the recent revelation about his neighbor's popularity with school administrators.

Chairman Marinara finished, and a large group in the front of the auditorium clapped madly. Bunny whispered, "Those are Lou Marinara's trained seals. The woman Marinara handed the microphone is Emily Cusack. She's announcing she's won't seek another term on the school board."

The microphone blared Emily Cusack's words all over the auditorium, "Pressing family obligations don't permit me to seek another term, but I want each of you to know what a privilege it has been for me to serve you these last five years."

Tom recognized Emily's voice as the angry lady outside the bathroom.

Again, Bunny leaned closer to Tom, "Emily's husband gave her an ultimatum. She either leaves the board, or he's divorcing her. For the past year, Emily has shacked up with Elliot Rush, the district's human resource director. Rumor has it Emily's pregnant, and when her husband finds out, he's going to throw her out of the house. Such a shame, they have three young kids."

"How did it happen?" said Tom and Bunny flashed him a look, "You're joking, right?"

"I mean…"

"Each school board member heads a committee. The school board chairman hands out the committee assignments. Emily chaired the human resource committee, and Elliot Rush was the human resource director. They spent too many late hours together putting Lou Marinara's cronies in jobs."

"Who's this guy Rush?"

"He's been here four years and has quite a past. Elliott Rush was the principal of the most prestigious public elementary school in Manhattan. He had it made. Teachers liked him; parents loved him that is until one day a first grader's mother found her daughter dead in the family brownstone, battered by the little girl's father."

"Dead?"

"Yes, the father physically abused the little girl for over a year. The child came to school with bruises and cuts on her arms, legs, and face. Teachers reported the cuts and bruises to Rush."

"Did he investigate?"

"Listen. Elliot was scared shitless of the little girl's father. 'The little girl probably just fell,' Rush told the teachers.

"Why was he scared of the father?"

"Today, a principal's position is very political. The girl's father held a respected reputation with city leaders. The mayor sought his advice, and the City Schools Chancellor came to the house for cocktails. This father had juice. No one wanted to come up against him."

"What eventually happened?"

"The day they found the child's body everyone ran for cover. Poor Elliot tried to run but had no place to hide. His world collapsed. Investigators appeared everywhere. Reporters huddled at every exit, and the State Board of Regents came to the school and discovered the teachers had reported the abuse to Elliot."

Tom interrupted, "Whoa, slow down, Mrs. Krouse."

"To make a long story short," whispered Bunny, "Lou Marinara, a second cousin once removed to Rush stepped in and had Elliot transferred here to the boondocks. Bringing Rush to our district accomplished two things for Lou, his extended family owed him, and he gained a grateful ally as the head of HR. Elliot Rush would follow orders and appoint whomever Lou wanted."

Tom felt uncomfortable with Mrs. Krouse whispering in his ear but didn't know how to avoid it. Bunny leaned still closer; Tom couldn't think of anything to say so he took his father's sage advice and kept quiet.

"Tonight, all eyes are focused on Emily Cusack. Tomorrow, every tongue in town will wag in the supermarket," Bunny declared, with no glee in her voice. "I'm no fan of Emily Cusack but..." Tom could see Bunny took no pleasure in Emily's misery.

Bunny, no stranger to heartache, lost her husband, Sal, when he fell fifty-five floors on a windy, March day. The skyscraper project employed the first all-woman construction crew in the city's history. Sal, the token male, hated his co-workers and the feeling was apparently mutual.

Bunny feared little in life, but after Sal's death, Bunny was on her own, and scared. The only child of parents who were only children, Bunny had no aunts, uncles, cousins, nieces, or nephews. Sal had even less family, a few distant cousins scattered across the country. When they married, Bunny and Sal agreed they'd have several children. This way their kids would have relatives. Sal wasn't supposed to die, and Bunny wasn't supposed to be left alone with five school-aged children.

"Until a few minutes ago, I only ever said hello and goodbye to Mrs. Krouse," chuckled Tom. "Now, I'm speaking to her like she was 'Bunny from the Block' and she's schooling me who's screwing whom. Life's funny."

§

The committee reports ended, and Lou Marinara asked for scheduled speakers to come to the podium. "Those of you who telephoned the school board office during the week and requested speaking time will be called in the order you phoned the office."

A young mother stepped to the podium. "My name is Liz O'Brien. Please excuse my nervousness." Mrs. O'Brien explained her daughter was 'on the spectrum.' Bunny whispered to Tom, "On the spectrum means autism." Tom's education courses discussed autism, but he kept it to himself. He wanted to hear what this mother had to say.

Mrs. O'Brien explained, "My daughter received an incorrect placement from the district for the second year in a row. The school put my thirteen-year-old in a regular education class for half the day and the other half in a class for the emotionally disturbed."

Mrs. O'Brien had everyone's attention. "My daughter is autistic, not emotionally disturbed. She doesn't belong in a regular education class or an emotionally disturbed class.

Mrs. O'Brien's voice cracked with emotion as she continued to tell the whole auditorium how her daughter had been the butt of terrible bullying from her regular education classmates. "Boys bump into her and touch her inappropriately."

Tom looked around the room to see the crowd's reaction and glimpsed the creepy guy who'd blocked the bathroom before. The guy nodded to the chairman from the back row. Tom later discovered this guy was Eddie Fisher and the nod indicated Eddie would be following Mrs. O'Brien all over the place attempting to find dirt on her and her daughter.

Mrs. O'Brien expressed the pain she and her child experienced this past year. "I received no help from my daughter's school or the parents of my daughter's tormentors."

Tom turned to Bunny, "Now, will the lady receive help?" Bunny didn't answer and continued to listen.

A parent on the other side of the auditorium loudly heckled Mrs. O'Brien. A group of obnoxious PTA parents joined in.

Bunny explained, "Those pieces of garbage feel special educational programs take away from important school activities such as football and dance club."

The cruel heckling continued for what seemed an eternity. Tom almost jumped out of his seat. "How can the chairman permit this outrageous behavior? He's not saying a word."

Finally, Marinara told Mrs. O'Brien, "This isn't the proper venue to discuss your problem. You have to speak to your school's assistant principal. He handles special education."

"But, I've conferenced with him, and he won't listen to me."

"I find that hard to believe. It's the assistant principal's job."

Rocco Pinzone, the district's superintendent, spoke up. "The school board doesn't involve itself in individual cases. It makes policy for our schools. The board leaves the micromanagement to individual school principals. If you can't resolve your complaints with him, you can always file a petition with the state board of education."

The chairman took the microphone from the superintendent. "I'm sorry, but your time's up. May we have the next speaker?"

A woman two rows in front of Tom screamed, "You receive all the services in the world, but you're never satisfied. You people always want more for your kids." Another mother looked over at Mrs. O'Brien and called, "School board members dedicate their time and efforts to our children. You should be grateful."

Tom glanced at Bunny's face and imagined Bunny leaping over the rows and smacking the woman, but Bunny disappointed him and remained seated. Tom wanted to say something to this loud-mouth but reconsidered it. He figured he better get the lay of the land before jumping into a fight.

Tom looked around an auditorium filled with rude, calculating, arrogant people. "Where are these people from?" He was learning more tonight than in any education courses he'd taken.

§

Speaker followed speaker, each uttering little more than extravagant praise for either the chairman or the board. Whenever something good was said about one of the board members, the school aides clapped so hard Tom's ears hurt. He still didn't understand the chairman planted these cheerleaders in the audience to protect himself from would-be trouble-making parents.

"Lou Marinara interviews potential employees this way," explained Bunny. "The sole activity required of these people consists of listening for any criticism of Lou Marinara in the schools, help him snag votes at election time, and give a donation twice a year to Marinara's favorite charity, The Fund-For-A-Better-Marinara."

The chairman called, "If we missed anyone, please step up now."

A black man dressed in clerical garb approached the podium. He and eight other black ministers were the only people of color in the room. All eyes watched the clergyman walk from the rear of the auditorium to the podium. Whispering tongues followed Reverend Jonas Thompson down the center aisle.

Bunny saw Tom's befuddled expression. "These men from small black churches across the district's southern tier came tonight to ask the board for the umpteenth time to distribute services equally throughout the district. I heard tonight they plan to be more vocal. The board shortchanges their schools with supplies, with programs, and with competent teachers.

"Will they be successful?" asked Tom.

"No, they won't. The ministers' problem is they don't have anyone on the board who owes them anything. The black community never elects anyone to the board, and the board remembers their impotence when it comes time to provide services."

As the prominent, burly minister came close to the podium, Tom recognized Reverend Jonas Thompson, the father of his childhood friend, Jeremy. Reverend Thompson, a tall, two-hundred-twenty-pound middle-aged man approached the speaker's podium and politely attempted to verbalize his group's reasons for being there tonight.

The Reverend began, "Thank you for the opportunity to present..."

"Excuse me, sir, but it's customary for a speaker to introduce himself before he speaks."

"I apologize. I'm Jonas Thompson, Pastor of God's Pentecostal Church on 5th Street."

The all-white PTA members and more than one board member snickered.

Bunny's face turned beet red. "Those bitches! Imagine how hard it is for a black man to come here and speak in front of these white racists, ask for something, and then have people laugh at him?" Although furious, Bunny said no more. Tom worried Bunny might take a stroke right in her seat.

"Mr. Thompson, I don t see your name on my list as having contacted the school board requesting speaking time."

"But, Mr. Chairman, I telephoned the office and spoke to the secretary on Monday."

"Well, I don't see any record of your request; therefore, I can't allow you to speak." Marinara paused, then pointedly asked, "You sure you're not mistaken, Reverend?"

Ignoring the innuendo, Reverend Thompson replied, "Mr. Chairman, I'm sure I contacted the school board office and spoke to your secretary."

"There's always next month," yelled one of Lou's trained seals, giggling loudly.

The minister asked the chairman to allow him to speak, and tomorrow the school board clerk could verify the error.

Lou mustered his usual arrogance and pronounced, "I'm sorry. That isn't possible. We follow the rules here."

"Does the Board think I'm lying?" asked the Reverend.

The chairman shrugged his shoulders, and said, "Are there any other speakers who have properly applied for speaking time?"

A white man in a V-necked undershirt chanted, "Liar, liar, liar."

A young black man sitting with the clergy jumped from his seat and charged across the auditorium. In seconds, he faced his father's tormentor.

"Holy shit, I know that guy," Tom gasped.

"You know the guy in the undershirt?"

"I know the other one. Jeremy Thompson is his name. I played little league with him. We were close."

Tom didn't believe his eyes. The white guy punched Jeremy in the face, and within seconds all hell broke loose. People screamed, stood on their seats, and threw papers.

Others grabbed their coats and quickly ran for the exit.

Bunny pulled Tom's arm. "It's time to leave. I've been to this party before."

§

Bunny locked arms with Tom and pointed, "Look, over there, the guy with the blue suit and red tie. He's one of the people running for the board. He's Vince Miller. Nobody can figure out what he does for a living. Someone said he buys bowling alleys and uses them to launder money for Asian gangsters in Chinatown."

Tom looked and saw a man of forty-five, swarthy, salon-tanned and immaculately dressed, chatting up a blousy, middle-aged blond. "Who's he talking with?"

"She's Lettie Grimes. She announced this afternoon she's running for a seat."

"Will she win?"

"Lettie Grimes is the parent associations' fair-haired darling. She headed the district PTA when her kids were in school. She'll win for sure. That leaves three vacant seats."

"But I thought all seven seats were up for grabs."

They are, but the incumbents, Marinara, Father Grant and Ted Kowalski will keep their seats."

"Is this Lettie Grimes any good?"

Bunny rolled her eyes. "I served on quite a few committees with Lettie. I put her in her place more than once, but she'll be good for the kids if she doesn't fall into the trap Emily Cusack did."

Three mothers, each twenty pounds overweight, wearing elastic waist pants said hi to Bunny and gave Tom the once over. Teachers and supervisors greeted Bunny with great respect. Mrs. Krouse was a force to be reckoned in the district.

"Tommy, we need young blood. Why don't you run for one of the vacant seats?"

"Me? I don't know anything about the job."

"You think those seven clowns on the stage know anything? You told me you receive your Master of Education next month. You know more than you realize. Look at those two." She pointed to Lou Marinara still standing on the stage talking with Ted Kowalski. "Those two have been on the board six years and don't understand the kids are the reason a person serves on a school board."

Tom looked at Lou Marinara, a man with no cheeks, only jowls, weighing two hundred and forty pounds and standing 5 foot 7 inches. A cheap suit, an inexpensive toupee and a pasty face added to his dashing appearance.

The chairman walked off the stage, his gait more waddle than walk. Lou Marinara believed serious facial expressions gave his windbag speeches gravitas. He wants to be taken seriously, and when presiding over a public school board meeting, perched high atop a stage, microphone in hand, talking to a nervous parent with no microphone, he is. Lou seemed a man of strength on these occasions, but at closed school board meetings, with the other six of his elected peers, not so much.

"What's Kowalski like?"

"He's vice-president of the board. Ted's like a Miss America runner-up. If for some reason Lou can't make a meeting, Ted fills in."

"Do you like him?"

"Ted disgusts me. He scratches his crotch and assumes no one sees him. He's oblivious."

"Does he always look disheveled?"

"A former board member who sat next to him gabbed, 'Ted's dandruff is so bad if a bug crawled across his shoulders, the bug would leave footprints on his jacket.'"

"What a group."

"This is why we need someone as smart as you. I've watched this group for years, and each one has an angle."

"I don't have the time or the interest, Mrs. Krouse."

"Don't kid me. I saw your face when Marinara shut the minister out of speaking time, and I saw the disgust in your eyes when the special education mom tried to explain her problem."

"I'm beginning my career. It takes a lot of time."

"Sure, start your career in education, but what better way to gain the inside scoop? See how and why decisions are made."

"But…"

"Hold on Tommy. Here comes Lettie Grimes."

"Bunny Krouse, who do we have here?"

"Tommy Foster, this is Lettie Grimes."

Ignoring Bunny, Lettie continued. "What brings you here, young man? What a fine addition to this sad group."

"Tommy finishes his master of education degree next month. He came to check us out."

"Well, Tommy Boy, if you need any help checking anyone out, I'm always available. Let me give you my number." Lettie rummaged through her purse for pen and paper.

Bunny quickly broke in, "Tommy has to go. I'll give him your number. He lives down the street from me." Bunny grabbed Tom's arm and ushered him away from Lettie.

"See what I mentioned before. We need Tom Foster. See the trash running for our school board."

Tom stayed silent trying not to trip as Bunny pulled him away from Lettie.

"She said, 'Tommy Boy.' I guess it's time for me to stop using Tommy and call you Tom."

"It might be better, Mrs. Krouse."

"And, it's time for you to call me Bunny."

The principal of Bunny's local high school, Frank Fontaine, passed and gave her a big hello. "Bunny, I hope we'll see you tomorrow at the meeting. It's in my office."

"I'll be there. See you at one o'clock."

Frank winked and continued on his way.

"Mr. Fontaine's the new principal in town. He's great. I fought hard to get the job. The Board almost vetoed him for this other guy who's connected to Lou."

"Mr. Fontaine seems like a friendly guy."

"He's more than friendly. He means business and the high school is almost up to where it should be."

Tom noticed a softening in Bunny's voice.

"Frank will do what's necessary to make his high school the kind kids deserve. Drugs have all but disappeared. He's made it the safest high school in the district."

"How did you help him?"

"I made sure he wasn't one of Marinara's flunkies."

"What's his pedigree?"

"He understands life. He's a widower, no children."

Tom sensed a spark in Bunny's eyes as she talked about Frank Fontaine.

§

Bunny and Tom reached the parking lot and her friend Esther Portnoy had taken up a new post handing out blood drive reminders. Tom watched as these loathsome people spilled out of the school into the parking lot and chatted in small groups. Evil seemed reluctant to end the evening. These parents were out for the night without their kids, having a ball, and weren't eager to return home.

Bunny commented again about the school board election, "It doesn't look like many people plan to run for the board this time. The only new ones so far are Vince Miller and Lettie Grimes and a few candidates from different PTA groups around the district."

"Did you mention a priest on the board?" asked Tom.

"Yes, Father Grant. Initially, he caused a stir, the whole church, and state thing, but it quieted down. The religious groups, Catholic, Protestant and Jewish all have schools in the district. Their schools are entitled to funds from the state and federal governments, like busing, non-religious books, and supplies."

"They're also entitled to some part-time non-religious teachers," remembered Tom from one of his courses.

"For years these schools received almost no services. The parent-teacher associations made sure they didn't. As a result, each religious school decided it needed someone on the school board to watch out for its interests. The group decided to put one of their people on the board. Father has district-wide support from every religious group. He wins easily. His group is capable of electing four out of the seven board members if they wanted. The PTA parents realize they better keep their mouths shut or they'll find themselves outnumbered on the board."

"What type of guy is Father?" asked Tom.

"He's a class act. He tries to stay above the fray, and he leaves any infighting to the other board members. When it's time for the religious schools to receive their lawful share of the educational pie, Father visits the superintendent. They meet on a quiet afternoon and Father makes damn sure his groups receive the services they deserve. He's also an attorney and the only one on the board respected by everyone. People may not agree with him on certain issues, but they know he doesn't play games with their kids' lives. He's also the only one on the board who even considers the concept of right and wrong in making a decision."

"I'm surprised no senior citizens run. They have the time."

"They should. Seniors sure have an incentive," said Bunny. "Each year their school taxes go higher and higher."

"You should get your older friend, Esther Portnoy, to run."

"Funny you say that. I've tried for years to get her to run, but she says she'll think about it, then when the time comes she says she is too busy with her kids."

Tom looked at Bunny more than a little surprised. "She has kids in school?"

"Yes, but they're her grand-kids. Her daughter and son-in-law crashed their car into an eighteen-wheeler over on the interstate and she's been mother and father to her three grand-children ever since."

"You don't know anyone else?"

"I know a lady, Mary McMurray. She has her hair done in the same place I have my nails done. She retired a few months ago from an executive position in a large corporation. What a pistol! Mary McMurray doesn't hold anything back. I thought I'd ask her to run for the board. She has the time now."

Tom was half listening. His eye caught something a hundred feet away. "That's quite a car Mrs. Grimes hopped into."

Bunny strained her eyes in the dark parking lot. "The red Mercedes she jumped into is Vince Miller's. Lettie's a slut."

A horn beeped, "There's my son, Norris. He passed his driving test last week and considers himself a big deal picking me up. I don't want him double parking."

Tom waved to Norris. As Bunny ran to the car she yelled, "Tom, stop by my house this week. I want to talk more about you running. If I don't hear from you, I'll stop in to see your mother on Friday."

Tom watched Bunny's seventeen-year-old son floor the gas and pull onto the street, banging the curb as he drove away.

"Run for the board! Not in a million years!" Tom insisted.

§

Tom stood in the dark parking lot dazed by tonight's events. A young black man hurried past, and Tom recognized his boyhood friend, Jeremy Thompson. "Hey, Jeremy, are you alright?"

Jeremy looked back at Tom. Big smiles appeared on the both their faces. "Tom, how the hell are you? It's great to see you."

The two hugged. "You ok? The jerk gave you quite a shot."

"I'm okay, but I'm mad as hell. You saw what happened to my father and the other ministers tonight."

"I couldn't believe it. The way they treated your father and that lady with the special education daughter made me so freaking angry I wanted to go up on the stage and give that Marinara guy… "

"Tom, I know how you feel. Those bastards are something. They have all the power, and we have none. We need people like you on the board. People who react the way you do. Listen, let's have coffee and catch up. Maybe, I can talk you into running for the school board. My ride is here, and I don't want to walk home. Are you free tomorrow morning?"

"Sure. What's a good time?"

"How's 11 o'clock?"

"At Starbuck on Main Street."

"Perfect. Tom. I miss our talks."

"I do too, Jeremy."

A horn beeped from across the parking lot.

"Have to go. See you tomorrow."

Tom watched Jeremy head for his ride. It felt good seeing his old friend again.

§

By now, Tom's car was one of the few cars were in the parking lot. He looked around and saw the short guy from the bathroom walk out of the school and walk toward the far corner of the lot. For the first time, he noticed a small group of young men standing in the shadows, leaning on two dark-colored cars.

A security car drove by and blinked his headlights at Tom. The driver yelled from his car, "It's time to head out, young man."

"I'm leaving, officer," Tom responded.

The patrol vehicle pulled beside Tom. "What's a nice young man like you doing at a school board meeting anyway?"

"It's what I've been wondering for the past two hours," Tom joked.

The guard waited for a more definitive answer.

"I have a paper to write for a graduate course. Unfortunately, I picked school boards as a topic." The guard flashed Tom a grin and said, "Good luck, son. Better go. It gets dangerous around here after everyone leaves."

The security car sped towards the far end of the lot and pulled next to a dark green SUV. The guard exited his vehicle and spoke to the four young toughs and the creep from the bathroom. The guard pointed over in Tom's direction.

When one thug lit a match, Tom recognized him. Yesterday, Tom went to the library to do research for tonight's meeting. As he headed for the library door, he passed this punk and a cluster of teens. The thug gave him a look of annoyance that signaled Tom had rudely interrupted an important speech in progress.

Tom tried to avoid eye contact with the thug, and when he reached the lobby, he noticed a guard looking out the window at the same punk. "Some group," remarked the guard.

Tom responded, "Who is that guy?"

"Luis Gomez."

"What's his story?"

Before the guard answered, a deafening scream bellowed from a lady leaving the library with a small child in hand, "A rat! Look over there. It ran across the floor."

The guard rushed over to calm the lady and child.

Tom continued to the library's education section and forgot about the thug outside, but tonight from across the parking lot, Luis Gomez gave him the same menacing glare. The problem was this time it was dark, late and Tom was alone.

Tom jumped into his car, slammed his foot on the gas, and left the parking lot with the smell of weed floating into his partially open window.

Driving home Tom's mind returned to the crazy meeting he'd just attended. All the names Bunny Krouse mentioned raced through his mind: Lou Marinara, Lettie Grimes, Miller, Vince and Ted Kowalski.

The only name even remotely familiar was Mary McMurray. "The name is familiar. I'll ask mom. She knows everyone in town."

§

Although breakfast dishes cluttered the breakfast table, Tom Foster's meticulous mother didn't care. Alice was just happy she caught Tom before he left for the day. Having her son home from school, made Alice Foster feel young. Everyone teased, "Tom's your favorite," but Alice denied it with the usual parental response, "I have no favorites. I love all my children the same."

"How was the board meeting last night?"

"Outrageous! I've never seen anything like it. The school board members were animals and the audience worse."

Alice laughed, "I remember those meetings."

"Good thing I met Mrs. Krouse. She helped me navigate the storm."

"What did Bunny have to say?"

"She had a lot to say, but most troubling was her suggestion I should run for the school board. Bunny feels the board needs new blood."

Alice Foster said nothing.

"And, Bunny," Tom continued, "It's what she wants me to call her, wasn't the only one who expressed it last night."

"Who else said it?"

"Remember Jeremy Thompson? I used to hang around with him when we were kids."

"Sure, I remember Jeremy. I liked him. Why was he at the meeting?"

Tom told his mother how Jeremy's father attempted to speak and how some jerk punched him in the face.

"Poor, Jeremy."

"The guy gave him quite a sucker punch."

"What made Jeremy think you were interested in running for school board?"

"I made the mistake of saying how disgusted I was with the arrogant disregard shown parents when they asked for help. Jeremy wasted no time saying I was the type to make a difference."

Alice waited for Tom to say more. When her son offered nothing, she said, "So, are you interested?"

"I can't believe it, but I considered it," answered Tom. "I'm meeting Jeremy at eleven o'clock at Starbucks."

"You are running for a seat on the school board is not the worse idea I've ever heard. You may have a Master's Degree in Education, but the school board experience would teach you more about education than any degree. You'd meet people from all over the metropolitan area, the movers, and shakers in education."

Tom had no response.

Alice continued, "You want to go into education to help people, and a seat on the school board would give you a chance to make real changes in our district and, as a side benefit, develop job opportunities in other districts."

Tom looked at his mother as if her halo had fallen off.

"Don't look at me that way! You have to be practical, Tom. You don't have to give up your idealism, but sitting on a school board would develop contacts for the future."

Tom said nothing.

"I bet you'd find a job quickly sitting on the school board."

"But I can't work in the district if I am on the board."

"Correct. But you can work in a neighboring district."

Alice saw Tom consider what she said.

"Tom, you'd be an asset to any school as a teacher. One last thing, I'm your mother, and I know better than anyone you need to be involved in things which gives you the chance to help people. You were like that since you were a kid."

Alice looked at the kitchen clock. "I'm late for work," she lied. "Have to go. We'll talk, later."

Tom's mother gathered her coat and pocketbook. "Where are my car keys? You borrowed the car last night."

Tom looked in his pocket and pulled out the keys.

"Tom, we have a big family, and we're friends with a lot of people. I can contact your aunts; they'll be thrilled to help. You were always ready to help everyone, and if you decide to make the leap, everyone will gladly pitch in. It'll be fun."

"Thanks, mom. I appreciate your support. It won't be easy. I haven't been in many organizations like I'm sure the other candidates have.

"Did Bunny mention anyone who is running?"

"There are three incumbents, Father Grant, Ted Kowalski, and Lou Marinara. I met a middle-aged woman named Lettie Grimes who's running. Bunny mentioned a retired businesswoman, Mary McMurray. I think I know that name from somewhere. I can't remember."

Alice smiled, "Well, I remember Mrs. McMurray. You're sure you don't. Think, Tom, think."

Tom looked at his mother and saw her enjoy his apparent memory lapse.

Finally, she said, "Remember kindergarten Sunday school?"

Tom's mind was still blank.

"You acted up…"

Tom's mind clicked, and he laughed. "She threw me out of class the second week. She scared me so much; I wouldn't go back until I was in first grade."

"Mrs. McMurray was great. She came to the house to see if she could convince you to return to Sunday school, but you wouldn't even come out of your room."

"I must have sublimated the whole thing. I didn't remember it until right now," Tom chuckled.

"When you went back the next year, Mrs. McMurray wasn't there. I met her at the twelve o'clock mass a few weeks later, and she told me her job had become so demanding she had to give up Sunday school. She told me she didn't think she was cut out for teaching. We both laughed, and I wished her luck with her job. Over the years I heard she was promoted again and again until she became second in command at Everything Foods."

"I could see her playing hardball with the big boys," said Tom. "What a small world."

"I have to leave. We'll talk tonight."

"Do you know any of the others?"

"I've heard of a few of them. But I have to leave, speak tonight. I want to hear about your talk with Jeremy Thompson."

Alice Foster hurried out the door before her son asked why she was leaving early this morning.

Tom called out to his mother, "Do you think the years have mellowed Mrs. McMurray a bit."

Tom's mother yelled back, "The years have mellowed all of us."

§

After his mother left, Tom sat at the kitchen table thinking. At twenty-six, he had a good sense of himself. He realized he was lucky, born with good wiring, good looks, good personality, athletic ability, loving parents, supportive siblings, and a close extended family. He appreciated his support system and recognized the huge head start he had in life. Usually, Tom accepted all these advantages without question, but last Sunday something clicked.

The priest said it all. "Life's a poker game. It deals you a handful of cards. The cards don't determine if you are a winner. It's what you do with those cards." Tom admitted he had done little with his gifts. He always had an excuse. "I'm not old enough. "I have to finish school." "I have to find a job."

Maybe the school board was the place to start his adult life, stop making excuses, and use the advantages he received at birth to help people.

CHAPTER 2

MARY MC MURRAY LOOKED OUT THE WINDOW AT HER FLOW-erless gray garden. "Thank God, Mark planted those evergreens last year. They give some color and block the road."

Three months had passed since Mary McMurray left Everything Foods, and she was bored silly. "I miss the excitement and stimulation I had for thirty years? I miss my friend and mentor, John P. Stanford."

J. P. Stanford and Mary Elizabeth McMurray jelled from day one. Together, they built a winning team based on mutual respect and in the process accomplished a great deal, both for themselves and for the company they headed.

Few at Everything Foods knew Mary's exact role in the company or the hefty paycheck she received each month, but it was only a third of what John P. Stanford reaped.

Mary was tough as nails at the bargaining table. "I want more money. I help this company make big profits each year, and I deserve far more then I get."

Stanford tried to satisfy his friend with, "The board won't give you any more money this year, Mary. But I'll give you more power. I'm nominating you for a seat on our board of directors. You'll be the only woman on the board."

Thanks to Mary McMurray things changed for women during her time at Everything Foods. Mrs. McMurray was the first to defend female employees handed a bad deal. She leveled the playing field for many women in the company.

As the years passed, Mary turned into the eyes and ears of her CEO. Power fuels the will, and there was no stronger will than Mary McMurray's. Her official title was special assistant to the CEO of Everything Foods; her real role was second in command.

Mary's career ended one Thursday afternoon when Stanford didn't return from lunch. Her boss, her confidant, and her friend dropped dead of a massive heart attack on the paddle board court at the New York Athletic Club.

J.P. Stanford's death knocked Mary right out of the office. A month after J.P. died, the new CEO arrived in the office and behind him his shapely, twenty-four-year-old assistant, Tammy, with 6" heels, short skirt, and tiny blouse which covered little of her abundant breasts.

Mary left two weeks later. Everything Foods threw her a party and gave her a generous retirement package and generous cash payout, an amount larger than the company's comptroller had ever seen.

Mary accepted the fact her time was up and slammed the office door on the way out. She flew down Madison Avenue, surprised at how happy she felt to be out of Everything Foods forever.

§

Since leaving her job, Mary fell into the habit of sitting on the window seat in the dining room in late afternoon drinking a cup of hot tea. She'd sit and muse about her future, trying not to think about becoming older. Mary didn't want to admit she felt real fear for the first time in her life. Old age was the monster living in her mind.

Mary's one living child, Ellen, lived in New Jersey with her husband, Todd, and their son, Harry. When Ellen told her mother, Todd had been reassigned to New Jersey five years ago both Mary and Ellen cried for one day straight.

Being home all day left too much time for unpleasant memories to creep into her mind. Since retiring, thoughts of what happened thirty-two years ago here in this dining room plagued her. At ten o'clock on July 15, Rodger, a nine-year-old who lived next door, climbed the high fence in his backyard. From her kitchen window, Mary watched the young boy reach the top of the fence and grab the adjacent tree's lowest branch. Rodger's both hands held the branch tightly. He was ready to play Tarzan, King of the Jungle.

Rodger swung from the oak tree branch. His left hand reached for a nearby wire, then his right hand. The wire sparked and crackled, and the light shone for blocks.

The electrical current whipped through Rodger, waving the little boy's body back and forth like a flag blowing in a storm. Rodger's frail frame shook so violently his arms separated from his hands and he fell twenty-five feet to the hard ground.

Veronica, Mary's older daughter, watched from the dining room window. Mary heard Veronica let out an ungodly, inhuman scream. She ran to her daughter, but Veronica kept screaming and screaming.

Mary grabbed her little girl and engulfed the child in her arms. Veronica shook violently for a minute and then fell limp. Mary scooped her ten-year-old into her arms, ran to the phone and dialed 911.

Seven minutes later sirens screeched outside the house as Mary held little Veronica tightly in her arms. By the time the ambulance arrived, she knew Veronica was gone. The medics gently pried the child from Mary. The EMT guys worked on the little girl for forty minutes. Mary sat there staring numbly, knowing her baby girl born with a severe heart murmur was gone forever.

§

Mary pulled a clean tissue out of her dress pocket and wiped her eyes. "Retirement isn't for me. I'm retiring from being retired."

Mary McMurray needed a new challenge, a fresh start, and an opportunity to be an integral part of something again. She reached for the local newspaper lying beside her. A small notice on page five read, "New Senior Center opens next week on Twentieth Avenue."

The ad encouraged seniors to get involved now. "The Center needs experienced organizers to develop activities." The notice made Mary uncomfortable. She didn't dislike old people, but she felt little in common with them.

Mary turned the page quickly and saw an article for the upcoming school board election. Mary had an attack of nostalgia, her mind harkening back to when Ellen and Veronica were in grade school. Mary yearned for those years when she, Mark and their daughters sat at the dinner table as a family.

"If I had children in school, I might try to win a seat on the board, but I don't. That ship sailed years ago."

An editorial on the same page explained the importance of attracting people of integrity to serve on school boards. The editorial emphasized, "Candidates do not need to have school-age children to run. We encourage all citizens with or without children to seek a seat on the board." The editor also encouraged parents of students in private and religious schools to serve.

The editorial concluded with a list of organizations interviewing candidates who wanted their support in the upcoming election. A list of civic, religious, and political organizations provided candidates with times and dates to appear.

The first interview listed was next Tuesday at eight o'clock, in the conference room of the Raccoon Lodge. For years Mary passed the Raccoon Lodge and never failed to get a kick out the six-foot snarling statute of a male raccoon sitting in front of the ugly building.

Mary decided she'd skip the Raccoon interview and wait for the PTA ones the following week. Then she thought, "No, damn it, if I do this, I'll put all my effort into it." She vowed not to miss a single interview, not even the ridiculous Raccoon one, and besides, she'd finally see the inside of the hideous looking building. "This will be fun. I have a lot more to give before the Grim Reaper appears at my door."

§

Mary waited impatiently for Mark to return home from work. Finally, Mary heard her husband's footsteps on the porch. Mark knocked on the front door. "He forgot his house keys, again. Well, he'd better remember them in the future, or he'll be spending a lot of time sitting outside."

As soon as Mark took off his coat, Mary told him she had a decision to make, and she wanted his input. As soon as Mark heard the word 'input,' he knew his wife had already made her decision.

Mark and Mary had this ritual since they were married. Out of love and respect for her husband, Mary always tried to make him fancy he was a part of her decision-making process. Mark helped perpetuate this simple ruse, a ruse he secretly enjoyed.

Mark said, "You have my full support, and I want you to know how proud I am of your community spirit. This town has no idea what's in store for it. I love you Mary and will do anything I can to help. We'll apply for a second mortgage to pay for your campaign. The sky's the limit where my Mary is concerned."

Mary walked over to Mark and gave him a big hug. "I love you."

As happy as Mark was that his wife had a new focus in her life, he knew the world of politics was rough. He remembered his two years as a political party committeeman and cringed how quickly nice people changed when given even a little power. "If anyone can resist the temptation, it's Mary. Her moral compass always points in the right direction."

"I have to find out who my competition is."

Mark didn't mention there was a glossy poster of a candidate named Vince Miller on the telephone pole by the deli. Mark thought the guy looked slick and wasn't thrilled with the prospect of Mary rubbing elbows with this guy, but then he reminded himself this was Mary and that she could handle someone like Vince Miller blindfolded.

§

No matter how finely tailored or expensive his clothes, Vince Miller made any garment look slick, pretentious and showy. His hair perfectly in place, his fingernails sharply manicured, his wristwatch properly bejeweled, Vince Miller walked through life always looking for the next mirror.

Vince liked women, and a particular type of woman liked him.

Miller had a PAST, and he was desperate to keep it hidden. He tried to maintain a certain level of sophistication in speech and manner but failed to do either. Vince's educational background obtained on the streets of the city didn't add to his appeal. His school sweater read, "School of Hard Knocks."

Vince's sophistication came from deals made in a world where horse heads were placed in beds as incentives to close a deal. Vince drove a red Mercedes, wore thousand dollar shoes, and five thousand dollars Italian made suits, made by a tailor who had absolutely no taste.

Vince knew why he wanted to be on the school board. He wanted to get his hands on the spoils of public office, and the school board jobs he intended to sell would provide those spoils.

Miller knew that ordinarily the higher the elected office, the more jobs there were to give out, but the lowly school board was the exception to this rule. School board members had far more patronage opportunities than any other local elected officials. School jobs numbered in the thousands and Vince salivated every time he thought of doling out each job for a price.

§

Alice Foster pulled out of the medical building parking lot, sore from the biopsy. She arranged the procedure before work. "This way no one needs to suspect anything is wrong. I don't want to die. I want to see the rest of my kids get married and take my grandchildren to the park. Please, God let me survive."

The prescription drug lessened Alice's pain, but it still hurt when she arrived at work. "Tonight, I'll order pizza for dinner."

"Dr. Shawn didn't seem too worried when he said, "The test will be back soon. We will know nothing until then."

"If the test is positive," asked Alice, "Will you operate right away?"

"Yes."

"I prefer to wait until my son, Tom, makes some decisions."

"What decision is more important than your health?"

Alice hesitated, "He's thinking about running for the school board."

The doctor looked at his old friend from elementary school, "Alice Jennings, I mean, Foster, if the test is positive and the growth is small enough I plan to have you in surgery within twenty-four hours."

Dr. Shawn Hayes saw a tear appear in his friend's eye, but continued, "If the growth is too large to operate on now, we'll give you a month of radiation to shrink its size. If the test is inconclusive, we'll wait and see."

"I don't want Tom to worry about me while he's deciding to run for the school board."

"Don't worry about Tom. If he decides to run, he'll win in a landslide." The doctor paused and said, "Alice, do you remember when you and I ran for class president and vice-president in fourth grade?"

Alice smiled. "Those were the days, not a worry in the world. It would be nice if it were always like that, Shawn. I'm so glad I shared my mom's chocolate chip cookies with you at lunchtime. Fourth grade was so long ago, but you haven't changed a bit."

"Alice Jennings Foster, now I want to repay you for those delicious cookies."

Walking to the parking lot Alice thought about the cookies Dr. Shawn remembered so clearly and her mouth watered. She had an urge for a cup of coffee and something sweet. "I'll make a quick stop at Starbucks and buy a cup of coffee and something sugary. I'll eat them at my desk.

Alice parked in front of Starbucks and got out of the car then she remembered Tom was meeting Jeremy there. She couldn't recall the time of the meeting, but she didn't want to take a chance of running into her son. Disappointed, she drove to work with neither coffee nor cookies.

§

A cold wind whipped down Main Street as Tom Foster arrived at Starbucks. He made sure he arrived early enough to find a table in the back. Starbucks was between breakfast and lunch, so there should be plenty of empty seats.

As Tom walked to the back of the store, he saw two tables occupied by six guys all dressed the same. In the center, sat the Gomez thug he ran into at the library and again in the parking lot last night.

The entire Gomez group gave Tom the evil eye. Tom attempted to nonchalantly turn and go to the front of the store without being noticed. He knew he'd failed when he heard the group laughing.

§

Jeremy walked into Starbucks right on time. The two friends hugged each other and sat down, unsure where to begin. Jeremy asked, "What the hell were doing there last night?"

"I'm writing a report for school," Tom explained. "Last night was the first school board meeting I'd ever attended. And I don't want to go back anytime soon."

"It was a trip," laughed Jeremy.

"Two old friends who haven't seen each other in a long time should start by asking each other what they've been doing for the last seven years, but under the circumstances, I'll ask what the hell was last night about?"

"First, Tom, it's great to see you."

"Same here, Jeremy, I've missed talking to you."

Both knew the other meant what they said.

"Tom, it's been a while since little league, but the basics haven't changed much. The district constantly shortchanges African-Americans, the same way as when you and I were in school. Remember when you came to my elementary school to see my science project. I saw how surprised you were to see the peeling paint on the walls and the leaks in the ceilings. The day you came, it rained cats and dogs. I was embarrassed about showing you my project with water dripping from the ceiling. The ink on the poster smeared so badly you weren't able to read it."

"I remember."

"You were great. You made a joke how the dripping water from the ceiling made my Mississippi project look realistic."

"We had fun that day, Jeremy. I remember your mother was head of the bake sale, and she slipped us a big piece of her apple pie, and we didn't have to pay."

"Sometimes, I wish we were back in elementary school."

"Me, too."

"So, again, what happened last night? Everything suddenly spiraled out of control."

"Tom, it's the way they treat us. We go to a meeting, and they figure out some reason why we can't speak. The meetings are all pre-rehearsed. Everything is scripted at the closed meeting the week before."

Tom listened intently.

"If you noticed, our little group had the only black faces in the place. It's hard for people who aren't black to understand how it feels to be the only people of color in a room of two- hundred whites. I wish I didn't feel that way Tom, but it's the way most black people feel when they're in a room of all whites. When they snickered and mocked my father, I wanted to stand up and give it to someone, but I couldn't decide who to go after. There were so many, but when I heard the guy chanting, 'Liar, liar…,' I had to do something."

Tom put his hands over his ears and bent his neck toward the table, "Holy shit, the rudeness, the disrespect, the freaking nerve!"

"It happens all the time, and I won't pretend it doesn't hurt. We contact the school board office to find out how to file a simple complaint, and they hang up on us. We go to the office to complain, and the secretary tells us there's no one there even though we see the people walking around. They don't care. They know we can't do anything. We've no one to help us."

"Why don't you run for the board, Jeremy? You're an articulate guy. People like you."

"They might like me, but they won't vote for me."

"There are a lot of African-Americans in the district. They certainly would vote for you once they met you. You'd receive white votes, too."

"Yes, some white folks would, but I can't get enough of those votes to be elected. I can't march into the local Elks Club and ask for votes. I probably wouldn't even get in the front door, and if they did let me in, they would be so freaked out, they wouldn't listen to me. They may not lynch me, and they may even be polite, but vote for me, not a chance."

Tom knew his friend was right.

Jeremy continued, "Let's say they allow me to speak, and then someone like you gets up after me. Who do you reckon they'll support?"

"The white guy, but if I went around and introduced you to these people, bring you to my family's clubs, you'd reap a lot of votes."

"No disrespect Tom, but it shows how little you know about what it's like to be black. With all the advances you might think have happened in society, our neighborhoods are very separate, very far apart. When a black man or woman strolls into a restaurant in a white area, he doesn't see anyone whom he resembles."

"I agree," said Tom.

"If a black family moves into a white area and wants to go to church, the family is the only black family in the church. After a few weeks of being the target of odd looks, they decide it's too uncomfortable to continue to go. Black people want to at least speak to God in peace."

"But you have to admit; the world is changing."

Jeremy gave his friend a look. "Tell me, Tom. How many black families are at your church each Sunday? I bet there isn't one."

Tom tried to picture a Sunday church service to counter Jeremy.

"Tom, stop racking your brain. The answer is one black family, occasionally. I checked your church, and five or six others in the school district's northern tier, and you know how many had any blacks in regular attendance? *Nada*. None. In this day and age, segregation is alive and well, even in church. Someone wrote the most segregated hour of the week is eleven o'clock on a Sunday morning."

"What about black voters? If we campaigned hard in the district's southern tier, we'd pull the vote out for you. Don't forget Jeremy; there are seven seats on the board. Even if only you are elected, it would be a start. The board would have to at least listen to you."

"The black vote doesn't come out for school board elections. We're lucky if they come out to vote for president or governor. The black turnout for school board elections has been so small in the past; the white board members see that and ignore us. But if you run we could get out the vote. Tom, do you want to help us?"

Tom didn't answer immediately. He tried to express his determination with, "Sure, Jeremy, but I want to see you on the board. You're so much more knowledgeable about what's going on."

"Tom, I appreciate your confidence, but the number of votes I'd pull from my area will be minimal. If we add the voters you will convince to vote for a black man, we'd lose so badly the members elected would be more emboldened to continue ignoring the southern tier of the district."

"So, this is where it ends? We do nothing. We let those bastards continue to fuck with you. We let them deride any black man who wants a fair share of the educational pie?"

"No. It's not what I mean."

"What the hell do you mean, Jeremy?"

"If you want to help, run for the board. You'd be a shoe in. You would attract young voters, especially the girls, with your good looks. They'd presume they voted for that movie actor, what's his name. I mix up all the pretty white guys, which one again?"

Tom pushed Jeremy good-naturedly. "Oh, and you with the Denzel good looks would do the same."

Both laughed. It broke the tension.

"Seriously, Tom, you're twenty years younger than any other candidate. I'd be able to convince more black voters to vote for you than for me. The black community is tired of putting its eggs into a losing basket. I know I'd convince them they were backing a sure winner, one who would be on their side."

Tom assured his friend, "I'll think about it."

"You don't have much time. The board of elections starts distributing petitions in two weeks. You'll have a month to collect enough signatures of registered voters, Republican or Democrat, to get on the ballot. We have less than two months."

"I'll call you tomorrow. I can't promise anything. I came to a meeting at my old high school last night as research for a report to finish my Masters, and in less than twenty-four hours, two people are pushing me to run for the school board. I have to look for a job. I'm twenty-six years old and starting a new career. I have student loans, and I still live in the house where I was born. I sleep in the same bed, in the same room I did when I was five."

Jeremy ignored Tom's rant. "Who else asked you to run?"

"The lady you saw me with last night at the school board meeting. I'm headed over to meet a principal she introduced me to last night. He might give me a job."

"You know you can't work in the same district that you are on the school board?"

Tom didn't answer but stood and headed for the door.

"I'll call you tomorrow, Jeremy. We'll talk more."

§

Luis Gomez and his posse were still in the back of Starbucks when Jeremy and Tom left.

Luis turned to his second in command, Elmer Rodriguez and joked, "What's the black boy up to now?"

"I'll check it out."

"I guess he didn't learn his lesson the last time," said Gomez.

Luis and Elmer were interrupted by another gang member. "I got a call from the high school. There's a problem. Someone complained about the product's quality."

The whole group rose in unison and walked out the door.

§

The day after Mary McMurray's decision to run for school board, she jumped out of bed and called her friends and neighbors to tell them of her plan to run for the school board. Mary's calls met with a great deal of enthusiasm.

One friend Mary planned to contact was Ernie Spikes, her next-door neighbor and a friend of thirty years. Ernie worked at the local cemetery as assistant cemetery director. Ernie belonged to many organizations in the community and was a well-liked guy.

Mary and Mark had a long history with the Spikes. The Mc Murrays were there to console Ernie when his wife, Martha, died.

Mary looked out her kitchen window and saw Ernie in his garden. She quickly threw on some clothes and ran out to speak to him before he turned on his leaf blower.

After a big hello, Mary broached the subject. Ernie responded, "Mary, that's great. I wanted to run for the school board when the district was much smaller, but once they combined all the districts into two, I gave up any idea of running. But I'm thrilled you are considering it and you know I'll do anything I can to help."

"I appreciate it, Ernie. I knew I could depend on you."

"When and where do I report for duty?"

"I'm not sure, but I need to have a certain number of people sign a petition with my name on it. I read they have them at the election board."

"They do but don't worry. I'll pick the petitions up for you."

"Why go to the board of elections?"

"Mary, this is a real election, run by the board of elections. Our school district is the size of a congressional district. If you win, you'll be an elected official of our state. You can use the title Honorable before your name. Sounds good doesn't it, The Honorable Mary E. Mc Murray."

"Mary chuckled, "You always make me laugh, Ernie. I can't tell you how you've already helped put me at ease."

"How long have we been friends?"

"It's a long time, Ernie."

"So, it's settled. I'm the official petition person for the future Honorable Mary McMurray. I'll distribute and collect your petitions. Mary, this will be fun."

Ernie's enthusiasm touched Mary. "I feel funny at my age going door to door asking people to sign a petition. I hate asking anyone for help. It's against my religion," Mary joked.

"No problem. You won't have to; I'll do it. Mary, helping you will be a pleasure."

"Thanks, Ernie, you're terrific."

"We'll knock them dead."

"Ernie, are you looking for more business? Isn't your cemetery busy enough?"

Both howled at the silly joke.

Mary walked to her back door relieved Ernie would get the signatures, but uncomfortable relying on someone else.

After talking to Mary, Ernie felt his stomach rumble. "It's lunchtime." Ernie went into the house, made himself a ham and cheese on rye and sat down to read the newspaper. An article caught his eye about last night's raucous school board meeting. "Darn it; Mary missed a school board meeting last night." The article described the black ministers' outrageous behavior and how they had disgraced themselves. Ernie shook his head and thought, "These people are never satisfied."

§

When Jeremy Thompson arrived home from meeting Tom Foster, he ran upstairs and peeked into his father's small office. His father was working on Sunday's sermon, preparing, tweaking and changing things ever so slightly.

Congregants of God's Pentecostal Church expected to be spellbound each week by their pastor's words, and Reverend Jonas Thompson never disappointed them. His sermons were the reason God's Pentecostal Church was packed to the rafters every Sunday morning.

Jeremy remembered how proud he was when his father won that special award last March from the state NAACP. The words of the director rang in Jeremy's ears. "Reverend Thompson, you're a treasured asset to the black community. The nine black ministers in your county nominated you unanimously for your tireless efforts in helping the poor and disadvantaged in your town."

Jeremy was accustomed to seeing stacks of papers piled on his father's desk. Today, he saw one sheet sitting atop Jonas' mahogany desk. Jeremy knew his father focused on one topic at a time.

Reverend Thompson was upset. The school board encounter last night bothered him more than anything Jeremy could recall. His father and the other black clergy planned to present a proposal for rehabilitating the schools in the district's southern tier.

After the meeting, Jonas said, "The only thing I accomplished was getting my son into a fight with some racist jerk."

Jeremy remained silent as he entered the office, unsure if this was a good time to interrupt his father. His father looked up and beat Jeremy to the punch, "Morning, son."

"Morning, Pop. Have a second?"

"Sure. What's up?"

The heat had come up, and Jonas' second-floor office was warm and inviting. Jeremy took a seat in a big, comfortable, brown leather chair across from his father and told him about meeting his old friend, Tom Foster, last night and about his meeting this morning.

"I remember the Foster boy. I always liked the kid. There was something different about that white boy."

When Jeremy finished asking his father about the possibility of Tom's running for the school board supported by the black community, Reverend Thompson sat silently. Jeremy knew his father never shot from the hip. He would mull the ramifications involved in supporting a white kid and how his decision would affect the community.

"Is Tom strong enough to help us if he's elected?"

"I believe so."

"You know, son, you have this problem."

"I know, Pop."

"Those gang members over on Smith Street can't be ignored. You had them pretty angry when you reported them to the police last year. They never forgave you. The gang had to move their operation to another part of town. Reverend Mackey defused the situation to some extent, but the threats are still out there."

"Pop, I know."

"You go around with a white boy, and it'll raise suspicions you're up to something again."

"I'll be careful, Pop. I'll make sure they know it's about school matters and education. They have no interest in either."

Both smiled. "That's for sure," said the Reverend. "Nevertheless, Jeremy, I hoped you would go out to your aunt and uncle's place in California. You want to be a screenwriter, and there's no better place to start."

"I know Pop, but I want to do this first. We'd make significant progress with Tom on the board. He's young, smart and his heart is in the right place. This chance may not come again for a long time. I promise, after we do this, I'll go out to California. This experience will give me the material to write important stuff."

"Let's set up a meeting with Tom and the other pastors."

Jeremy paused. "Sir, I didn't mention to you, Tom hasn't exactly agreed he'd run."

Reverend Thompson looked at his son with a raised eyebrow. "Maybe, we should find out before we do anything else."

"Tom promised to give me an answer tomorrow." Jeremy paused, "Well, maybe not a definite answer, but he assured me he'd give me an idea of what he was thinking."

Jeremy's father gave his son a look only an exasperated parent gives.

The phone on the desk rang. Jonas reached for it, and, Jeremy took the opportunity to leave. "See you later, Pop."

Jonas picked up the phone. "Hello, Reverend Thompson, here." Silence rang from the other end of the phone. "Who is this?"

The phone died. The Pastor slowly placed the phone back on its cradle and sat for a minute remembering the barrage of anonymous calls which stopped only a few months ago. He rushed to the office door. "Jeremy." Jonas waited and yelled again. "Jeremy, are you still here?"

Reverend Thompson returned to his desk and tried to finish his sermon, but he couldn't keep his mind off the telephone. The calls stopped only after the Baptist Pastor, Reverend Mackey, contacted his uncle, a bigwig in the police department. His uncle spoke with Luis Gomez, the gang's leader.

The calls ended, but the basis of the truce was Jeremy keeping a low profile in the neighborhood. The phone calls had upset the whole Thompson house except Toby, the youngest Thompson.

Footsteps coming up the stairs distracted Jonas from his thoughts. "Jeremy, I'm glad I caught you before you left. I've something; I want to say." But instead of Jeremy entering the room, Toby flew in. Jonas Thompson found it difficult expressing the enjoyment his special needs son always gave him. Toby was still sweet, always grateful, always the same. Toby was a gift to the whole family.

"Pop, you wanted Jeremy. I saw him go out." Toby came over and sat on his father's lap. Jonas Thompson hugged his son tightly.

Although Toby seemed too old to be sitting on his father's knee, Jonas encouraged it. "Oh, how I love you, Toby." Jeremy was a great kid, but Toby was special.

Rev. Thompson sat with his youngest son, and his mind slipped away from Jeremy's problems. Born with Downs Syndrome, Toby gave his parents more joy than their other children combined. "Unless you have a child like Toby, there's no way you can know the joy," Jonas often told people.

§

Felicia Estes was late picking up Betty Kramer for their meeting with Frank Fontaine at the high school. Betty stood at the curb outside her house. She couldn't believe the way her cousin, Emily threatened her last night. Betty shivered, not sure if the cold December air or her cousin's words caused her shaking.

Finally, Felicia pulled up in her new Escalade, and Betty quickly hopped in the car.

"You're late, Felicia. You're always on time. What happened?"

"I had some business to finish. But before I tell you about it, has your cousin Emily done anything to Arnie's car yet?"

"No. Has Emily tried anything with you?"

"Let her try," Felicia replied

"Okay, what little business has you late?"

"Well, you know the new girl who recently came into my daughter, Kim's first-grade class? She's the kid whose mother thinks who she is?"

"No, I can't picture her."

"I told you about the mother who marched into school and tried to take over the PTA. She's only here two months."

"So, what did you do?"

"I heard yesterday she's having her daughter's birthday party this afternoon. She invited all the PTA officers' kids to the party."

"I assume your Kim wasn't invited."

"You assume right. I was furious. What nerve."

"But you're not an officer, and you're not active in the elementary school anymore. Kim's your last. You're mostly in the junior and senior high."

"It's not the point. Who does that bitch think she is coming in here and trying to take over?"

Betty Kramer didn't answer the question, but asked again, "So, what did you do?"

"You know the new thing with the first graders is they don't want their mothers to stay for a party. They feel they're not babies anymore."

"Sure, it's been happening for a few years."

"I bought my cleaning lady a burner phone, and I arranged for her to call the police at four o'clock, and report there's a dangerous condition at the house, right as the party ends."

"Oh, my God. So Felicia, as the parents arrive to pick up their kids from the party, the first thing they'll see is a bunch of police cars with flashing lights in front of the lady's house."

"The parents will be hysterical."

"And, they'll never let their kids have a play date with the birthday girl again."

"You got it."

"I can't believe you did it. You're one tough cookie. So, I guess you aren't worried about Emily's threat to get you."

"What do you think?"

"Emily better watch out for you."

"Who do you think will show up for the meeting today?"

"You can bet Bunny Krouse will be there."

§

Bunny arrived early for her appointment with Frank Fontaine the day after the school board meeting. Even Felicia Estes and Betty Kramer hadn't arrived. Rego Park Memorial High School was quiet, not like two years ago when kids were hanging out the windows smoking. Bunny dragged herself up the school's large marble staircase. She felt tired from last night's school board meeting but still enraged at the board's arrogance. "The way they treated those ministers, and the O'Brien woman with the autistic daughter, was unbelievable."

"Are you here for the meeting, Mrs. Krouse?" asked Ruth Torres, the principal's secretary. "Yes, Ruth. How have you been?"

"Fine, Mrs. Krouse. Thank you for asking. Mr. Fontaine is in his office. He instructed me to send people in as soon as they arrive."

"Thanks, Ruth. I wish you'd call me Bunny."

Ruth quickly responded, "Mr. Fontaine prefers we use parents' surnames. So, per his request, I use last names for all parents."

Frank sat at his desk not at the large conference table and as soon as he saw Bunny, he rose from his chair.

"Oh, good you're alone, Frank, I want to speak to you before the others arrive."

"It was some meeting last night," interrupted Frank. "When the white guy punched the young black kid, I couldn't believe it."

"It's why I wanted to talk to you. We need a few reasonable people up there on the stage. You saw the young man I was with last night?"

"You mean the good-looking guy standing next to you when I passed?"

"That's him. His name is Tom Foster, and he is good looking. He was even as a child."

"I'll admit I was a little jealous until someone told me he was a kid from your block."

"Well, he isn't a kid anymore. I told him he should run for a seat on the school board. By the end of the night, I think he considered it."

"Does he have a chance?'

"Are you kidding? He'd win in a minute. His family is so well-known, Tom would win any election he entered. His good looks alone would ensure his win. I asked him to stop by today to meet you."

"Great, I'd like to talk with him."

"I'll stop by to speak to Tom's mom on Friday. If his mother is on board with his running, we're in good shape."

"This Foster kid doesn't have a chance of not running with you pushing him."

"If he runs, can you help with some votes and if he doesn't, will you help him get a job in some school in or out of the district."

"I can certainly try."

"I don't want you to get into trouble."

"I don't care. The superintendent scheduled a principals' meeting for tomorrow afternoon. He put in his email subject line: "STAYING NEUTRAL IN UPCOMING SCHOOL BOARD ELECTION."

"Meanwhile, he'll do all he can to help Marinara win."

Frank said, "I'll ask around and see who I can trust to help us. At least a few of the other principals will help and some teachers. Of course, it will have to be on the sneak, but we have to do something about Marinara putting his garbage into every position that comes up."

Bunny looked at him with a twinkle in her eye. "Thanks, Frank."

"Now, what about us Mrs. Krouse? Will I see you this weekend?"

"I don't see why not if you don't mind spending part of the time at a Boy Scout Jamboree. Norris has a few more months until he receives his Eagle Scout Medal. He's volunteering this weekend helping out with the Jamboree."

"You know I enjoy the kids more than you," joked Frank.

"Now, I'm the one who's jealous."

Noise in the secretary's office alerted Bunny and Frank the rest of the committee had arrived.

"Frank, what's the main thing on today's agenda?"

"Gangs."

Bunny quickly took a seat in front of Frank's desk as he walked behind it. Both giggled like teenagers hiding something from their parents. The mothers sauntered into the meeting, and Principal Fontaine greeted each with a big grin, "Good afternoon, Mrs. Estes, Mrs. Kramer, Mrs. Portnoy..."

§

Since the death of his wife five years ago, Frank had avoided romantic relationships with anyone, never mind a spitfire of a woman like Bunny Krouse, but from the first time Frank Fontaine saw Bunny across a crowded auditorium six months ago, he was hooked.

Frank and his wife had been college sweethearts. Every time Frank saw Bunny, those familiar feelings returned. Frank Fontaine wanted to marry and take care of Bunny Krouse.

§

Esther sat next to Bunny as Principal Frank Fontaine discussed curriculum, drugs, gangs in the school district and how with the help of the parents of his school, gangs and drugs have all been eliminated.

Bunny whispered to Esther, "Ask how the PTA can help elect candidates who will be responsive to all the parents of the district, not to just a hand with big mouths who come to meetings."

Esther Portnoy hated Felicia as much as Bunny did, so she had no trouble looking directly at Felicia Estes and voicing the question. Felicia and Betty Kramer bristled. Bunny sat straight in her chair ready to pounce if either lady dared say anything in response to Esther's question.

Principal Fontaine watched each woman and when he was sure all the posturing at the table had reached a safe level, he addressed the matter diplomatically. "As you know Superintendent Pinzon has instructed the principal of the district to refrain from involving themselves in the election except to encourage all parents to vote." He then told about the new science curriculum being implemented this school year.

During the meeting Bunny received a text from Tom. "I apologize, but I have to skip the meeting with Mr. Fontaine. My girlfriend, Jen, has a minor emergency and I have to go help her." Bunny smiled and remembered the 'minor emergencies' of young love. She was a drama queen at that age, too.

Meanwhile, Tom rushed to Jen's side and found her and her disabled grandmother upstairs in a bedroom. Tom saw Jen swinging a large broom at a terrified squirrel. The critter jumped around the room, on and off the bed, while poor Granny lay there, paralyzed with fear. The one window in the room was wide open without a screen.

Tom grabbed the broom from Jen and swung it in the squirrel's direction. The critter flew around Grandma while Tom tried to bat it without bruising the old lady. Tom's efforts only encouraged the rodent to become more active. The old lady screamed like an insane person, and the squirrel climbed off the bed and jumped out the open window.

Jen ran to the window and slammed it shut. Poor Grandma stopped screaming but lay on the bed in a catatonic state. Jen's cries subsided.

Tom sat at the foot of the bed and waited for sanity to prevail. The incident reminded Tom why he never cared for camping.

"I know I don't want to be a Forest Ranger. Maybe the school board is the way to go!"

§

Driving Esther home from the meeting with Frank Fontaine, Bunny decided to press her friend to run for the school board this time around. Before Bunny said three sentences, Esther interrupted with, "Bunny stop. I can't run. I have to find a job. I've run out of money. Alysia is getting out of school this year and any financial aid she gets will not be enough to pay the tuition and board."

"But what about the local scholarships from the district and some of the large businesses in the area. Kids coming out of our high school usually do well in getting some pretty substantial support, especially if they are smart and near the top of her grade like Alysia is."

Esther looked with a raised eyebrow and said. "Sure, if they aren't Jewish."

Bunny felt stupid. She knew first hand the sting of prejudice. She had experienced this first hand when she and Sal first moved to this community. People immediately thought because Bunny's name was Krouse she was Jewish. It took a while for people realized she was Irish and her husband was German on his father's side and Italian on his mother's.

"Esther, forgive me. I wasn't thinking. They always pass the Jewish kids up."

"I have to get something full-time and close to home so that I can get home right after work. My two, younger grand-children have after-school activities and are old enough to stay by themselves for an hour or so."

Bunny tried to think of something to help her friend and started to say maybe we can ask one of the school board members to help find something for Alysia. She got as far as, "maybe one of the board members could speak…" Then remembered not one member of the board were Jewish.

"Father Grant is the only member inclined to help and obviously he isn't Jewish," said Esther.

"Sure. He's the one who is backed by the parochial schools including all the yeshivas in the district. I could ask him if he knows any ways to get some help."

Neither friend said a word as they pulled in front of Esther's house.

Bunny said to her friend, "We'll figure something out." She hugged Esther and waited until her friend disappeared into the house.

Bunny looked at the dashboard clock and saw she had an hour before she had to pick up the kids. She decided to drop in to see Alice Foster. She hoped Tom's mom would help encourage her son to run for school board. Bunny knew Alice Foster worked only three days a week and Bunny was sure this was one of Alice's days off.

Bunny rang the bell and waited for Alice to answer. When no one came to the door, Bunny rang again. This time she heard footsteps.

"Hi, Bunny, sorry I wasn't quick to answer, but I was on the phone. I'd been waiting for the call since this morning. I …I…how've you been? Come in."

"Are you busy?" said Bunny feeling she'd interrupted Alice at a bad time. "Alice, can I talk to you about something?"

"Sure, Bunny, come on in."

Bunny followed Alice into the kitchen and noticed Alice looked wobbly.

"What brings you by today?"

"Alice, are you all right?"

Bunny watched as Alice sat down and cried uncontrollably. Bunny went to her friend and put her hand on her shoulder.

"I just got off the phone with my doctor's nurse, and she said I have to have more tests. I haven't told anyone, and I'm not going to until I find out some answers. My doctor was called out of town last night. His mother-in-law died and he and his wife had to leave right away. He won't be back for a week. There's nothing I can do until then."

Bunny continued to comfort Alice until she saw Alice was ready to start a new topic. Then Bunny jumped right to the point and explained how she'd met Tom last night at the school board meeting. "Alice, Tom was shocked at the school board's behavior. I suggested he seek a seat on the board. I stopped by today to ask you what you think."

"Bunny, I worry about Tom. "

"I don't know why Alice? He has the whole package."

"He has a great deal, but he and I know he wants more."

"Alice, I don't understand."

"Since Tom was a kid, I knew he was special. The fact he has the whole package might be the problem."

"He seems fine to me."

"The problem isn't now; it's in the future. Unless Tom does something with his gifts, he'll never be content."

"Running for a seat on the school board might be a start. Tom could do a lot for the community, especially the parts of the district the present board ignores."

"Going to last night's meeting and talking with you may be a sign the school board is the right direction for him. I told him he might also find a job through the contacts he makes."

"Those are two reasons to run, do some good and find a job."

"When I mentioned it to him, he bristled. Tom isn't sophisticated enough to know the world is all about contacts and there's nothing wrong with making your profession and your outside activities blend. Of course, there's a fine line you have to watch you don't cross. Tom can be black and white in his thinking."

"Alice, we do our best with our kids. Ninety percent of the qualities a person possesses are present at birth. Ten percent is the nurturing environment a child receives from his parents. We're off the hook, especially when kids become serial killers." Both women saw the humor there. "That's it, Bunny. Tom received a lot of advantages at birth. He can't sit back on them for life."

"Okay, so we better convince him to run." Bunny got up from the chair, "I have to go pick up one of my brood. Speak to Tom and tell him we'll all help, and he'll learn more about life sitting on a school board than he can imagine. He'll meet people he never supposed existed."

"Thanks, Bunny. Speak soon."

"Alice, I want to help Tom, too." The two women agreed with their eyes to help Tom.

CHAPTER 3

SCHOOL BOARDS HAVE MANY SECRETS. ONE SECRET IS THE existence of private investigators on staff.

"Initially," said Lou, "We hired a PI as a money saving tool to check on the residences of students in our district. Our attorneys told us hiring a full-time PI would pay for itself."

"How?" asked Rush.

Lou figured he'd better take the time to school the district's new human resources director about the district's PI on different projects. "Our district spends about thirty-five thousand dollars a year educating each student. If a child attends one of our schools illegally, the district is out the money."

"What do you mean by illegally?"

"Students often try to use a relative's address to register in one of our schools."

"Why don't these students want to go to their neighborhood schools?"

"Elliot, you'll see as you are here longer, some of our schools are top notch, especially in the northern tier of the district."

"How do the illegals get back and forth to school?"

"Sometimes these students live close enough to the district's geographical border to walk to and from school each day.

"How do you catch them?"

"If the district thinks a student lives outside the district, the PI follows the student after school to see where the student lives. If the PI finds a discrepancy between the address the student gave when he registered and where he resides, he reports it to the superintendent. The next day the kid is thrown out of the school.

Lou watched Elliot digesting the words and continued, "If it's too far for the student to walk home, the student might stay at the relative's house until someone picks him up and drives him home in the evening. The PI watches to see if the student is picked up and he follows the car that picked him up. It requires more surveillance hours, but the extra cost is nothing compared to educating a non-resident child."

"Is the use of the private investigator encouraged by the state Education Department?"

"Most certainly," Marinara said forcefully. "Our PI is Eddie Fisher. You'll be working with him on occasion."

"That's great," said Elliot to his benefactor.

But after Lou Marinara left his office, Rush thought, "The use of a PI may be legal and often appropriate, but the dangers a PI could pose in the hands of the wrong people..." Elliot bet Lou often misused this guy, Eddie, to uncover dirt about the superintendent, principals, and school board members.

§

Eddie Fisher saw himself as a mixture of an FBI and CIA operative. His assessment made him dangerous, delusional, and paranoid. Everyone thought Eddie Fisher wasn't important enough to be on anyone's radar. No one thought of him as anything more than a person hired to do odd jobs around the district.

Eddie wasn't an ex-cop, although he told people he was. Eddie was an ex-security guard at a Macy's in Greenvale. Eddie received a dishonorable discharge from the Army for sneaking into the commissary and stealing cigarettes which he sold to his fellow recruits.

Eddie wasn't a good-looking man. He drank vodka on the rocks so no one could smell liquor on his breath. He frequented strip clubs and knew his way around the internet's dark and dangerous sites. He developed several impressive investigative skills which he used to keep track of the lovers, the movers and the shakers in his school district. Eddie tracked down those guilty of adultery and relished it. Emily Cusack and Elliot Rush didn't have a chance. Eddie never missed someone's slip-up.

§

Emily Cusack barged frantically into Elliot Rush's office two days after she announced her decision not to run for another term on the school board.

"Emily, I wasn't expecting you."

"I had to come. Henry promised he wouldn't drive over here and break your nose before we leave for California. He's one angry man, Elliot. We leave for the Coast for two weeks to visit his parents. Hopefully, he'll calm down by the time we come back."

"I want to be responsible for the baby, if it's mine, Emily."

Emily chuckled, "I had the baby's DNA tested, and you're not the father. I showed the results to Henry, and it was the only reason he didn't charge over and beat the shit out of you."

Elliot looked relieved.

"Do you imagine for a second I wouldn't have had an abortion if the baby was yours?"

Elliot claimed, "I'm happy for your sake."

"For my sake and yours."

Elliot Rush shook his head in agreement.

"My plane leaves in two hours. I came here to make sure you know it's over between us. I have one more public school board meeting before my term ends and I don't want to see you there."

"But the superintendent insists all district office staff must be in attendance at all public meetings."

"I don't give a crap what the superintendent wants. Call in sick. Do what you have to, but don't be in the audience. I won't come by the district office so there's no chance I'll run into you again. I was an idiot ever to become involved with you, but I've learned my lesson."

"Emily, I care for you a lot."

"Bullshit! You only cared about the sex. You were a selfish lover who was only interested in satisfying yourself and convincing me to vote for whatever Lou Marinara wanted. When I think of the times I voted to put principals into schools who I knew were incompetent jerks. I only wanted to please you so that you could please Marinara. I want to die. I'm so ashamed of myself." Emily stopped and forced herself not to cry.

Emily, you were a good board member who …."

"Don't try and bullshit me, Elliot. We both know who we put into jobs in this district, from teachers to principals, but it's in the past. I can't do anything about it." She stopped speaking again, afraid the tears would start.

"Emily you weren't the only one who voted for those people. What about Father, Ted Kowalski, and the others?"

"They're bad, too. Father was only interested in the religious schools receiving their share of the pie and Kowalski is an idiot. The others will have to live with themselves." This time Emily didn't hold back her tears.

Rush sat in his seat, not knowing what to say.

Emily gained control and continued, "Let me warn you right now, if you ever try to contact me, I'll call some law enforcement agency. I don't know which one, but I'll find out, and I'll tell them to look into you and what you do for Lou Marinara. I'm sure the papers will also like a follow-up story on what you've been doing since you left your old school. You know the one where the little girl died. Elliot, you're a reprehensible pig. To think I almost lost everything for you."

Emily slowly walked over to Elliot. She spits in her ex-lover's face, then raced out and slammed the door.

§

After Emily Cusack left Elliot's office, she had one more thing to do before meeting her husband and children at the airport.

She stopped at Kramer's Clothing Store. Emily knew her cousin Betty wouldn't be working today. Betty volunteered for all of her kids' class trips. Today, her cousin chaperoned her daughter's trip to the Teddy Roosevelt Museum in Oyster Bay. Her cousin wouldn't be back before dark.

Emily parked the car in front of the store and hurried in to speak with Betty's husband, Arnie. Emily knew her cousin Betty wasn't the one responsible for the jam she was in, but she blamed Betty for bringing it to a head by telling Felicia Estes about the baby. Emily wasn't forgiving Betty, ever.

Emily entered the clothing store and waved to Arnie Kramer. She liked Arnie and often wondered what a good looking guy like him saw in a drab woman like Betty.

Emily shifted through a rack of dresses until Arnie finished with a customer. He came right over and gave Emily a peck on the cheek.

"What brings you in here today?'

"We're leaving for California for two weeks to visit Henry's parents. His mother hasn't been well lately. I was packing, and I realized I need something a little dressy if we go out for dinner. I figured I'd run in and look."

"I have some things in the back of the store. They may be what you're looking for today."

Emily followed Arnie to the back of the store. "Arnie, I have a dilemma."

Arnie looked quizzically and asked, "Can I help?"

"Well, you know how much I always liked you." Arnie looked curiously but was silent. "Arnie, I've debated whether I should tell you something about my cousin. Henry says you have a right to know."

Arnie stared at Emily. "Arnie, I wouldn't tell you if half the town wasn't talking about it. I'm talking about people who come in here, your customers."

"I don't know what you're talking about."

Emily looked at her wristwatch, "Arnie, I have to leave. So, here goes. Felicia Estes and Betty are having an affair."

Arnie turned white as a sheet.

"I hope, I did the right thing by telling you, Arnie." Emily ran for the door and missed Arnie yelling, "Fuck you, Emily."

§

Eddie Fisher walked into Elliot Rush's office minutes after Emily Cusack stormed out.

"I'm busy Eddie. I have to finish a report."

Eddie ignored Rush and sat down in front of Elliot's desk. "What was that about, Elliot?"

Rush looked up from his report. Eddie's adult acne was breaking out, and Elliot tried to avert his eyes, but Eddie stared right at him. "What are you talking about, Eddie?"

"Emily Cusack. She just ran out of here. What did she want?"

"Eddie, it's personal. There's nothing to report to Phil Turner."

"When a board member storms out of the human resource office, I want to know what happened. I'll decide what Mr. Turner should know."

Elliot knew Eddie wouldn't leave until he heard the story. "Mrs. Cusack wanted me to know she and I were through, simple."

"I want to know if she threatened to call law enforcement on you."

"You eavesdropped? You have some nerve."

"Stop the crap. I happened to be passing and heard a few things."

"With your ear to the door."

"Stop the dramatics, Elliot. Did she threaten to call any law enforcement about the district or not?"

"Yes, but nothing specific."

"Anything else I should know?"

"Nothing except Superintendent Pinzon is about to come in the door, and he doesn't like you coming in and disturbing the peasants."

"Shut up. I was leaving anyway. I have to see Phil Turner."

"And tell all I told you."

"You bet, and by the way, Phil wanted to know about the report on what job vacancies we expect in the next year. He wants the figures broken down month by month."

"Is it Turner who wants them or is it, Troy Burns?"

Elliot saw Eddie Fisher's face go beet red. Eddie walked over to Rush, grabbed him by the tie and pulled him halfway out of his chair. "If I ever hear you mention Troy Burns' name again, I'll kill you?" Eddie let go of Rush and let him fall back into the chair.

On the way out Eddie slammed the door so hard Rush was sure the glass broke.

§

Next, to Troy Burns, most scumbags look good. A con artist since he fell out of his mother's womb at the local K-Mart, legend has it baby Troy lay on the K-Mart floor screaming, "Get me a lawyer. This floor is wet."

Troy holds the esteemed elected position of councilman for the county. He sits on the council with five other nipple-slurping individuals with a combined eighty years of sucking the government tit.

Troy's years of public service provided him with far more money than if he worked in private industry. Troy recognized his many limitations early in life. Those limitations made him more suited for government service than for real work.

Burns' career as a public servant began at Donovan's Bar on Main Street. Troy sat on a barstool and watched the five o'clock local news as a reporter interviewed a retiring municipal government employee. The reporter hailed the retiree for his long career as a public servant.

Troy thought it cool whenever he heard a city worker was paid each week for thirty years; then, upon retirement was congratulated for a long, illustrious public service career as if like the worker been an unpaid volunteer. Troy felt a perverse thrill when he thought how this worker would now sit home and receive a monthly paycheck often equal to the amount he received when he worked in public service.

"It's a great con," Troy commented to his fellow drinking partner.

Young Troy felt a kinship with retirees. He understood that 'the government's tits taste sweet,' and he decided this was his career path. Before Troy could ponder his next move, a breaking news alert announced police discovered a local councilman in a seedy hotel in Manhattan with a teenage prostitute.

The man on the barstool next to Troy commented, "I guess there will be a councilman's job up for grabs. I wonder what crook will win that prize."

Within days, four local candidates emerged for the seat vacated by the disgraced councilman. Troy Burns read everything written about the story. One article said, "The governor will appoint a person to fill the position until the general election next November," Troy calculated the person appointed by the governor and serving in the position until the election would have the best chance of winning in November.

Within three weeks of the governor's appointment, Troy found the location of the lucky individual's office. He hauled his butt over to the new councilman's place and volunteered to help the appointee with his election campaign.

The newly appointed councilman was a forty-four-year-old man, trim and energetic, with an easy going personality. Troy enjoyed working for him. The councilman appreciated Troy, and they soon became friends.

During the next few months, Troy Burns volunteered as much as his day job at Command Car Rental permitted. True to plan, he became invaluable to the new councilman and in the process became the face of the council office. The paid employees were happy to have Troy helping with the workload. Burns hoped if the acting councilman won the seat, he'd offer him a cushy municipal job.

Community outreach programs organized by the council office gave Troy entre into all community organizations, clubs, teams and neighborhood projects. Soon, Troy was the go-to-guy for all these groups.

As the election drew near, petitions had to be circulated to have the councilman's name placed on the ballot. Troy organized the entire petition campaign. The councilman's name appeared on the ballot with signatures to spare. As usual, there were other names on the petition for minor party offices, district leaders, representatives to the nominating convention, etc.

Troy Burns' name was one of them put on the petition for an insignificant title. By law, truly a formality, a political party must have a person's name on the election ballot should anything happen to the candidate.

The councilman's staff strongly suggested Troy's name appear in the slot. The staff wanted to thank Troy for all his volunteer work, but no one would give up even one small party position such as representative to the county convention, and no one was about to give up the state convention slots. Troy was disappointed, but he understood human nature. He thanked the councilman and the entire staff for this perfunctory and meaningless pat on the back.

A week before the election, the councilman's wife telephoned the office. "I went into the bathroom this morning and found my husband on the floor. He must have gotten out of bed in the middle of the night, sat on the toilet and had a heart attack." Her brave front collapsed, and she cried uncontrollably into the phone.

Everyone in the office joined the councilman's wife in her sorrow. All were grief-stricken by their boss's death, but by lunchtime, they had returned to a functioning office. By three o'clock they realized Troy Burns would become their next councilman.

The other candidates had dropped out before petitions were due and the future councilman would be running unopposed. Now, their friend Troy would be their new boss. Long live the King!

§

The first time Lou Marinara and Troy Burns met they fell in love with each other's 'nesses': crookedness, money-grubbiness, and self-centeredness. They jelled immediately.

With few exceptions, most elected officials don't have the charisma, the personality or the ideology to convince people to give up their worldly possessions and follow them. Politicians need spoils, or no one will work for them.

Elected officials must be able to give their supporters jobs. A dilemma arises because most elected officials have only a few jobs to hand out. Their office staff is small, largely because the money an elected official doesn't spend on his community office, he can keep for himself.

What does a politician do about providing jobs for his supporters? He finds a good friend on a school board and has his friend provide jobs for his campaign workers.

Troy Burns quickly learned the 'isms' of public office. Everyone knows 'Patriotism' isn't one of the 'isms' needed for re-election; rather, 'cronyism,' 'nepotism' and 'favoritism' are the building blocks for any democracy and successful political career.

Troy Burns went to see his new-found friend, Lou Marinara.

"Lou, I need your help. I've got three campaign workers with no jobs. Can you find something for them in the schools? I'd be grateful."

"How grateful, Troy?"

"I realize we would work on a two-way street. So, give me some ideas. How can I repay you?"

§

Phil Turner earned his job as head of all school facilities as every Marinara employee obtained a position in the district, by doing just what Lou wanted, when and how he wanted. Most district office workers considered Turner a person in a class by himself, and he was.

Phil Turner was the only one in the district allowed to have his pit bull in the office. Phil's pet was named Eddie Fisher, a junkyard dog if there ever was one. Eddie was unpleasant to look at, and nasty as hell to be around. Few people saw or knew much about Fisher, but everyone knew his boss, Phil Turner.

Everyone in the district saw Phil as the go-to-guy when you needed something. Most people considered him indispensable, likable and reliable. His presence in the district office seemed 24/7. The information he possessed in his secret files allowed him to get away with murder. Regina Moriarty, the school district's deputy superintendent, called him J. Edgar when he wasn't around.

Turner was hot-to-trot to find something he could hold over the head of the ambitious Regina Moriarity. If he found something

damaging about Regina, he'd be a happy man. Everyone knew Regina
Moriarity drank, but no one cared. She had a good personality, and most
people liked her. Regina kissed ass like no one in the district.

§

After leaving Elliot Rush's office, Eddie called Phil Turner. He
described Emily leaving Elliot's office and the threat she threw at her
former lover.

Turner immediately instructed Eddie to watch Emily. "There may
be nothing to it," added Turner, "But you never know. A scorned lover
can be a fierce warrior."

"I can't start tonight. I have a dermatology appointment after work.
I never know when I'll finish there."

Phil pictured Eddie's skin doctor working on Fisher, not a pleasant
sight. Phil tossed the cookie he was eating in the trash can. "While I
have you on the line, is there anything new on Ted Kowalski?"

"I'm waiting to gather more information before I give you a
report."

§

As promised, Tom called Jeremy the day after their meeting at
Starbucks. Unfortunately, Jeremy was in the supermarket when he
saw Tom's name on his phone. "The noise in the store and the poor
reception might make this important conversation difficult, but if I
don't answer, Tom might be unavailable when I call back." Jeremy took
the call and went to a quieter part of the store. "Hi, Tom."

Jeremy listened as Tom told him he'd need more time to consider
running for the board. Jeremy heard Tom say he wanted to make sure
he had the time, the votes and the nerve to do it.

Jeremy reminded Tom, time was running out. "I spoke to my father
about garnering support from the black congregations. He assured me
he'd do all he could. My father has a meeting of all the black clergy in
the district, and he's added your name to tonight's agenda. My father is
sure the ministers will follow his advice and back you." The two ended
with a promise from Tom to decide by "early next week."

Jeremy put his phone in his pocket and continued shopping. Waiting was always a problem for him. Since last night, Jeremy was on pins and needles waiting to hear from Tom. Waiting until next week would be challenging. Jeremy knew exercising patience and controlling his emotions were two obstacles in his path to success. His father had always told him about the importance of both. "It makes life a lot easier."

Waiting for Tom to decide might be a test of his maturity, but explaining to Reverend Jonas Thompson why Tom was playing Hamlet would be more difficult.

§

After hanging up with Jeremy, Tom felt bad not giving a definite answer, but he couldn't yet. Tom walked to the kitchen and made himself an espresso. He sat down at the table and tried to relax. The house was empty, and the quiet felt good.

"If I run for public office nothing in my past is that bad, no affairs with married women, no barroom brawls, no romps with local prostitutes…"

"On the flip side, I don't have any record of doing anything positive, no civic endeavors, no volunteer projects, no high school football championships, nothing, nada. Someone like Jeremy has much more experience with community involvement. Jeremy should be the one running and winning. Instead, Chairman Lou Marinara wins a seat with no trouble and treats the public like garbage. What a fucking disgrace."

CHAPTER 4

LOU MARINARA'S MOTHER, ANNA, TURNED EIGHTEEN THE YEAR he arrived. The birth caused great pain to the young girl. Lou's proud father passed out cigars to his gangster friends when he heard his firstborn was a boy.

Anna recovered after ten days of total bed rest and bounced back to have three more kids in the next five years. Soon after the birth of child four, Anna Marinara developed a constant cough. The doctor diagnosed the cough as the beginning of tuberculosis. During the next eight years, the TB spread into her other lung. Breathing became more difficult for her, and Anna knew she had to do something.

Anna asked her doctor, "Please, look into more aggressive treatments."

"I received some literature on a new treatment for TB this week," said the doctor. "Saranac Lake in Upstate New York opened a state of the art facility to treat TB in some unique ways. The program requires patients to travel to the facility and be prepared to stay for up to six months."

Anna was desperate. She had four children under fifteen. Thoughts of dying and leaving them without a mother made Anna cry herself to sleep each night. Lou's father, Carmine, loved his wife and hadn't slept a whole night for the last year. Both of Lou's parents were desperate.

Carmine contacted Saranac Lake, and they told him there was a place for Anna, but she must be there by next week.

"Anna, how will you go to the facility?" asked Carmine. His small specialty Italian meat store was a one person business. "All our relatives are in the same boat. The women take care of the kids: the men remain in the store."

Anna figured a way to go upstate. "Carmine, Lou will come with me. We'll take the train to Albany, change trains and from there we'll travel to Syracuse. A train from Syracuse will take us to Lake Placid; then, a bus ride will take us to Saranac Lake."

Carmine wasn't thrilled with his wife's idea, but before he spoke, Anna put her foot down. "There's no one else to take me but Lou. He's mature for his age."

"But he's a small child. What if someone tries to rob you or…?"

"Don't be silly; nothing will happen."

Two days after the big decision, Lou and his mother began the first leg of their long trip to nowhere land. Watching his mother say goodbye to his siblings ripped Lou's heart open. He looked at his mother and knew she was thinking, "Will I see my babies again?"

Lou's brothers and sister waved goodbye as he and his mother walked down their street. Lou and Anna turned and waved, but Carmine had closed the door. His mother held back tears. The strain on her face made her features look distorted; a memory young Lou would never forget.

The express train arrived in Albany in three hours. "There's an hour layover," said Anna, "Before we board the train to Syracuse."

The second leg of the journey passed through rural towns, over small rivers, and through tall mountains. The heavy, gray sky of Central New York reflected the young boy's emotions.

Lou and his mother talked for a while, and both fell asleep halfway to Syracuse. The conductor woke them, "You have to get off here to catch your connecting train to Lake Placid."

On the last leg of the trip, the train stopped six times, but no one came aboard. The closer Anna and Lou came to Saranac Lake, the more Lou hoped he wouldn't break down and upset his mother.

When Anna and Lou arrived at the medical facility, they ate dinner. They were starving. Within a half hour of eating, the Head Nurse told Lou it was time to leave. Lou kissed his mother goodbye. Both cried and held each other close, and then she was gone.

The Nurse-in-Charge asked Lou's age. When he told her fourteen, the woman gave him a sad look, one filled with pity. "You're a brave young man." Then she said, "If you have to go to the bathroom, go now."

When the young boy declined, the nurse told him, "You have to leave now to catch your train." The Nurse took Lou's hand and brought him to the car. The cold Adirondack air blew through Lou's black windbreaker.

The young boy walked to the waiting car. He opened the door and saw a disturbing looking man behind the steering wheel. "Have a good trip back to New York," called another nurse from the large doorway.

The car was heated, and Lou rode in comfort to the train station. He was happy to exit the vehicle and get away from the scary man behind the steering wheel.

Lou's train back to New York was a milk run. It went straight to Grand Central Station. No changes were required, but the train stopped at thirty-nine stations. Lou felt sick by the time he arrived in New York.

As the train pulled into Grand Central, Lou cried behind a scarf pulled over his face. The full impact of the last twenty-four hours hit him. He had brought his mother to a place far from her family and left her there. Lou was shaking with fear thinking about what was happening to his mother and what would happen to him and his siblings if his mother never returned from Saranac Lake.

A month after Lou made the grueling trip up-state, his mother died of TB.

§

Jeremy came right home after Tom's call. He wanted to keep his father apprised of what was happening, but before he could open his mouth, Reverend Thompson began. "Jeremy, before you tell me what happened with your friend, I have to talk to you about something important. I received a call after you left from Bishop Patterson informing me my presentation before the Synod Conference changed from the last day of the convention to the second day. I can't go. My ninety-five-year-old parishioner, Mary Temple, is being buried the day after tomorrow."

"I'm sorry to hear about Mrs. Temple," said Jeremy. 'She was always extra friendly to me."

"Mary Temple has been a pillar of our church her entire life, and I have to perform the burial service."

"Where is the convention?"

"It's down in Miami, and I need you to go to the conference in my place. You're the only one I can trust to accurately express our congregation's position on certain matters for possible discussion."

"But Pop, I can't just up and leave."

"Well, you'll have to."

"How long is the conference?"

"It's a week, but you can be out of Miami in three days. I need you to attend the lectures scheduled for the second and third day." The second day concerns itself with education in the inner-cities, and although technically we don't live in the inner–city we have the same problems of neglect."

"What's the next day's topic?"

"I want you to read a paper I wrote titled, 'Have African-Americans Given Up At the Ballot Box?' Both topics are undoubtedly relevant to our community, and especially to the question of our supporting Tom in the election. I want you to listen for any new ideas."

"The topic of black people giving up on the ballot box is the reason why I need to stay here and help Tom. His election could mean a big change for our community."

"I know, but go for three days. Tom's election isn't in danger because you left for such a short time. You can fly down to Florida tomorrow and be back two days later."

Annoyed, but resigned, Jeremy headed upstairs to pack, but turned back to his father, "But Pop, Tom needs my moral support now. I'm afraid he might bail on the whole thing and then where are we? He's our last chance to hitch our wagon to someone who can help our kids."

At that moment, Jonas felt great pride in his oldest child. He smiled and said, "I am very proud of you son for being so passionate about our people, but a few days, either way, won't make a difference."

Jonas Thompson could see by Jeremy's expression his son disagreed. Jonas continued, "Jeremy, you don't know how joyful I am you want to help our kids make new strides, but as much as it would be great to have Tom on the board, I can't forget my first responsibility is to my parishioners. If it's meant to be that Tom Foster runs, it will happen; if he doesn't, I'll be as disappointed as you. But I also believe God will show us another way to accomplish our mission."

Jeremy looked at his father's face and knew his father was right.

"I'll buy the airline ticket this afternoon and make arrangements to have Deacon McGee drive you to the airport."

"Do you have the speech ready? I'll go over it this afternoon."

Jonas never doubted Jeremy's willingness to help. His son was a special person, and Jonas silently thanked God for his boy.

"Son, one more thing, I'm meeting with the other ministers tonight, and I plan to introduce the idea of backing a young white boy for school board. I want you to stop by for a few minutes in case the ministers want you to answer some questions about Tom."

"I can't, Pop. I have to go up to Toby's school and help out. They have tryouts for the district's Special Olympics Program tonight."

"I forgot. I'll dial your cell if something comes up I can't handle." Jonas walked to the stairs and hugged Jeremy, "I love you son." Jeremy hugged his father and enjoyed the security of his father's arms.

§

Jeremy Thompson was wiry and energetic. His complexion was caramel color, a mixture of Jonas' deep black African skin and his mother's lighter brown coloring making Jeremy a big hit with the girls.

Jeremy toyed with a decision to follow in his father's footsteps, but Divinity School didn't compare with Hollywood's allure of a career as a screenwriter. Jeremy felt the movies provided a more effective path for him to change people's minds. Mass media is a powerful tool for change.

When Jeremy was a young child, he sat for hours in church on Sundays mentally acting out the Bible readings his father read to the congregation. Jeremy took the biblical characters and made believe these characters lived on his block. The young boy made up stories about how these characters helped him to make life better for his neighbors.

As he grew, Jeremy acquired the tools of grammar, style, and rhetoric. Reverend Thompson encouraged his son to develop this gift of writing. Soon, Jeremy was giving ideas to his father for sermons. Jonas Thompson saw a future for his son in the clergy, but fate seemed to have a different path for his son to follow.

Jeremy loved his father and appreciated all the sacrifices Jonas made for his family. He understood his father would never ask him to go to Florida if there were any other alternatives. Jeremy would go to the Convention and make his father proud.

CHAPTER 5

URING HIS FIRST FEW YEARS IN THE U.S., LUIS GOMEZ MADE many acquaintances, but no real friends. Luis figured, "I don't need friends."

Luis' grand–aunt insisted he enroll in classes. "You're too young to be finished with school." A month after arriving, Luis was sitting in a seat in the local high school without understanding a word the teacher uttered. After a week, the Guidance Counselor placed Luis in a Spanish speaking class. Luis' attendance during the rest of the school year was sketchy, going to class an average of three days a week. During the second year, Luis' attendance rate dwindled to twice a week.

When not in school, Luis busied himself hanging out on the streets or watching TV in fellow truants' homes. Soon Luis was smoking weed and taking prescription drugs. In a short time, Luis's out of school activities not only included taking drugs but dealing them also.

Luis hadn't found a friend, and he continued to say he didn't need one. He only required bodies to help him distribute product. It wasn't until he crossed paths with Elmer Rodriguez that Luis made his first real friend in the United States.

Elmer and Luis met one day when Luis went to school. Luis had nothing else to do and was hoping he might meet a pretty girl. Instead, he met Elmer Rodriguez. The two hit it off immediately. They were what Latinos call 'simpatico.'

Both Elmer Rodriguez and Luis Gomez were born in El Salvador, but Luis came from San Michel's in the east and Elmer from Santa Ana in the western part of the country. Their personalities complemented each other perfectly. Elmer was outgoing and talkative. Luis never let his right hand know what his left hand was doing. Both found refuge in the time they spent together. Neither had any siblings living in the United States.

Elmer, unlike Luis, rarely missed a day of school. Elmer enjoyed school and wanted to learn English. Elmer realized knowing his new country's language would open doors for him. Luis's attendance improved somewhat after meeting Elmer, but his still erratic attendance caught the eye of Eddie Fisher, the truant officer/ PI. Eddie wondered, "How did a student like Luis fall through my net?"

Eddie saw no advantage of spending time figuring out how he missed this kid; rather he'd attempt to harass the student into officially dropping out of school. "I'm sure the kid's illegal and with some pressure, I can get the kid to disappear permanently and have him off the school's roster."

Fisher cruised the neighborhood streets looking for truant students and Luis was now on Eddie's radar. After a few days of observing Luis on the streets during school hours, Eddie pulled over to the curb, rolled down his window and waved for Luis to come over to the car.

Assuming, Eddie was a dealer, Luis walked over.

In Spanish, Fisher asked Luis, "Why aren't you in school?"

Luis replied, "I'm on my way to the doctor."

Eddie told the kid, "Stop the bullshit. I'd better see you in school tomorrow."

Luis was surprised to hear a person from the school using such words. Luis walked away from Eddie and headed to the next block. The following day Eddie went looking to see if Luis was in class. Luis was sitting in his seat. Eddie was disappointed. He'd hoped to find the kid on the street again and pressure him to withdraw from school and become another kid the district didn't have to waste money upon this school year.

Luis skipped classes the next day and was back on the street with a few other kids who scattered as soon as they saw Fisher's car. Luis didn't move, patiently waiting for his distributor to arrive with some product.

Eddie gave Luis a look and continued driving down the street. Eddie parked a block away, walked back toward Luis and watched as the kid finished paying for the drop. When Gomez saw Fisher, he flipped him the finger. The gesture was a mistake on the young boy's part. Eddie was a person to take seriously.

Eddie returned to the school and called his friend, Detective Weiner, at the local Police Precinct. Eddie told the detective he suspected drug trafficking close to the school and the two devised a plan. If Luis Gomez came to school the next day, Eddie would call the Detective and have him visit the school. If Luis were absent, Detective Weiner would troll the streets, pick Luis up and bring him to school.

Fisher and Weiner would speak to Luis in Eddie's office, and between the two adults, they would terrify the young student. They would search Luis and hopefully find pot on him. They would send Luis back to class, and they'd split the pot.

This day Luis was clean, much to the disappointment of Weiner and Fisher. While the two men pressured Luis, Wiener received a call and immediately left. Eddie and Luis sat staring at the other, both trying to decide what came next.

Eddie finally asked, "How much do you make from your drug sales each week?"

Luis surprised the truant officer by answering, "Four hundred a week."

Eddied asked, "Is that after you pay for the drugs?"

Luis shook his head, "Yes."

Eddie was flabbergasted this young kid made so much money for only a few hours a week.

"Do you sell any in school?"

Luis answered, "No."

Eddie knew the kid was answering truthfully but wanted to hear it again to make sure.

The kid quickly added, "If you let me sell in schools, I'd be rich."

"What do you mean?"

"The guys selling in school make real money. I make chicken feed."

"Is there a lot of shit sold in the high schools?"

"Si, and in the junior high schools also."

Eddie tried not to show his surprise. He watched Luis to see if the kid was bullshitting him. Finally, Eddie inquired, "How do they get away with it?"

"No problemo. The teachers don't say anything."

Eddie replied, "All the teachers?"

Luis was finished speaking, and Eddie knew there would be no more talk today. "Go back to class. I'll be watching you and your new friend, Elmer Rodriquez. I want to meet you here in my office on Friday and see how you're doing. Make sure you don't skip class on Friday or Detective Weiner, and I will go looking for you. When we find you, you'll spend the weekend in jail."

Luis left the room with a great deal of swagger.

Eddie picked up the phone and dialed Phil Turner, one floor up. "Phil, do you have a second? I have something interesting to tell you."

§

Luis treasured his grand-aunt for trying to fill the void caused by losing his mother. His grand-aunt tried to ease his transition to life in America. He appreciated all she did for him each day. She cooked his favorite Salvadorian meals, cleaned his clothes and made sure he had a warm and comforting home to return to each night. She never complained about his loud music or the mess he sometimes made. All she wanted was for Luis to be happy.

Until the day she died, Luis loved her dearly, and when she was dying, he cared for her day and night for four straight days. When the end came, Luis was crushed. He arranged a beautiful funeral for her with money he had earned on the streets. After leaving the cemetery, Luis went home and remained in the house for a week mourning the loss of his only source of emotional comfort. Luis stayed home until he was sure he had control of his emotions. He knew from his father, "You cry in private."

§

Gomez sat in Starbucks sipping his latte and proudly thought of how far he'd come from his poverty-stricken village in Central America. He smiled thinking about sitting here holding court with his gang. Only his friend Elmer heard him say, "America is truly the land of opportunity."

Elmer Rodriguez was an invaluable asset to Luis Gomez's business operation. Elmer always had Luis' back and often saved him from disaster. Luis realized how much Elmer meant to him and Elmer was the only one he allowed himself to rely on. Luis wasn't softening; rather, he was maturing. Luis now understood he needed a good friend like Elmer in his life.

Elmer Rodriguez turned sixteen only a month before he crossed the border into Texas. Elmer's half-brother, Juan, sent him ten thousand dollars for his trip to the United States. A guide called a 'coyote' arranged the trip and received most of the ten thousand dollars.

Juan sent the money only after his father sent letters begging his son to bring his half-brother, Elmer, to the United States. At first, Juan ignored his father's requests. He resented his father for leaving his mother for a younger woman, and he resented the children his father bore with this new lady. But Juan's tree-trimming business rapidly grew and with it his need for cheap labor.

Eventually, Juan saw an advantage of bringing Elmer to the U.S. He put his resentment toward his father on a back burner and sent the money, but Elmer would have to repay the money by working for Juan cutting trees. Elmer would live with Juan and pay for rent and food.

The trip from El Salvador took three long weeks, walking through Guatemala, traveling slowly through Mexico. The trip terrified Elmer.

Mexico posed a multitude of dangers for a young boy. Robbers, kidnappers, rapist were at every stop.

During the long journey, Elmer lost fifteen pounds from his already thin frame. He had successfully eluded the Border Patrol, and after crossing into the US, he walked to the nearest town, El Paso. Elmer called his half-brother, Juan with the cellphone his half-brother had sent with the ten thousand dollars.

Juan immediately flew to Texas and brought Elmer to New York.

Juan, his wife, and two children welcomed Elmer into their home. Elmer was expected to work for his brother six days a week, twelve hours a day during the summer and after school in the fall, winter and spring and attend Juan's Pentecostal Church four evenings a week. On Sundays, Elmer accompanied his new family to church for the entire day.

When Juan first arrived in New York, he joined a church congregation to make connections and to create business opportunities. During his years as a church member, he became a respected trustee.

Juan refused to permit Elmer to go out in the evenings, even on weekends. Elmer fought with his half-brother and then refused to attend church. After two years of this cloistered lifestyle, Elmer wanted out. He wanted friends his age, some fun, and a girlfriend. Finally, after months of arguing, Juan threw Elmer out of the house.

Elmer had no place to go, but luckily it was late spring, and the weather allowed him to sleep in the park. After a few days, Elmer met Luis, his friend from school at the park. Luis noticed Elmer stayed sitting on the bench after everyone went home. He told Elmer, "Come back to my house for the night. I have the room."

After they arrived at the house, Luis and Elmer stayed up drinking and talking. A special bond formed that night, one which would last a lifetime. Elmer lived with Luis until months later when he left to move in with a girlfriend.

§

Eddie knocked on Phil Turner's office door and tried to open it. The lock was on, and it took a few minutes for his boss to let him in. As he entered, Turner's secretary squeezed by him and nodded. Eddie flashed Heather a knowing grin.

"What is so interesting you had to rush down here?"

Eddie related Gomez's drug story, emphasizing the seemingly unexpected sale of drugs in the district's junior high schools.

Turner grilled his subordinate on specifics and dismissed him without fanfare, but when Eddie left, Turner called his Boss. "Lou, I have to see you right away. It's important."

Lou told him to drop by his office after work.

§

Lou Marinara's interest in the suspected drug use in the district schools had increased dramatically during the past five years. But this past year, he had been approached by friends eager to get in on the action.

Sales to junior and senior high school students had always been high in the southern tier of the district, and recently the northern tier showed signs of increased drug use. The days of the Little Red School House were numbered, even in affluent neighborhoods.

Marinara instructed Turner, "Have Eddie do a study on the drug operation in each of the junior and senior high schools in the district. Let's get the lay of the land, and then devise a plan."

"Where will we get product?"

"Don't worry about it. My friends will provide us with all we need. We have to plan carefully and efficiently. Security is the key. We're dealing with schools, not factory loading docks."

"I'll call Eddie as soon as I get home. By then he'll be back from the dermatologist."

Lou and Turner spent until midnight trying to devise a workable path to taking over the drug trade in the schools.

§

Eddie worked tirelessly investigating the state of drug use in the schools. He visited all the senior and junior high schools, interviewed every principal and hung around the perimeter of the school buildings after school. Eddie enlisted the help of Luis Gomez to fill in any blanks in his report.

Eddie rewarded Luis' help by promising him less hassle and a vague reference to assistance if Luis wanted to expand his business.

Eddie's final report on drugs in the district exposed widespread use and sale among students of all neighborhoods. Each school seemed to have between two and five dealers, depending on the size of the school. Each dealer had his clients and operated with his own distributor.

Many of the small operations were vestiges of businesses passed down from sibling to sibling over a twenty-year period. None of the older operations wanted to grow beyond the previous siblings' established base.

§

One day Luis decided his gang needed a name change. After a week of thinking about many names, Luis came up with the G&R Gang, G for Gomez and R for Rodriguez. Luis waited until he was alone with Elmer before he casually mentioned the new name.

"Elmer, my amigo, I've decided we'll call ourselves the G&R Gang." Elmer looked at his friend and laughed, "What brought this on?"

Luis turned serious, embarrassed by Elmer's reaction. He knew his friend wasn't disrespecting him. Disrespect would be a big deal, even with Elmer.

Luis waited for Elmer to realize what the initials G&R represented. Finally, Elmer beamed, "You honor me."

The two men hugged each other as brothers do.

§

Jeremy called Tom to tell him about the conference in Florida. Jeremy crossed his fingers hoping this wouldn't give Tom an excuse to say he wasn't running.

"Hey, Tom."

"Jeremy, you have to give me at least a few days to decide. I thought I made it clear. I need to give this decision a great deal of thought."

"Tom, I'm not calling to bother you. I have to go to Florida to represent my father at a conference. I'll be gone for three days. I won't be in town to bother you, but I wanted you to know I'm not off on vacation. I'll be back in three days, and we can talk. "

"Thanks for the space, Jeremy."

"Listen, Tom, whatever you decide, I'll respect your decision. I know you don't have an obligation to take on the troubles of the black community and if I pressured you, I apologize."

Jeremy didn't tell Tom his father planned to meet with the ministers that evening, or that his father intended to pressure the ministers to help with the election.

"Tom, I'll see you in a few days."

"Enjoy Florida and make sure you don't get too sunburned."

"Funny, Tom. Goodbye."

§

The ministers met in the basement of Reverend Thompson's Pentecostal Church. All the ministers had attended the other night's school board meeting, and all came tonight ready to discuss what to do about their intolerable situation.

"I want to thank you for coming on such short notice."

Another Pentecostal minister spoke first. "After that meeting, we have to do something, Jonas."

A Baptist minister added, "We can't let them continue to ignore us. Those white, racist idiots won't even let us speak."

"Amen, amen" intoned around the entire table.

"I've asked you here tonight to discuss a specific plan that can give us a voice in this school district."

Reverend Thompson paused before continuing. The Congregationalist minister jumped in. "Jonas, you know you'll have all our support."

"Thank you, Pastor Dobbs. You and your church have always been at the forefront of progress. But wait before you commit. You may not agree with my proposal. I'm not completely sure how I feel, either." Jonas told the eight about Tom Foster and how this twenty-six-year-old white boy could be the answer to their prayers.

"But you say this Foster boy isn't definite?"

"Part of Foster's indecision is the doubt he has enough support to win an election. In reality, he'll win with or without our support. Tom Foster has a big family living throughout the district."

The Methodist minister interrupted Jonas. "They live all over the district, except in the southern tier."

Jonas looked at his dear friend and voiced, "Jim, in part, it's the problem before us."

"Sorry, Jonas, I couldn't resist."

Reverend Thompson continued, "Foster has a good chance of bringing more young people into the election process. He's young enough to attract his high school friends, many still living in the neighborhood. Foster's father is a member of many fraternal clubs around the district. His mother is head of Catholic Daughters over at St. Regina Parish. She's prominent in the district-wide Rosary Society. They're nice people and seem to be liked by everyone. If he runs, he's a shoe-in."

"So, why does he want our support?" asked one minister?

"Because Foster is young and inexperienced and he's scared. He needs encouragement. My son, Jeremy, is his friend since childhood and the one who suggested Foster run. At twenty-six, Foster is still idealistic, and he's green enough to be upset by racial injustice. Tom Foster is our best bet. In the short run, we don't have any other options."

"What do you want us to do?" asked Gideon Rollins, Pastor of the Church in the Sky.

"I want you to invite this young man to your Sunday services and introduce him to your congregations. Invite him to your mid-week services. Let your people see what a fine kid he is."

"You know Lou Marinara won't be happy when he hears we're not staying out of the election. He doesn't want our support, but he doesn't want anyone else to get it either," asserted the Methodist cleric.

"Lou Marinara can go you know where," remarked Reverend Thompson. All the pastors joined in with another round of "Amen, amen."

"You know how hard it is to convince our people to go out to vote. We know from experience we can barely pull them out for a black candidate. How can we do it for a white boy?"

Jonas answered, "It's exactly the point. We can't pull the vote out in great part because our black candidates always lose. We'll explain to the people we can't lose with Tom Foster. We'll explain this when we go around to their homes. Tom Foster will explain it to them when he comes to speak at our services. Everyone wants to back a winner, and with Foster, we'll finally be backing one."

§

Jonas Thompson, the man, was much like Jonas Thompson, the man of God. His personal life merged well with his lofty position in the community. Jonas Thompson was the real deal, not some fake preacher into religion for the money.

Jonas received insurance money from his parents' automobile accident. He was nineteen when his parents' car crashed through the guardrail of a small bridge in upstate New York. The insurance paid double the money because his parents' deaths were an accident.

When Jonas graduated from State College at twenty-two, he headed for Divinity school to pursue a life of helping people find God. After receiving his theological degree, Jonas returned home and took over a local community church from a retiring clergyman who saw potential in the newly ordained Jonas Thompson.

The insurance money Jonas received gave him financial wiggle room. He purchased a brownstone building in the more desirable black side of town. Jonas' new block was all white when he was a kid, but over the years, white flight increased as crime rose in the district's southern tier.

After Jonas settled back into the neighborhood, he joined the Kiwanis and Elks Clubs and the local NAACP chapter. He tells everyone, "It was the luckiest day of my life. It was the day I met Miss Nora Jones."

Jonas Thompson walked into the NAACP offices on Tremont Avenue and sitting at the receptionist desk was his future bride. Nora asked, "How can I help you?" Jonas smilingly replied, "By agreeing to have a cup of coffee with me after you finish work."

Nora discerned the guy standing in front of her desk wasn't a wise guy looking to strut his stuff. So, she smiled right back and agreed to go for coffee.

This pretty, delicately figured girl of twenty-three with the beautiful blue eyes and lovely smile became Jonas' bride nine months later.

CHAPTER 6

THE SUN SHINED BRIGHTLY ON THE TARMAC AS JEREMY boarded a jet to Florida. The 707 plane had two seats on either side of the aisle. Jeremy immediately noticed the attractive young lady in the aisle seat of his row.

Jeremy wanted to appear cool but became flustered, and instead of waiting for the young woman to stand and let him pass, he tried to climb over her, lost his balance and wound up on the girl's lap. Jeremy apologized for his clumsiness, and the young girl replied, "I should have stepped into the aisle, so you had room to pass."

Relieved the girl wasn't crushed, Jeremy settled into his seat. The young girl introduced herself, "My name is Theresa." Jeremy replied with a nervous response. Both settled into their seats, and Jeremy opened his briefcase and took out the papers he needed to review for the conference.

Theresa noticed the conference's letterhead and asked, "Are you attending the Christian Conference in Miami?"

Jeremy stuttered, "Yes, I'm representing my father. He isn't able to attend and asked me to present his paper at one of the committee meetings."

Theresa was thrilled to tell her fellow traveler, "I'm attending the same Conference representing my parish, St. Dorothy's."

"I gather you're Catholic?"

"Yes, what religion are you?"

"I'm Evangelical."

The flight attendant came on the loudspeaker and said, "We will be taking off any minute. Please, fasten your seatbelts."

Jeremy didn't say another word as the plane raced down the runway. He gripped the arms of his seat and looked straight ahead. Beads of sweat appeared on his forehead. Jeremy's torso became rigid and missed seeing the grin on Theresa's lips. Yearly vacations to visit her father's family in Europe made a short trip to Florida a breeze.

After the plane leveled off, the pilot took to the intercom. "Welcome to Toga Airlines. Your flight to Miami should be uneventful." After a short pause, the pilot added, "There's always the chance we'll experience some turbulence, but if we do, don't be concerned. Have a good flight."

The flight attendants began their trip down the aisle with refreshments. Theresa saw her fellow traveler's vise grip on the armrests but did not comment. Jeremy finally loosened his grip by the time the attendant asked what beverage he preferred.

Theresa answered first, "I'll have lemonade, please."

"Same for me," added Jeremy.

"Where are you staying in Florida?" questioned Theresa.

"The Hilton, it's right in Miami.'

"Me, too."

After an awkward silence, Jeremy mustered enough courage to ask, "Maybe we can split a cab to the hotel? I made no arrangements to be picked up. My coming was a last minute thing."

"Neither did I," lied Theresa. Her father had hired a car to drive his daughter from the airport to the hotel. Lou Marinara never took a chance with Theresa.

The rest of the flight to Miami the two talked of things young people discuss: music, school, and parties. They spent their time being young together.

§

Tom's cell phone vibrated on the nightstand. He ignored the intrusion and let his down comforter lull him back to sleep. Ten minutes later his cell rang again. "It's probably Jeremy." Then Tom remembered his friend was on his way to Florida.

Tom reached to answer it and knocked the phone off the nightstand. While he reached to pick it up off the floor, it stopped ringing. He checked to see whose calls he missed.

Tom redialed his good pal, Ed McNally. "Tom, I'm sorry to call so early, but Vanessa left a message. She wants to know if you and I want to go to Boston this weekend. It's a spur of the moment thing, but that's how she is."

"Thanks, Ed, but I have a lot to do. I'm seriously considering a run for a seat on the school board. I have to spend some quiet time deciding if I'm jumping into something over my head."

"Tom, you'll do a great job. We'd all be behind you. I want to talk more, but I have to go."

§

The cab pulled up to the hotel, and two bellhops jumped to attention. Jeremy and Theresa exited the air-conditioned car into the bright Florida sun. The warm air filled the two with a sense of serendipity. Coincidently, Jeremy and Theresa's rooms were on the same floor of the hotel, six doors apart.

Theresa went ahead while Jeremy took extra time at the registration desk because the reservation was under the name, Jonas Thompson. Jeremy explained to the desk clerk he was filling in for his father at the convention. The man assured Jeremy, "No, problem, sir, but it will only require some adjustment in the paperwork." Within minutes Jeremy followed the bellboy to the tenth floor.

The sun-filled room matched Jeremy Thompson's spirits. "This trip rocks-sun, sand and the beautiful girl on the plane." Jeremy planned to meet Theresa in two hours at the first lecture of the afternoon.

Two hours later, Jeremy sat in an all-glass conference room listening to the Very Reverend Elias Stone speaking on a topic dear to his heart,

GOD IN SCHOOLS. Sitting in the chair next to him was his new friend, Theresa.

Jeremy listened as Reverend Stone considered hypothetical problems, gave possible solutions and shared meaningful anecdotes. Jeremy and Theresa shared an interest in religion in schools. When the lecture ended, the applause for Reverend Stone shook the auditorium.

Jeremy talked excitedly about the lecture and Theresa doted on his every word. When the two reached the crowded lobby, Jeremy asked, "How about something to eat?" Theresa immediately answered, "Yes."

"The bellboy told me Shake Shack opened a place a block down on Collins Avenue."

"Let's go, Jeremy. I'm starved."

The two young conference-goers slipped a hand into the others. Afterward, neither knew who had made the first move, but both agreed it was the right one.

§

After moping around for an hour, imagining what fun he'd have if he went to Boston, Tom called Ed McNally back. "Hi, Ed, I changed my mind. Tell, Vanessa; I'm in." Ed's voice told Tom how glad he was Tom had changed his mind. "Great, I'll call you back with the details."

Tom reminded himself. "Good friends like Ed are hard to find," Feeling a little guilty for going away for the weekend, Tom reasoned, "My mind needs some downtime. Why not go? It's for two nights, and there are no interviews this weekend. Things are happening too fast. I don't want to make decisions I'll regret later."

Tom sat on the bed and enjoyed a wave of relief. Hanging out with old friends in Boston would be a nice break.

§

Theresa and Jeremy enjoyed their favorite bacon cheeseburger at Shake Shack. They talked and talked and never seemed to run out of words. Neither Theresa nor Jeremy wanted to return to their hotel rooms alone.

The following morning, Jeremy was scheduled to deliver his father's paper. He planned to read the paper on the plane and practice reciting it in the hotel room. So far, neither had happened. All he thought of was Theresa, and not going back to the stuffy hotel room by himself.

When they arrived back at the hotel, Theresa solved the problem for Jeremy. Her Aunt Pena left a message at the front desk saying she wanted to see her niece in the hotel's coffee shop when Theresa returned from dinner.

Reluctantly, Jeremy said goodnight and dragged himself up to his room knowing he'd have a tough time keeping his mind on his father's paper. Theresa promised him she'd be at the lecture tomorrow morning in the front row. Although this pressured Jeremy, he was thrilled with impressing Theresa with his oratory skills. Jeremy planned to knock Theresa's socks off but realized he didn't even know his new love's last name. "It doesn't matter. What's in a name?" he waxed poetically.

§

Theresa headed to meet Aunt Pena. Her aunt moved to Florida two years ago with her husband, Vito who daydreamed about moving to Florida his whole adult life. Vito turned sixty-five on a Sunday, and by the next Saturday, he and Pena boarded a flight to Florida.

Vito ran from the plane, knelt on the ground and kissed the Miami dirt. Poor Pena tried to keep up with her strapping, energetic husband. They arrived at their new condominium in a beautiful retirement community, and within a week Vito had signed up for the bowling team, the golf team, and the hiking club. Pena seemed to need a new pair of dancing shoes every week. The activities at the retirement village never seemed to end, dinner dances, late buffets, movie nights. Vito was having the time of his life.

Pena enjoyed a few activities, but she didn't have the need Vito had to join everything. Pena missed her three daughters and her six grandchildren. She had spent her life catering to her husband's demands. Initially, Vito forbade her to work outside the home. Then his brother, Lou, said, "I needed a full-time person to keep my books at the office. It has to be someone we can trust, someone like Pena."

Vito agreed, but he required his wife to continue to put a hearty dinner on the table every night and feed his entire extended family a traditional Italian meal each Sunday. On Thursday nights she vacated the house to accommodate Vito's men's club meeting.

Not long after Vito became captain of The Florida Pin Crushers, his bowling team made it to the club finals. Everyone who was anyone in the retirement village attended the big event. The bowling alley reverberated with hoots and howls from all the retirees.

Vito stepped up to the alley with the aplomb of a professional athlete. Bronx and Brooklyn's cheers continued to ring from the rafters. Vito picked up his specially crafted red bowling ball and methodically prepared to roll the ball down the lane. Positioned in the middle, ten feet from the foul line, Vito threw the ball perfectly. As the ball moved closer and closer toward the pins, all eyes focused on the ball. The ball crashed into the pins, and the pins fell like dominoes. Vito jumped into the air. The crowd erupted. No one saw Vito's jump ended with his body falling to the floor, lifeless, dead, but smiling.

It wasn't until things quieted down and everyone returned to their seats that Pena saw her husband dead on the bowling alley floor. She ran to him hysterically, but with a sense of freedom, she hadn't felt in forty-five years. She loved Vito, but she was sure she was headed for the cemetery herself if she tried to keep up with him for another week.

For months, after Vito left for the condo in the sky, Pena spent her time figuring a way to get back to New York, and to the life, she didn't want to leave two years ago. So, when Pena's sister-in-law, Angie, called to say Theresa was in Miami, Pena planned to enlist her niece's help.

Theresa walked across the lobby to the coffee shop. A man looked at her and quickly turned away. She thought she might know him from New York, but didn't stop and check.

There was a line to be seated, but Pena waved her over to a booth in the corner. Theresa hugged her aunt tightly. Pena asked, "Are you hungry? I sure am."

Theresa answered, "Yes," although there was no room in her stomach after Shake Shack.

"Theresa, you have to help me. If I don't leave this old-age hell, I'll die."

Theresa didn't know what to say. Pena barely took a breath and continued, "I didn't want to come here in the first place. I only came because it was your Uncle Vito's dream. It's been my nightmare. I have no one else to ask but you. Your father is the head of the family which I rely on to live. The family business has always put food on my family's table, but when we left New York your father wasn't happy. He thought Vito was abandoning the business. Your father made it clear once Uncle Vito left, he couldn't come back and join the business again."

Theresa remembered her father wasn't thrilled with his brother's decision to leave New York, but she did not understand how the family real estate business worked. Her father never discussed business in the house. Her days at a private convent school isolated Theresa from her father's world. When Theresa was at home studying, there was little time to dwell on what her father did for a living.

"Theresa, please help me return to my family, my daughters, and my grandchildren. I'll be so grateful to you. There will be nothing I won't do for you." Pena cried softly.

Theresa sat there not having the faintest idea of what to do.

Pena's tears dried. She looked at her niece. "Please?"

"Aunt Pena, I'll do anything I can to help." Theresa always loved her aunt and was determined to do what she could to help her.

"How long will you be in Miami?"

"Another three days."

"Come to my house tomorrow, and we can talk more."

"I can't come tomorrow. I have to present a paper for my church group," she lied. Tomorrow was the last day Jeremy would be in town, and she hoped to spend the whole day with him. "Can I come the next day?"

"Fine, I'll send a car for you. I can't thank you enough, Theresa. I love you."

"Aunt Pena, I love you, too. Don't worry. Everything will be fine."

"I have to leave before I start balling." Pena threw a fifty dollar bill on the table. "I'll call tomorrow and leave my address and telephone number." Pena left the coffee shop hopeful.

"This is turning out to be some trip, first Jeremy and now Aunt Pena," Theresa thought.

§

The next morning Theresa sat front row center for Jeremy's lecture. The conference room held a hundred people, and ten minutes before the lecture began people filled every seat. Jeremy walked into the room, and immediately applause rang out. Once on the stage, the butterflies in Jeremy's stomach flapped their wings, and he feared he'd open his mouth, and instead of words, butterflies would fly out.

Jeremy felt young as he explained his intention to present his father's paper and apologized for his father's absence. "My father had no choice. And, I can assure you, I had no choice either." People in the large crowd who knew the Reverend Jonas Thompson laughed heartily. Jeremy looked out at the audience and saw Theresa in the front row. Instead of making him nervous, her presence calmed him.

The paper read so clearly, so interestingly, and so thoughtfully, Jeremy had no trouble keeping the audience's attention. Forty-five minutes later, Jeremy asked if anyone had a question. No one raised a hand. Jonas Thompson's lecture was so clear in content, no one asked a question. Jeremy descended the stage to a fine round of applause. He headed for Theresa and was pleased to see how proud she was of him. Theresa threw her arms around her new love and gave him a congratulatory hug. Jeremy floated on cloud nine. Theresa's warm embrace made him feel good like no one ever had.

"My plane leaves at three. We've only a few hours."

"What do you want to do? I'm here for a few more days. So, you decide."

"I'd just like to stroll along the beach and…"

§

Jeremy and Theresa stood by the curb outside the hotel as the cab pulled up. Theresa put her arms around Jeremy and squeezed. "Have a safe trip." Jeremy squeezed back and reluctantly let go. "I'll call you Saturday when you're back in New York."

Theresa leaned toward Jeremy and kissed him softly on the lips, lingering longer than she should. As Theresa pulled away, Jeremy pulled her back and returned the kiss, harder and longer. Both stopped, and Jeremy hopped in the waiting car. He waved as the car drove away and he hoped Theresa didn't see the tears in his eyes.

Riding in the cab to the airport, Jeremy thought only of Theresa. He prayed he'd miss his flight and be forced to return to her. Jeremy recalled each detail of those last moments before he jumped in the cab. Each detail lingered indelibly in his mind. Corny maybe, but he had fallen deeply in love, entranced by a single wonderful kiss.

§

Theresa arrived at Aunt Pena's home the next evening hoping for homemade lasagna. When her aunt opened the front door, Pena's sauce wafted into Theresa's nose. Hugs, kisses, and the smell of homemade pasta brought back fond memories of Uncle Vito and Aunt Pena. Both had been a large part of her childhood. Theresa accepted a glass of Chianti and sat in the kitchen while Pena prepared dinner.

Pena wasted no time bringing up moving back to New York. She needed Theresa to convince her father to let her return to her job as bookkeeper for the family business. "You must convince him it was his brother, Vito, who dragged me to Florida. Tell him I didn't want to go. Explain to your Father how painful it was for me to leave my family and friends to come to this hell hole. My grandchildren are growing up without a grandmother, and my heart breaks every time I hang up the phone with them. Please, Theresa, help an old woman return to the life she loved so much."

Theresa didn't know how upset her father was when Uncle Vito announced he was moving south. She remembered hearing him say Pena knew the whole business operation and must spend one week a month in New York until he found a suitable replacement. "My wife is coming with me, and not on a part-time basis."

"Your father flew into a rage when his brother refused to allow me to come up and at least supervise the person replacing me. Your father and I tried to convince Uncle Vito to let me fly up to New York once a month for three or four days. My husband refused even to discuss it. Your father threatened him, but my husband wouldn't budge. Your father hated his brother for leaving and worse, he was disappointed in me for not successfully talking Uncle Vito into staying."

Pena's eyes filled with tears, "I better serve supper. We can talk and eat."

While Pena put dinner on the dining room table, Theresa watched her aunt pour another glass of wine for herself, the fourth since Theresa arrived. "I'll be right back. I forgot to put the dressing on the salad." Theresa watched as her aunt walked unsteadily into the kitchen on her four-inch heels.

Theresa tried to remember her parents talking about Pena's importance to the business. She did not understand her aunt's involvement. When Aunt Pena came back into the room, Theresa asked, "What exactly did you do for my father?"

Pena smiled, "Honey, I watched the money. I made damn sure no one was stealing from your father. I was the one who had been around since the beginning, and I knew how, when and where your father made money and where the money went."

"I see why my father was so upset over you moving to Florida."

Theresa tried to change the subject, but throughout dinner, Pena continued to explain to her niece what she wanted Theresa to tell her father to convince him to let her come back to New York, to her family and her old job. Pena asked one last thing before her niece said she had to leave.

"Tell your father I've been speaking with some of my old friends who still work in some schools in the district. They have been telling me about some business opportunities he might find very interesting."

Theresa thanked Pena for the delicious dinner and walked out of her aunt's house with a lot of questions.

§

Alice Foster left work at four o'clock headed for a doctor's appointment. She never remembered being so scared. The drive to the doctor's office took fifteen minutes, and Alice controlled her nervousness by biting hard on her lip. She thought she tasted blood, but she looked in the dashboard mirror and saw bite marks, no punctures.

Alice told her boss she had an emergency at home, and he told her to see about it, but he was anything but happy. This was his busiest time of the year, and things quickly get behind schedule.

Dr. Sean Hayes assured Alice, his elementary school chum, that although patient office hours ended at three o'clock, he'd wait for her to arrive. The parking lot of the medical building was empty, as was Dr. Hayes' waiting room.

Dr. Hayes met Alice at the door of the reception area and escorted her to his private office. "Come in Alice. Please sit down."

Alice took a seat and waited for her friend to lower the boom.

"I don't have anything good to tell you." Alice's heart sank. But Shawn quickly added, "I don't have anything bad to say either. The test results were inconclusive."

Alice's heart was beating so fast she could say nothing.

"I am not going to do anything for two months. I don't want to operate if it isn't necessary. We'll do the tests again to see if anything changes."

Sean Hayes looked at his life-long pal and saw the fear in her eyes. "Alice, the two-month delay won't change the chances of recovery if it turns out we have to operate. There's also a fifty, fifty chance this could be something remedied with medication."

Alice got up to leave, and the tears flowed. Shawn pulled his friend close and waited until all her tears dried, and then sent her home.

§

Tom and his friends reserved rooms at Boston's oldest hotel. Entering the Parker House Hotel's grand lobby, Tom felt transported into a world of quiet luxury. Brown leather couches; green suede winged-back chairs, and thick red Persian rugs met his gaze. Wall sconces lit the lobby giving the deep mahogany wainscoting a rich glow.

A sign at the registration desk informed guests the famous Boston cream pie, and the equally delicious Parker House Roll was served here first.

After a day of sightseeing Tom, Ed, Vanessa, and three other friends took time to sit in the hotel lobby and enjoy reviewing the day. After an hour, the group decided it was time for a joint.

Tom's room was tiny. The older hotels, even the luxury ones, had what today's travelers would call a 'half room.' It was half the size of today's average hotel room, but not half the price.

Vanessa and her sister had the largest room of anyone in the group. Everyone headed into her room and lit up. The group was on its second joint when a loud knock on the door startled them. The girls giggled, the boys were less amused.

Ed McNally opened the door, and an older man in uniform yelled, "What's happening in here. Smoking is prohibited in our hotel rooms."

The girls' giggling turned to howling. "But officer we weren't smoking cigarettes."

"First of all, I'm not an officer; I'm hotel security. Second, what the hell do I smell?"

Vanessa's sister offered, "I don't smell anything, Mr. Security Officer."

This older guy took a deep breath and tried to place the smell streaming past him and into the corridor. He put two and two together, the smell, the laughing, and the size of the cigarettes. "Don't try and kid me, you're all smoking weed, and I'm reporting you to the police." These words caught the group's attention.

Tom was the first to speak up, "We're sorry sir. We knew nothing …"

Ed McNally interrupted Tom. "Sir, can I speak to you outside?" Ed walked over to the security guard and gently ushered him outside.

Everyone grabbed the stash and ran into the bathroom, dumped the grass into the toilet, and Vanessa flushed it all down the drain. Ed walked into the bathroom and announced, "Well, it's taken care of."

"What did you do?" asked Vanessa.

"I gave him two hundred dollars."

"That's a lot of money," said Tom

"It sure is, but I wasn't taking a chance of him calling anyone."

§

When Tom arrived back in his room, his cell rang. The cell ID showed Tom's favorite Professor, Chris Powers. The Professor was returning Tom's call from two days ago. Tom and Professor Powers spent many evenings drinking beer off campus at the Wanna Drop Inn, a favorite college watering hole.

Tom hoped to talk to his mentor about the possible decision to run for a school board seat. The Professor was in Ireland enjoying a six-month sabbatical, studying the history of public education.

Although Tom preferred speaking with Professor Powers in person, the cell phone would have to do. "Congrats, Tom I commend you for even considering a run for school board. The position holds great importance, great power, and great pain. I'm sure you'll do a wonderful job if elected. If you allow me, I want to share something with you."

"Share away."

"School boards are identical throughout the United States. School boards attract the same types of candidates whether you're in New York, Kansas, Mississippi or California. Most people who serve on a school board profess their devotion to children. Each declares, 'I want to contribute to the community. I want to give.' BULLSHIT. What they want is power, power and more power. These good people want to control the lives of others. Many see money to be made through their selfish community service".

Tom chuckled at Professor Powers' ability to come right to the point.

The Professor continued, "Most people begin a political career with at least a modicum of idealism, but soon each falls prey to the allure of power. Don't kid yourself, Tom, school board elections are as politically charged as any election."

Tom replied, "What is the essential qualification for a potential candidate?

From across the Atlantic came, "The most important qualification is the ability to count to four."

Tom responded, "What?"

"The majority rules on any board. Most school boards across the country have seven members. If you have four votes on your side, you control the board. On five-member boards, three controls and on the occasional nine-member board, five takes the cake. Do you see where I'm going with this?"

"I do," said Tom.

"You have to have a majority, four out of seven board members on your side to accomplish anything. Another key component concerns the superintendent. Why? Because he's on the job all day every day, and if he is on your side, it's a great advantage. He can finesse certain situations. If he is antagonistic, he can sneak behind the board's back and thwart the members' plans. Tom, I'll be back in a few weeks. I'll call you then."

Reluctantly, Tom bid goodbye to his former professor.

Tom's group was meeting in the Lobby to go to dinner. He washed and dressed, and as he came from the bathroom, he heard a knock on his door.

"I'll be right there, Ed."

The knocking continued, so Tom quickly put a comb through his hair and opened the door.

Standing there was the security guard from Vanessa's room. "Your friend took care of some of the problem, but I need more."

Tom looked at the old man dumbfounded. Tom towered over him and proclaimed, "Well, you aren't getting any money from me," and pushed past the surprised guard.

§

Jeremy waited a few days after he arrived home from Florida to call his friend. Tom's phone's message informed the caller he'd be in Boston for a few days. "Please, call back in a few days. Leave a message at the beep." Jeremy decided not to leave a message. He'd call back tomorrow.

The next day, Jeremy's cell rang. The ID read Tom. "Hey, Tom, how was Boston?"

"Never mind Boston, how was Florida? Did you get burned?'

The two friends spent several minutes exchanging stories of their trips.

Tom surprised Jeremy by saying, "I'd like to meet with your father and talk about running for the school board. Please, set up a meeting."

Jeremy was over the moon with delight, but only said, "Sure, Tom, right away."

§

The next day Jonas sat in his office working on Sunday's sermon, waiting for his one o'clock appointment with Tom Foster. Jonas looked forward to discussing the black community's needs with Tom.

Of all the white kids his son brought home, Tom was by far his favorite. Reverend Thompson felt comfortable talking to Tom; he suspected most people did. Tom seemed comfortable with himself which allowed others to feel the same way. Tom had good wiring, a natural flair for leadership in politics. Jonas predicted a sure win with the voters.

Jeremy waited by the front window for Tom. The doorbell sometimes got stuck, and Jeremy wanted to make sure Tom wasn't waiting outside for someone to answer the door. He saw Tom walking down the block admiring the hundred-year-old brownstones. Jeremy opened the door before Tom reached for the bell.

"I can't tell you how I enjoy looking at the endless detail these buildings have. You're a lucky stiff living here, Jeremy."

"I'd much rather be living in your neck of the woods, clean streets, good schools and little crime."

The awkwardness this exchange may have caused two other people did not affect Jeremy and Tom. They'd long understood the reality of the neighborhoods in which they lived.

Tom removed his coat in the alcove off the living room and followed his friend up the curved mahogany staircase. "My father is upstairs in his office. We can talk more privately up there." Tom heard Jonas Thompson practicing his sermon. Jonas' deep voice was a gift from God.

When he saw Reverend Thompson, Tom declared, "If I had your voice, I could become president."

Jonas quickly responded, "If I had your good looks, I'd be the happiest guy in town."

Jeremy interjected, "We're off to a good start." All three agreed.

"Tom, I'm excited about you running for school board. We'll do what we can for you. I met with the other ministers, and I've convinced them you'll do all you can to represent the whole district, not only the northern tier. They want to help you in any way they can."

"I appreciate it, Reverend Thompson."

Jeremy remarked, "Tom, there are some things you'll have to do to garner the support of all the ministers' congregations. Some parishioners will support you on the word of a particular minister, but we need to reach the entire parish. What you'll do is go to the churches and speak directly to the people."

"Jeremy is right, Tom. You'll have to speak at all the churches on Sunday mornings. You'll get up on the altar and let the people see the guy Jeremy and I know. You must convince them you can win. Explain how you will help our unrepresented part of the school district receive what it deserves."

"Don't worry, Tom. You can do it," encouraged Jeremy. "In black churches even if the audience hates a person, they're always polite, but I know they'll love you."

Reverend Thompson suggested, "When you speak at the churches, be specific. Tell the parishioners if you're elected, you'll make sure the schools in the southern tier receive their share of supplies and services."

"You'll begin at my church, and after you speak, I'll get on the pulpit and emphasize the importance of their support. I'll tell them you are their best chance to put someone on the school board who'll be on their side. I'll tell them about all the support you already have, and they should be wise enough to go out and vote, and bring their neighbors and friends with them."

"You can do three churches a Sunday. Jeremy will educate all the ministers on how to obtain valid petition signatures. Jeremy will be responsible for picking up the petitions at the ministers' residences before they're due."

Tom looked overwhelmed, but grateful to the Thompsons.

"There's another thing we have to talk about," mentioned Thompson. He paused, and Jeremy took over. "Pop, let me take it from here. The rest is about me. Last year, I was determined to clean up the local high school. I wanted the vermin hanging out around the school and playground gone."

"I was proud of you, son."

"Well, I wish it turned out differently. First, we received anonymous phone calls, then threatening ones. The next thing we knew, a brick came crashing through our front window and whenever I left the house at least one gangbanger followed me. If I went to the police station, they saw me. If a detective came to the house, those guys knew about it. One Sunday, five jerks came to our church. These hoodlums sat in the back of the church. They remained through Pop's sermon, then noisily got up and left."

"That's fucked up."

Jeremy continued, "Those gangbangers monitored my activities real closely. I stopped reporting information to the police. We weren't sure if the cops were on our side or theirs. We're sure someone tipped off the bad guys every time we filed a complaint.

"Members of my congregation came and told me they felt intimidated coming to church," said the Reverend. "Wednesday night service dwindled to three people."

"We didn't know what to do," said Jeremy. "We were afraid for my brother, Toby. The gangbangers were showing up at three o'clock outside his school. My mother couldn't take it any longer." Jeremy choked up and cleared his throat.

"Sometimes you have to know when to quit, not forever, but for a time. Luckily, a minister friend had a relative in the police department with a pipeline to the gangbangers. He tried to cool things," said Jonas. "Using the pipeline, the minister's uncle let the gang's leader, Luis Gomez, know Jeremy was quitting his do-gooder career and taking courses in 'minding his own business.' A few weeks passed, and the gangbangers disappeared. Things have been quiet since then," finished the Reverend.

"It won't affect the school board election. We're not trying to convince these thugs to vote for me, right?"

Jeremy and Jonas both laughed

"Good, because I'm nervous enough, having to speak to so many congregations the next few weeks without worrying about dodging bullets from gangbangers."

"Tom, Jeremy and I didn't want to scare you, but we felt we had to tell you about this. We don't want to overwhelm you, but we want to give you examples of the problems in our schools. The high schools in the southern tier are drugstores for dope. The northern tier is a victim to misuse of over the counter medications and prescription pills. There are other drugs in the north, too, but not nearly as much of the hard stuff as in the south." For the next hour and a half, Jonas and Jeremy gave Tom an earful.

Jonas looked at his watch. "I have another meeting in ten minutes." He excused himself. "You're welcome to stay and continue talking."

Tom said, "I have to be leaving."

"Tom, it was great seeing you, and I hope we're successful in helping you get elected. You'll need a lot more support than we can give you. So, try to obtain the endorsements of some fraternal and civic groups in the district. I read the first one is The Raccoon Lodge of America. Get all the support you can. We need you to win."

CHAPTER 7

TOM HIT THE CAMPAIGN TRAIL WITH AN INTERVIEW AT THE storied Raccoon Lodge in the center of town. He kept telling himself. "The interview is the reason why I feel so uneasy. I'm not used to public speaking." But deep down Tom knew some of his uneasiness was because he would run into his childhood Sunday school teacher, Mrs. McMurray.

Tom stepped through the big, wooden doors of the Raccoon Lodge and into a long, brown tiled corridor. A sign scotch-taped to the wall showed a red arrow pointing toward the interview room. At the end of the corridor, Tom saw an older lady sitting on a bench. Tom walked over, sat next to the lady and said, "Hello."

The woman looked Tom up and down and decided he was all right.

"Hello, I'm Mary McMurray. Are you here for the interview?"

Tom replied, "Yes, I am."

"What is your name young man," asked Mrs. McMurray.

"Tom Foster."

Tom could see the lady's mind working overtime.

"Tommy…Tommy Foster…"

"Mrs. McMurray, I was in your Sunday School class for a short time and …

102

Mary's eyes lit up, and she howled. "Tommy Foster, I've thought of you often during the years. I felt so bad about what happened. I went to your house and spoke with your mom. I wanted to see you, but you wouldn't come out of your room."

"I remember it well," said Tom.

"I hope you've forgiven me after all these years."

"It's good to see you, Mrs. McMurray."

"Please, call me Mary."

"I will, and you can call me Tom."

Another candidate walked cockily down the hallway, nodded and sat next to Tom. "I'm Vince Miller." The new arrival put a damper on Tom's conversation with Mrs. McMurray.

Tom looked at a photo on the wall across from him of angry looking men wearing raccoon hats. The three candidates sat on the bench waiting for what seemed an eternity until a young secretary came out of the conference room opposite them.

"We'll begin the interviews. The panel will interview you together." Tom looked relieved all the attention wouldn't be on him. Mrs. McMurray seemed annoyed she must share the spotlight. Miller cared less. When McMurray, Tom, and Miller sat, the panel of six men began.

"Good evening, and welcome to the Raccoon Lodge. Please, state your names for the record."

"My name is Vince Miller."

"My name is Tom Foster."

"My name is Mary McMurray."

Tom's wobbly knees prevented him from moving off the chair. Mrs. McMurray sat next to Tom; her erect carriage projected a confident air. Vince Miller sat on Tom's other side, and looked in charge, ready for anything the questioners threw at him.

When the interview ended, the panel's chairman thanked all three for coming. Tom wanted to crawl in a hole, but on the way out Mary saw Tom's face and said, "Don't worry. You'll get better after each interview. All it takes is practice."

Tom felt like he did when he took his driver's test as a teenager. He remembered getting into the car and remembered getting out of the car, but had no memory of the test itself. The time between was a blank. Now, although still in a fog, he slowly recalled the confident, gravelly voice of Mrs. McMurray answering the panel's question. "If elected to the school board, what experiences would you bring to the position, and in particular, what business experience, what personal experience and what financial experience will you bring, Mrs. McMurray?" Tom could still hear Mary's many lengthy examples.

Tom also remembered Vince promising to bring entrepreneurial and parental experience to the board and added he had a wife, Linda and three children. Tom didn't offer to tell the interviewers his business, life or parental experience because he had none.

Tom cringed when he remembered offering his recent traveling experience to Boston as an example of his sophistication and how travel had broadened his worldview. He told them how he had learned Boston cream pie and Parker House rolls were invented at the hotel where he stayed for the weekend.

As Tom, Miller and Mrs. McMurray exited the room, in walked Lou Marinara. As Lou went into the interview room, Tom heard, "Lou, it's good to see you. How've you been?" Then the door shut behind him. Tom came out of the bathroom and saw Mr. Marinara walking swiftly down the hall toward the Lodge's front door. The Miller guy called after.

Vince ran down the hall calling, "Excuse me, Mr. Marinara. Mr. Marinara."

Marinara stopped and asked the caller's name. Lou was sorry he had acknowledged Miller. He'd kept his wife, Angie, waiting in the car and she'd be pissed off if he took any longer.

"Mr. Marinara, my name is Vince Miller. I hoped to ask your advice on a few things. Do you have time this week to talk?"

"What do you want to talk about?"

"I hoped you'd fill me in on the problems we have in the school district. You've been involved for years, and I need help learning about the most serious problems we'll be facing during the next three years."

"Sure, but I have my wife waiting in the car. Contact me tomorrow. We'll set up a time. Contact the school board office for my number. I have to go."

§

Mary McMurray walked toward the front door and came up behind Vince Miller, "Quite an ordeal."

"It sure was," replied Vince Miller disingenuously.

"We better get used to it. We've another twenty to go. Are you going to the district PTA interview tomorrow?"

Vince answered, "I want to make as many as I can. But my business won't allow me to go to all of them. I'll be away most of next week. I'm afraid I'll miss several of the interviews."

"If I were you, I'd try to make tomorrow's interview. It's an important one. All the PTA presidents in the district will be there."

"I hear they're quite a group."

Mary laughed, "I've met a few, and they're something else."

"I met one at a party last week. I've never met a pushier person," added Vince

Miller noticed Tom coming down the hall. He didn't want to get stuck talking to this young kid. He didn't want to waste time on competitors who had little chance of winning.

"Mary, let's talk soon. I have to go."

Mary headed for the front door. She decided she didn't like Miller and knew she must be careful with him.

Tom Foster came up behind Mary. She jumped when he tapped her on the shoulder. She saw sweat running down Tom's neck; his cheeks were flushed.

"Are you alright?" Mary asked sympathetically. She liked this young Tom Foster from her past, but he better buck up if he wanted to win a seat on the board. Mary wasn't putting any money on his chances, not a cent.

"You survived. So, go home, relax and get some sleep. You'll feel a lot better in the morning."

Tom asked, "Can anyone go to the PTA interviews tomorrow?"

"Yes, starting at two in the afternoon. It's probably the most important interview in the whole campaign. Several years ago the State divided the district in half; thirty-five of the schools will have PTA Presidents present."

"What about the other half?"

"It seems they aren't as active." Mary wasn't about to educate Tom Foster on the racial problems in the district.

Tom interrupted, "I didn't see anything on the school district's website which showed the district divided."

Mary rolled her eyes, and Tom knew he sounded infantile.

"Tom, my new friend, you have a great deal to learn. If you want to win in this election, you'd better learn quickly."

Mary decided she'd take a few minutes to give her former student a short lesson on race. "The district isn't divided on paper, but it's divided nevertheless."

Lettie Grimes, the school district's delusionary *femme fatal* interrupted Mary. If matronly is the new sexy, then Lettie was this year's hot tamale.

"What are you two up to?" asked Lettie. "Plotting already?"

Mary rolled her eyes and headed down the hallway. "Phone me tomorrow, Tom. We'll talk."

"So, what's up with the old lady? Are you two teaming up so early in the game?"

Tom gave Lettie a puzzled look.

Lettie flirted, "If you team up with anyone, you should consider jumping on my bandwagon. I can give you a lot more than that old lady." The dirty smile on her face made Tom nervous.

Satisfied with Tom's expression, Lettie quickly added, "Tom, I didn't mean that, you dirty boy. I meant I know all the PTA presidents at this end of the district. Maybe, I can help you get some of their support."

Tom silently filed Lettie's comment 'at this end of the district' for future reference. Tom couldn't listen to Lettie a minute longer.

But Lettie wasn't finished. She looked straight at Tom and teased, "A good looking guy like you can call me anytime, and if you want, we can campaign together. We could take turns driving each other home after late night interviews?"

Tom ignored the suggestion, and Lettie Grimes sashayed down the corridor.

§

Lettie Grimes always had a lot on her plate. There was her mother, her twenty-two-year-old daughter and her twenty-eight-year-old son living in the basement. They all depended on Lettie for food, shelter, and clothing. A brother showed up every few months and stayed in the attic for several weeks and then left without a word. Lettie's husband took the cake. He cheated on her from the day he uttered the words, "I do." Luckily, Pete Grimes was seldom home, and it was okay with Lettie.

Lettie had given up on Pete. He drank, caroused, cursed and blamed everyone else for his shortcomings. First, he blamed his parents, then his siblings and finally his friends. If you ever wondered what happened to the kid in your elementary school class who blamed teachers, classmates and parents for everything wrong in his life, wonder no more. That kid grew up to be Pete Grimes.

§

Tom waited until he was sure Lettie was out of the building then cautiously went out to the parking lot. On the far side of the lot, he saw a sleek red Mercedes and a fire-engine red Chevy parked next to each other. Tom glimpsed Lettie talking to some man. Her car obstructed the man's face, but Tom had seen Vince Miller drive up in the red Mercedes.

Theodore Kowalski, a candidate seeking another term on the district's school board, sprinted across the parking lot headed for the front door. Ted Kowalski was running as an incumbent on Lou Marinara's record because Ted Kowalski's tenure on the school board was an echo of Marinara's wishes.

Ted planned to tell the Raccoons as little about his background as possible. He had no intention of telling them what he went through in his life. Ted's father's destructive behavior caused young Theodore Kowalski more pain than Ted could relate in a year.

§

Ted Kowalski was shy by nature, but after six months working at the Deli, the fifteen-year-old had gained a lot of confidence. Ted took care of his customers in a pleasant, respectful manner. He grew into a favorite with his customers, his coworkers, and his boss.

Unfortunately, Ted vividly remembered the afternoon his father walked into Hans Becker's Delicatessen while he was cutting cold cuts behind the counter. Young Ted was patiently waiting on an older Italian lady having difficulty ordering.

As Ted helped the lady with her purchases, Ted, Sr. walked in the door, spotted his son and from fifteen feet away screamed at the top of his lungs. "You son of a bitch, you sided with your mother. I'll show you."

The deli owner came running from the back of the store and saw Ted's father about to go around the counter and hit young Ted. Assisted by one of his other employees, the boss thwarted Mr. Kowalski's attack and ushered him out the front door.

Once on the sidewalk, the deli owner calmed Ted's father and sent him on his way. Ted finished his shift and went home. He never returned to the deli, not even as a customer. His father's actions humiliated him so badly he remained in his room for a week, shades drawn, and lights out. Ted's mother filed for divorce the next week. Her husband's abuse of Ted and herself ended that day.

§

Mary couldn't wait to tell her husband, Mark, about the Raccoon interview. Mark waited at home to hear all about it. He knew Mary would have no trouble with the interview. "What's the place look like anyway?" was the first thing he asked. "Did you make it out of the interview without breaking up when the furry raccoon hats began asking questions?"

After a few laughs about the interview, Mark asked, "Did you meet any other candidates?"

"Yes. And the group wasn't impressive. They're pretty low on the food chain. I met a former student of mine. He's green, but he's sweet, and his heart seems to be in the right place."

Mark looked at Mary puzzled. "You were a teacher?"

Mary reminded her husband of her brief Sunday School career and her experience with Tommy Foster.

"I seem to remember something about it. Maybe you can go to some other interviews with Tom. I worry about you traveling around at night without someone with you."

Mary objected to Mark's suggestion, but quickly realized he had a point. It would be wise to go around with someone else.

"Mark, you're right. I gave him my number if he had any questions, but I won't wait for Tom to call. I'll call him tomorrow and test the waters. I wrote his number down on a piece of Raccoon literature. Mary grabbed her purse and pulled out a piece of paper with a raccoon face at the top. Tom's number was under the raccoon's chin.

Mary and Mark looked at the raccoon face and howled.

§

The next morning Mary called Tom Foster and asked if he wanted to drive to the candidate interviews together. Tom quickly said yes. He didn't want to repeat the Raccoon Lodge experience. He needed moral support, at least for now. Mary offered to drive, but Tom insisted he would do the driving. Mary said they'd discuss it. After seeing Mary McMurray pull out of the parking lot last night, there was no way he was letting her drive while he was in the car.

Mary suggested they campaign at some of the senior centers. Tom agreed. He heard percentage wise, seniors vote more than any other group. They talked for more than an hour about the school district and the problems they'd face if elected. This odd couple hit it off right away. Both seemed oblivious to the wide gap in their ages.

"Mary, I have to go. I'll call you tomorrow, and we'll talk some more." Both hung up knowing they'd each made a new friend.

§

A few days before the interviews at the Raccoon Lodge, Eddie Fisher called one of his friends on the interviewing panel, "Let me know who shows up for an interview." Fisher wanted to know who was running for the board.

The day after the interviews his friend called. "Eddie, there's a retired business lady who was impressive, two incumbents Lou Marinara and Ted Kowalski. Of course, we'll endorse Lou and whoever he wants. No one was terrible except this young kid, Thomas Foster. He was way out of his league."

Eddie's friend chuckled. "This Foster kid had nothing to say during the interview, but at the end, he became nervous and started telling us about his traveling experience which amounted to a trip to Boston last weekend. It was sad."

Eddie was born in the Boston area and knew the town well. "Did Foster say where he stayed?"

"The kid mentioned something about a hotel that had invented a type of roll and a special kind of pie. We didn't listen. We had more people coming in for interviews."

Immediately, Eddie knew the hotel was the Parker House. He thanked his Raccoon friend, hung up and called his old buddy, a security guard at the Parker House Hotel. The operator told Eddie his friend was off today, but reluctantly gave Eddie the guard's cell number.

Eddie's friend picked up on the third ring. "Oscar, it's Eddie Fisher."

"How the hell are you, Eddie? "

The two chatted for a while, catching up on things. Finally, Eddie said, "I need some information Oscar, and I want to pay you for it."

Eddie's friend perked up. "Sure, what can I do for you?"

"You had a guest named Thomas Foster recently. Would you look him up on the Hotel Registry and give me any information about credit cards, other people in his group, anything at all?"

Oscar chuckled, "I don't have to look it up, I remember the guy." Oscar told Eddie about the marijuana and the quick two hundred he made. "But the Foster kid, he doesn't scare easily. Watch out for him."

Eddie told his friend a money order would be in the mail. Fisher hung up, pleased with himself. No wonder his boss Phil Turner was impressed with the creative ways he found dirt on people. "One of Turner's goals for me this year is to find out as much about the candidates as possible."

§

Bunny Krouse passed Tom's house on her way to the district's PTA interviews. Bunny knew Tom didn't have a chance of being endorsed by any PTA. "They rig the process, but both Mary McMurray and Tom will benefit by seeing what they'll be dealing with."

Tom stood in his driveway with the car hood open. Bunny pulled over and opened the window, "Need a ride?"

"I'll call the garage."

"Hop in. There's no time. If you come late, it'll make it easier for the PTA to come up with an excuse not to endorse you."

As soon as Tom hopped in the car, Bunny minced no words giving him the scoop on the group. "Traditionally, the PTA is the most powerful force in a district because they potentially can pull out more votes than any group."

"I thought you said the other night the churches and the synagogues brought out the most votes."

"They do. The PTA has the most members, but many of them don't come out to vote."

"I get it."

"The PTA is made up of women who say they want to be home with their children, but the real reason they're home is they can't find jobs or keep them."

Bunny saw Tom didn't understand.

"They don't have any particular skill, and if they did, they were so obnoxious they'd get fired. One woman told me the boss asked her to work from home after she broke the office toilet bowl. This woman dropped something heavy in the bowel and broke the porcelain."

Tom laughed.

"First, the water poured from the bowl at an alarming rate, the turds flowed out of the bathroom into nearby offices, into the lobby and finally into the elevators."

"You made this up," chuckled Tom.

"I didn't. The boss brought the lady into his office and told her, 'I value your work but starting tomorrow, I want you to work from home."

"Most of the office heard the boss and would have taken a huge sigh of relief if they weren't holding their noses from the smelly turds swimming past their desks. This woman was insulted by her boss's suggestion and quit."

"What did she do next?"

"She joined the PTA. Her husband earned a decent salary, so they just took fewer vacations. What's missing in the PTA is mothers who have their shit together; women who are out advancing their careers, struggling to be good mothers to their kids. Those mothers appreciate education, but don't want their kids' school to be their exclusive social life."

Tom sat in the passenger seat silently, overwhelmed by all that Bunny Krouse told him. She thought she should throw something encouraging at Tom before he turned and ran for his life. "The good news is you'll have at least one person at your interview who isn't looking to sabotage your candidacy. I called my friend Esther Portnoy. You know she's the one you thought was a hundred and too old to be at a school board meeting. I told her to make sure she got on the interviewing committee. I told her to watch out for you and make sure that those PTA bitches don't rough you up too much."

"I think I can handle a few mothers at a school interview."

Bunny gave Tom a smirk, "Let's revisit that thought after the interview."

Tom Foster ignored Bunny Krouse and asked, "Bunny, before we arrive at the interview, please explain why the district's so big, and why it has so many schools?"

Bunny sighed knowing she didn't have the time to explain before arriving at the interview. "I'll give you the short version. School taxes were sky high. The people were fed up, and the politicians realized they were an election away from being thrown out of office. Relief came in the form of combining the many individual school districts into two large ones. Dividing the districts reduced the administrative staff, saved money and reduced taxes."

"When did it happen?"

"Six years ago, there were fifty-four school districts in this county. Some districts were so small they had five schools: two elementary, one junior high and one high school. None had more than ten schools. Each had a superintendent making over 300k, an assistant superintendent making almost as much and each district had a full office staff."

"I have one more question before I go into the interview."

Bunny waited for Tom's big question.

"Why am I running? I don't have kids."

"Neither does Mrs. Mc Murray, nor Father Grant. Mary's daughter is grown. The priest hopefully doesn't have any kids. If all the members of the school board had kids in school, the only thing we'd see in the budget is football and cheerleading. After-school activities would include babysitting accommodations for the parents who spent their time at school meetings. The budget would be spent by the mothers with the power, and it would only include what they wanted for their kids."

"So, how would Mary McMurray be the right person for making school district educational policy?"

"She pays school taxes. Why shouldn't she have a say in where her money goes?"

"But…"

"But nothing, those PTA bitches taxed some of the older folks out of their homes so their darling kids can be on a synchronized swimming team, but we'll talk more on the way home. We're about to pull into the parking lot, and I don't want to get into an accident with any of these crazy mothers."

Once inside the school, Tom followed the signs to the interview. Bunny Krouse headed for the bathroom.

§

Tom sat next to a young woman, no older than nineteen, He introduced himself, and the girl gave him the once over, then a big smile and an extra loud chew of her bubble gum. She didn't offer her name, but said, "I hope this won't be all day. I'm meeting my friends. We're strategizing my campaign."

Tom asked the nameless young lady if she was nervous. She replied, "Oh, no. I've seen everything. The interview will be a breeze. They want someone under a hundred on the board. You know, to like give a different perspective."

"Well, to tell you the truth, I'm nervous," said Tom. "This is my first time running for office since high school."

A motherly tone came to the young girl's voice, and she put her hand on Tom's knee assuring him, "Don't worry. They'll like you. You're so cute."

One of the PTA people came out of the conference room and mumbled a name from a sheet of paper. The girl pulled a card from her bag and gave it to Tom. "Call me." Tom couldn't help admire the little wiggle the girl gave as she entered the conference room. He looked at the card and read the name, "Candy Caine."

§

Mary McMurray stormed through the door hunting for bear. The sole reason she came to the interview was to show the PTA hags she didn't intend to take any of their crap during the campaign and to bring them down a peg or two.

When her kids were in school, Mary despised the women of the PTA. Since then she had heard about their recent shenanigans at school board meetings, their cliquishness and arrogant airs, and stories of how they ignored working parents who didn't fit in with their little group.

As Mary approached the waiting area, she saw Tom walk into the conference room for his interview. She uttered a little prayer for him. Mary knew her friend felt the pressure of the interviews; they spoke on the phone last night of ways to plow through the process.

§

The PTA person pointed to a seat at the top of a long rectangular oak table. Tom looked around the room and saw only unfriendly faces. Then he spotted Esther Portnoy standing by the window. She gave him a nod and flashed a smile.

"Welcome and thank you for coming. I'm the President of Presidents' Panel of the district's PTA." Quite a title thought Tom, and immediately thought of the Head of the Raccoon Lodge introducing himself as the Grand Raccoon Tail; now it's 'the president of the president...' These thoughts relieved his nervousness until the Grand Head of the PTA asked her first question.

The first question, "Tell us about yourself, Mr. Foster," was followed by "Do you have enough time to devote to your duties as a school board member?"

The question was a difficult one for Tom because it hit at the core of his indecision to run for this position. He struggled for an honest answer but was distracted by the smugness seen on the faces of the people around the table. The rolling eyes, the smirks on their lips, the same behavior he'd seen at his first school board meeting.

Sensing weakness, the questioner proceeded, "Really, Mr. Foster. Do you think a young boy like yourself has the time or inclination to devote the huge amount of time necessary to do a good job if elected to serve on the school board?"

Tom started to answer when another mother jumped in with, "Mr. Foster, do you know anything about schools because…"

In a loud voice, Esther interrupted the questioner. "Ladies and I use the term ladies loosely, this man has come here today not because he is on trial for murder but to ask for our support for his candidacy to our school board. So, please, don't be as rude as you usually are." Esther turned to Tom and said, "Mr. Foster, you were about to answer a question when you were interrupted. If you are ready, please continue."

Emboldened by Esther's support and by the arrogance of the banshees around the table, Tom gave his first response as a politician. "I'll give my total effort to the school board. It will be the centerpiece of my life, I assure you."

The mothers and one father in the room seemed flustered. They realized they didn't have the young kid they thought they had. Intimidation wouldn't be easy. After a few more questions Tom was escorted from the room with a half-hearted, "Thank you, for coming."

§

Although Mary had arrived at the PTA interviews after two of the other candidates sitting on the bench, she politely asked the two women if they'd allow her to go ahead of them. "I have a doctor's appointment, and I've waited for weeks for it. I won't be able to stay if I have to wait."

These two women knew they were guaranteed to receive the endorsement of the PTA, so they agreed. When the usher came out for the next candidate, Mrs. McMurray rose and walked toward her. "These two gals have been kind enough to let me go ahead of them." Mary gave the usher no time to speak. She entered the conference room and sat down at the head of the table.

The group greeted her and Mary returned the greeting in kind. The mothers rustled papers looking for the questions they wanted Mrs. McMurray to address.

Mary sat looking at the oak table in front of her. She smiled, sure some of these gals' bottoms had helped give this table its beautiful shine.

From time in memoriam, there has always been a conference table in a school principal's office for principals to speak with a worried mother or an underachieving teacher. The length of the table usually measured about eight feet. The table could accommodate even the largest PTA President. Aside from the participants, few knew any wear marks on the table resulted from a certain type of friction unrelated to educational matters.

The biggest problem Mary had with the interview was appearing to take these women seriously. "Mrs. Mc Murray, I mean Mary. You don't mind us calling you Mary, do you?"

Mary quickly responded, "Mrs. McMurray will be fine."

After the questioner regained her composure, she asked a few preliminary questions, Mary's background, career experience, and education. Mary answered these pedigree questions agreeably, graduated from Smith College, married, one daughter, worked for thirty years as executive assistant to the CEO of a large food conglomerate."

Out of the blue, one parent asked a question Mary would never have expected. "What is your personal view on abortion?" The rest of the mothers smirked.

This silly woman concluded she had trapped Mary McMurray because Mary was Catholic. Mrs. McMurray immediately recognized the trap laid by this stupid mother. Mary smiled, looked at her questioners and coyly joked, "I'm flattered by the question, but surely you know I'm over sixty-five years old and most probably won't face this difficult and complex issue.

The ladies of the PTA waited for the rest of Mary's answer. "It would be presumptuous of me to weigh in on this serious topic. Furthermore, as a candidate for a seat on this local school board, I will never have to address the issue of abortion. And with that, ladies and gentleman, I must take my leave. I have a doctor's appointment I can't miss."

As Mary rose to leave, one woman offered a polite, "I hope it's nothing serious."

Mary replied on her way out the door, "Nothing serious, but after the last question, I'll certainly inquire of my doctor whether he recommends my husband use protection. Good-by, people."

§

In Eddie's world, the chain of command was simple, Lou Marinara to Phil Turner to Eddie. Lou insulated himself from Eddie Fisher. Lou, buffeted by Turner, had the best of both worlds; a sneak to do his dirty work, and a Chinese wall to protect him from liability.

As Eddie was leaving for lunch, Phil caught him in the hall. "Come to my office."

"But boss, I was just going for lunch."

"This will take a second."

Once in the office, Phil explained to Eddie, "Lou needs help finding dirt on Vince Miller. He's thinking of supporting him in the election. If Lou hooks up with Vince, he wants some leverage in the form of information to use to pressure him into voting his way."

A lucky break came in the person of an old pal of Eddie's who worked in the Manhattan Hall of Vital Statistics. His friend said, "Miller must have changed his name." Eddie suggested, "There's no way Miller is his name, not with his sallow complexion."

Eddie conjectured Vince's last name resulted from some Irish Health Inspector's misspelling Vince's grandparent's name coming through Ellis Island. Often the Inspectors could not spell some Eastern European surnames. A name like Mikaloff became Miller.

Eddie's friend at Vital Statistics could find nothing in the Ellis Island Data Bank, but when the friend searched recent name changes, he located an application for a name change in the Borough of Manhattan fifteen years ago. A male named Vinkolas Mikaloff changed his name to Vince Miller. Attached to the application was a photo of a young Vince Miller smiling for the camera with a short biography giving three previous addresses and a copy of Vince's birth certificate.

Eddie's friend typed Vince Miller's name into other databases, and the criminal history of Vince Miller appeared on the screen. Eddie was delighted with the results of his investigation.

§

Lou Marinara and the district superintendent, Rocco Pinzone, waited in the school board office for Ted Kowalski. Ted voted with Lou on most matters that came before the board during the past term.

Lou hoped to fill one more school principal position before the present term concluded. Lou wanted to continue his complete control of the district's personnel roster but feared he might have to compromise with the next board. Two of his close allies decided not to run for another term.

"After I receive Ted's commitment on the principalship, I'll bring up your contract extension. While we have him here, we might as well kill two birds with one stone."

When Ted finally arrived, Lou held his temper. "Hey, Ted how's it going? Are you having any trouble getting signatures for your petitions? If you are, remember I can help."

"No, I'm good, Lou. Thanks anyway."

"I asked you to meet today to talk about the principal's position at Jefferson High School. I wanted to fill the position before our term ends. The community is anxious for the next principal to start right away. I have a favorite."

Ted interrupted Lou. "You always have a favorite," sighed Ted. "Don't you think it would be refreshing if we had a more open door policy, at least sometimes? You decide the positions before we even advertise."

Lou held his cool. "Ted, we can't take chances."

Ted looked at Lou, not sure what he meant.

"That's right, Ted. You've been on the board long enough to know my way works."

"I'm not sure I know what you're talking about."

"You remember. We hired someone right off the street to fill the vacancy after old man Mullins' retirement. The candidate knew no one on the board. Remember what happened, Ted? The parents in the top school in the northern tier got up in arms over their precious little kids getting C's and D's on their second term report cards."

"I remember, I thought we'd have a riot during the emergency meeting at the school," recalled Ted.

"Do you remember what we did so we could get out of there without being skinned alive?"

Ted offered no answer.

"We lied, Ted; that's what we did. We told the parents the computer misread the scanner and we apologized for upsetting them, then we had the teachers change any unpleasant marks. Do you remember what happened next, Ted?"

"No, Lou, I don't."

"We called the principal into the district office and told him in no uncertain terms if this ever happened again, he'd be the first occupant of the new Rubber Room we were building."

Ted agreed, "We never had any trouble afterward."

"Correct. Word traveled fast, and the other principals fell in line."

"What about the principals in the southern tier?"

"I don't know. Frankly, no one cared. No one complains there, and if anyone does, we ignore them. We'll do what we always do when we can't do anything else. We LIE, LIE and LIE," roared Lou. "So, do I have your vote or not for the principal's position, and I almost forgot, the vote for chairman?"

All Superintendent Pinzon and Chairman Marinara heard from Ted was mumbling as he hurried for the door.

§

After Ted left the school board office, Lou yelled at Rocco Pinzone, "He didn't give me an answer, did he?"

"No, Lou, he didn't. You also didn't bring up the matter of my employment contract."

Lou left Rocco Pinzon sitting by himself in the office.

Rocco wondered if he just witnessed the beginning of the end for Lou's long reign of absolute power, or a small bump in the road until a new board was elected. "At any rate, I had better look to the new board members for at least some support."

CHAPTER 8

THE FLIGHT FROM MIAMI TO NEW YORK WENT SMOOTHLY, NOT a bump, not a rattle, not a roll, but Theresa Marinara didn't notice. Her mind spun trying to decide what to say to her parents.

When Theresa exited the plane, Angie immediately bombarded Theresa with questions. "Were the lectures interesting? How is Aunt Pena? Did you meet any interesting people? Was there any people from New York?"

Theresa gave one-word answers. She didn't know how to answer most questions her mother asked without starting World War III.

Theresa wanted to answer, "Yes, I met someone interesting. I'm in love with him, and by the way, he's black," but decided to say, "I visited with Aunt Pena. She's miserable. She wants to come home and work at her old job, and she wants you and me to help her."

Angie wasn't the only one with questions. Theresa also had questions. "What does my Father's business have to do with schools? I thought the school board was his way of contributing to our community?"

Angie quickly changed the subject to how they could help Aunt Pena.

§

Thirty years ago, Lou Marinara practiced real estate law from a rented office in Corona, New York. Lou still occupies the same office, but now owns the building and the entire block. Lou traded his real estate business for a more lucrative criminal law and commercial litigation practice.

One afternoon the young Marinara received a call from Tony Govi, a criminal attorney with an office down the block from his. Lou's father and Tony had been childhood friends back in Italy. Tony always liked young Lou, and after Lou's father passed away from cancer at age forty-nine, Tony tried to help Lou out by giving him all the real estate business which came through his door.

One day Tony called Lou and told him, 'I've decided to retire and move to Arizona next month." Lou was a little sad, and a lot scared. Lou relied on the extra business Tony sent him. Lou now had a wife and a little girl to support.

Lou arranged a retirement luncheon for Tony and invited the local merchants on the block. All the good wishes from the business people he'd worked with for years touched Govi.

After the luncheon, Tony called Lou aside and asked him to do him a favor.

"Lou, as you know I'm leaving for Arizona the day after tomorrow. I have a former client who needs someone to represent his son in a domestic violence case. The kid violated an order of protection to stay away from his girlfriend. The girl refuses to cooperate with the DA's Office, so they don't have a case."

"Thanks for thinking of me, Tony, but I never do criminal cases, and I don't want to screw it up for you. You've been so good to me."

"Don't worry. There's nothing to it. All you have to do is make an appearance a couple of times and say the kid will go for counseling. They'll offer to adjourn the case for six months, and if he stays out of trouble during that time, then the case will be dismissed."

"Okay, Tony. I'll do my best."

Lou got the kid off after the first conference with the assistant district attorney. The ADA saw the witness wouldn't testify, so he dropped the charges right then and was happy to have one less case.

Luigi Costa, the father of the kid, thanked Lou. "I'll call on you, again." And he did. He called the following week and the week after, and the week after, until Lou became his go-to guy in criminal matters and eventually in civil ones. "Lou, I want you to take over all the business I used to give Tony. You can do all the legal work my large law firm can't do."

Lou asked who the other firm was.

"It's Bologna, Blatt & Campanelli. There's plenty of work for both of you. They have fifty lawyers and a hundred support people. They can do the heavy lifting."

Lou thought he hit the jackpot.

When he and Angie looked for a house, Luigi Costa gave him the down payment for a small one in Corona. When their daughter, Theresa, started school, Costa opened a college fund for her.

The money showed how grateful the Costa Family was for Lou's efforts in making sure all their money got properly cleaned.

§

Forty years ago Luigi Costa sat at the bedside of his older brother, Anthony, at Polyclinic General Hospital watching his brother cling to life, tubes in his mouth, nose, and arms. Doctors held little hope of Anthony Costa lasting the night. The Priest had been called to administer the Last Rights of the Church, and the Giordano Funeral Home was notified. The Costa Family owned The Giordano Funeral Home. The Giordano family, who operated it, had been close friends of the Costa family for fifty years.

Luigi saw his brother Anthony at their mother's house every Sunday. Homemade ravioli and lasagna brought all the Costas back home for dinner. Sitting beside his brother Anthony's deathbed, Luigi marveled how little he knew about his older brother, other than he was into things Luigi swore to his wife he'd never be apart.

Three days ago Anthony was at Aqueduct Raceway placing a bet on a horse called Tomahawk when he collapsed. Two EMS guys were fifty feet away and revived him, but Anthony had taken a massive stroke, and by the time the ambulance arrived at the hospital, he was brain dead.

Anthony was a strong-willed, arrogant, and stubborn man who refused to die. Luigi was the designated family bed-side representative for the night. Two policemen stationed at the door were there to make sure no one tried to kill Anthony.

At three-thirty-two, the monitors above Luigi's brother's bed flat-lined. Luigi rang the buzzer for a nurse. Nurse Claire checked for a pulse, found none and removed the tubes from Anthony's dead body. There was no wife to contact, but plenty of girlfriends. Luigi called his mother and two sisters. He left the hospital quickly, eager to return to his normal life with his family.

After the burial at First Calvary, as Luigi walked back to the limousine, three of his brother's friends pulled him aside and offered their condolences. They asked Luigi to meet with them the following night at the Savoy, a local Italian restaurant.

Luigi remembered meeting these three guys a few times over the years. "Fellas, can it wait. The next few days I'd like…"

The broadest of the three said, "Luigi, it can't wait. Be there tomorrow." The three shook Luigi's hand, and each gave him a man hug.

Luigi watched the three cross an expanse of green grass and get into their limo. Luigi knew he'd better meet these guys tomorrow night, or he'd be seeing them at his front door.

The restaurant was untouched from the 1950's, red and white checkered tablecloths, bent-back chairs and chianti bottles with candles dripping multi-colored wax. Luigi sat with his three new friends at a table in the corner.

After the obligatory hugs and hearty handshakes, the spokesman said, "We want to extend our condolences again to the entire Costa Family."

Luigi waited for the other two individuals to say something, but neither of the two men uttered a word. During the entire meeting, only one man spoke. "We have a problem Luigi, but you've got an even bigger one."

Luigi looked at the men, waiting for some revelation. He didn't have to wait long.

"You have a contract on your head for five-hundred thousand dollars."

The speaker of the group waited until his words sank into Luigi's mind.

"But why me?"

"You weren't involved with your family's business, but your brother kept so tight-lipped about who was in and who wasn't, the other crime families assumed you were an active participant.

"But I knew nothing."

The speaker ignored this comment and said, "Certain organizations would like to try and take us over but hesitate because they assume we have a new head of the family business, you. They think if they kill you before you take over, it will be easier for them to walk in and absorb us into their organization."

Luigi didn't know what to say.

"We know you're shocked, but you can't stall. You have to act."

For the next two hours, Luigi listened to how his brother's crime family operated.

Fearing for his family, Luigi accepted the first suggestion offered him, protection for him and his family, armed guards around the outside of his house. Luigi agreed to the second suggestion only after intense pressure from his three dinner partners. His new friends would put out the word "Luigi Costa has assumed leadership of the Costa Family upon his brother's death, and he intends to operate the business as usual. A smooth transition would result from a well-developed plan constructed by his brother, Anthony Costa, a year ago."

Anthony Costa had developed a plan for transition, but it differed from the one announced by his three captains. Anthony's plan was Luigi would take over the leadership in name only. Within a month, Luigi would become gravely ill and give up leadership of the family to Vito Costa, Anthony's bastard son. Vito, with experience as the family consiglieri, would take the organizational reins. Luigi would move to Italy with a guarantee of lifelong support for him, his wife and daughters.

The problem occurred when Vito was killed in front of his house one Tuesday morning leaving Luigi still the boss, but by this time Luigi liked the role of Don, along with the respect, money, and women the job provided.

§

On Saturday Jeremy called Theresa as he promised. His legs felt as weak as they did after Theresa's kiss. The overwhelming feeling of joy returned when he heard her say, "Hi Jeremy." The Heaven-on-earth thing his father always talked about in church now had new meaning.

Theresa told Jeremy all the information she heard during the lectures he missed. Jeremy absorbed little, his mind floating in a world inhabited only by Theresa and him.

Twenty minutes later Heaven was still here on earth for love-struck Jeremy when this angel named, Theresa, apologized for cutting the conversation short. "I have to go food shopping with my mother." The call ended after quick plans were made to meet the next day after church.

Theresa hung up with Jeremy and saw her mother standing next to her with hat and coat on ready to go.

"Who was it?"

"Someone I met in Miami."

"A boy?"

"Yes Mama, a boy."

"Is he nice?"

"Yes, Mother, he is nice."

"What's his name?"

"His name is Jeremy."

"When will we meet him?"

"He's a friend and wanted to know about the lectures he missed. He had to leave after the second day and return to New York."

"Oh, he lives in New York. Anywhere near?

Theresa waited to answer. "How far am I willing to go with this conversation?" she asked herself. She went with, "He lives right here in the County. I'm not sure of his address. I only have his cell number." Theresa grabbed her coat and headed out to the driveway.

In the car, Angie was dying to ask Theresa more about this boy she met in Miami but held off.

Theresa brought up the subject of Aunt Pena reminding her mother, "She wants to come home. She hates Florida. She wants her old job back, and she pleaded for us to help convince Daddy to take her back."

Angie kept her mouth shut until her daughter finished.

"I'll do what I can." Theresa knew her Mother would help her.

Theresa wanted desperately to tell her mother about Jeremy. She never kept secrets from Angie and didn't want to start now. Theresa wanted her mother to know she had found the man she planned to marry.

After buying out the grocery store and putting all the food into the SUV, Angie started up again with question after question about Jeremy. Angie was relentless.

Theresa told her mother, "Either you cool it with the questions about Jeremy, or I'm getting out of the car and taking the bus home."

Angie pulled out of the parking lot and immediately hit traffic. Mother and daughter sat quietly, inching along the crowded road. After ten minutes, Angie came at Theresa with a new burst of energy. Angie peppered her daughter with questions. Theresa sat wondering what would happen if she turned the tables on her mother and announced, "Mom, Jeremy's black." Theresa could predict what would happen next. Her mother would go into the house and tell her father. Theresa could hear the conversation that would take place. Her mother is crying, "I don't know what we'll do, Lou. Our daughter is dating a black man."

Her father would twitch as he yelled, "Please, stop crying and let's plan to end this quickly." Lou would call his daughter into the room and say, "I forbid you to see that N…. again,"

Theresa knew what she'd say back, "I'll see him anytime I want."

Angie would continue, "What can we do, Lou?

"We'll force her to stop seeing this N…"

"What if Theresa brings him over for you to meet?"

"He's never going to step a foot in this house."

Angie would moan, "We'll lose our little girl, Lou. You have to do something."

"Don't worry; I will."

Theresa often heard her father say, "Don't worry, I will," but in this scenario, those words had a scary ring.

§

Tom climbed the six-step stoop and rang the Thompson's bell. Tom accepted Mrs. Thompson's invitation for dinner with lightning speed. He remembered what a good cook Jeremy's mother was. Tom thought for sure he smelled Mrs. Thompson's pot roast when he stepped foot on her block. Tom pictured Nora Thompson's dark brown gravy covering the pot roast, the mashed potatoes, and the red cabbage.

Tom and Jeremy lived a mile from each other. The professional blacks lived closer to the border of their white neighbors. Tom loved Jeremy's block, a row of well-kept brownstone, lined with sycamores.

The stark difference between the block Jeremy lived on and the rest of the district's southern tier immediately smacked an observer in the face. The sycamores abruptly stopped at First Avenue, so did the neat, stately brownstones. First Avenue was called the Mason-Dixon Line by the old timers in the County.

Tom remembered how at first his anxiety increased walking into Jeremy's neighborhood. Stares from the people standing around on the street corners smoking weed made him want to run. When Jeremy walked to Tom's house, the trip attracted equally uncomfortable stares.

Beginning in October, walking home alone made Tom tense. He never failed to misjudge the time when he played at Jeremy's house, and darkness often settled earlier than he anticipated. Tom was fearful when the streets got dark. Often a worried look remained on his face when he arrived home.

One time his mother, Alice, asked, "What's wrong?" But Tom sat silently at the kitchen table and instead of answering his mother's question he substituted, "What's for dinner?"

At the end of junior high both Tom and Jeremy quit baseball and a natural parting of the ways occurred. They would see each other occasionally at school, but it was uncomfortable when they met each was with a group of friends. Tom's all white friends looked suspiciously at Jeremy's all black friends and vice versa. Tom's mother asked about Jeremy a few times, then stopped, understanding the natural, but unfortunate, course of events where friends like Jeremy and Tom were concerned.

So many memories raced through Tom's mind as he approached Jeremy Thompson's door. He was happy for the invitation, and Tom always looked forward to seeing Reverend Thompson. When Tom was here last for dinner, Jeremy's brother, Toby, wasn't born. He looked forward to meeting the young boy.

Jeremy answered the door. "Welcome, it's been a long time since you've been here for dinner."

"It seems like it was a week ago. The same wonderful cooking smells bring back memories."

"Yes, Mom's still at it."

"I always liked sitting on your stoop talking."

A fire burned in the living room, and its flames lit the mahogany fireplace giving a warm glow to the leather couch and armchairs in the living room. "Come into the kitchen. Mom is putting the icing on a cake."

"I loved her tomato-soup cake with the chocolate frosting."

"I remember. You would always take a piece home with you."

"Delicious. Absolutely, delicious."

"Pop will be downstairs in a minute. He's putting his Sunday sermon to bed."

They stepped in the kitchen, and Nora Thompson hurried over to Tom and gave him a big hug. "It's so good to see you, Tom. It's been a long time. You're still a good looking boy."

With that, Reverend Thompson walked into the kitchen and shook Tom's hand vigorously. "Welcome, Tom, it's good to see you again."

"Same here Reverend Thompson."

"What can we get you to drink?"

"A glass of red wine, please."

"I'll get it, Pop." Jeremy rushed to the bar for the drinks.

Tom and Jonas Thompson sat on the couch asking about each other's families, but when Jeremey returned with the drinks, Reverend Thompson wasted no time in asking Tom, "If you win a seat on the school board, what will be your first project."

"I was hoping to receive some guidance from you tonight."

"Our son Toby has Downs Syndrome. He's typical of Special Education students in the southern tier of the district. They receive less than the basics."

"What does Toby need?"

"Toby needs services the school district refuses to provide for him and many other children in the southern tier. In Toby's case, he needs a behavioral therapist to help him gain the social skills he needs to succeed in everyday situations. Toby won't need AP Physics or Chemistry. He won't take Pre-Calculus. All we ask is the district take the money saved from having fewer science, math and violin classes and give special education students classes which develop the skills they need to function in life."

Tom nodded in agreement. "It makes sense."

"The attitude the principals have toward parents in the southern tier is disrespectful and often abusive. They know they can say and do anything to us. These guys were hand-picked by Lou Marinara, not because they're capable educational leaders, but because they're either related to him or are friends or cronies."

"There have been rumors," said Jeremy, "Principalships in the southern tier junior and senior high schools cost twenty-five thousand dollars, slightly less for an elementary position. I don't know about the northern tier schools. I assume it's a lot more."

"You're joking?"

"No joke," said Jeremy. "It's worth the money. The salaries and benefits, plus pensions, are well worth the initial investment."

"What about the other jobs in the school system?"

Jonas fielded this one. "Tom, that's a whole other story. Although principals' jobs are important, it's the rank and file workers in a school who make the real difference. The district office puts the worse teachers, aides and ancillary staff in minority schools."

Jeremy glanced at Tom to make sure he was keeping up with him. "Tom, I'm sorry we're hitting you with everything all at once, but it's important."

"No, no, I'm shocked, but I'm with you. Go on."

Jeremy took Tom at his word and continued, "I'll tell you about my friend who was hired last year in a school at the far end of the district's southern tier. Poverty is deep in the neighborhood. School services are almost non-existent."

Jonas continued, "The district placed Jeremy's friend in this school as a remedial reading teacher. The school needed one desperately, and I guess none of Marinara's friends wanted the job."

"Pop, let me tell this part," said Jeremy. "The same day the district appointed my friend, they also filled another position. They sent an origami teacher. Out of all the services needed in this school, why they would fund an origami position, no one knew."

"Months later," Jonas interrupted, "The origami teacher slipped and announced how grateful she was for her Uncle Lou's help. 'I graduated from college with a degree in art history and couldn't find a job in the next county, but thanks to Uncle Lou I got a job here.' "

"The girl lasted a semester," said Jeremy. "She couldn't take it, and one day she stormed out of the school never to be seen again. The money had already been appropriated for the position so they asked around and no one wanted the job. They kept the origami position on the roster in case some other of Lou's relatives wanted it up the road."

"Does the district keep a list of applicants for positions who are qualified and waiting for a job?" asked Tom.

"They keep a list of people they've no intention of hiring," said Jeremy. "They show this list to anyone inquiring about a position. When Marinara doesn't have anyone who needs a job, the head of HR takes the first person off the list. My friend got the job this way. He waited two years. Finally, they reached him. My friend informed me Lou bragged for a month they chose a black candidate off the list."

"How did your friend do?"

"He gave us a window into how things worked. The needs of the students in the southern tier are overwhelming." Jeremy's eyes filled. Jonas and Tom waited for him to continue. "Pop, tell Tom what happened when they experimented with busing three years ago."

Tom watched as Reverend Thompson struggled with his words. Jonas cleared his throat. "Do you know how hard it is for a black third-grader to march into an all-white school, past the staring eyes of unfriendly parents and their children? Well, I can tell you, it's not easy. The parents and kids who try not to make the new black kid uncomfortable are so uptight the air fills with tension. Now, add those people who resent this black intrusion, and you have an atmosphere which is less than ideal for learning." Jonas paused, and Jeremy took up the story.

"Tom, there was a small attempt at making the northern tier more diverse, the board and the district's office of pupil personnel bused kids from a school here over to an all-white school in the far end of the northern tier. The school went to third grade, but there were fights among the bussed black students and the white students. Some white parents secretly encouraged this behavior. The bullying of the black students was so intense, the district discontinued all future attempts at diversity. Seldom is one side all right and the other all wrong."

Tom looked puzzled by Jeremy's 'one side' comment.

"At a subsequent school board meeting," said Jeremy, "Some white parents reported to the school board that bullying had increased eighty percent since the district began busing black kids to their school."

"But, wait the white kids bullied the black kids."

"That's the point. The subsequent report didn't say the white kids did the bullying. The report just said bullying went up eighty percent. The newspapers got hold of the story, and further spread the false impression the black students were at fault. You can't win in a debate like that."

Tom kept silent. Jeremy continued, "This noble experiment ended at the half-year mark. Both sides were relieved."

"There's nothing to be said," muttered Tom.

"The answer is action, and action won't happen until someone like you runs for the board," added Jeremy.

§

Angie never stopped asking about Theresa's new guy. "When will we meet this person you say is 'only a friend'?"

Theresa bristled at her mother's attempt at being cute but held her tongue. "I'm sure Jeremy will come over when he has a chance."

"What does Jeremy do for a living?"

"He helps his father with the family business, and he's also a writer when he has the time."

"It's nice his family has a business."

"Yes, they have about one hundred and fifty clients." Theresa wasn't sure she could keep a straight face when she thought of Jeremy's father calling his congregants 'clients'."

Theresa was sure if she continued this conversation, there would be a great deal of discussion, all unpleasant.

"Mom, I have to go. Antoinette is waiting for me at the Mall. We'll go to lunch, and then look for her wedding dress." The word wedding was a sure fire way to change the subject.

"How lucky Antoinette's mother is. Her daughter found a man she can settle down with and give her grandkids. I wish someday I'm as lucky."

"See you tonight mom. Maybe some of Antoinette's good fortune will rub off on me. Maybe I'll find someone soon." She wanted to tell Angie she'd already found the right guy.

"Will you be home for dinner? I'm making homemade ravioli, the kind you and your father love, the ones with the ricotta and spinach filling."

§

Angie Marinara haunted her daughter for weeks to ask her new friend over for dinner. Finally, Theresa had enough, bit the bullet and invited Jeremy. "Next Sunday Jeremy is coming to dinner," she told her mother.

Unfortunately, Theresa's plans to mention Jeremy was African-American never materialized. The time never seemed right. Theresa grimaced, "There will never be a right time." She knew her parents' reaction would be explosive and prayed any explosions would be postponed until after Jeremy left.

As Sunday came closer, Theresa had second thoughts about inviting Jeremy. She wished she'd arranged the meeting in a more neutral place, a restaurant perhaps or maybe a police station in case her father tried to kill Jeremy, or her.

Theresa Marinara's heart hurt when she thought what her father might say when Jeremy walked through the front door. Theresa knew his temper and also knew how much her father hated black people.

On Wednesday, over lunch, Theresa prepared Jeremy for what was coming. The two sat in a booth at Pinkus Luncheonette on Main Street. The dark wooden booths lining the restaurant's wall provided more privacy than the open tables in the center of the room. The old ice cream parlor dated to the 1940's and the owner attempted to keep the place looking like it did when the luncheonette first opened.

Over the years many couples sat in these booths and declared their young love for each other. Theresa and Jeremy weren't the first couple to fear their parent's reaction to the news the couple planned to become engaged or were already married.

"Jeremy, I'm worried about Sunday. My parents are old school. They always expected I'd marry an Italian boy. When you walk in, I don't know what they'll say or do. I love you, and I don't want you hurt by their reaction."

"I know your parents will be shocked I'm not Italian. They're going to be more shocked I'm black. I can handle it. My parents will be surprised too, but I know once they meet you, they'll be fine."

Theresa realized how clueless Jeremy was about her family's prejudice, to how cruel they can be. Her parents grew up on daily doses of prejudice. She remembered as a little girl the racial slurs both her grandparents used when they spoke about other nationalities: Mick, Kike, Nip, Chink, and Pollok, the list went on and on.

There were so many things Theresa wanted to tell Jeremy about life in her world. She knew in practice both her parents and grandparents had developed relationships with other white nationalities, even formed friendships with some. Other nationalities lived next door over the years or became clients, and some insight into these strangers showed her grandparents and her parents, all non-Italians weren't necessarily monsters. With this said, Theresa's friends and family constantly told her that Italians were still the preferred family over all others. Theresa remembered the real hatred, the savage language, was always saved for people of color, particularly blacks.

Theresa realized part of the reason blacks never became friendly with whites was they were never allowed to live next door, never allowed to join the same clubs or churches, or allowed to attend the same schools. There were exceptions, but these exceptions were few and far apart in her grandparents' day and even to a great extent in her parents' time.

"How could someone like Jeremy suspect the truth? Sure, he'd experienced the obvious slurs used to describe blacks by many European Americans, but she doubted Jeremy heard the term 'mulignan' used by Italians to describe black people. The Italian word 'mulignan' means a black, shiny vegetable with a reflection of purple, an eggplant. The word by itself doesn't sound so bad unless you heard the tone of voice used by the speaker, then it became degrading, vile and upsetting. Even as a child, Theresa sensed the repugnance in the word.

Jeremy's voice brought Theresa back to the present. He was still going on and on how everything would be all right once he and her parents sat down over Sunday dinner.

Theresa couldn't stand it any longer. "Jeremy, you've no idea what you're saying. My parents will explode. In the remote chance, my parents wait until you leave before they go through the roof, the minute you pull away from the curb, the roof is off the house. They won't stop yelling for days, months, years."

Theresa was frustrated. Jeremy did not understand what a dangerous road lay ahead or how determined her father would be to break them up.

CHAPTER 9

ON THE WAY TO HER REGULAR SATURDAY APPOINTMENT AT Lulu Belle's Beauty Salon, Mary McMurray dropped off a campaign election poster at the hardware store across the street from Lulu's.

Her husband, Mark was a regular customer at the hardware store, and when he asked Frank Ramirez if he'd mind putting an election poster for Mary in his store window, Frank was happy to do it. Mary thanked Frank for the free advertising.

As Mary left the hardware store, Frank called after her, "Mary, if you win you have to do something about my school taxes, they're going through the roof."

Mary answered, "I'll do my damnedest."

Mary crossed Main Street and arrived right on time for her hair appointment. As usual, everyone in the beauty parlor was glad to see her. When Mary Mc Murray was in the house the atmosphere was brighter, the room filled with something extra. People called it charisma. Her sharp tongue gave everyone a laugh unless directed at them. Mary's bite was always directed at those who merited it, never at someone weaker than she.

Today the salon was packed. Everyone saw Mary carry a poster over to Lulu Belle. Mary had called Lulu yesterday and asked if she'd put one of her election posters in the salon window. No one knew what the poster read. All the ladies watched to see what was up. Lulu took the sign and immediately went to the front of the salon and placed it carefully in the window.

Lulu Belle turned to all the customers and announced, "Ladies, can I have everyone's attention." The place quieted, and LuLu continued, "I'm happy to announce my friend Mary McMurray is a candidate for a seat on our school board." A loud round of applause sprung from the crowded salon. Many of you have known Mary for years. She needs all the help we can give her in this new endeavor." A murmur of agreement filled the salon.

A customer called out, "How can we help?"

"First of all, each candidate must collect signatures of registered voters in the district, Democrat, Republican or Independent. It doesn't matter. So, Mary needs help with collecting signatures. After Mary hands in the required amount of signatures to the board of elections, they put her name on the ballot for Election Day. And to show my support for Mary, I'm offering anyone who comes to the salon and signs a petition for Mary and takes a whole sheet home for friends and family to sign will receive a gift card for a free manicure."

Again, the salon filled with applause. "Thank you, ladies. Now I know you want to return to letting us make you beautiful. Thanks so much for your show of support and I'll see you next week with more details."

Mary hugged Lulu and sat down to have her hair colored. Lulu put a long plastic cape on Mary's shoulders, tied it around her neck and applied the coloring. No sooner was Mary's head half covered with dye than Lulu Belle's cell phone rang.

"Mary, I have to take the call, my son is at the dentist, and I have to okay an extraction." While Mary waited for Lulu to come back, she contented herself by looking out onto Main Street. She could see Frank's hardware store across the street. As she watched, Frank reached into the window display and removed Mary's poster.

Lulu returned and looked upset.

"Is everything all right?" Mary asked.

"The call came from Felicia Estes. Look out the window. She and Betty Kramer are standing across the street looking over here."

"Who are they?"

"They come in every so often for manicures. When they do come in, all they talk about are their kids and the PTA, and how they're on the district's PTA board. They brag how much power they have, and about the important people they meet at the Inter-County PTA Board Galas."

"Why did they call?"

"They threatened me if I didn't take your poster out of the window they'd picket the salon starting now. They swore they'd stand there and wait until I removed the poster from my window."

Mary saw red. She looked out at the two women across the street. "Now, I understand why Frank Ramirez yanked my poster out of his store window."

Mary rose from the salon chair and headed for the front door, plastic covering around her neck, half her head wet with reddish brown dye #10. Mary was on the sidewalk in seconds, and across the street in a flash.

The whole salon rushed to the window as Mary marched across the street and approached her prey. Mrs. McMurray's hands waved in every direction, and the salon patrons swore they never remembered seeing anyone's mouth open that wide. The ladies watched the scene waiting to see someone's head bitten off."

The patrons were unsure what Mary uttered when she pointed toward the hardware store. The next thing the ladies saw was Felicia Estes, and Betty Kramer headed for Frank's hardware store. Mary stood at the curb's edge, hands on hips, waiting, watching.

The two PTA mothers disappeared into the hardware store. A minute later, Frank appeared at the window, sign in hand. He looked over at Mary and gave a wave. Mary returned the gesture and headed back to finish her dye job. For the third time, the applause sounded throughout Lulu Belle's Beauty Salon.

When things quieted down, Lulu Belle asked, "So, what did you tell them?"

Mary's responded, "Nothing."

"Oh, come on Mary. Tell me."

Without lifting her head, Mary said, "I told them I was contacting my lawyers and then I was contacting their husbands to tell them what assholes their wives are and if their wives ever come near me or even speak to me again, I was instructing my lawyer to file suit for damages equal to every penny they have. Then I told those two bitches to move their sorry asses into the hardware store and ask Frank to please put my sign back in his window, and I told them to do it now."

"And off they went. You're something, Mary. You'll be a great candidate. This campaign is going to be fun."

§

Ernie Spikes, Mary Mc Murray's neighbor, and her new Petitions Coordinator worked hard at the town cemetery, a proud member of the United Cemetery Workers of America. Ernie chaired the local chapter of his union and his co-workers at the Evergreen facility liked and respected him.

Ernie made friends easily; he's a guy older men called a 'straight shooter.' Ernie would pressure none of his coworkers into supporting someone they didn't want to support, but after volunteering to help Mary with petitions and signatures for her campaign, he naturally figured his friends at work would help him.

Mary and her husband, Mark came through for him when he needed help. As soon as his wife, Millie, fell ill, Mary and Mark McMurray were there for him. Ernie tried not to let his eyes water at the memory of those sad days before Millie passed away.

Luckily for Mary, the monthly union meeting met the next day right after work. Ernie arrived at the union hall the next day at 5:15, earlier than usual. The smell of stale cigarettes made him feel comfortable. The union hall's old wooden floors oozed cigarette smoke from a thousand past meetings. The smell made him feel good.

Ernie Spikes smoked for a good part of his adult life but gave it up after Millie died. Although the doctors never said his smoking in their house contributed to Millie's death, Ernie couldn't shut it out of his mind. It was fifteen years since his last smoke, but even a whiff of a cigarette still made his day.

Meetings scheduled for 6:00 sharp never began before 6:15. The group wasn't formal. Ernie knew why he enjoyed being chairman. No one gave him a hard time. The large clock on the wall read 5:50, and Spikes already had 21 men who agreed to help Mary Mc Murray.

Only two men said they couldn't help. One was scheduled for an operation in the next few weeks, and one had a sick wife requiring all his free time. Ernie remembered how he suffered when Millie fell ill. Ernie recalled the pain and offered to help the guy anyway he could.

By 6:15, six more union men walked in the door. Five of the six verbalized they'd help, which made twenty-six. Four more walked in. and before Ernie could ask for their help, one of them mentioned: "We were down the block at Foley's Bar and this guy, Vince Miller, bought drinks for everyone, and we volunteered to help him win a seat on the school board." Ernie just smiled and was grateful he had so many guys who said they'd give him a hand with Mary's petitions.

The meetings always began with the members reciting the Pledge of Allegiance, followed by a treasurer's report. After the Treasurer finished, he asked for the floor. "Some of us will support different candidates in the upcoming school board election. I hope this won't be a problem," he continued looking over at Ernie. "We don't want to take time from the meeting to discuss the school board election, so if any of you are interested in hearing about another candidate, meet me at Foley's Bar at the end of the block."

Ernie knew the treasurer was a good friend of Lou Marinara, but Ernie was confident his group could collect the required number of signatures to put Mary's name on the ballot.

Mary gave Ernie a list of her friends and family, and Ernie contacted them for help. All were happy to volunteer. Ernie's plan consisted of visiting their homes and giving each some idea on how to help his friend. Ernie smiled to himself, "I'll offer a ride to anyone who needs one on Election Day. I also gave Mary a list of senior centers to visit starting immediately." Ernie was hyped.

§

Tom Foster pulled up to the Shady Pines Assisted Living Facility in the northwest section of the district with Mary McMurray riding shotgun next to him. Mary had an old friend who was the Director of Nursing Services at the facility. The residents at Shady Pines had their wits about them and moved to an Assisted Living Facility because of loneliness. Shady Pines provided the company of other people, something they didn't have at home.

"This is fertile ground for you to get votes, Mary."

"You too, don't forget each voter can vote for seven people. There are seven seats up for grabs. I'm not the only one the old people will vote for, wise guy. Old people appreciate handsome young fellows and pretty young girls, too. There are no pretty young girls running, so you are the handsome one looking for votes."

Tom feigned being embarrassed as they walked from the parking lot.

Mary's friend from college, Sara Jane, met them in the lobby, brought them to the day room of the facility and asked the residents to welcome the guest speakers. The applause was enthusiastic, but not loud.

Mary spoke first. Tom saw the attention she immediately received from the hundred and fifty seniors. Mary explained she and Tom were trying to win seats on their school board and they were here to ask for their votes. A man in the first row asked how the election concerned them. They didn't have kids in school.

"It's a good question and one which older people should be asking," said Mary. She explained, "Most people assume only parents of public school children should be on the board. But, I realize now this would be a disaster for the rest of the population."

More than a few faces in the audience looked shocked by Mary's strong statement. Mary had their attention which was her goal. "Older people need representation, so the parents of school-aged kids don't go crazy raising taxes for things which are over the top. Some young people forget many of us are living on fixed incomes."

Now the faces in the room nodded in agreement. Mary knew her audience. "Older people need someone to make sure the money coming into their school district earmarked for us, goes to us."

Puzzled faces peered up at Mary. "You didn't know money is given to the school district to encourage the students to go out into the Community and perform for senior citizens, and for seniors to come to the schools to help enrich the curriculum with their experiences."

A fashionable lady toward the middle of the room raised her hand. Mary acknowledged her as the lady slowly stood. "Mary, with all due respect, why are you running?"

Mary stood at the podium without answering. Tom saw his friend debating how she should respond. Finally, Mary put her mouth close to the microphone and softly uttered the right words. "I've been telling people; I want to do something for my community and my years in the business world will help me make the sound financial decisions a school board member has to make, and that is true. But standing here with you, my peers, I'll tell you something I don't usually admit when I answer the same question before PTAs and civic organizations, not even before church and synagogue groups. Most of the people I speak to are younger than I, and they won't understand my answer the way I'm hoping you will."

Mary paused for what seemed an eternity. Finally, she continued, "I want to be relevant. I want to feel needed. I spent thirty years with people who came to me for advice both at work and at home. Then, suddenly, no one asked me anything. My daughter moved to New Jersey for her husband's job. I encouraged them to go although I knew I'd miss them."

Mary's voice choked, but she continued, "It's the natural course of life. I was no longer at work, so no one asked my opinion. I'm the same person I was a short time ago when no one in my house could do anything without my help. Ladies and gentlemen, I want to be needed. I am in good health, and I have a lot to give and that, my friends, is one of the main reasons I'm here asking for your vote. Thank you for understanding why I'm running for this position."

Slowly, the residents of Shady Pines rose from their seats and clapped harder than they probably should have. Some would have sore hands in the morning, but you could see they didn't care. Mary introduced Tom, and from the side of his mouth, he whispered, "Thanks a lot, Mary. How do I follow that?"

Mary finished, and Tom found himself in front of a sea of seniors.

A very old man's hand shot up first. "It's good to see a young man like you stepping out and trying to make a difference in your community." The man sat down without asking a question. Tom thanked the gentleman and pointed to a man in his late sixties. Tom had learned the skill of approximating ages.

This senior began, "Of course, I want to make sure every kid in our school district gets a good education, but I don't want to wind up in the poorhouse doing it."

Applause echoed in the speaker's ears.

The man continued "Cut budget expenses. For example, my wife and I work three days a week. We leave pretty early in the morning and often find ourselves behind a school bus. We enjoy watching the young kids hopping on the bus We don't mind waiting, but while sitting there, we've noticed many young mothers come out to the bus with their kids, a steaming cup of coffee in one hand, and their child's hand in the other. Often these ladies have a jacket over their pajamas."

A woman in the back of the room took the spotlight. "Why should we pay, so some lazy mother doesn't have to get up off her ass and drive her kids to school?"

A new round of applause deafened Tom. He couldn't believe his ears. These old people were something.

"We have time for one more question," said the nervous coordinator. A man in the front raised his hand. "Jake, you get the last question."

"Mrs. McMurray, what's your take on the present school board chairman, Lou Marinara?"

Mary was taken back for a moment, "I don't know much about him. I've only seen him from a distance."

"Well, watch out for him."

"No personal comments, please," said the coordinator whisking the mic from Mary. "We want to thank you both for coming today," said the coordinator surprised at the deafening applause from the audience.

Tom gently pulled the mic from the coordinator and said, "Be assured if elected Mary and I will address your concerns with vigor" Again, the applause rose to levels rarely heard at the Center.

As they drove away from Shady Pines, Mary kidded Tom, "And as usual, you triumphed big with the ladies. They kept on trying to guess what movie star you looked like."

Tom suggested no name.

Mary pressed, "Come on Tom, tell me who they meant."

Blushing and exasperated, Tom responded, "Ask Bunny Krouse."

Mary took Tom's answer to mean the conversation was over. The two had developed a rapport in the short time they'd known each other. Both felt comfortable enough to show their feelings without repercussions.

Mary sat back and thought, "I'll kill myself before I go into one of those places."

§

Tom saw his cell ID, but he couldn't take Mary's call. Jen waited on the couch for him to return from her kitchen with a fabulous bottle of wine and two glasses. Tom's relationships with women his age had taken a beating since he met Mary McMurray.

Campaigning night and day, collecting enough signatures to have his name placed on the ballot, then the grueling trips to senior centers, churches, and clubs had poisoned three budding relationships.

Tom's cell showed Mary left a message. "Sorry, Mrs. McMurray, no school board talk tonight."

His new girlfriend, Jen, smiled as Tom sat down and put his arm around her. Jen pressed play on the DVD and the old classic movie, *Love Story*, appeared on the screen. Its romantic theme song played while the credits rolled.

The next morning neither Tom nor Jen remembered much about the movie.

§

Rocco Pinzon had been district superintendent for five years. Rocco realized the toll his position as superintendent had taken on his life. He began the job with a wife who loved him, and who he thought still did until unexpected divorce papers delivered to him at work said differently.

Last year a man thrust an envelope into his gut in the corridor of the district office. The note attached to the divorce papers requested he "Refrain from entering his house or coming within two hundred feet of said dwelling."

"I'm fifty-five years old, and I'm alone. My kids are grown and living on the other side of the country."

Rocco was a resilient type of guy and after thoughtful inspections in the bathroom mirror, and noticing more hair on his brush each morning, he had a facelift and a hair transplant. "If I'm in the game, I have to look at it."

A three-week vacation, a plane ride to Brazil, and miraculously Rocco looked ten years younger. Some uncharitable people quipped, "After all that work, Rocco looks like a fifty-five-year-old man who had a facelift and a hair transplant." But the majority of people agreed the change was apparent. Rocco looked younger than before.

"Now, I'm ready for action." Although Rocco was on the prowl, to his credit, he had no intention of 'shitting where he ate.'

Rocco saw too many friends and colleagues fall prey to the easy 'pickins' available in the PTA. There are women desperate for a kind word; women stuck in the boredom of households where there was neither time nor desire for affection, women who'd hop onto the conference table in the principal's office quicker than you could shut the door.

Mary McMurray, being kinder than most, especially when someone was down, commented after seeing him for the first time, "I give Rocco Pinzon credit, good for him."

Pinzon was too young to retire and was ready to jump back into the dating game. If he wanted to keep his three hundred and fifty thousand dollar a year job, he had to be on the top of his game, ready for all the challenges this cesspool of a district handed him.

When Rocco took his job as superintendent, he'd hoped it would be a stepping stone to a seat on the State Board of Regents. That position would be a perfect way to end his career. But meanwhile, Rocco looked around his large, spacious office and thought, "This isn't such a bad job." His reverie was soon interrupted by the assistant superintendent, Regina Moriarity's entrance through his office's open door.

"Rocco, here's the report you asked Phil Turner to write. He did a good job uncovering who is supporting whom for the school board. Phil Turner investigated one half of the district and his lackey, Eddie Fisher, the little bastard, did the other half."

"Regina, is that any way to talk about our esteemed colleague?"

"That bastard is one dangerous individual."

"Eddie's alright as long as Phil keeps his leash tight."

"The guy worries me, and he should worry you, too." Regina tossed the report on Pinzon's desk and left.

"You're worried about Fisher? Well, I'm more worried about you."

§

Regina Moriarity wanted to be superintendent, and she was prepared to do anything to make it happen. The one thing Regina couldn't do was hide her ambition from Rocco Pinzon. There was only so much ass kissing she could pull off with him.

Regina was fifty-one, six feet tall, solidly built and could have played football if girls were allowed on the field back at James Madison High School in Flatbush, Brooklyn. Regina's face was weather-beaten from her long-time whiskey drinking. Regina smoked like a chimney. Her voice was gravelly and when she laughed her hearty good humor was infectious.

Regina was a party girl, not in the sense of loose sexual morals, but as a girl who wanted to have fun, plain good-time partying. She never married and lived with her sister, Marge, who also never married.

At her beach house on the south shore of Long Island, Regina reigned as Queen of Fun. The house looked over the Great South Bay. She and Marge bought it many years ago after their parents left them some money. Then, the prices weren't exorbitant for waterfront property.

The Moriarity Girls knew how to throw a party, especially for people who could help their careers. The liquor flowed, the music played, and the food abounded. There were no holds barred when entertaining school board members. Big crowds came, everyone except her rival, Rocco Pinzon.

§

"Mom, what will we do about Aunt Pena," said Theresa, "She's so miserable down in Florida."

"Let me see what I can do."

"Thanks, mom. I have to do something; after all, she is my godmother."

Theresa got up, "I'll be in my room if you decide on something."

Angie remembered the decision to have Lou's brother and his wife as godparents. Angie wanted her sister, Connie, but Lou insisted, "We can't ask Vito without asking Pena. You can have your sister for the next one." But there never was a next one.

Angie always felt a slight strain when she and Pena were together and could never put her finger on it. Angie always suspected Pena knew her first choice for godparent was Connie.

The discomfort wasn't helped by Angie's slight jealousy of Lou's reliance on Pena in his business. Pena was a big help to Lou. He often joked, "Pena is the accountant who keeps us all out of jail." Angie recalled not understanding what her husband meant.

Angie didn't want to prevent her sister-in-law from returning to New York. Pena had always been nice to her and Pena deserved her help. Angie called to Theresa, "I'll speak to your Father tonight. I'm sure he'll agree."

Angie didn't mention to her daughter this might take more than a little effort. Lou was furious and very hurt over Pena and his brother leaving New York.

§

"Lou, I want to speak to you about something."

"Make it quick. I have to go out in a few minutes."

"At least come and sit down." Angie waited until her husband reluctantly took a seat on the couch. "When Theresa was down in Florida for the religious conference she visited with Pena."

"You told me."

"Pena isn't happy down there without Vito."

"So, what am I supposed to do?"

"Pena told Theresa she wanted to come back to New York."

"Why should I care? She didn't care about leaving us in a lurch to go down there."

"You know, Lou, it was all Vito's decision. Pena wasn't crazy about leaving everyone here."

"But she did."

"She had no choice. Vito insisted they go to Florida and that was the end of the discussion. You of all people should understand."

Lou gave no response, but Angie knew she had hit a cord. "Lou, she thinks she needs your approval. Pena might be able to help you put some things in order. I hear you complaining to everyone you can't find anything, and you expect to be audited."

Lou remained silent, but Angie saw the wheels turning in his mind. "Lou, she's family and Theresa says she wants to help her godmother."

Finally, Lou promised, "I'll give it some thought."

Angie smiled. She knew Pena would be coming home soon.

As Lou was leaving the house, he called to his wife, "Tell, Pena to come home, and she can have her old job back if she wants."

§

Angie lightly knocked on Theresa's bedroom door. "Honey, are you awake?"

"Come on in, mom. I'm doing my nails. "

"I wanted to tell you the good news. Your father told me he had no objection to Pena coming back to New York and she can have her old job if she wants."

"That's great. I'll call Pena right away." Theresa picked up her cell phone off the nightstand, but before she dialed, the phone rang. Theresa knew who it was. She texted Jeremy she'd return his call in fifteen minutes.

She quickly dialed Florida. Pena answered on the third ring, "Hello, this is Pena."

"Aunt Pena, this is Theresa. I've good news. My father wants you to come home."

Angie could hear Pena's squealing from across the room.

"Aunt Pena, I have more good news. He wants you to have your old job back."

This time Angie heard weeping. Angie took the phone from her daughter. "Pena this is Angie. We all missed you, and we look forward to you coming back. I miss your homemade Ravioli."

Angie and her sister-in-law talked non-stop. After several minutes Theresa looked at her wristwatch. Jeremy would be expecting her call. Finally, Theresa motioned to her mother; she wanted her phone back. "Pena, I got to go. The phone is Theresa's, and she needs it back. I'll call you tomorrow, and we can make plans."

"Your aunt is over the moon. I'm happy for her."

"I'm happy too, but I need to make a call."

"Hmm, sounds important. I know when to leave."

Theresa held her tongue and made no retort.

As Angie closed the door, Jeremy called again. "Is it a good time?"

Theresa's heart skipped a beat. She lay back on her pillow, happier than she ever remembered.

The conversation went on for hours. Angie passed Theresa's door several times to catch a word or two of the conversation. All Angie heard was an occasional giggle.

After a while, Angie gave up and went to bed.

§

Saturday evening Tom and Jen rode out to Long Island to the annual Fireman's Fair. Traffic was light, and Tom zoomed along the expressway at sixty miles an hour.

"What's your favorite carnival game," asked Tom?

"The Goldfish Game," replied Jen. "What's yours?"

"I'm a sucker for The Basketball Hoops. They're rigged, but I still like to try."

"I remember my father telling me that when I was a little girl. I always thought he made it up because he wasn't very good at shooting baskets."

"And you never told your father. You made believe he could do anything. What a good daughter."

The couple pulled into the parking lot and saw the giant Ferris Wheel. Both felt the excitement of the bright lights, the sound of the calliope and the smell of popcorn and cotton candy.

Parking was easy to find, and the line for tickets was short. "Tonight's going to be fun," thought Tom.

The couple strolled down the Midway playing games. Twenty dollars lighter, they headed toward the first ride of the night, the Cyclone. The Terminator and the Avenger followed. Exhausted and thirsty, they headed to the food court for some cold beer.

Energized by tonight's break, Tom and Jen hurried to their favorite ride, the Ferris Wheel.

Tom considered a ride on the Ferris-Wheel the most romantic attraction in an amusement park. "It's my favorite ride," said Tom as the operator man punched their tickets.

"I know your type," said Jen. "You enjoy when you get to the top of the Ferris Wheel, and the operator starts letting people off one car at a time. You look out over the whole Fair, then, you put your arm around a girl, and you kiss her."

Tom blushed and knew it was true.

"And that's why it's my favorite ride, too," said Jen squeezing Tom's hand as they boarded the ride.

As he looked out at the moonlit sky, Tom's spirits soared. He glanced at the beautiful girl sitting to his left and felt terrific.

Eddie Fisher watched the happy couple from the ground and he too felt his spirit lift.

§

Arnie Kramer observed his wife for the next week looking for any sign she was a lesbian, but he saw nothing. He noticed no change in their sex life. It was just as rusty as usual. Arnie monitored how often Felicia Estes called and how often she and Betty went out. Arnie saw little out of the ordinary.

Kramer secretly asked a friend, experienced in surveillance, to tap his home phone. He listened to the taped conversation between his wife and Felicia Estes. He heard nothing suspicious, only a great deal of gossip about the school district. After two weeks Arnie was sure Emily lied, the rumor made-up.

"What reason could Emily have for telling me this horrible story?" He needed to know. "Betty did you and your cousin, Emily, have a falling out?"

Betty was visibly upset. "Why do you ask?" was all that came out of her mouth.

"I just wondered. Emily hasn't called the house lately. You haven't mentioned her name in a while."

"Nothing's wrong. I guess we've both been busy."

"Good to hear. You know you can always tell me anything."

"I know Arnie." She broke down crying.

Arnie said nothing. He waited until his wife cried herself out. "Betty is spreading a vicious lie about you and Felicia Estes. Is that what you're so upset about?"

Betty looked puzzled, and Arnie was sure Emily made up the whole lesbian story.

Arnie told his wife what Emily told him. Betty cried again, "Emily swore she'd get even with me, but I never thought she'd go this far."

"The whole school board stuff sucks. Maybe you should consider becoming less involved for a while. The kids are doing well in school. They don't need your involvement as much as they did."

Betty cried again, and Arnie yelled, "Grab the kids. I'm taking you out for dinner.

§

The Sage Diner was the favorite 'comfort food' place in the neighborhood.

After Mary and Ernie Spikes settled into a booth at the diner, Ernie wasted no time, "I've some bad news, Mary. I passed out your petitions at the union meeting last week, and I discovered you'd got competition for my union guys' votes.'

"Who is that?"

"A guy named Vince Miller. He bought drinks for the men down at Foley's Bar. The good news is if he's lucky he'll only win a quarter of the votes from my members. The rest will go to you."

"Ernie, I don't want to cause friction between you and anyone in your union."

"There won't be. Seventy-five percent offered personally to carry your petitions. A few guys were too busy with sick wives, children, and mothers-in-law, but they assured me they were more than willing to sign your petitions and vote for you on Election Day."

"That's terrific, Ernie."

"Mary, do you know anything about this guy, Miller?"

"The word is he's a bit shady."

"Meaning?"

"I heard through the grapevine he may be into some illegal activities, possibly money laundering and prostitution."

"Hold on a second, Ernie. I see someone sitting over by the door. I want to get her attention. Mary smiled over at Betty Kramer. Betty quickly turned toward her husband making believe she hadn't seen the lady who scared the shit out of her last week outside the beauty parlor.

§

When Betty looked away from McMurray, she gazed in the other direction and saw Elliot Rush seated at a table on the opposite side of the diner. Across the table from Elliott sat the attractive new secretary from accounting. "Holy cow! Doesn't he ever learn? The whole Emily thing isn't even cold…"

Betty looked back at Mary and said to her husband. "I can't take it, Arnie. McMurray on one side, Rush on the other."

Arnie saw his wife was beside herself. "Are you alright?"

"No, not really. There are too many people I don't want to see here. Can we go to McDonalds?"

"Okay, we're leaving. Let's go to Mickey Dee's."

A chorus of cheers went up from the kids, "Hurrah! McDonalds."

The Kramers got up from the table and made a hasty retreat out the diner door.

§

Ernie Spikes had just arrived home when his cell phone vibrated in his side pocket. He tried to pull it out before the call went to voicemail. "Hello, this is Ernie."

"Ernie, Lou Marinara here."

"Lou, it's been a while. How the hell are you?"

"I'm fine, except I hear you're helping someone who is running for school board against me."

"Lou, there're seven seats open. You never asked my help before, so I figured there would be no harm in helping my longtime friend and neighbor. Mrs. McMurray could be helpful to you if she's elected."

"You remember, Ernie, how you asked me to find a job for your nephew who had an interest in politics. I called my friend Troy Burns, the councilman. Burns gave your nephew a part-time job in his office, and do you remember how your nephew needed another part-time job because one political job wasn't enough for him to pay his bills."

"Of course, Lou, you got him another part-time job. And I was very grateful."

"Well, Troy Burns has a lot of supporters who need jobs, and I try to help him out, but I can't unless I have the right people working with me on the board. Do you understand, Ernie?"

"I do Lou, but…"

Ernie could not finish the sentence before Lou yelled, "Stay out of it, Ernie," and hung up. Ernie sat in his chair dazed by the call.

CHAPTER 10

TOM AND JEREMY HEADED INTO MANHATTAN TO GET AWAY and talk campaign strategy with no one interrupting them. As Jeremy drove over the Queensborough Bridge, he was surprised to see how many new buildings had sprung up in Long Island City.

"Can you believe all this construction on this side of the bridge? The buildings are beginning to block the Manhattan Skyline."

"It still looks spectacular on a day like this. The bright blue sky gives the East River a deep blue hue."

"They've done a great job of cleaning up the water in the past ten years."

Once in Manhattan, Tom found a parking lot near the subway. He and Jeremy walked south on Lexington Avenue. The sun reflected brightly off the glass buildings making Tom wish he'd brought sunglasses.

"Jeremy, let's start down to the Staten Island Ferry. We can ride it over and back. The water will be beautiful, and I always enjoy looking at the Lady in the Harbor. She never gets old." They hopped on the 6 Train and were downtown in twenty minutes.

The two friends emerged from the subway at the Bowling Green Station at the very tip of Manhattan. A foghorn blasted, signaling the ferry's next departure in five minutes. The two friends took off full speed, barely arriving at the ferry before the gangplank lifted.

Out of breath, but invigorated, the two headed up to the beverage counter for a cold beer. It was the weekend; the empty ferry gave Tom and Jeremy plenty of space to talk privately.

"There she is," Tom pointed to the Statue of Liberty.

"She is beautiful," said Jeremy.

"I've been meaning to ask you, how does your father feel about you going to California and starting a new career in the movie industry? Is he disappointed you're not following in his footsteps?"

"I'm very lucky. Pop and mom are very supportive. They believe I've got some writing talent and I should pursue it, but deep down my father is disappointed. He thinks any natural gifts I have are better suited for the ministry. He asks for my input when he writes his sermons, and he believes with practice; I might develop the oratory skills to win over a congregation. He says I'm good at convincing people to do things."

Tom laughed. "You sure are. You took an innocent schoolboy like me and convinced him to run for school board."

"I didn't convince you. You were in the right place at the right time. It was fate. We better change the subject."

"I have meant to ask you, what exactly do you want to say in your films?"

Jeremy became serious and answered, "Whether we want to admit it or not, our country is changing. My father's world is different from the one you and I'll get old in. There's a break down in the barriers which kept groups apart. Today, there's a growing portion of black men and women who've gone to college and have good jobs that pay a decent salary. These black men and women are often second generation professionals. Their parents went to local colleges, and their kids went to even better ones."

"I've seen it."

"But where do they live?" asked Jeremy,

Jeremy allowed Tom a second," and continued. "I do know many of them are living in areas which cost far less than they can afford. It's a concept no white person can imagine. Do you know any of your white friends who live in areas that cost less than they can afford?

"I never thought about it."

"And why would you?"

Not wanting to continue to put Tom on the spot, Jeremy ended with, "These overachievers live below their means. They still live on the wrong side of the tracks either because they don't feel comfortable moving into an all-white neighborhood or the real estate brokers are reluctant to sell to them."

Tom knew his friend was right. No one on his block would consider selling to a black family.

"Movie and TV history is replete," said Jeremy, "With examples of how films can neutralize feelings of prejudice and fear. "Going back to the seventies when Archie Bunker was outraged a black family moved in next to him." Jeremy stopped to see if Tom was still with him."

Tom said, "So, what is your point?"

"It's this. We see how once a racist like Archie Bunker got to know his new black neighbors and saw they were decent people, he couldn't, no matter how he tried, hold onto his childhood prejudices. He'd have to think of some other reason to dislike his new neighbors other than the color of their skin."

"What exactly will be your goal?"

"I want to write scripts which will convince black people who are on their way up the ladder of success to take a chance and mix in with their white friends from work and college. I want to encourage them to move into nice houses in the all-white neighborhoods, attend all-white churches, and eat at all-white restaurants. Let their example trickle down to other blacks who are on their way up the ladder of success. Let the trickle become a geyser."

"It's a terrific idea, Jeremy."

"I don't know how terrific it is, but I do know real progress won't happen until blacks and whites take a chance and invite each other into their homes and their lives."

Tom thought about the story his grandfather told him about a black man walking into a white man's bar. The black man immediately faced cold, threatening stares. Most of the time, the black man would leave immediately, but when he didn't, the bartender reluctantly poured him a drink. The other patrons watched the barkeep carefully to see what happened to the black man's glass after he left. "To the relief of all the remaining patrons, the bartender broke the glass. If he didn't, the bar would be out of business in a day."

Jeremy watched his friend thinking about something. Finally, Tom asked, "Won't people criticize you for saying you're zeroing in on a small portion of the black problem?"

"Probably, and also, I have to try to convince the target audience they shouldn't forget the folks left behind in the old neighbor. I have to encourage this upwardly mobile group to invite their old friends to their new neighborhoods and expect them to conduct themselves in a manner that won't embarrass themselves or their hosts."

Tom interrupted, "Slow down, Jeremy."

Jeremy ignored his friend and went on, "Also, the upwardly mobile can't allow any of their people to intimidate them with names like Uncle Tom or Uppity Black or the most common taunt, "Who the fuck does he think he is?"

Tom laughed heartily. "Jeremy, I'm lucky to have you as a friend. You're a pisser."

"It's time to get to work and figure out what we need to do to get you elected."

"The petition signing is going great. Every Sunday we get more than five-hundred signatures outside the Catholic churches in my area. My friends and family have a slew of petitions filled out, and they are still collecting whole sheets from other friends."

"We shouldn't stop collecting," said Jeremy. "Each signature has an address next to it. The more people who sign your petitions, the more people we can contact when it comes time to get out the vote. I'll set up a command center where we can stuff envelopes with reminders to go out and vote. We'll mail the reminder to all your petition signers a few days before the election. I heard Lou Marinara organizes carpools to drive the older voters to the polls," said Jeremy. "He gets Councilman Troy Burns' campaign workers to help."

"We're in good shape, my aunts have the carpools covered," said Tom, as he put out his fist for a bump.

"Let's get off the ferry and go for a drink. Someone told me of a new place that just opened a few blocks from where we get off the ferry."

"It sounds good to me."

§

In the spring and summer, the G&R Gang hung out in Trenton Park right off Cornish Avenue. In the fall, they grouped under the train tracks near the river. In winter, they met in The Koch Houses Youth Center. For small meetings with only the chiefs, Starbucks was the place of choice.

Luis called Elmer in the morning and asked him to meet at Starbucks at seven-thirty that evening. Elmer waited for Luis at a back table. When Luis arrived, the two gave the appropriate shakes and man hugs.

Both men were always glad to be with each other, but with the increase in business; they saw each other less and less. Drug sales increased dramatically in the past few months, especially in the high schools. The main reason involved their new partner, the small guy named Eddie.

"Thanks for coming, Elmer. Something came up, and I needed your help in figuring it out. You remember Jeremy Thompson?"

"Sure, he's the preacher's son. He's the one we almost whacked last year. I thought the minister over at the black church swore he'd keep Thompson in line. What's going on with him now?"

"I'm not sure. That's why I need your help. All I know is Thompson has been hanging around with this white college guy from the northern part of town. Nelson, Alejandro, and Jose say the two of them have been all over the place together and they're always carrying lots of papers with them. Nelson saw them outside the Elks' Club. Enrique saw them over at the state offices. They came out with sheets of papers."

"If Thompson is up to something, he'll be sorry."

"What about the white guy? Who is he?"

"Jose found out his name is Foster. Put some of your guys on it. Let's find out what's going on before anything happens."

"Luis, there's one more thing. Eddie says we can have another high school, but he wants a bigger cut of the sales."

"Negotiate him down as far as you can. We want to try and keep the money relationship the way it is."

"Good. You know we haven't been out with each other for a while. How about you, me, Carmen and Rosa go out to Club Havana Saturday night?"

"Let's do it; We'll have the girls call and make plans."

Luis didn't mention where he was going after Starbucks. He'd tell Elmer this weekend. Elmer walked down the block one way, Luis, the other. Elmer was on his way home. Luis had a long night ahead waiting in the bushes for an old man to come home drunk.

Luis didn't know why this old man's sons wanted their father killed, but it wasn't his concern, not when they were paying him ten thousand dollars. Luis smiled, "Won't Elmer be surprised when I give him five grand Saturday night? We'll have a ball."

§

Luis waited in the bushes for hours, but the old man never came home. Luis' butt was sore from sitting on the hard ground. His cell phone went dead four hours ago, and he could not call Jose, one his captains, to tell him to cool it with the Foster guy.

At dawn, Luis went home distressed at not earning the ten thousand dollars, but he was keeping it anyway. He needed a cup of coffee and a place to charge his cell. He walked into Starbucks and saw Tom Foster sitting at a table reading the newspaper.

Luis couldn't tell from Foster's body language if Jose tried to scare him last night. While his phone charged, Luis watched Tom carefully. If Luis had to bet, he'd guess Jose did nothing.

§

Jeremy called Tom to meet and discuss Tom's visit to his father's church. Neither friend suggested Starbucks. Both agreed they wanted to avoid running into Gomez and his thugs.

"Let's meet at my house," said Tom. "It's easier. Besides, my mom's been bugging me to have you over. She wants to see if you're the nice little boy you used to be. I told her the little boy she remembers has grown up and fights at school board meetings."

Jeremy howled. "I always thought your mom was great. Tell her I look forward to seeing her."

"See you tonight at eight."

§

Jeremy arrived promptly. Alice Foster answered the door. Alice hugged Jeremy and ushered him into the living room. "Jeremy, you're all grown up."

Alice Foster peppered Jeremy with questions for ten minutes. Finally, she said, "I'm going upstairs to give you two some privacy. There are snacks and drinks set up in the kitchen; you can serve yourselves. I'll come down when you're finished." She gave Jeremy another hug. "It's great to see you."

"Same here Mrs. Foster."

Tom asked what his friend wanted to drink.

"Nothing right now, maybe later, thanks."

"So, prep me for Sunday."

"First of all everyone will be extremely polite to you."

"Good.".

"But it doesn't mean they'll be happy with what you have to say."

"What should I say, or not say?"

"Often, it's the way a person says something which is offensive, rather than what they say."

"Why not give me a script. I won't be offended if you tell me exactly what to say."

"Tom, you'll be fine. Be yourself. Don't try to insinuate you know what it is to be black or how it feels. So many people come around and say how sympathetic they are to the plight of black folks. Those words don't go over big. Just tell them, if you're elected, you'll help their children receive the services they're entitled. That means the same services the white kids receive in their schools."

§

As usual, the next Sunday the congregants of the God's Pentecostal Church expected to hear a sermon both interesting and well-delivered by the esteemed Reverend Jonas Thompson, and Jonas Thompson never failed to give them both.

Jonas began, "Everyone's mind is a superhighway of ideas, one lane going one way, the other lane going in the opposite direction. Good ideas wiz past bad ideas at an alarming rate. Good travels east, Bad speeds west. In life, we travel east, in the Good Lane and a few hours later we find ourselves going west in the Bad Lane. Often, we don't remember when we decided to change lanes. Good choices put us in the Good Lane. Bad choices put us in the other lane."

Tom's stomach churned, and his hands shook as he sat nervously on the church altar waiting for his turn to speak. He looked down at a sea of unfamiliar faces, each one a different color than his. Tom told himself this shouldn't matter, but bullshit, it mattered.

Tom didn't know what to expect. He was never the only white person in a group this size. The overflowing pews filled with parishioners from neighboring black churches showed the community's interest in Tom. "They've come to check me out." Panic gripped him for the hundredth time since he entered this church. "Please, God, let Reverend Thompson's sermon go on forever."

Reverend Thompson concluded his moving and eloquent sermon and introduced Tom. "Ladies and Gentleman, I want to present to you this morning a young man who has promised to help us in our struggle for equality in our schools." Applause rippled through the church.

"You've heard about Tom Foster in the past few weeks from your local pastors, and they have explained how Tom Foster can help us improve our schools. Tom has come here today to tell you about himself and ask for our support in the upcoming school board election. At this time, I turn the podium over to my friend, Tom Foster."

The time had come for Tom to stand tall and do what he'd come here to do. Tom prayed, "Lord, please don't let my legs give way when I try to stand, or my voice fail as I open my mouth to speak, but most importantly let my pants remain dry, at least until I reach the pulpit." God heard Tom's prayers, and Tom arrived at the podium upright, able to speak and dry.

Tom stood high above the crowd and smiled. In return, beautiful smiles appeared on the faces of all the congregants. Tom's shoulders loosened, his stomach calmed, and his breathing eased. Tom knew he'd be all right.

"My name is Tom Foster, and I'm here to ask you to help me win a seat on your school board." The rest of his speech was a breeze. The people in Jonas Thompson's church saw a young man whom they hoped would help their children acquire the educational services to improve their lives.

After the service, Jonas told Tom, "These people will help you all they can. They liked you, Tom. They saw in you a chance for change."

§

Emily Cusack returned from California after two weeks of vacation. Her whole family came back relaxed and rested except Emily. She spent the entire time in California worrying. "Is my husband going to leave me when we get home?"

Leaving Emily was the last thing on Henry's mind. He loved his wife and wanted to keep his family together, but Emily was acting irrationally. Whether she was on a beautiful white sandy beach or in the vast waters of the Pacific, her mind obsessed with the mistakes she made during her tenure on the school board.

Guilt clouded Emily's mind and caused her to obsess about how her lust for Elliot made her vote for terrible people for solely because Elliot Rush wanted to please his benefactor, Lou Marinara? Emily asked herself the same questions repeatedly. "Did my voting decisions permanently harm students in the district? Did I favor the district's northern tier because Lou wanted more funding for the white students? I know I didn't vote for supervisors, principals, and assistant principals because they were the best qualified for the job. I voted for them because they were friends or relatives of Lou. I voted the way Elliot asked me to vote. I ignored what my vote did to the kids in my school district."

Since Emily returned home from California, Eddie observed her carefully Emily's twisted expression since she returned was easy to read. Pain and depression were written on her face. Emily Cusack was desperate, and Eddie knew from experience desperate people were dangerous.

Emily called people in the district office she was friendly with during her term on the board. She quizzed them on after-school positions, allocation of funds and after-school programs. She asked them for specific names of people who received these positions. Her requests included questions about which schools in the district received federal program money. Emily appeared to be frenetic and obsessed with her investigations.

Her district office friends immediately told Superintendent Pinzon who told Phil Turner of Mrs. Cusack's requests. Phil Turner called Chairman Marinara. Lou knew what his former colleague on the board wanted, and he told Phil, "You better tell Eddie to ramp-up the surveillance on Cusack."

Eddie obeyed immediately and followed Emily exclusively. When Emily walked, Eddie slowly followed in his car. He sensed something was different on the third day of his souped-up surveillance. He had followed Emily five blocks from her home when she turned into a single family dwelling on Turnip Drive.

The quaint house occupied a twenty by a hundred piece of land. Emily rang the doorbell, and someone buzzed her into the house. A small, discreet sign indicated this was the office of an M.D.

Eddie googled the doctor's name, and Dr. Randolph Duganne, Psychiatrist, appeared. Eddie waited outside Dr. Duganne's office for an hour. When Emily exited the building, she hurried toward Main Street, turned right on Main, and entered a local pharmacy.

Emily left the pharmacy twenty minutes later with a small prescription bag.

Eddie decided not to continue following Emily. He parked the car at a meter and went into the pharmacy. Eddie knew the pharmacist well. He was always a great help to Eddie when his adult acne flared up. Eddie was a frequent customer, and when he walked toward the register in the back of the store, he was greeted with, "Hi Eddie. Good to see you.

"Good to see you, Gene."

"Eddie. Let me see how the new ointment is working."

Eddie was long past being embarrassed in front of Gene. The pharmacist had seen the rash, the redness and the pimples often, so neither man felt any discomfort. Fisher was grateful for Gene's help, and he told the pharmacist this often. Gene enjoyed being thought of so highly by a customer. The two frequently talked for hours about sports, politics, and women.

"Gene, I have a question about the lady who was in here a few minutes ago."

Eddie surprised Gene with his interest.

"Can you tell me what prescription you filled for her?"

Gene hesitated for a moment, and then said, "It was for Zoloft, quite a high dosage. She must be in tough shape. Doctors don't prescribe that high a dosage unless a patient is near the edge."

Eddie realized Gene told him this as a favor. No questions asked.

"Gene, I owe you one." Eddie left quickly. He also wanted to see if Emily went straight home.

As Eddie pulled away from the curb and proceeded down Main Street, he saw Emily a half a block away, window shopping. Her eyes seemed glued to an array of cameras for sale. He pulled over to the curb and watched as she went two doors down and went into Mom & Pop's Luncheonette.

Eddie pulled into a parking space right outside the eatery. He saw the waitress place a glass of water in front of Emily, and he watched as Emily tore open the little pharmacy bag, frantically unscrew the cap, pop a pill into her mouth and wash it down with the glass of water.

Eddie watched Emily change her mind about staying for lunch. She popped up and headed for the exit door. As she reached the exit, a young black man and an older black man entered the restaurant. Emily recognized the man and talked animatedly to him. Emily frantically searched her purse and took out a pen and a piece of paper and wrote down something.

Emily tenderly patted the man on the arm. Eddie recognized the man as the minister who'd caused such a commotion at the school board meeting. The younger man was his son, the guy who got punched in the nose by one of Lou's cronies. Eddie became distracted by a blousy, bleached blond middle-aged woman paying her bill at the cash register and missed Emily's exit from the coffee shop. As Eddie got into his car, he saw Emily walking toward her home. Eddie watched Emily for another block when he saw her stop to talk to an older lady he recognized from school board meetings.

If Fisher was able to eavesdrop on Emily and Esther Portnoy's conversation, he would have heard Esther ask a question, one she knew the answer by Emily's bulging eyes and slurred speech.

"How are you doing, Emily?" Although through the years they were rarely on the same side of inter-district struggles, there was something about Emily she liked. Looking at Emily today, Esther was saddened how Emily's life had changed by serving on the school board.

Suddenly, Emily burst into tears and threw her arms around Esther whispering, "I'm at my wit's end, I have no one to confide in, no one I can trust. I'm so depressed I feel like..." Esther stood on the sidewalk hugging Emily while she sobbed uncontrollably." People walked around the two staring, but Emily didn't seem to care. She just held on to Esther for dear life."

Fisher continued to watch until finally Emily let go of Esther's neck and walked home. Eddie drove back to the office; he had a lot to tell his boss.

§

As soon as Eddie arrived back at the district office, he went straight to Phil Turner's office. He was relieved. Phil's new protégé, Ginger, from funded programs, was nowhere to be seen.

Phil was in great spirits. "Ginger must have just left," thought Eddie, but his boss's mood instantly changed when Eddie related his recent observations of Emily.

"Are you sure the pharmacist told you she must be in desperate shape to warrant such large a dosage?"

"He did."

"And you saw her exchanging notes with Jonas Thompson?"

"Yes. His son, Jeremy, was with them."

"I thought when Emily didn't get far with her little investigation, we'd be rid of her. Thanks, Eddie, that will be all for now."

Eddie hated when his boss dismissed him like he was a schoolboy, but he knew Turner wanted him out of his office right away so he could call Lou Marinara."

§

Phil didn't call Marinara as Eddie predicted. Instead, he dialed Luis Gomez's cellphone.

"Luis, I have something for you to do."

Gomez waited for the details, but Turner said, "I'll give Fisher a package to give you tomorrow. Meet him at the usual pickup point. The name, address and 20k will be in the package."

"Don't think you're getting that money back."

"I don't want it back; I want a clean job on this one. Remember, it has to look like an accident or a suicide."

§

Later that day Esther Portnoy called Bunny Krouse to tell her about running into Emily on the street. Both women felt bad about what Emily was going through; they understood how being involved in their school system often took its toll. Both knew how life could change overnight and you found yourself alone not knowing what to do next. Both planned to take Emily out for lunch the following week. Bunny tried to change the topic. "Did you hear anything from the job resumes you sent out?"

"I started to call you a million times. I got a job as a bookkeeper on the other side of town. The pay is good and I need it for the first payment of my granddaughter's tuition. I took it temporarily; it's too far to get home at a decent time for the other two grand-kids. I'm looking around for something closer to home." Frustrated, Esther added, "Everyone thinks all Jewish people are rich." Bunny remembered growing up hearing this myth all the time.

Next thing Bunny heard was a loud bang and Esther yelling, "I told you not to carry all those dishes at once. Got to go Bunny. We'll speak soon."

CHAPTER 11

TOM LOVED ALL HIS BROTHERS AND SISTERS EVEN THOUGH each had a different temperament. His three older sisters were pretty and popular with positive, upbeat personalities. His quieter older brother married the girl down the block last year, and instead of losing a son, his mother gained a daughter-in-law. The newly married couple was at the house all the time. Alice Foster commented, "My son is around more than when he lived here."

Tom's younger brother posed a challenge, not because he was gay, but because he was often reckless in where he socialized.

Most people knew or suspected Randy was gay, but it never seemed a problem for anyone, probably because the Foster family represented such a force in the community. The Fosters were generous, active, well-known, and respected. Although all of Randy's siblings were protective of him, the real duty fell on Tom as the sibling closest in age.

Randy was always ready for some fun, always joking around and Tom enjoyed his brother's company.

Randy's friend Travis Baker was another story. Although Travis had grown up in the neighborhood a few blocks from the Fosters, Randy and Travis just recently became close. Alice Foster encouraged the friendship because she knew Travis came from a good family. It wasn't apparent if their friendship was platonic or romantic.

Tom had hung out with Travis' brother, Roy, in high school. They had been in the same clubs and sports teams. Roy joined the local police department at nineteen, the earliest age allowed by state law.

Since Roy joined the police force, his name appeared in the local newspaper all the time. Roy saved lives, delivered babies, helped old ladies find their stolen wheelchairs. He belonged to the local political club, and many at the club saw Roy Baker as a rising star in local politics.

Tom wasn't surprised at Roy's celebrity and felt no one deserved it more. In high school, Roy Baker organized the fundraising drives for everyone from victims of hurricanes to children of drug addicts. Roy was a natural do-gooder.

A few days ago Roy stopped by the Foster's to pick up his brother, Travis. Tom answered the front door, and there was his old friend standing there smiling. "Roy, how are you? Long time no see." The guys hugged and kidded around like they had seen each other just the other day. "It's so good to see you, Roy."

"Same here, Tom."

"Come in and have a beer. We've some catching up to do." The two old friends sat drinking beer for twenty minutes before Travis and Randy came down from Randy's room.

"Travis, we have to go. Mom made a big fancy dinner for Pop's birthday, and we're already late." Roy stood and gave Tom another bear hug. "Let's grab a beer next weekend."

Randy interrupted, "You better postpone that beer Roy until after the election or my brother will rope you into helping him win a seat on the school board."

"Tom, you're running for the school board?"

Tom hesitantly nodded, "Yes."

"Sure, I'd be glad to help. I enjoy the excitement of politics. I even belong to the local political club. I've toyed with the idea of eventually running for something."

"I would certainly appreciate your help."

Travis glanced at this watch and reminded his brother they were late for the birthday dinner.

Tom and Roy planned to meet later in the week to discuss election strategy.

Tom overheard Randy and Travis discuss going to a new club tomorrow night. Tom never heard of the place and figured he was out of touch with the local social scene.

After the Baker boys left, Tom commented to his brother, "Roy Baker is a great person. Is Travis like his brother? Randy answered, "Not really."

Alice called into the living room, "Dinner is on the table." Tom made it a point to tell Randy he'd like to go for a drink later.

§

After supper, Tom and Randy headed to Joe's Pub, two blocks from their house. Tom knew that during the week the place would be empty. On the weekends, you couldn't get near the bar and revelers jammed all the tables. Randy sat in a booth and Tom went up to the bar and ordered two Bud Lights.

"How are you, Tom. Long time no see. I hear you're running for the school board. That's great. Roy Baker was in here with his dad a minute ago. Everyone is on your side. We'll make sure we do our part of mobilizing the troops," assured the bartender.

"Terry, you're terrific. I appreciate your help. I bet I receive more votes from your place than from anywhere else."

"It's our pleasure. You and your family are the best." Terry waved to Randy and turned to Tom. "You're a good brother, Tom, and I hope Randy appreciates it."

"He does, Terry," responded Tom and walked back to the table.

Both brothers took a big gulp of their beer. "The corned beef made me thirsty."

"Me too."

"I'm glad we have a little time to spend together. The campaign already takes up a lot of time, and I feel we haven't connected in a while."

Randy nodded but was silent.

"It was good seeing Roy again. He's a great guy. What is his brother Travis like?"

"He's good, but occasionally he can go wild. He's into things I have only heard about."

"Like what?"

"Tom, I don't want to talk about it. I've problems of my own."

"What can I do to help?"

"Tom, you've been a great brother, but there're things I have to get straight in my mind, and you don't have the expertise. I don't mean you aren't smart. You know a lot, but what I need is to talk to someone about…"

"Randy, please go on. I may know someone."

"I need to find out where I stand with things like God, life, my future…Our parents raised me Christian, but it seems I don't exactly fit the profile of what I was taught growing up."

"I'm honored you shared it with me. I struggle myself with some religious aspects of my life. Gay isn't the only issue people struggle with."

"But it's the issue I struggle with."

"Let's find someone who can help, someone whom you can discuss it. Maybe after we find someone for you, we can find someone for me."

Randy smiled at his brother. Tom was the best.

§

As promised, Roy Baker put his money where his mouth was. He called Tom three days later to confirm plans to help with the election. Tom asked him to come over that afternoon.

Roy barreled into the Foster house ready to win Tom's election single-handedly. His enthusiasm energized Tom. "Thanks for coming over, Roy. I appreciate it."

"Tom, I've some knowledge of the petition process from working at the political club. Let me distribute them and instruct everyone on how to collect the signatures accurately.

"That would be great. I've some signed petitions, but I need someone to organize them.

Roy warned, "The political machine thwarts many good and honest candidates because newcomers don't understand the process. I have a good working knowledge of how to make sure you've got the required number of valid signatures."

"I don't know what to say."

"Don't say anything. Give me the names and addresses of all the people who are carrying your petitions. Give me the names, addresses and phone numbers of any other people who are likely to sign, but can't collect signatures because of time, shyness or they just don't want to do it."

Tom's head spun at the shotgun speed of Roy Baker.

Roy and Tom bounced ideas back and forth. Tom asked, and Roy answered questions for hours. Both needed a break, "How about a cold beer? I'm ready for one."

Roy agreed, and the two walked into the kitchen and cracked open two Bud Lights.

"Fill me in on what's happening in your life. Do you enjoy being on the force?"

"I like the job. In high school, I thought I would follow my father into finance. He had the connections to help get the first job. But I realized over the summer of my junior year I hated working on Wall Street."

"Why?"

"Many reasons, number one, the materialism. Don't get me wrong, I appreciate nice things as much as anyone, but the jerks I worked with that summer were over the top."

"In what way?"

"For starters, you'd be walking down an aisle of desks to go to the bathroom, and some young jerk would pass, grab your tie and turn it over to see the label. If the label didn't display a popular designer's name, the jerk would announce it to the whole office, and everyone would laugh and yell, "Dick."

"What assholes."

"At lunch, the other interns would parrot their bosses or their fathers. 'It's all about the bottom line.' Another favorite was, 'Your only responsibility is to the stockholders.'"

"I repeat, what assholes."

"You and I are a lot alike, Tom. It must have been the way we were brought up. A week later, I quit."

"Good for you. You were always a stand-up guy. I remember you fighting bullies way before anti-bullying became a cause."

"You too, Tom. If you remember, it's how we first met. Those idiots in gym class made fun of the clumsy Latino kid. We both told the other kids to leave him alone, or we'd beat the shit out of them after school."

"We certainly had balls," laughed Tom. "Those guys could have beaten the crap out of us by sheer numbers.

"Well, it worked, and it didn't hurt our reps either."

"I'm sure glad you're on my side, Roy."

"Same here, my friend."

Roy finished a swallow of beer. "I'm out of here. I'll stop by and pick up the names tomorrow, if you're not home, leave them in the mailbox."

"Thanks again, Roy."

"Tom, I'm glad to do it. I'll help in any way I can. Politics in this town can be difficult. Being on the force, I see and hear a lot. One problem involves some of your future colleagues on the board. I'll give more details as I hear them. I don't want to scare you off. The town needs you."

§

Most Sundays during the campaign, Jeremy and Tom went to the black church services. They also went to mid-week services on Wednesdays.

The pastor of each church pre-warned parishioners of Tom and Jeremy's visits. Jeremy did most of the talking initially, but Tom always gave a ten-minute speech followed by questions. As soon as Tom asked for questions, hands immediately went up.

"Yes, Pastor Rollins."

"Can you give us specifics of how this will affect our kids on a daily basis?"

Tom quickly answered, "It's a good question, and I'll tell you exactly how providing the proper services affects our young people. First of all, basic janitorial services will make our children comfortable. The bathrooms in some of our schools are dirty because funds aren't allocated equally among the schools in the school district."

A young woman in the back pew asked, "Please, give specifics."

"The bathrooms in many minority schools are cleaned every three days, which turns out to be once a week. The neglect causes the bathrooms to smell. Toilet paper and hand towels are at a premium. The doors on the toilet stalls hang off their hinges; often they fall off completely. The toilet seats are cracked or non-existent. If the seats crack, feces become embedded. Last year all the anal infections reported were from the southern tier of our district."

Some older women in the first pew gasped.

"The halls are cleaned on the same schedule as the bathrooms. Papers and trash clutter the hallways. If someone spills a juice box in the corridor, it stays there for three days or more. The cafeteria has vermin crawling around."

"That's enough my boy," interrupted Pastor Rollins. "We get the idea. You've certainly answered the question." The Pastor continued to speak. Tom sat down in a chair next to the altar.

"Ladies and gentleman in speaking with Tom and Jeremy before services today, I've been enlightened on what other services we miss: Outdated books, broken computers, incompetent teachers, crazy bus drivers, uncaring principals and assistant principals, broken musical instruments. The list goes on."

Rumbling from the audience forced Pastor Rollins to end his speech and told the people the conversation would continue in the lower level dining hall.

After the service, Tom and Jeremy went down to the Community Room and answered more questions. If the Pastor hadn't stepped in, they would have been there for the rest of the day.

As had become Jeremy's custom when they left the churches, he told Tom how well they had done. But for the last two Sundays Jeremy's balloon was partially deflated by the sight of three gang thugs standing across the street from the church. Jeremy did not point this out to Tom.

§

Jose, Nelson, and Enrique reported back to their leader, Luis Gomez, what they saw on Sunday mornings at the black churches. As Luis listened to his three scouts, Elmer walked into Starbucks with his woman, Carmen. Luis and the others greeted Carmen with affection, but Luis signaled Elmer he wanted to speak with him privately.

"Carmen, please see if my sunglasses are in the car and could you stay there until I come out?"

Accustomed to this behavior Carmen understood there were things she'd better not hear. She smiled at Luis and the others and went to the car.

After telling Elmer about Jeremy and the white kid in church today, Luis waited for Elmer's reaction. "What do you think all the papers are for?"

Between the two, they decided maybe a little warning to the Thompson kid and his white-bread friend might be in order.

"We better be careful," added Elmer. "You know how the police react to us doing anything to one of their color."

"We'll be careful," assured Enrique. Jose and Nelson nodded in agreement. "We'll be careful."

§

Luis met Elmer at the Hacienda Bar and Grill, and each ordered a shot of Tequila.

"To friendship," toasted Luis. Both men swallowed the Tequila in one gulp.

Two young women on the other side of the bar made no pretense at being interested in Elmer and Luis. Both men smiled but continued to talk about why they were there. The men had no time for any distractions, as pretty as those distractions might be.

"I didn't want to go into too much the other day at Starbucks with Enrique and the others, but I'm concerned about Thompson and this guy, Foster. I got word from Eddie; Foster wants to be on the school board, and Thompson is breaking his neck to help him. Eddie said it wouldn't be good for our business if this Foster guy got elected. Tonight, we must make a plan to stop Thompson and Foster from upsetting things. We have a good thing going, and I want to keep that way."

"We have to do something to change their minds, Elmer. We can't let them get involved with our schools, but it isn't going to be easy. Foster is protected by his white skin and by his family and friends. One scrape on his little toe, the cops will be all over our asses. I am more worried about the black kid. The white kid we can probably scare off."

"Besides," said Elmer, "When he's on the school board, he'll only worry about the white section. He'll string Thompson along, get any votes he can from the blacks, and once he's on the board, he won't even remember Thompson's name."

"I'm not so sure you're right, Elmer. I hear this young white guy is different. He'll stick with the blacks."

"You don't know white people like I do, Luis."

"How do you know what white people are like," laughed Gomez. "You haven't spoken a word to whites except, "Yes, sir. No sir. What can I do for you, sir?""

Elmer looked at his friend with a serious face, and Luis hoped Elmer wasn't insulted. Little by little Elmer's mouth showed a grin, and a second later he broke up laughing. Both friends howled. The Tequila worked.

"Bartender, another round here for my friend," ordered Gomez.

Luis and Elmer's meeting at the Hacienda Bar and Grill produced little more than big aching heads the next morning. The following week they were back at the Hacienda determined to have one drink and make sure they left with a plan. The two took a seat in the back of the bar and settled down to business.

Luis took the lead, "I've decided we have to go after both Foster and Thompson and..."

"But..."

"No buts. We go after both of them. It will be a warning. No one will get hurt, but the warning has to be strong enough to do the job."

"Be careful with Foster," Elmer persisted. "Enrique and Jose have been keeping an eye on him. He's all over the place. He knows everyone, and everyone likes him."

"We'll be careful with him. The whites get the message a lot quicker than blacks. We have to go much harder on Thompson. Nothing physical, just something that will scare the shit out of his whole family."

Elmer responded with gusto, "You take Foster, and I'll handle Thompson."

Luis saw the question on his friends face. Luis grinned, "You follow Foster because you have so much experience with white people." Both cracked up laughing.

When they stopped laughing, Elmer responded, "Let's talk details."

§

Tom had enough signatures to appear on the ballot. People were happy to sign, neighbors, former schoolmates, and team members. His parents were related to so many people all over the County and had so many friends that between his parents and siblings, signed petitions poured into the house.

Tom went home earlier than usual, hoping to organize the stacks of paper for Roy and then catch a little sleep. The house was empty. Tom remained silent listening to a house he'd never heard so quiet until this moment. With so many siblings he was never alone anywhere in the house. "We never have any privacy," was the most common complaint in the Foster home.

He felt uneasy standing alone in the living room.

Boom! Tom heard a loud noise on the ceiling. His first thought was the heat must be coming up. The old fashion heating system with the cast iron radiators made a great deal of clanging and banging when fired up. The bustle in the house from everyone going about their business usually masked the noise, but at night it was a different story.

Tom would have no trouble handling himself in a fight if it was an intruder and not the noisy pipes. His heart beat faster as he started up the stairs banging his feet on each stair so if there was an intruder he'd jump out the window.

He reached the landing and waited, Tom heard another bang on the floor. When he went into his room, his desk drawers were on the floor, and his bedroom window was wide open. Tom rushed over and looked out. He and saw a man climbing the fence to the neighbor's yard then taking off down the street. The guy looked familiar.

Tom took out his cell and dialed 911. "Someone just ran out of my house a minute ago. He jumped out the second story window and took off down the street."

The 911dispatcher inquired, "Is there anyone in the house now?

"No, I already told you, he jumped out the window?"

"Was anything taken?"

"I'm not sure."

"Is there any danger, presently?"

"No."

"I suggest you go in person to your local precinct and file an incident report.

"You mean the police won't be coming?"

"That's correct, sir."

"If there's no immediate danger, we ask citizens to go to the Precinct regarding the incident. That way, our officers can respond to real emergencies."

Tom hung up, now angrier with the police than the intruder.

The next day he went to his local precinct and made the report. When he told his father and mother, his parents took the break-in in stride. "It's the price of doing business in the city."

Tom couldn't help trying to think of who the burglar resembled. "The walk and shape of the bastard was very familiar."

CHAPTER 12

NORA THOMPSON LIT THE OVEN, WAITED FOR IT TO PREHEAT, and, carefully placed the uncooked pie in the oven to cook at 400 degrees. Nora Thompson had everything required to serve a delicious meal for her family right there in her kitchen. The image of her apple pie, topped with vanilla ice cream, made her mouth water. She imagined the smiles on her family's faces, especially Toby.

Toby came barreling into the kitchen and asked if he could help with dinner. As always, Toby's presence made his mother feel extra fine. "Can I help, mom?"

"I've all I need, Toby. I made your favorite apple pie, and I have plenty of vanilla ice cream to put on it."

Nora saw her son's expression change. "What's the matter, Toby?"

A sad expression darkened Toby's face. "Me and Dad finished the ice cream last night before we went to bed." Tears appeared in Toby's eyes, and Nora put her arms around her son and gave him a big hug. "Don't worry, Toby. I'll run down to the grocery and pick up another half-gallon."

Nora headed for her coat when she remembered she had the pie in the oven. She made it a habit of never leaving the house while the stove was lit, even for a ten minute trip to the grocer.

"Toby, I'll wait until the pie cooks, then I'll go."

"Let me go, Ma. I can go for it."

"No, I'll go as soon as the pie finishes." Nora saw the disappointment on her son's face. "How many times did I say no to Toby growing up?"

"Toby, don't feel bad. While I'm gone, you can set the table." There was no change in her son's disappointed face. Nora looked out the window and saw how quickly it was getting dark. Toby never left the house alone at night. Before Nora could change her mind, she grabbed her purse and took out a ten dollar bill. "Here, Toby. Ask Mr. Sanchez for a half-gallon of vanilla ice cream, the extra creamy kind. Don't stop to talk with anyone. Go right there and come right back."

Toby's face immediately brightened. "Thanks, Mom. I'll be back in a flash, like Superman." Toby grabbed his coat and flew out the door. Nora Thompson looked out the kitchen window and watched the sky get darker by the minute. A feeling of pride at how far her son had come made Nora relax. She quickly set the table so Toby wouldn't have to do it.

Nora looked out the window. It was now dark. She put the last dish on the dining room table and sat down on one of the cushioned dining room chairs.

Nora tried to give Toby the freedom all kids need, at least when she could. She carefully picked the times and the places when her son could venture into the world by himself, a walk to the local grocery store to buy a container of milk during the day, a trip to the local barber two blocks away from the house or over to his cousin's on the next block. Numerous supervised practice trips preceded these outings. Each snippet of freedom prepared Toby for more.

Nora looked at the clock and thought, "Is he taking longer than he should?"

§

As soon as Toby Thompson entered New Hyde Hospital, Dr. Eugene Pagano carefully examined the young boy's chest to see where the bullet had entered. The radio dispatcher reported a young boy was shot in the chest, but when Dr. Pagano cut the shirt off his frail body, Pagano saw no gunshot wound on any part of the boy's torso.

A nurse ripped off Toby's pants, exposing a bullet wound in the right leg. The wound bled all over the examining table and onto the floor. The Doctor pressed a cloth on the wound and instructed his team, "Call the OR and tell them to prepare a room as quickly as possible. We have to stop the bleeding. This tourniquet won't last long."

They wheeled Toby from the emergency room onto the elevator up to the OR.

Jonas and Nora Thompson rushed through the electric door as Toby rolled onto the elevator. As the doors closed, all the Thompson's could see was their son's closed eyes and a group of worried medical personnel surrounding him.

Nora Thompson cried hysterically. Jonas tightened his large arm around her shoulders. Both parents rushed toward the elevator, but an alert nurse stopped them. "Are you Toby's parents?"

"Yes. Where are the nurses taking him?" cried Nora.

"He's on his way to the operating room. When your son first arrived in the ER, we thought the bullet entered at his chest, but thankfully it entered his leg." The nurse avoided telling the Thompsons the bullet severed an artery in Toby's leg.

Terror gripped Nora's vocal cords. "Can we see him?"

"You won't be able to go into the operating room, but an operating room nurse will keep us updated. Nurse Woo is Dr. Smallson's surgical nurse. Dr. Smallson will operate on your son and his assistant will be down in a moment to help you fill out the surgical consent form."

Nora couldn't stop crying. Jonas held back his tears for his wife's sake. He loved his son so much. Both parents felt guilty over the years because this young boy was their favorite. Nora's guilt reached its limit a year ago. She went to see a psychologist.

Sitting in the hospital today, Nora reminisced about her visit to the psychologist and how she confessed she loved her son, Toby, more than her two older children. "I enjoy my time with Toby more than I ever did with Jeremy or Catherine. I must be a terrible mother."

"Mrs. Thompson, first of all, you're not a bad mother for feeling this way. Feelings don't make a person good or bad. What counts is how you deal with those feelings."

Nora's shoulders relaxed, and the psychiatrist continued. "Parent's don't necessarily love one child more than the other, but we're human. We enjoy spending time with people who aren't hitting us over the head each time we're with them. Your son, Toby is more enjoyable to spend time. It's that simple."

"I see your point, doctor."

"Parents hear on TV, and they read in the latest child-rearing book, they should love all their children the same. Well, in most cases parents probably do. They just like one child more than another. Is it realistic to expect parents to enjoy being with kids who are a royal pain the butt? Why should parents assume something is wrong with them because they don't like being hit on the head all the time? Of course, you prefer the company of a childlike Toby who gives you only pleasure?"

The psychiatrist paused, gauging Nora's reaction. "Usually, by this time a parent is in shock at what I've said," he thought. Nora didn't reach for her coat to leave, so he continued. "Maybe the truth is parents don't have unconditional love for their kids, but rather the unconditional love, if there's such a thing, is given only to a special child, like Toby." Again the psychiatrist paused, then added, "And maybe to a dog."

Nora smiled at her doctor's attempt at humor. "When you walk into the house after you come back from the store, Toby is happy to see you. There's no attitude, no sulking, no problem a cookie and a glass of milk can't fix. Let's face it, Nora, we're human. Accept it."

"But…"

"No buts. Both you and Jonas love your son, Jeremy, and your daughter, Catherine, but be honest; there are times both can be pains in the rear end."

Nora Thompson's attention returned to the present by a short, chubby nurse standing by the elevator calling. "Is there someone from the Thompson family here?" Jonas practically dragged his wife over to the nurse. "We're Toby's parents."

"Follow me."

The three weaved their way past the busy nurses' station and turned into a small conference alcove of the large emergency room. "Please, take a seat, Mr. and Mrs. Thompson. My name is Nurse Rizzo. I'm the ER supervising nurse. I'll do my best to keep you informed about the progress of your son."

The Thompsons dropped into their seats. Nurse Rizzo squeezed into the chair opposite them and began. "Your son is being operated on as we speak. He has a gunshot wound to his right leg. The bullet grazed the artery running up the leg to his stomach. The bleeding is extensive, and Toby has already lost a considerable amount of blood. A team of doctors is working to stop the bleeding."

The Thompsons stared at Nurse Rizzo looking for some word of encouragement. Rizzo felt it best to be frank with them. "I won't try and fool you, Mr. and Mrs. Thompson, your son's condition is critical."

Jonas asked, "When will the operation be over?"

"It depends on how quickly the doctors patch the artery. It could be a few hours. In the meantime, I'll bring you upstairs. There's a waiting room right down the hall from the OR. You can wait there. It's more comfortable than down here, and there are a coffee machine and water cooler in there."

With some difficulty, Nurse Rizzo squeezed out of her chair. Jonas and Nora followed Rizzo into the emergency room and tried to snake their way to the closest bank of elevators.

The ER rang with the cries of patients, visitors, and staff. It was hard to tell the relatives and friends from patients. There was pain on the faces of everyone in the room, and Nora felt their pain. She knew only too well many people would return home tonight without their loved one. Nora prayed she and Jonas would be the lucky ones.

§

Elmer frantically called Luis' cell ten times over the last hour. Each time Luis' phone went right to voicemail. Elmer's five texts went unanswered. Finally, he tried Rosa's cell. "Hola."

"Rosa, this is Elmer."

"How are…"

"Rosa, where is Luis?"

"When he went out this morning, Luis mentioned he'd some business up north but didn't say when he'd be back."

Elmer's call waiting beeped. Elmer hoped it was Luis.

"Rosa, I think Luis is calling me on the other phone. Thanks."

She wanted to say, "Tell him to bring home some milk," but the line went dead too quickly.

"Luis, my boys screwed up. Enrique and Jose walked on Thompson's block. They saw his kid brother by himself. They figured this was their opportunity. Without saying anything to Enrique, Jose took out his gun and pointed the gun in the air. Enrique pushed Jose's arm down to stop him. The gun went off and hit the kid. Jose only planned to shock the kid. They didn't know what to do so they took off, pronto."

"I can't talk, Elmer. I'll call you later. I'm doing a job for Turner up north."

Elmer got off the phone more panicky than before and quickly headed to the hospital.

§

Jeremy sat beside Toby's hospital bed staring at the tubes in his younger brother's arm, nose, and mouth. Jonas and Nora drank black coffee in the cafeteria to keep awake for a long night ahead.

Jeremy planned to stay by his brother's side until his parents returned from the cafeteria, but Toby's doctor came into the room accompanied by an entourage and asked "Jeremy, could you step outside? We'll be about a half hour."

The doctor assured Jeremy, "Don't be concerned. My colleagues and I want to give your brother a thorough examination."

Jeremy joined his parents in the cafeteria. As soon as he stepped off the elevator, he saw Reverend Charles Mackey talking to his mother and father at a table in the center of the room. Jeremy missed seeing Elmer Rodriguez online buying a cup of coffee, staring over at the Nora and Jonas Thompson with sheer panic in his eyes. Rodriguez needed to know what was happening to the young boy.

Reverend Mackey asked Jonas what the police had to say.

"The emergency room nurse told us, "The police took off as soon as we arrived at the hospital. No one from the local precinct has been by to ask questions."

Nora interjected, "I'm calling them as soon as we get home and demanding to know what they've done to find out who the shooter was."

"Don't get your hopes up, Nora," said Reverend Mackey. "You know they don't do much when they see the victim is black or when they hear a victim comes from our part of town."

"They shot my nine-year-old son. I can't let them get away with it."

"Why can't we get all the black ministers in the district to organize a demonstration at the police precinct," said Jeremy. "We can invite the white ministers to join us."

"We could also invite the Catholic priests in the district to help us get the attention of the media," said Reverend Mackey. "They have some juice in this diocese."

"I'll make a list of the Catholics parishes and the synagogues," said Jeremy. "Reverend, if you could take the Protestant churches and Pop, you call or go down to the police station and demand answers about what they're doing. While you're there, mention our organization has big plans for a rally on Saturday."

"What rally?" asked Jonas, before realizing his son was bluffing. He enjoyed the take-charge attitude of his son. "Yes, sir," said Jonas. "I'll go as soon as Toby is out of danger."

Jeremy told his parents what the doctor had said, and they all headed back up to Toby's hospital room.

§

Roy Baker picked up Tom's petitions as promised. The board of elections gave each candidate twenty petition sheets to start. Roy photocopied another fifty, confident of Tom's popularity in the Community.

Tom gave Roy the list of names and addresses of individuals he thought would collect signatures for him. Roy made sure he called each person on the list to make sure they would help. He did not want to embarrass anyone into helping. "All but two assured me they would be happy to help. The two who declined told Tom they would be out of town on business for the next two months, but they would request an absentee ballot from the board of elections."

Roy made an appointment to bring the petitions to each person's house. If they were unavailable to meet him, he offered to leave the petitions in their mailboxes with detailed instructions of how to approach a potential signee, how the signature should be written on the petition and when he would return to pick them up. He emphasized the fact there was a limited time to collect the signatures and return them to the board of elections. Roy was smart, organized and driven, a mix hard to beat.

At Tom's request, Roy kept in contact with Ernie Spikes. Tom wanted to make sure Mary landed on the ballot also. He didn't look forward to sitting on the school board without her.

§

Cellphone signals pinged off cell towers in the district all day. Within forty-eight hours all religious groups in the county swore on a stack of bibles they'd send representatives to Saturday's demonstration in front of the police station, half a block from the Thompson home.

Friday night came, and Jeremy conferenced with his father and Reverend Mackey. "Everything is set for tomorrow. Speedy Printing did a great job. Mom will pick them up at nine in the morning and distribute them as people arrive."

"I can't believe the support we received from all the groups," said Mackey. "It restores your faith in people."

"We made so many contacts to use for future projects, we are in good shape." said Jeremy."

The two Reverends rolled their eyes at Jeremy's youthful enthusiasm. "We want to get through tomorrow, son. I can't think past tomorrow."

Both ministers ignored Jeremy's befuddled expression.

The phone rang, and Jonas excused himself. "Hello, Jonas Thompson, here." Jonas was silent. After a minute, Jeremy and Reverend Mackey heard, "Goodbye."

Jeremy waited for his father to say something, but Jonas had trouble collecting his thoughts. "It was the police captain from our precinct. They caught the gunman. They have a signed confession."

"Who was it?" asked Mackey.

"A teenager from the neighborhood."

"Why did he shoot Toby?" asked Jeremy

"It was an accident. The captain said the kid found a gun in the dumpster near the Sky Bar. He played with it, and it went off."

The three men sat in silence trying to get their heads around the last five minutes.

"What should we do?" asked Jeremy

We better get on the phone and call the churches and synagogues and tell them the good news and don't forget to thank them for their help. I'm sure word of our demonstration put a fire under the cops to figure this out."

All three had an uneasy feeling in their stomachs. Jeremy expressed all their concerns. "I hope this is the real end of it."

§

Tom's favorite relatives arrived for dinner. His aunts came one by one with their husbands and kids. Tom's cousins were much younger than he because his aunts were a lot younger than their older sister, Alice.

His grandmother had one child, Tom's mother. "When I was three, the doctor diagnosed my mother with cancer. For ten years Grandma fought this horrible, debilitating disease. Gratefully, she won the battle and resumed her life by having four more children, your aunts, Rosalie, Una, Patty, and Ethel.

He had seen none of his aunts for over a year. Tom's last year of grad school took up most of his time. His infrequent visits home, confined to short stays, prevented him from visiting with his aunts. Tom missed them. They were closer to his age, more like sisters than aunts. "It's going to be a great day."

Aunts Rosalie, Una, Patty, and Ethel doted on Tom as a child. Early on they all formed a close affection for each other.

As they arrived, each aunt rushed over, gave Tom a big hug, and told him how excited they were to be here to help him win.

Aunt Rosalie squeezed him the hardest, "How proud I am of you."

Una whispered, "I always wanted to run for some office but was too scared. I'm so glad my favorite nephew is doing it." Patty and Ethel expressed similar wishes. Patty asked, "Where are those petitions?" Ethel demanded, "Hand me a pen, I want to be the first to sign."

Una yelled over the din, "I'll take a blank sheet and have all my friends sign. Rosalie grabbed a bunch and yelled, "I'll take ten sheets for myself, and I'll make copies and bring them over to everyone's house. We have to make sure our boy wins big."

Tom's family had a great afternoon, eating, drinking and laughing. When his aunts left, Tom felt sad. Aunt Una was the last to go. She kissed Tom on the cheek, "I wasn't kidding when I told you I always wanted to do something similar to what you're doing, but I was afraid. I made all sorts of excuses. I said I have children. I have a job and on and on. But I knew the reason was, I was scared. I'm older now, and I still can't do it. I'm still too afraid to do a lot of things." She wiped a tear from her cheek and ran out after her family.

Aunt Una wasn't the only one getting older. Tom saw all his aunts had a few more lines on their faces than they did last year. Seeing Patty, Rosalie and his other aunts aging took some of the wind out of Tom.

Tom felt flattered his aunt shared her feelings with him. "Either you're in the game of life, or you're not. Most people postpone their dreams by using some excuse." Tom appreciated his aunts sharing how happy they were their nephew would not be like most people.

The aunts didn't know how much their support meant to him. Their words of encouragement gave him the courage to go forward. Tom thought, "I stand on their shoulders, and I will make them proud. I'm in the race from here on in, one hundred percent. I'll make a difference, and no one will stand in my way. I'll kiss as many babies as it takes to win this election. Whatever it takes, I'm in."

§

Roy Baker called two minutes after Tom's aunts went out the door. "Tom, sorry I am calling so late, but I wanted to check you're not goofing off instead of campaigning."

"I worked all afternoon wining and dining some of the best campaign workers there are," Tom explained what he was up to with his aunts. They arrived early and stayed late; they were so excited about me running. They brainstormed what they could do to help, and they stayed until they finished."

"Great."

"Roy, have you heard anything down at the station house about Jeremy's brother?"

"All I know is I received a call last night saying they canceled the demonstration because they found the gunman."

"Who is he?"

"He's a seventeen-year-old kid from around the neighborhood."

Tom heard no response and assumed the line was dead. "Are you there, Roy?"

"I'm here."

"What's going on?"

"It's very hush, hush down at the precinct, a lot of closed doors all over the building. I get dribs and drabs, a word here and there, but nothing I can piece together."

"What do you think…?"

"Tom there's no sense asking me. I don't know. I'll call you tomorrow. Maybe, I can learn something by then. I'm getting a call from Travis. I better see what he's up to."

"I think Randy's out with your brother."

"Got to go."

CHAPTER 13

"**R**OY, I NEED YOUR HELP. I'M AT VOLTAIRE."

"You're where?"

"At Voltaire, it's a Club in Jamaica. There are some people here who want to beat the shit out of me."

"Where exactly is this place?"

"On Evergreen and Thirty-First Street, it's right on the corner. You'll see the flashing purple lights from two blocks away."

"I'll be there."

"I'll be in front of the bar hiding in the bushes. When I see your car, I'll run over to you."

"Is Randy Foster with you?"

"No, he left about an hour ago. I met someone and didn't want to leave."

Roy heard a Rap Group playing in the background, accompanied by laughter and cursing.

"I'm leaving now. Sit tight. I'll be there as fast as I can."

Roy drove his SUV for ten minutes before the streets got darker, dirtier and more dangerous. His brother sounded as if this time wasn't the usual call for a ride home. Roy resisted using the ancillary blinking lights he had on his car. If stopped he could always show his shield, but the streets were empty, and the flashing lights wouldn't gain him any more time.

Roy sped into Voltaire's graveled driveway and slammed on his brakes sending gravel in all directions.

Seconds later a woman in six-inch heels, skirt four inches above her knees, hair teased eight inches above her scalp, makeup, and lipstick like pudding, headed for his car. She reached the locked passenger door and banged on the window.

"Just what I need," thought Roy," as he shook his head no; he wasn't interested in what she was selling. She kept banging on the window. Roy cracked the window open and told this working girl, "I'm a cop, so get the hell out of here before I arrest you."

A voice came back, "It's me, Travis." Roy's brother whipped the wig off his head and under the heavy makeup, and lipstick Roy saw his brother's face.

Roy quickly unlocked the door. "Get in."

Travis cried, and Roy held off giving his brother a piece of his mind.

"They planned to kill me as soon ..."

Roy looked at Voltaire's entrance and saw some men standing at the half-open door.

"What did you do that made them so mad?"

"Nothing, the bastards cursed at Randy and me."

"Where is Randy now?"

"He took off as soon as they first started with us."

"Why didn't you leave with Randy?"

"I was supposed to meet someone, and he hadn't arrived yet. Right after Randy took off one of the thugs joked around about Randy's brother and how he went to church a lot, and the others pushed me around. They promised they'd do all sorts of things to me. I made believe I had to go to the bathroom, but instead I went outside and hid in the bushes."

Roy said nothing more the rest of the ride home. His mouth couldn't open; his mind was incapable of forming words.

Travis assumed his brother was pissed beyond belief, so he was silent.

When Roy drove the SUV into their driveway, the house never looked better. Only a few miles from Voltaire to home, but the distance seemed like a plane ride away.

Travis waited to exit the car and gradually opened the car door slightly. Roy asked, "What are you waiting for?" Travis uttered no words at first, then begged, "Please, Roy. Go in and find a pair of pants, a shirt and some shoes for me."

Roy realized his brother didn't want to go in the house dressed as if it was Halloween. "I'll be right back, and I'll bring a washcloth so you can wipe the crap off your face."

Travis held his tears until his brother closed the front door.

§

Jen offered to put a bright orange colored sign on her car's roof, "Tom Foster for school board" with the date of the school board election. Jen thought it would be fun. Tom thought Jen was wonderful.

Jen's sign attracted a great deal of attention in the neighborhood during the three days the sign was on the roof of her car. Greeted by waves and applause by many motorist and pedestrians, Jen felt lucky dating this good-looking, popular man-about-town.

For the past few weeks, Jen thought of a possible future with Tom Foster. He wasn't rich, but Tom would always make a decent salary in education. Jen could see herself with Tom and maybe two kids.

Jen stopped at a red light, and two kids with smiles on their faces came over pointing at the sign on her car roof.

She opened the passenger window and said, "Don't forget to tell your parents to vote for…"

But the kids beat her to it. "This is for Tom Foster," and with that, the kids threw a whole pack of lighted firecrackers into her back seat.

The firecrackers made a sound that forced Jen from her car. When she got out, the boys threw more firecrackers at her feet. Finally, some older men and women saw Jen and came over to help.

One of the older men let Jen put her head on his shoulder until she stopped shaking. Some women offered to take her home, but she refused and returned to her car and drove directly home.

When Tom saw Jen the next day he asked, "Where did the sign go?" Jen told him her local insurance agent saw the sign and insisted she had to take it off the car or there'd be a huge increase in her insurance premium.

§

"What's happening to the neighborhood?" said a neighbor of Emily Cusack.

"What do you mean," asked another neighbor.

"You didn't hear? They found Emily Cusack hanging from a rafter in her attic."

"You're kidding?"

"No. The cleaning lady found Emily this morning. The kids were at school, her husband, Henry, left for work about nine, and the cleaning lady arrived at ten. When Emily didn't answer the bell, the cleaning lady used her key, went in and began working. An hour later she needed the heavy duty vacuum Emily kept in the attic.

The cleaning lady climbed to the attic and saw poor Emily swinging from a rafter. There was a breeze traveling through the roof, and the maid told the police Emily was swaying back and forth.

"Was there a note?"

"No, it doesn't seem Emily left one."

"I know she hasn't been herself since she came back from California. We met on Main Street. She told me she was coming from her psychiatrist."

"A psychiatrist?"

"She told me the doctor gave her medication to calm her nerves. To tell you the truth, it didn't seem the meds were too effective. She looked terrible."

"Do they have any leads?"

"The maid told the police she saw a Latino looking guy walking down the path from the house as she arrived. She thought maybe he was a delivery man, but there was no package outside the door."

"Maybe it was Emily's brother; I know he stops by occasionally."

"The maid said she couldn't be sure if he had come out of the house or not."

"Did she say if she'd be able to recognize him?"

"She told a neighbor she was too far away to get a good look at him."

"I have to finish shopping. How are the tomatoes? Are they ripe?"

"I haven't been in the produce department, yet."

"Are you going to the school board meeting tomorrow night?"

"I plan to, that is if my husband doesn't give me too much grief about it."

"See you tomorrow night."

§

Tom went to the Thompson home to visit Toby and to tell Nora and Jonas Thompson what Roy had related to him last night.

After talking to Toby for a half hour, Tom left the boy lying on the living room couch, propped up with pillows. Tom motioned to Jeremy he wanted to speak to him away from Toby's hearing.

Nora stayed with Toby while Tom and Jeremy walked casually into the kitchen. "Listen, Jeremy; I have some pretty tough things to tell you."

"Okay, shoot."

"Roy Baker has been trying to find out the full story about the kid who shot Toby. Originally, he told me everything was hush, hush at the station house, but last night, his partner didn't show for work, and he partnered with an older cop. He was a detective, named Weiner, on the force for twenty-five years. Weiner knows everyone. The captain gave Roy and Weiner a special assignment, overnight surveillance. As soon as they got settled, this Weiner breaks out a bottle of Jack Daniels and starts drinking. This older guy pounded the bottle pretty well. He told Roy, 'This is the way I can get through this type of boring night.'"

"About three in the morning, Roy was about to doze off. Weiner started bragging how he saved the Captain's ass the other day. Roy perked up and listened to this blow-hard tell him a story:

'We got word those black bastards were going to picket the station house. The captain went ballistic. He has a year left before retirement, and he doesn't want to see himself on camera during the eleven o'clock news being called clueless about who the fuck shot the little black kid. The captain asked me to call my contact at the school district office. I have a friend over there, a little guy who stays under the radar. He and I sometimes work together. I called him and gave him names of some teens with criminal charges pending. This little guy looks at their school records and sees what kind of trouble they've been in at school, and while he's at it, he looks at their family situation. He gives me the names of kids with the worst records and with the least supportive family situations.'

Tom stopped to see if Jeremy was still following and then continued.

"When Weiner sees he has Roy's attention, he starts up again. By this time Weiner is slurring his words, with an almost empty bottle in his hand. Roy was afraid the detective would pass out before he finished the story, but Weiner continued, 'I meet with one of these teens and make a deal with him. I tell the kid if he confesses to finding the gun and shooting it off by mistake, I'll get the DA to quash the charges he has pending and get the accidental shooting charge down to a violation. The kid pays the fine, and that's it. The kid bites. I go to the captain, and he's thrilled. Everybody wins.'

"Roy says to Weiner, 'You're telling me the guy who confessed lied?'

"The Detective gave Roy a big smile, and took a last gulp of Jack Daniels and fell dead asleep. Roy waited till dawn and went back to the station-house, parked the patrol car in the lot, and left Weiner snoring in the passenger seat. Roy called me as soon as he got home."

Jeremy let this unbelievable story sink in. "I'm not telling my father, not now anyway. My parents are just calming down. Toby is recovering, and this information won't help them, today. We still don't know who is responsible. They'll just worry. Right now, I'll handle it."

Tom nodded in agreement.

Jeremy stood up and said, "Tom, let's get going. We have an election to win."

§

When the lush green grass grew to an inch and a half, Ernie Spikes ordered the men to rev up the lawn mowers and begin cutting.

Ernie stood by an open grave instructing two new workers on the proper way to lower a casket into the ground. He emphasized to the men how important it was to do it with the greatest respect. He reminded the workers, "Someday, you'll be the one going in there. Handle the casket with the greatest of care. Families entrust their loved ones to us. We must honor their trust by our actions. The corpse could be your mother, your wife, or your child."

The new men's first interment was the hardest and the men with Ernie today hung on his every word, secretly afraid the childhood ghost stories might come true. Ernie didn't discourage their imaginations. Routine would soon harden their attitudes, but for today the dead would receive the reverence they deserved at least from these two workers.

One of Ernie's fellow foremen walked over and asked, "Got a second, Ernie?"

"Sure, Tim, what's up?"

"Someone called me and asked if I would relay a message."

Ernie waited to hear the rest.

"The person told me to tell you he wants you to screw up the McMurray lady's petitions. He doesn't want her on the ballot."

"And I bet the person was Lou Marinara."

Tim frowned and walked across the green lawn.

Ernie waited before he returned to his men. His mind raced thinking what Lou Marinara would do if he didn't obey his order. One thing Ernie knew was his nephew would be unemployed.

Ernie saw in the past the influence Lou possessed. Men lost overtime work and sometimes lost their jobs. Co-workers shunned the object of

Lou's disapproval. Sometimes bones got broken. Ernie put it all out of his mind for now.

Ernie's thoughts were interrupted by one of the new men calling, "Help."

Ernie looked over and saw one of the new workers struggling to pull the other out of the hole in the ground.

"What a day."

§

Ernie ended his eight hours at the cemetery, and by four-thirty he was on his way home. Riding in the car Ernie felt his blood pressure rising to the point he was ready to explode.

As soon as he got into the house, he went to the refrigerator and grabbed a cold beer. He sat down in his lounge chair and picked up the phone. He dialed Lou Marinara's office.

Lou's secretary answered, "Marinara Law firm."

"Let me speak to that boss of yours."

"Excuse me. Who is this?"

"It's Ernie Spikes."

"Well, Mr. Marinara is not available."

"Then tell him Ernie Spikes called and tell him Ernie says, Fuck You."

§

The interviews and their venues blended for Team McMurray-Foster. Today was the fifth church group this week, second for the day. Traveling between interviews required a person who knew how to use a GPS.

Mary was glad she had taken Mark's advice and teamed up with Tom before anyone else did. Lettie Grimes and Vince Miller were now hot on Tom heels to form an early alliance.

Tom and Mary parked the car with great difficulty. The handicapped spots outnumbered the regular parking spaces, and Mary and Tom had to walk a distance to the entrance of the Saint Pancras Senior Center.

The Center in the basement of the Catholic school was buzzing. Wheelchairs sped along the linoleum floor. Crutches, walkers, and wheelchairs were most members' transportation choices.

A large, smiling eighty-year-old woman greeted Mary and Tom. "Welcome to St. Pancras Senior Center. My name is Lillian Walsh. How may I help you?" Mrs. Walsh asked their names and politely said, "Why are you here?"

Mary told Mrs. Walsh who they were and assured the lady, "We called ahead and made arrangements to speak with the seniors about the upcoming school board elections."

Ms. Walsh looked befuddled, and Mary repeated herself just as a man in clerical garb approached them. Mary's eyesight prevented her from recognizing Father Grant, member of the present school board and a fellow candidate for the upcoming election.

Tom recognized Father Grant immediately. He and Father originally met at the Raccoon Lodge interview and several times since. Tom liked the priest's easy manner and quick, broad smile.

"Father Grant would win." thought Tom, "Even if he didn't have most of the votes from all the religious institutions in the district."

It's nice to see you, Father."

"Good to see you both. Welcome to St. Pancras."

"What brings you here, Father?" Mary asked. "We only see you at non-sectarian places; I hear you have all the religious places wrapped up."

Father Grant laughed and said, "I have some support in that area, but I'm here because this is my home parish."

"Everyone here is voting for Father Grant," said the old lady. "We all love him."

Father's face reddened, and he interrupted, "Nonsense, there will be people here open to your message."

Mary replied, "Maybe we should go. The seniors may be annoyed that we even came."

"I insist you stay. I'll introduce you both as my friends, and tell the members to vote for you. I'll remind them they can vote for more than one candidate."

Father ushered Tom and Mary into seats in the large auditorium. "The meeting will start in a few minutes."

While Tom and Mary sat waiting, Tom looked around the room at the posters on the wall. One old poster caught his eye. It was an advertisement for last year's New Year's Eve Party at the senior center. It read, "Come to our New Year's Eve party. Dance the night away from 3:00 to 6:00 PM."

Tom poked Mary "Look at the sign."

"I can't read it."

Tom read it to Mary. They both broke up laughing.

Father Grant introduced Tom and Mary and asked the seniors to give them a big round of applause. The seniors clapped wildly. Tom could see they'd do anything Father Grant asked.

Tom spoke for two minutes, Mary for one. The group immediately embraced the newcomers for their brevity so they could start their Bingo game. Father asked the group, "Friends, if you go out and vote for me, please vote for my two friends here. You can vote for more than one candidate. Another round of applause went up, and out came the Bingo cards.

Mrs. Walsh took the microphone and called the Bingo numbers. "B-22…"

Father walked Mary and Tom to the exit. The three talked about the election and some candidates they'd met. Father asked if he could speak to Tom privately.

"Of course, Father. Tom, I'll wait in the car."

Tom handed Mary the car keys.

"Mary, I'll only keep Tom a minute. I promise."

When Tom arrived at the car, he had a big smile on his face."

"What was so private, Tom?"

"I'm going back to high school."

Mary looked curiously at her young friend.

"Father asked me if I would chaperone one of his parish youth club dances."

§

After Tom and Mary left Saint Pancras Senior Center, Mrs. Walsh came up behind Father Grant and tapped him on the shoulder. Father had been avoiding the sweet old lady all morning, with little success. He knew what Mrs. Walsh wanted to talk about, and he wasn't thrilled with the topic.

Lillian Walsh's second husband, Ben, made a great deal of money on Wall Street. Lillian promised she'd marry him if Ben agreed to live in her beloved St. Pancras Parish. Lillian's suitor reluctantly agreed, "But I insist you let me build a new house where I can entertain my Wall Street friends and clients."

The year after Ben married Lillian he purchased the two adjoining homes, tore them down and built one of the first McMansions.

Lillian and Ben had no children and contented themselves with raising Lillian's son by her first husband. Ben loved Billy as if he was his biological son. When it was time for college, Ben pushed Billy to go to his alma mater, California Institute of Technology.

Ben and Lillian's son agreed to go to Cal Tech, but he never returned to New York. The newly graduated student met a girl from Sacramento and put down roots in northern California.

Billy had two sons who Lillian saw when she and Ben flew out to the west coast to visit their son. Unfortunately, air travel was difficult for Lillian because of an inner-ear problem which made flying painful. Trips to California were few.

Billy and his wife were always too busy to come to New York, even after Ben died. Years passed, Billy's wife died, and three years later Billy passed away of a massive heart attack at age fifty-two.

After their father died, the grandkids woke up and realized their grandmother was a wealthy woman. They didn't know she was worth ten million dollars, but they suspected she was loaded.

The older grandson wrote a short note to Lillian and mentioned he was coming to New York on business, and he'd love to see her. The grandson arrived at Lillian's door, saw her big house and the valuable items in it and he conveniently declared his grandmother feeble.

He called his brother, and they devised a plan to convince Lillian to give them power-of-attorney. Their problem was Lillian had a good lawyer who stopped them in their tracks.

A court case which lasted a year extricated Lillian from the would-be clutches of her grandchildren, but Lillian's attorney told her, "These bums are your next of kin, and if you don't want them to inherit your money, you better draw up a will. You have to tell the court where you want your money to go."

After much thought and prayer, Lillian intended to bequeath her money to her beloved St. Pancras Parish and her favorite priest, Father Grant. When Lillian approached Father with her plan, he thanked her but indicated he wanted all the money to go to the Church.

Lillian gushed, "Father, I want you to have some of my money. I know you don't have a retirement fund. You're a secular priest, and secular priests don't take a vow of poverty, just obedience, and chastity." Lillian blushed after saying the word chastity.

"I don't want your money, Mrs. Walsh."

"You may not want the money, but you need it. I bet you don't have more than a few dollars put aside for your retirement. I know our diocese doesn't plan for its priests' latter years like the Dominican and the Franciscan Orders do. "

"I don't feel right about it," said Father. "I would prefer you give my share to the parish or some other charity."

"I told you before if I can't leave some of the money to you, I'm not leaving anything to the Church."

Father Grant had been struggling for two weeks with the issue. He knew he must decide, or Mrs. Walsh planned to have her lawyer draw up her will leaving everything to SAVE THE WHALES FOUNDATION.

Father Grant asked Lillian to meet him in the back of the auditorium after confessions. "I won't be long." Lillian sat at a table by the exit and watched Father escort the last senior out of the Center.

When Father Grant returned, Lillian wasted no time getting to the point. "So, what should I do, Father? My lawyer says I can't wait any longer. If I die tonight, my money goes to those rotten grandchildren of mine. I'm meeting with my lawyer tomorrow to make a will. I can't take a chance those grandkids get any of my money."

Father sat down next to Lillian and said, "I want you to know I appreciate you wanting to leave me some of your money for my old age."

"So, can I leave you some money or not?"

Finally, Father said, "I'll leave it up to you Lillian. Leave me what you want, but please give most of it to St. Pancras Parish."

§

Theresa Marinara prepared the dining room table for dinner. Jeremy was due in a half an hour, and Theresa wondered, "Why am I bothering to put these beautiful Lenox plates on the table, when within the hour they'll be flying through the air, smashing against the walls."

Theresa knew five minutes after Jeremy came into the house he'd be hit with the words, "If you don't stay away from my daughter, you're a dead man." Theresa put everything out of her mind and went upstairs to finish getting dressed.

Angie suspected problems with Theresa's new boyfriend. This morning she warned Lou to be prepared for some surprises with his daughter's new friend.

"I'm pretty sure he isn't Sicilian and probably not even Southern Italian. He might be from the North. The boy may not have the best heritage, but on the bright side, she met him at a prayer conference in Florida. He's probably a good person. So, let's not judge him until we know him a while."

"Angie cut the crap. When we meet him, we'll know right away if he's good for Theresa. After he leaves, we'll talk about him." Angie knew this was the end of the conversation, so she uttered a quick prayer and went downstairs to prepare for dinner.

Angie was glad she hid Lou's gun before he got up this morning. She lifted it from his bottom drawer and brought it up to the attic.

§

Theresa sat on the loveseat facing the fire. The heat from the burning log failed to warm her feet or her fingers. Nothing would. Angie sat on a chair behind her daughter pretending to read a book. Lou banged around the kitchen waiting for their guest.

The bell rang, and all three froze. Theresa walked to the front door, prepared for all hell to break loose. The young girl's heart flew into her mouth.

Theresa felt the man she loved on the other side of the door, and she would do anything to make sure she'd be with him for the rest of her life. No one, not even the father she loved dearly, would change her mind about Jeremy. Theresa flung the door open, and Jeremy stood there, dark caramel skin, wearing a big smile. Theresa threw her arms around her love, almost knocking him off his feet.

Angie's saw her daughter's new boyfriend, and instantly her feet became glued to the floor. Lou's eyes dilated so wide, it took a week, and several bottles of eye drops to return his corneas to normal.

Theresa dragged Jeremy across the threshold and into the center of the living room.

"Mommy, Daddy this is Jeremy. Ma, you were so anxious to meet my new boyfriend. Well, here he is."

Jeremy put his hand out and shook Lou's hand heartily. Angie looked over at her husband's red face and was sure she'd be a widow by dessert.

Jeremy turned to Angie and shook her hand like he was pumping water.

"Please, sit down on the couch, Jeremy," requested Theresa. "What would you like to drink?"

"A glass of juice is fine."

Afraid to leave the three alone, Theresa asked Jeremy to help her in the kitchen.

Once in the kitchen, Theresa gave Jeremy a big hug. "I'm so glad to see you."

"You're parents seem nice, maybe a little surprised."

"Don't worry a bit. We'll eat and go for a ride. It's going to be a beautiful evening."

Theresa went back in the living room and suggested, "Let's have dinner. Jeremy and I are famished."

Lou and Angie staggered to the dining room table and fell into their seats. As soon as Lou sat, he developed hiccups. Theresa looked up in the air. "Thank you, God. It's pretty hard to yell when you have a case of the hiccups."

Angie poured Lou a glass of Chianti and with great difficulty, asked Jeremy if he cared for some wine.

"No, thank you. I don't drink alcohol." His smile showed no sign of smugness.

Lou jumped out of his seat and mumbled something about going upstairs for medicine. That's the last anyone saw of him. Lou never came back to the table.

After a while, Angie excused herself to look for her husband and a few minutes later, Jeremy heard a roar. Theresa said, "It's the TV."

Angie came down and told Jeremy and Theresa, "Daddy is resting. He won't be down for dinner."

Jeremy and Theresa ate quickly. Jeremy thanked Angie for a delicious meal and asked her to give her husband his best wishes for a speedy recovery.

Theresa grabbed Jeremy by the hand and pulled him out the door. Walking down the driveway, they heard another roar from the second floor of the house. Jeremy turned to Theresa and asked, "The TV again?"

§

The ride in Jeremy's car relaxed them both. The dining experience this afternoon did nothing for their stomachs. But as they drove further from Theresa's house, their bodies relaxed.

"So, how did it go, my dear Theresa?"

"Oh wonderful, my love."

"They hated me, didn't they?"

"They did."

"Did what?"

"They hated you, and you'd better get used to it. There's no way we're going to win my parents over."

Jeremy felt a stinging pain in his heart. He knew once again he was judged by the color of his skin rather than by what was in his soul. His father told him many years ago, "God is the only refuge for peace."

§

"Lou, calm down, or you'll take a heart attack."

"I should be so lucky. What will people say when they hear our daughter is dating a *mulignan*?"

"Maybe, she'll get sick of him."

"Sure. And maybe pigs will fly."

"Alright, what should we do?"

"I'll kill him."

"Don't be ridiculous."

"I mean I'll have someone do it for me. Can you picture holidays sitting around the table, with this *mulignan* grabbing for the antipasto?" Lou rubbed his stomach and headed for the medicine cabinet for another antacid.

Angie was sick. She knew her husband's temper, and she knew how much Lou hated blacks. Angie wasn't a civil rights activist, but she didn't have the desire to kill all black people like so many of her friends and relatives did. Angie never understood how one group of people could hate another group with such passion.

"I'm telling you, Angie, you better make sure after today Theresa knows she's forbidden to go near that black bastard again."

Angie rolled her eyes anticipating Theresa's response to that directive.

When Theresa was growing up, Lou never helped Angie with the baby. He was always out of the house doing something. When Lou came home, Theresa was in bed. If she was up, he patted her on the head and said, "Good girl," and went into his office and locked the door. Instead of having a child, they should have bought a dog.

"Now, he expects me to say, 'Your father forbids you to see the love of your life.'" Angie couldn't believe she was more upset with Lou than with Theresa and Jeremy. "Let him tell his daughter." Angie snatched her purse off the kitchen doorknob and went out to the car. "I'm going to my sisters and get drunk."

§

When Theresa was born Lou looked at her in the hospital nursery and prayed she'd never had to experience the pain he felt the day he left his mother at the clinic in Saranac Lake. Lou wanted to protect his little girl but was unsure how.

The day Angie and Lou brought Theresa home from the hospital, Lou drew away. Little by little Lou found excuses not to hold his little girl, not to play with her and not even be in the same room with her.

Angie gradually noticed her husband kept a distance from Theresa, both physically and emotionally. "Lou, are you afraid of the baby. You know she won't break."

Lou smiled, "I don't want to hurt her. You know how clumsy I am. I might drop her."

Angie brought the baby over to him. "Hold her. I'll be right here to catch her."

Lou had no choice but to take the baby from Angie. "See, Lou she didn't break."

Lou could feel himself relaxing. He looked down at his little girl. She fit perfectly in his arms. The feeling was indescribable.

"Lou, she's smiling at you. She knows you are her father."

Lou handed Theresa back to Angie more determined than ever to make sure he didn't let Theresa become too close to him.

CHAPTER 14

THE DANCE THEME, STARS WE ADMIRE, FEATURED TEENS IN elaborate costumes. The theme required everyone to dress as their favorite Rap, Movie or TV Star. The members of Father's teen group insisted if they had to have chaperones, they couldn't be over a hundred years old, meaning no one over thirty, except Father.

Father Grant tried to recruit chaperones fitting this requirement. First, he attempted to commandeer people from within his parish but had no success. In desperation, Father tackled Tom Foster that day at the parish senior center.

Tom told Father he'd be happy to help if no one expected him to dance. Father assured Tom of a 'no need to dance policy' for chaperones, then said, "And you're welcome to bring someone as long as she's under thirty."

"Were you afraid I'd bring Mary McMurray?"

Both laughed, and Father added, "It did cross my mind. You two have become quite a team."

"We have, and we intend to continue if we are elected. The problem is, Father, we need some more players to join us. Without a team of four players, we lose every vote and don't accomplish anything. The district has a lot of problems."

Father looked serious. "I agree, and I am ashamed to say I haven't kept up with much of what's going on lately in the district."

"But Father, if you excuse my frankness, you've gone along with Mr. Marinara a lot."

"My voting with Lou Marinara is a habit. When I first arrived on the Board, I figured Lou wanted the best for the district. He lived here. His family and friends were here. Why wouldn't he want the best for the district?"

"Lou does have a lot of friends, and they all appear to be on the school district payroll."

"I have no problem with hiring individuals you know. He has helped a couple of people in my parish find employment in the schools."

"Were they competent, Father?"

"Of course, I would never recommend anyone who couldn't do the job."

"That's the point. I hear Lou seems unconcerned if a person he puts in a school can't do the job. Lou hires family so he won't have to support them, and he hires friends to help him at election time, and I hear our good friend, Lou, hires a third group, people whose only qualification is they helped Councilman Troy Burns win election."

Father listened silently.

Tom waited for a reaction. None was evident.

Jen returned with three glasses of punch on a tray. "What are you talking about that looks so serious?"

"We were discussing the hiring practices of the school district."

"I'm glad you reminded me. I have a good friend who wants to transfer to our district. She's working in Upper Manhattan, and the commute is two hours each way. She can't do it much longer. Is there any chance of you two pulling some strings?" Jen asked coquettishly.

Tom asked, "Is she qualified?"

"She sure is. I went to college with her. She graduated Phi Beta Kappa and went on to receive her Masters from Columbia Teachers College. Every year, her principal evaluates her above average."

"What's your opinion, Father? Can a woman find a job in our district without being related to Lou Marinara?"

The DJ played a slow dance and Jen grabbed Tom's hand and pulled him toward the dance floor.

"I can't dance. I have two left feet."

"Well, tonight you'll dance with me, or you won't be trying any other moves later."

Tom blushed in front of Father. Father turned his head as if he heard nothing.

Father watched the two chaperones glide across the floor. "It seems Tom Foster has been modest about his dance moves," thought Father.

When Tom and Jen walked back to Father Grant, he clapped heartily.

Tom mentioned he'd heard something disturbing while on the campaign trail. "I heard there was a decision to keep the drugs in the southern tier of the district, or at least try to."

"Of course it means in the black part of the district," Father said disgustedly.

"No matter how many years I live," said Jen, "I'll never be able to wrap my head around people like that, people who'll target a certain group for destruction."

"You have a lot to learn girlfriend."

"In this county, there's one death a day from a heroin overdose," said Father Grant. "There are two school districts in this county. We have five deaths in our district for everyone in the neighboring district. And the southern tier of our district has three out of four of those deaths."

"There must be big drug volume to cause so many deaths."

"Business is brisk, and product laced with lots of other stuff adds to the danger of overdosing," said Father. "Drug profits feed a lot of families in the southern tier. The small-time sellers make money, but it goes to feed the rest of their family, here and in Central America."

"One small-time pusher," said Tom, "Has to take care of his mother, his baby momma, his father, the kids, mother-in-law, maybe more. These guys take chances, but they have little other options."

"Sad, it's sad," said Jen. "How do they get away with selling it? The area isn't that big. It's not the size of a state," asked Jen.

"There are four high schools in the southern tier and five in the white northern tier," said Father. "There's a lot of dealing in and around the junior and senior high schools. We know how they bring the drugs into the schools. The dealers use student dealers. But we haven't figured out how they're able to sell the drugs without anyone seeing the sale."

"I heard the suppliers hang around the school," said Tom, "And they give it to a group of students who sell it to the other students. We have metal detectors at the school entrances, but the metal detectors don't pick up drugs. How no one sees them is the important question."

"What does the school board do about it?" asked Jen.

The chairman is the head of a special school task force looking into this problem," said Father.

Before Tom could catch himself, he blurted out, "Isn't it a bit like the fox being in charge of the hen house?"

Even Jen felt the awkwardness of the moment and said, "The band is playing our song, Tom. Let's dance."

This time Tom didn't object.

§

In the car on the way home, Jen asked, "Will Father help my friend?"

"He wouldn't if it was a year ago, but now he's waking up."

Jen moved closer and snuggled up to Tom. She whispered in his ear, "Thank you."

As soon as Tom pulled into Jen's driveway, he glimpsed two men ducking behind Jen's red BMW.

"Wait, don't open the door." Tom clicked the door locks and sat staring down the driveway. Two young guys jumped from the front of Jen's car and ran off into her neighbor's yard.

"Stay here," ordered Tom as he grabbed a flashlight from under the drivers' seat. Tom slowly exited the car and flashed the light toward the

BMW. There wasn't a sign of anyone still hanging around, but closer inspection revealed all four tires were flat.

Tom returned to the car and motioned Jen to get out. She could feel her heart pounding in her chest as they walked quickly to the front door. As soon as Jen unlocked it, Tom pushed her into the foyer and slammed the door behind them. Jen's parents slept undisturbed on the second floor.

"That was scary, Tom. Am I glad you're with me, I don't know what I would have done if I were alone."

Tom thought, "If you weren't with me, this probably wouldn't have happened." But he said nothing to Jen.

§

Father Grant saw Tom the day after the dance at the Knights of Columbus candidates' night. "Thanks again, Tom, for chaperoning the dance last night. I was in a real bind."

"No problem Father, Jen and I had a good time, even though we were forced to take a reality check about getting older. Before we arrived, we thought we were so young."

"If I can ever return the favor, just ask."

"I will Father."

"Seems like all the candidates are here," said Father looking around the room.

Lettie Grimes listened from a few feet away.

"Father, if you ever need anyone to chaperone your dances. I'm always available."

Lettie surprised Tom and Father. They didn't realize Lettie was listening.

Father responded, "Thanks, Lettie but…"

Tom came to the rescue, "Lettie, the kids demanded an age cut-off of thirty,"

"Darn it; I missed it by a year. Couldn't I pass for under thirty?"

The Grand Knight's loud voice saved the day. "Everyone, please, take your seats."

Father and Tom rushed for their chairs leaving Lettie Grimes in their dust.

§

Tom had debated about asking Father Grant to speak to his brother Randy. So when he bumped into Father again a few nights later at the Elks Club candidates' night, he approached the priest and said, "Father, I have a favor to ask. It's about my brother, Randy."

"Sure Tom, what can I do?"

"I'd like Randy to speak with you.

"Can you give me an idea why you want me to talk to him?"

"Father, Randy is gay, and he's also religious. He went to Catholic school his whole life and enjoyed the experience. I hoped you could listen to what he has to say. He came out to everyone a few years ago, but he has never discussed the subject in a religious context. He's ready to speak to a person he sees as someone with connections to God."

"It would be my pleasure, but about my connection with God, I don't know."

"You know what I mean."

"Ask Randy when he wants to come to the rectory, and we'll make it happen. If you want to join us it would be fine, or you could make the appointment and tell him to ring the Rectory bell, and I'll be waiting."

"Thanks, Father."

§

Tom accompanied his brother to St. Pancras Rectory. Randy Foster rang the bell next to the big carved oak door.

"How can I help you?" asked the attendant.

"We have an appointment to see Father Grant," replied Tom

"Come in. Please, follow me."

Inside, the thick red carpet contrasted with a poorly lit vestibule, giving the room a warm, comfortable feeling. The attendant ushered Tom and Randy into a small conference room off the foyer. "Father will be right down."

"I forgot priests live in the same building where they work."

Father entered the room with a flourish, "Tom, so good to see you."

"Father, I'd like you to meet my brother, Randy."

Randy put out his hand and Father gripped it warmly.

"Tom, are you staying?"

"No, Father, I have an appointment with Jen."

"She's a great girl. Say hello for me."

"Randy, I'll see you, tomorrow."

After Tom left the room, there was an awkward silence.

"Well, Randy, it's good to meet you."

"You too, Father."

They sat in silence.

Finally, Father said, "So, you're gay?"

"Yes, Father."

"Why did your brother suggest we talk?"

"Tom thought it would be good if I told a religious person I'm gay, sort of a religious affirmation." Father smiled, and Randy burst out laughing. "Sounds funny, but I guess I'm looking for some validation for being gay."

When each stopped laughing, the tension in the room had dissipated. Both felt more comfortable and relaxed with each other.

"Was there something, in particular, you wanted to say?"

"No, I guess I wanted the Church to know."

"Well, although I'm a small part of the Church, I accept the position and your gayness is properly noted." Both saw the humor.

"But seriously, Randy, how can I help you?"

"You have already, Father."

"Do you mind if I ask, did you receive a lot of grief about being gay, especially in high school?"

"Some, but not what you'd expect."

"Why?"

"I have a big family that is well known and liked in the community. People accepted me. I guess they thought if my parents accepted it, they better not say much. The neighborhood respected my parents which helped. My mom and dad knew most of the families at school through Tom and my other sibling. Most of the kids had been in and out of our house for years. The kids my brothers and sisters knew probably told their younger brothers and sisters to leave me alone."

"You were lucky. I've heard some terrible stories of what gay students have to put up with at school."

"Don't get me wrong. I had to put up with a lot in general, on the street, at work. There were times I thought of suicide."

"Did you ever try to hurt yourself?"

"I considered it once, but it never got bad enough. I knew of two guys who tried, and one girl who succeeded."

"God rest her soul." Both were silent until Father added, "We should all respond to rudeness and cruelty with your gentleness."

Randy and Father were now completely at ease in each other's presence, and they did what people who feel that way do. They talked about interests, hobbies, and relationships, topics people talk about when they're friends.

§

For most of Father Grant's twenty-five years in the priesthood, he went through his day with a song on his lips and a prayer in his heart, but for the past year, he was troubled by doubt. He made a great effort to suppress this feeling, but since speaking with Randy Foster last evening, Father's gnawing doubts jumped to his mind's center stage. Unlike Randy, Father had failed to confront his troubles head-on.

During his four years in seminary, his teachers reminded him and the other seminarians of the promises they planned to make at their Ordination. The teachers emphasized Chastity the most.

No one could know what they were giving up twenty-five years ago at Ordination. Father and his fellow seminarians never imagined what a sacrifice a life without sex would be.

During the last year, he confronted the fact he'd die alone. He wouldn't know the companionship of a wife or the joy of children.

During their talk, Father compared the differences between his new friend and himself. Randy Foster related several difficult experiences he had with individuals who had tried to destroy him. It was only with the support of his brother, Tom, and Randy's other siblings he survived the pressures of being different. After the initial shock of their son being gay, Randy's parents were more than supportive.

Father's parents died when he was relatively young and his only sibling, a brother, died five years ago in a car crash on the Long Island Expressway.

All the support Randy had in dealing with being gay only highlighted to Father Grant the absence of anyone in his own life. He had no one to talk to about his present struggle or anything else. The day after Randy's visit whenever he was alone, Father Grant sensed a nagging, empty feeling creeping into his consciousness.

He needed to speak to someone. That night after supper, Father went back to his room and sat on his bed. He debated whether he would call Randy Foster. Before he could change his mind, he reached for his phone and called. "Hi, Randy, this is Father Grant? It was great speaking with you the other evening."

"Me too, Father, it was good. I appreciated you taking the time to meet with me. I never expected you'd be that cool."

"Same here Randy. Let's do it again?"

Randy was surprised by the priest's call, and that Father wanted to get together again.

"Sure, Father, when would be good for you?"

"How's this weekend? No. Wait. You're probably busy on weekends."

Randy interrupted the priest. "I'm free, or at least I can make myself free this Friday. How is seven-thirty?"

"It's fine."

Randy hung up and thought about what just happened. A priest called and wants to be my friend. Who would have thought it? It passed Randy's mind, "Maybe, Father was interested in him as more than a friend." He hoped not. Randy enjoyed his talk with Father last night, and the sex thing would only get in the way.

§

"He's been dead for at least sixteen hours," said the medical examiner to one detective standing outside the Baker house.

"The kid's name is Travis Baker," said the detectives. You know his brother, Roy? He's on the job, a great guy."

"Sure, I know him," said the Medical Examiner. "Roy gave me a hand last month with the Fire Department's clothing drive."

"Roy Baker's kid brother was into some strange stuff, drugs, gangs, and sex," said the detective. Roy came home from work and found his brother on the living room floor, called 911 and administered CPR until the EMS arrived and took over. EMS told us Travis Baker was probably gone for several hours before his brother came home."

"Is it possible this was a homicide and not a heroin overdose?"

"We'll see after I do the autopsy."

"Here comes the Captain. I better get moving. He doesn't like us talking to anyone at a crime scene, only potential suspects."

"But there aren't any suspects yet."

"It doesn't matter. The boss likes us to keep moving. See you later."

§

Randy arrived right on time at the Rectory door. The enormous carved doors weren't as frightening as they were the week before.

As soon as Father saw his new friend he knew something was wrong. Randy's eyes were red from crying.

"Okay, Randy, what's wrong?"

Randy didn't speak until both sat in the conference room.

"My friend Travis…" Randy couldn't continue. His eyes welled up.

Father waited until the young man regained his composure.

"They found him last night on his living room floor. He overdosed."

"On heroin?"

"Heroin and alcohol. The cops aren't sure if there was foul play. Probably not, but my brother, Tom, is a friend of Travis' brother, Roy.

Roy told Tom the detectives are looking into three causes of death, overdose, foul play, and suicide."

"Was it a suicide?" asked Father.

"Travis told me he had attempted it a few times, but I'm not sure if it was heroin, or someone killed him. He might have scored some heroin mixed with some nasty stuff or the people who Travis owed money to decided to make an example of him."

"I'm sorry, Randy, for your loss."

"Thanks. I loved Travis."

"Do you mind if I ask if you were involved with Travis."

"You mean sexually?"

"I mean what was your relationship."

"Well, he was my friend." Randy sat there deciding if he wanted to say more. Finally, he said, "No."

"I hope you weren't offended by my question."

"Most straight people imagine every gay has to be doing it with every other gay he knows."

"There's more than a little truth there."

"Well, we don't. Do straight people want to do it with every straight person they know?"

Father smiled impressed with new friend's ability to put things in perspective.

"You know, Father, people look at you and say 'This guy doesn't have sex. Father's such a nice person, and he's a young man, but he doesn't want to have sex. Something has to be wrong with him.' Those same people say, 'Randy isn't a bad guy, but he wants to have sex with the wrong people, there must be something wrong with him.'"

Father laughed, "There's no winning in this life." Father saw the ironic humor in what Randy was expressing so clearly. "Good analogy, Randy."

"Since we are being so open, Father, do you mind if I ask how do you feel about sex?"

Like Randy a few minutes before, Father wasn't sure he wanted to answer the question, but decided, "Why not."

"It's also about choice. I want relationships with people, but there's one relationship I've chosen to avoid, and it's the one which involves sex. My choice doesn't mean I don't desire sex; it just means I've chosen not to have it. The fact people don't understand is the problem."

"That's what we have in common. When I chose to have a sexual relationship with someone, it's my business. If I'm not hurting anyone, why does it bother anyone?"

"Do you think being sexually attacked when a person is young influences sexual orientation?"

Randy waited again, trying to decide if he wanted to go any deeper in this conversation. Randy hardly knew Father Grant.

Father saw the young man's hesitancy. "Randy, don't answer if you feel uncomfortable and I apologize if I was too frank."

Randy answered. "Father, I have an opinion, and I trust you enough, even though we only know each other for a short time."

Father waited while Randy gathered his thoughts. "I was violated when I was eight years old by a next door neighbor. One day I was in the backyard, and he called me into his house. He brought me into the kitchen for a glass of milk and a cookie. I walked in front of him and all of a sudden he was all over me. He…"

Father jumped in, "You don't have to say more, Randy. I get the picture. How terrible."

Randy teared up.

"Did it happen more than once?"

"Yes, several times that summer."

"What stopped it?"

"He moved away. He was a bachelor. He was an airline pilot, so he moved around a lot."

"Did it affect you being gay?"

"No, Father, it affected my becoming sexually active earlier than I probably would have. It jumped started something. I already knew about my sexual preference."

"So, you were born gay?"

"I was since I can remember and certainly before being attacked by the cookies and milk guy."

"Did you ever discuss any of this with Travis?"

"I did. Travis believed there was a connection between being gay and exceptionally good-looking children."

Father said, "And what was it?"

"Travis was exceptionally handsome like Tom. Travis' parents were always being approached to sign him up as a model, but they weren't interested. Travis read a magazine article which warned parents of extremely good looking children, both boys, and girls, to be vigilant about sexual predators stalking their children. The article explained, "Both men and women sexually attack a disproportionate number of these children compared to the average child."

"That's interesting. I wonder if it's true."

"Well, in Travis' case it was. He told me he was approached many times by all types of people; he couldn't count the number."

"Was he bragging?"

"Travis wasn't that type of person. I asked Tom about this, and he swore no one ever approached him."

Father listened intently and was pleased he had called his new friend.

Randy continued, "Travis' theory isn't disproven by Tom's experience. Tom's genes account for this. He had both good looks and exceptional emotional wiring. A predator instinctively knew he wouldn't be successful in trying anything."

Father listened as his new friend opened up a world of ideas for him.

"Father, my brother doesn't consider himself particularly good looking. He never had a gorgeous girlfriend, good looking sometimes, never gorgeous, never drop dead gorgeous. Tom's girlfriends always had a great personality, not great legs."

"Oh, but I met his present girlfriend, Jen. She's pretty."

"She's alright in the looks department, but what she has is a nice way. She's fun to be with, a typical Tom Foster girl. I don't know how many times growing up I heard a neighbor, a teacher, a family member say, out of Tom's hearing, 'Tom could do much better.'"

Randy saw Father befuddled by a subject new to him and changed the topic. "I hope Travis is in a better place, one where intolerant individuals do not haunt him, people trying to always take advantage of him."

"When is the funeral?"

"The Medical Examiner will release the body tomorrow. Travis' family is Catholic, and I'm sure they want to have a Catholic ceremony. Is there any law gays can't be buried in a Catholic Cemetery?"

"No, there isn't."

"Great."

"What about a funeral mass?"

"Travis' family isn't registered in any particular parish. Will it be a problem?"

"It could be. When a family goes to a church to ask about burial arrangements, the pastor will probably ask if they're registered parishioners. Occasionally, the pastor will say we can't bury you from this church, and other times he might say there's a five hundred dollar donation needed to have a mass offered."

"It's tacky."

"Maybe, but someone has to pay for the heat or air conditioning, the organist, the vocalist, the cleaner and everyone else who keeps the church running smoothly so when people come to ask if they can have a funeral mass, there's a place and people to make it happen."

Randy thought for a second and replied, "I see your point."

"If the Travis family wants to come here, I'll say the funeral mass and if they prefer I also will come to their local church. I probably know their pastor."

"Father, I'm sure they'll appreciate your kindness. I am delighted you called and invited me tonight."

"I am too. Let's go down to the kitchen and have a piece of home-made pie the cook made for supper. There was plenty left over."

§

Tom called Mary to tell her he was at Frank Fontaine's school to meet Bunny and Frank, "I'm here now. Are there any questions you want me to ask Frank?"

"Ask him how many mess-ups he was stuck with when he arrived at his school and does he know which ones have Marinara connections?"

"I'll call you tonight."

Tom went into the main office where Bunny and Frank were waiting. "How about a tour of the school before lunch?" asked Frank.

"It would be great."

Frank said, "Can you give me a second I forgot my keys and we'll need them to get into certain classrooms I want to show you."

Frank took off and Tom said to Bunny, I haven't seen your friend Mrs. Portnoy around the past month. Is she alright?"

"Esther is good, but she had to get a job and the only one she could find paying decent money has long hours and is on the other side of town. I asked Father Grant if he could put a good word in for her with the superintendent to get her a job at the district office or in a school close to her home and he said he would ask Pinzon."

"Sorry to hear it. I was getting to know her and there is something about her I like."

Frank appeared and said, "Are you ready to start the grand tour?"

"But before we start, Mary wanted me to ask you a question. Do you know which people in the school have Marinara connections?"

"Yes, and I had a lot to do to shape up this faculty because of them. Marinara put so many of his buddies in here they should have renamed the school the C.A."

"What's C.A.?"

"The Crony Academy. You wouldn't believe the characters Lou put on the staff of this high school?"

"It's no surprise," said Bunny. "Your predecessor was a relative of Lou's."

Frank added, "Let me give you an example. When teachers returned from summer vacation, each department schedules a meeting to discuss the curriculum for the fall semester. I decided to treat myself and attend the meeting for senior English teachers. I was an English teacher many moons ago, and I miss discussing what books the students will read during the coming semester."

"I didn't know you were an English teacher; I was an English Lit major. I knew we had a lot in common," said Bunny with a flirtatious smile.

Frank smiled back, and he continued, "I'm sitting there, ready to hear some discussion on what books the senior class will read when the chairman of the English department stands up and announces she has decided what should be read by the students during the fall semester."

"I've decided the students will start the semester off by reading the great Russian novel, The Brothers Kalamazoo."

Frank paused, and Bunny burst out laughing. "I'm sorry, but Kalamazoo is hilarious."

Frank continued. "I sat there dumbfounded listening to the head of the English Department. She was the member of my faculty who supervised a subject I hold dearest and a subject which all students need to pass to graduate."

"What did you do?"

"I left before I made a scene. The other English teachers watched the expression on my face. Many had been passed over by my predecessor for this chairmanship position, although they were far more knowledgeable, articulate, and well-read than this idiot who got the job because she had an in with Lou Marinara.

"What happened next?"

"I returned to my office and sent my secretary back to the meeting to tell that idiot chairwoman to come to my office, immediately."

Tom and Bunny were all ears.

"She came into my office and started to take a seat. I told her there was no need for her to sit. 'This meeting will take a minute.' She looked befuddled. I told her starting tomorrow Mr. Steiner was chairman of the English department. I informed her she should make a formal request for a transfer to one of the other high schools in the district for the next semester."

"Can you do that with the union rules? I'm sure she was on the phone with her friend, Marinara, as soon as she left your office."

"You're correct," said Frank. "An hour after she left my office, I received a call from the Lou Marinara demanding to know the reason why I treated his friend in such a manner. I told Marinara I was glad he called and I related the story of what happened. And before he said anything, I told him our senior class would not be reading the Brothers Kalamazoo this semester.

"What did he say?"

"Nothing, I couldn't pry a word out of him, he was laughing so hard on the other end of the phone."

Bunny and Tom broke up.

"When Lou finally stopped laughing, he said, 'She'll ask for a transfer first thing in the morning, effective right away.' And he hung up."

"Score one for the good guys."

"Mr. Lou Marinara has been extremely helpful since that conversation. He has helped me with supplies and added personnel."

"It's great, Frank, but watch him. Lou's a snake."

"Thanks for the advice, but I'm watching him as carefully as he's watching me."

Tom offered, "I recently met one of the board members who served on the last board, and I asked him why he didn't run for a new term. He confided, "I was sick of Lou dispensing all the patronage."

"Well, Tom, with you on the board, I'm sure things will change. Now, let's finish the tour and go to lunch. I'm starving."

§

Eddie Fisher always followed orders from his superiors, but when he heard the order came from Lou, the sky was the limit. When Mr.

Marinara was looking for information on Bunny Krouse, it was Eddie's pleasure to oblige.

Eddie's attraction to Bunny was strong. He knew her principal activities, but little more. He wanted to discover more about this attractive lady.

A few nights of surveillance proved informative. Eddie sat in his car, four doors from Bunny's Pine Hollow Drive home. The street was quiet except for the Krouse home. Eddie soon became bored watching the comings and goings of Bunny's kids.

On the third night, Bunny opened the door to a face Eddie recognized, Frank Fontaine, principal of one of the high schools in the district. Eddie's interest peaked.

He watched Fontaine ring the bell. Bunny appeared and invited him inside. Two hours later Frank and Bunny appeared at the door again. Bunny planted a kiss on his cheek and closed the door. The next day Eddie dutiful reported to his boss, Phil.

"Great job Eddie. Keep after her and find out how serious this relationship with Fontaine is. I want to see what she's up to, and who she's supporting for school board. Do what you can to make sure Krouse doesn't get any closer to the McMurray lady and her sidekick, Foster. Bunny Krouse knows more about the district than she should. If the three of them team up, they'll be big trouble."

Eddie promised to keep ahead of it. He intended to ask Phil about a raise starting this month, but Vince Miller walked in the door.

§

Superintendent Rocco Pinzon, the school district's educational leader, couldn't wait a minute longer. He dialed Lou, and when Marinara picked up, he didn't pause a second. "We have to fire, Regina. We have to find a way to get rid of her. She's up to something, and she's been drinking more than usual. It's only a matter of time before Regina Moriarity sees something and blabs it around the district."

The silence was the only thing Rocco Pinzon heard.

"Are you there, Lou?"

"What do you want me to say? I'm afraid of rocking the boat right now. Father and Ted like Regina. I'm not sure I have the votes to get rid of her, and if I did get rid of her, I might lose one of their votes for chairman after the election. We'll need both their votes and another vote from one of the new members to ensure your contract renewal."

"But Lou, she's going to ruin us."

"There's nothing I can do right now. Your contract comes up for renewal next year, and you want the votes, don't you?"

"Yes, but hers is coming up at the same time. And Regina wants to be superintendent. She'll find a way to push me out, I know it."

"Calm down, Rocco."

"You know, Lou, if Regina becomes superintendent there's no way she'll play ball with you or do your bidding like me. She'll be on the phone with the board members every two minutes trying to screw you."

Lou realized Rocco Pinzon was right. "After the election, it will be a different story, Rocco, but for now that's it."

Rocco found himself on the end of a dead phone line.

The superintendent dialed Phil Turner, but Turner didn't pick up. He phoned Eddie Fisher's line. "Eddie this is Superintendent Pinzon. Tell your boss I want you to investigate Regina. And tell Phil I want results this time." Rocco slammed the phone down as Lou did to him a few minutes before.

§

Lou and Vince differed regarding patronage. Lou wanted jobs for his neighbors and relatives. He wanted to stack the district with people beholding to him. The more incompetent the job holder, the more beholding they would be.

Vince wanted jobs for anyone who would pay him the right price. Vince's philosophy was, "You can make a lot of money selling jobs with great benefits, hefty pensions, and generous vacations to people with the money to pay."

When Vince mentioned this to Lou, Marinara would look like he was taking a heart attack. "We don't give any jobs away. Do you understand? The way to keep this group going is to never let anyone into the district who isn't one hundred percent on our side. Got it, Miller?"

Vince answered, "I get it, Lou." But thought, "Screw you, Lou, I want the money. You keep the loyalty."

Vince knew this philosophical difference between Lou and him would cause trouble up the road, but for now, Vince would pretend to agree with it.

"There are not only principal and assistant principal jobs, department chairmen, district office personnel, teachers, but also janitorial staff, kitchen staff, contractors, food vendors, school supply vendors. The list goes on," salivated Miller.

§

Four days before the school board election, Tom went to the mailbox hoping to find a check from a catering company for a job he did last month.

He saw an envelope with a handwritten address, ripped it open and pulled out a single white piece of paper. The letter began, 'Dear School Board Voter…'

Tom read the letter in disbelief. The author accused Tom of being both a drug addict and a drug dealer. The writer called him the 'Marijuana-Go-To-Guy' for the neighborhood and asked the reader if this person was the sort 'we want on our school board.' The letter concluded with, 'DO YOU WANT TOM FOSTER SELLING YOUR CHILDREN DRUGS?'

Tom received calls all day from friends and relatives assuring him the letter would not affect his election results. Tom was comforted to hear the encouraging words, but he knew the letter had to affect several people who would now think twice about voting for him.

When Tom's mother came home and read the letter, she told Tom, "There's nothing you can do about it. It's too close to the election to respond effectively. You have so much support; you can't lose."

Later in the day, Tom called Mary and told her about the letter. Mary was enthusiastic in her encouragement. "Tom, don't worry. You may lose some votes from older voters, but you'll make it up from all the young voters who'll think you're even cooler than they suspected. Tom, you'll win."

Tom hung up feeling a lot better. He might not be cool, but his friend Mary sure was.

§

The next day Tom's friend, Ed McNally, who brightened his spirits on the Boston trip, called and kidded him. "Tommy Boy, can you fix me up with some weed. I ran out last week, and I read you're the go-to-guy for the stuff."

Tom laughed, "So you received the letter, too."

"Everybody received it."

"How did they get the names and addresses of all my friends?"

"It's an old trick in politics. When my uncle ran for Alderman in New Jersey; the same thing happened. The bastards went to the board of elections and copied his petitions. They sent this type of letter to everyone who signed my uncle's petitions."

"Did it hurt your uncle?"

"It sure did. My uncle lost big time."

"Why didn't you lie and tell me he won?"

"Tom, the letter didn't hurt him. He was a crook. The letter reminded everyone what they already knew. In your case, no one will believe anything bad about you. Let's face it, Tom; you're stuck with a huge 'good guy' rep."

"I hope you're right."

"I called to tell you every one of your friends will be free on Tuesday to help us get the vote out for you. We will make sure every old lady who signed your petition has a ride to the polls."

"Ed, you're the best. I can't tell you how…"

"Never mind, keep your pot franchise going. I'm getting another call."

Tom promised to stop feeling sorry for himself and work his ass off to win the election.

§

Bunny Krouse's house buzzed with people going in and out. Bunny barked orders, "Today is Election Day, gang. We either do it today, or we lose. The two old ladies across the street need a ride to the polls. Norris, go over and give them a ride. Frank here's a list of people who said they'd vote for Tom. Please, call and remind them. Ask if they need a ride."

Across town, Roy Baker armed a small contingent of Tom's younger supporters. In the northern tier of the district, Tom's aunts prepared to go door-to-door to neighbors and friends who signed Tom's petitions offering rides and reminders to vote.

§

Election Day morning, Tom opened his eyes and the sun shined brightly through his uncovered window. He looked around the room piled with fliers, "Vote Tom Foster for School Board." His heart beat faster. He was ready for today's challenge.

The infamous letter sent by his opponents lay on his nightstand. Tom's anger rose, and he jumped out of bed, ready to win despite the embarrassment he still felt.

Randy came upstairs to wake his brother, and he was happy to see Tom already up. He called into the shower, "You'll knock the bastards off their feet today, Bro. Mom's got breakfast ready."

The whole Foster clan sat in a circle at the breakfast table ready to start their appointed rounds. Alice Foster reached for Randy's hand, and Randy reached for his sister's hand, continuing until the entire family physically connected around the table. Randy uttered the prayer, "God's will be done this day." The rest answered, "Amen." Tom's three sisters ate and left to cover polls in the northern tier of the district to make sure no funny business went on.

Randy and his father had a list of older men and woman who needed a lift to their polling places. Alice left to meet Bunny to supervise a bank of telephones at a wealthy supporter's law office, ten phones, and ten callers.

Frank Fontaine took off from work to shadow Tom for the day. He had arranged for Tom to visit six senior centers, shake hands and remind the people to vote.

"I spoke with Jeremy Thompson last night," said Frank. "And he's given each minister in the southern tier their marching orders for the day. Jeremy has ten friends organizing poll visits to make sure the voters are not turned away incorrectly.

So far today, no one mentioned the 800-pound gorilla, the letter accusing Tom of being a drug dealer.

§

The day after the school board election the candidates gathered at the district office for the results of the balloting. One by one they arrived. Lettie Grimes came first, followed by two candidates from the northeastern part of the district. No one had ever seen them at a school board meeting or any interviews. How they concluded they'd win was beyond everyone.

Next, Mary and Tom arrived. Lou and his wife, Angie, arrived a half hour after everyone. Father Grant never came. He knew he'd win and if he didn't, he'd have more time for his ministry.

Vince Miller didn't show until after Tom and Mary. The three candidates backed by the PTA President's Counsel huddled in the corner. No one noticed when they came into the auditorium. Candidate Candy Caine sat in the corner reading a magazine.

Lou turned to Angie and whispered, "We underestimated Foster. His voters came out in droves. His organization was much better than ours."

Angie Marinara softly responded, "One polling place was in the basement of a school, and I heard an old lady fell down the stairs. When the ambulance came to take her to the hospital, she refused to go until she voted for 'That nice young man, Tom Foster.'"

§

A man from the board of elections finally walked into the room filled with candidates. He apologized for the delay in announcing the election results but explained there was difficulty collecting the ballots last night after the polls closed. The school board results are always the last to be counted especially in a year when the governor and a Senator are on the ballot. We had a big turn-out this year, and I am sorry to say we won't have your results until sometime this afternoon.

Lou gave Angie a look and said. "I have to go back to the office," Angie said she would wait around and call if she heard anything.

Lou was back in the office for less than an hour when Vince Miller came barging in.

Marinara looked up at Vince and laughed, "Your little idea to knock Foster out of the box didn't work."

"I know. It probably increased Foster's vote," said Miller.

"He's a shoe-in," said Lou. "I am, and Father is. The rest of you will probably have to wait until they count the absentee ballots."

"Do you think that bitch McMurray will get in?"

"She'll get a lot of the older folks. She's the only senior running. She should get a large group from the beauty salon community throughout the county. If your hairdresser says vote for someone, you listen. Her friend Lulu is president of the county salon owners and she has been working like a dog spreading McMurray's name."

"I was sure my letter would work."

"Your letter only energized Foster's campaign. My poll-watchers called and said young voters came out in droves, Foster's high school friends, his siblings' friends, his parents' friends and his relatives will push him right to the top just under Father Grant."

Lou couldn't resist saying, "I hope you fill the last seat and not that young girl, Candy Caine."

Vince just shook his head and said: "I'm going back to the district office to see if there is any news."

Lou called after Miller, "Keep me informed."

PART II

CHAPTER 15

"**N**OW, LADIES AND GENTLEMAN, I'LL SWEAR IN THE SEVEN winners of last week's school board election. There were fourteen candidates for seven seats on the board. This year's election brought out forty thousand voters, a record number for our district and reflected nine percent of the district's eligible voters. Before I swear in the new members of the board, I would like to announce each winner's name in the order of the number of votes they received beginning with the highest:

Thomas Foster

Father Dan Grant

Lou Marinara

Mary Mc Murray

Lettie Grimes

Theodore Kowalski

Vince Miller

"I now ask the elected candidates to stand, raise their right hand and take the oath of office." After the group took the oath, the packed auditorium resounded with thunderous applause for all the winners.

The Master of Ceremonies invited the assembled friends and relatives of the new school board to go to the cafeteria, one floor below, for light refreshments. School security officers ushered the group downstairs.

Mary McMurray turned to Lettie Grimes and asked, "Why are the school district offices in a school?"

"This school doesn't have enough kids to fill it. If the school didn't have the district offices, it would have to close for under-enrollment. By placing the district offices here, the school and the district save money by not paying rent elsewhere."

"Someone was awake."

"This particular school is paradise; the kids are all white. The school is so small there aren't any discipline problems. The school is in the best neighborhood in the district."

Mary kept quiet but noted all Lettie said.

On the stairs to the cafeteria, Mary heard a voice call, "Congratulations, Mrs. McMurray, and you too, Mrs. Grimes."

Mary waited until she reached the bottom of the stairs to turn around, "Oh, Mr. Pinzon, thank you."

"Hello, Rocco," replied Lettie."

Mark McMurray reached his wife and greeted Rocco Pinzon. Then Mary said, "Lettie, this is my husband, Mark." Mark shook Lettie's hands.

Lettie replied, "My husband won't be coming. We never go anywhere together."

Mark grabbed his wife's arm. "It's good to meet you, Mrs. Grimes. Mary, Ellen and Todd are over by the food waiting. Tom's mother, Alice, also wants to say hello."

As the Mc Murrays left, Vince Miller came up to Lettie. "We did it, Lettie."

"We sure did, now, the hard work begins."

"And so do the spoils."

"What does that mean?"

"You know respect, prestige, jobs."

Ted and his wife, Martha joined Lettie and Vince. Ted introduced his spouse as Father passed.

"Hey, Father."

"Hi, Ted. Good to see you, Martha."

Always looking for alliances, Vince asked, "You know Ted's wife, Father?"

"Sure, and Lou's wife, Angie, too. Don't forget; this isn't my first term on the board."

Vince waved to his wife, Linda, as she exited the elevator pushing their oldest son in a wheelchair.

The caterer announced, "Please, come and eat."

Lettie Grimes headed for the refreshment table. Tom Foster and his family picked up plates and joined the line. "Tom, please introduce me to your lovely family."

"Sure, Lettie. This is my mother, Alice, my father, Fred, my brother Dan, my brother, Randy, my sisters, Nan, Erin, and Trish." They all shook hands, and Alice Foster said, "Congratulations on winning a seat on the board, Mrs. Grimes."

"Thank you, but you deserve the congratulations for raising such a fine son. Tom is a great guy, and I look forward to working with him."

Under her breath, Alice muttered, "I bet you are."

Bunny passed, and Alice used her as an excuse to end the conversation with Lettie Grimes.

"Hi, Bunny. Here, get in front of me."

"Thanks, Alice, but I'm not hungry."

"Just get in front of me," whispered Alice. "I've got something to tell you."

Lettie chimed in, "It's how she keeps her little shape."

Bunny gave Lettie a look and stepped in front of Alice.

Alice whispered, "When we get to the end of this line, walk back to the table with me."

Once off the line Alice grabbed Bunny's arm and pulled her close. "I was at the doctor's yesterday, and he told me my latest tests were negative. It was a cyst, not a tumor, and the cyst is benign?"

Bunny quietly squealed, "Thank God, Alice. I'm so happy for you. It's quite a day."

Tom walked over to the McMurray table, Mary jumped up and introduced Tom to her daughter, Ellen, and her husband, Todd Taylor.

"It's great meeting you, Tom. My mother speaks of you often," said Ellen.

"Ellen and I feel we know you," said Todd. "My mother-in-law talks about you all the time."

"Tom and I have developed a wonderful relationship in a short time," said Mary

"We sure have," Tom responded.

"Living in New Jersey," said Ellen, "We worry mom won't have anything to do without us."

"I miss all of you very much. But running for the school board has taken up so much time and energy, it's unbelievable. Tom runs me all over the place."

"On the contrary, your mom drags me all over the school district. She wears me out, but it's fun, and we believe we're about to do some good things for the students of the district."

"Tom has a new girlfriend, and she's starting to take up more and more of his time. I'll have to speak to her."

"Mary, please, you'll scare her away."

The group laughed.

"Todd, what type of work do you do?"

Mary and Ellen looked at Todd, not sure what he'd say. Todd often gave an evasive answer to this question, but after a short pause, he revealed, "I work for the FBI. I'm a Field Agent."

Tom sensed Todd's reluctance to answer this question. "I'm sorry, Todd. I didn't mean to be intrusive."

"No problem, Tom. I usually try to avoid telling people what I do. People either clam up or ask a million questions. Obviously, I can't go into any detail, but when a person like you asks, I answer the question."

"I appreciate it."

"Let's have a drink," suggested Mary.

"Mary, I can't. I have a date right after this, and I have to speak to some of my friends who came today."

"With the same young lady?"

"Yes, it's been two and a half months, a long-term relationship with me, lately."

"Tom, it was a pleasure meeting you. And thanks for all you do for mom."

"It's been great meeting you,' said Todd. "I hope to see you soon. I'd like to hear what goes on in the schools."

"Hope to see you soon."

After Tom left, Mary commented, "I'm lucky to have Tom with me on the board. So far, he's the only one I can trust."

"What about the priest?" asked Todd.

"Father's fine, but he's preoccupied with his parish duties and isn't as engaged as Tom and I."

"Tom's an impressive young man. Too bad he didn't choose the FBI as a career."

"It's my guess he'll stay in public service."

"I see him eventually seeking higher office," predicted Ellen.

"He's a natural," agreed Mary. "He has it all, looks, personality and enough friends and family to win. He had the most votes of anyone who ran, including Father."

"We should watch Tom Foster carefully," suggested Todd.

§

Tom saw Jeremy, his parents and their son Toby walk into the room while he was talking to Mary and her family. He quickly excused himself and walked over to bring them to the Foster table.

"Can you believe you did it?" asked Jeremy.

"We did it," said Tom.

Alice Foster stood up to kiss Nora and Jonas Thompson and to give Toby a big hug. "You look great young man."

"I'm almost completely better," said the young boy. Alice and the Thompsons chatted up a storm.

Jeremy glanced across the room and saw Theresa sitting alone with her mother and father. Jeremy's eyes zeroed in on her father's face. His eyes exploded with a million light bulbs.

Tom saw his friend's face. "What's the matter, Jeremy?"

Jeremy continued to stare across the room. Tom looked toward Jeremy's stare and saw Theresa Marinara give his friend a wave. Tom looked back at his friend's sickly face. "What's the matter, Jeremy? You look terrible."

Jeremy turned to Tom, "That's the man who gave my father and the other black clergyman such a hard time two months ago at the school board meeting. I didn't associate the name Marinara with Theresa or her father. When I think of it, I don't know if I ever heard Theresa's last name and I never connected that face when I went to dinner at Theresa's home. I was so nervous, plus I only saw him for a minute before he went upstairs to puke."

"I guess all old white guys look the same."

Jeremy didn't respond to Tom's joke, so he asked, "How do you know Theresa?"

"I met her in Florida. We've been dating since then. I love her, and the feeling is mutual."

Alice Foster walked over, "Tom, Mr. and Mrs. Vogel are leaving."

"Excuse me, Jeremy. I'll be back."

Tom didn't return for quite a while, by then Jeremy was gone.

Tom went over to his mother and asked if she'd seen Jeremy.

"He and his parents left about ten minutes ago. They had to leave, but Jeremy promised to call tomorrow. Tom, there go your friends, Ed and Vanessa. Catch them before they leave."

The rest of the reception passed uneventfully with all the board members meeting the friends and the relatives of the people they'd be fighting with the next three years.

§

On the way home from the swearing-in ceremony, Lou asked Theresa, "How does your mulignan boyfriend know the Foster kid?"

"Daddy, I hate when you use that word and by the way, that 'Foster kid' is the young man who cleaned all your clocks in the election. Tom Foster received the most votes in the election, and my 'mulignan' helped him."

Angie sat next to Lou in the front seat and saw Lou grip the steering wheel so tightly, she thought it would snap.

"Your father doesn't mean anything by it, dear. It's what the Sicilians call eggplant. When your father's family came to this country, they saw the Negros and called them *mulignans*."

"But Daddy gets angry when the Irish call him a WOP. What's the difference?"

Angie didn't answer. She let that fly ball go foul.

"The Foster kid will be a pain in the ass. He pulled votes from the dark areas in the district, and now they probably own him, big time."

"Tom Foster received votes from all over the district. He couldn't even begin to pay everyone back, even if he was so inclined." Theresa then quickly added, "Which of course he isn't."

"That's what you think little girl."

"Wherever Tom went on the campaign trail, he was a hit. Daddy, face it, you'll have to deal with Tom Foster."

"I want you to stay away from Foster and all the other board members."

"Why? Are you afraid I might agree with them on how poorly the district has run under your tenure?"

Angie sat in the car waiting for the pains in her chest to start.

§

The reception was over for everyone except Vince Miller and Lettie Grimes. After Lettie jumped into Miller's Mercedes, she immediately regretted her decision. Vince reached over and tried to kiss her, his hand on her thigh.

Lettie pushed his hand away. "Vince, what kind of girl do you think I am? I only recently met you." She paused, "Maybe in the future."

Vince smiled and drove to a secluded part of Forrest Park. He parked and turned the engine off. He reached over for a kiss. Lettie pushed him away again.

This time, Lettie wasn't so polite. "Get your fucking hands off of me. Drive me home immediately."

"I thought when you said 'maybe in the future,' you meant it encouragingly."

"Well, you were wrong." Lettie didn't say another word until they were in front of her house.

"Listen, Vince, you're an attractive guy, but we should wait a while before we start anything. For now, let's be friends. Most of the time, I'm all talk and no action." Lettie hopped out of the Mercedes even quicker than she got in. She waved when she got to the door.

Vince waited until Lettie's closed the door then gave her the finger.

§

Vince wasted no time after driving Lettie home to begin the critical task of forging alliances, building bridges and cementing relationships with his fellow board members. He already had calls into Ted Kowalski and Father Grant, and they'd only been sworn into office a few hours ago.

Vince immediately planned to secure a four-vote majority before anyone else.

Vince needed Lou Mariana's vote more than anyone's. An alliance with Lou needed fertilizer, and Vince knew the brand of fertilizer Lou liked the best: money. As long as Vince helped Lou maintain a supply of green grass, all would be well.

Vince rang Ted Kowalski's cell for the second time. Ted picked up on the first ring. "This is Ted. To whom am I speaking?"

"What an asshole," thought Vince.

"Ted, it's Vince Miller, your fellow school board member. How did you like the Swearing-In Ceremony?"

Vince listened to Ted complain, "The room was too warm, the food was too cold, the people smelled."

"Who smelled?"

"This woman sitting next to Martha and me at the table, she was a friend or relative of Lou's…"

Vince waited impatiently for Ted to stop talking; then he jumped in. "Ted, I called to say I look forward to working with you. You're a knowledgeable guy, and I know I can learn a lot from you. I won't keep you. It was a big day. We'll talk soon. I'm getting another call. Take care." Vince groaned, "What a windbag. The hardest part of working with Ted won't be convincing him to vote with me. It will be listening to his inane chatter."

§

Theresa Marinara's cell phone vibrated non-stop during the ride home from the swearing-in ceremony. Jeremy desperately tried to reach Theresa.

When Theresa arrived home, she did two things, visit the bathroom and look on her phone. Jeremy had called ten times. Theresa quickly dialed her lover's number. The phone rang once before Jeremy answered.

"I've been calling…"

"I know my love, but I was in the car with my father…"

"Lou Marinara is your father!" stuttered Jeremy. You can't let your father split us up, Theresa."

"Don't worry. It's not happening, ever."

§

Lou called Phil Turner the day after the Swearing-In Ceremony. He wanted Turner to help figure out a plan to get Thompson off his daughter.

Phil heard the desperation in his boss's voice. "Speak to Fisher; have him come up with something. I want Thompson scared off. If it doesn't work, I'll get someone else to ensure a more permanent solution."

"I'll get right on it, Lou. Theresa is such a beautiful girl. I can imagine how you feel."

"You have no idea how I feel. I'm ready to take a stroke. Get back to me in a few days with a plan."

Phil called Eddie into the office right away. Turner explained the situation and told Eddie to work his magic. "Plan something to convince Jeremy Thompson to leave Lou's daughter the fuck alone."

"Sure, I'll think of something. Give me a day or two."

After Fisher left, Turner admitted, "Eddie's quite an asset. I'd never tell him, but he always seems to come up with something." Turner sat down at his desk, covered with papers, and continued working. Ten minutes later Eddie was on the line. "I thought of the perfect plan, Boss. I'll be down in a few minutes and…"

"Eddie, don't bother coming down. I'm up to my neck in work. I'm sure your plan is good. Take care of it."

"Okay, Boss, thanks for the vote of confidence."

Eddie got right to work on an idea which might be the final solution to Mr. Marinara's problem. "An anonymous call at the right moment to the police may be the answer to Lou's problem."

§

The next day Phil Turner handed Fisher the names of the new school board members.

"Here are some people you've been following since they announced they were candidates. Now, I want you to keep an eye on them all. There's a lot at stake, and we can't take a chance of someone upsetting the apple cart. Both of our jobs depend on it. If anyone discovers what you do, you're gone in a second."

Phil Turner handed Eddie a list of board members and a folder.

"This is a report on all of them. Next to each of their names I have code words. We'll use their code names if circumstances prevent us from using their real ones."

Lou Marinara-*Boss*

Thomas Foster-*Kid*

Mary McMurray-*Bitch*

Lettie Grimes-*Lolita*

Theodore Kowalski-*BB* (ball breaker)

Vince Miller-*Slick*

Father Michael-Grant-*Outer Space*

"The first name on the list is Lou. So, you only have to watch six of the members."

§

A week later, Eddie Fisher handed Phil Turner a folder. Turner quickly opened it and read. "Tom Foster was the largest vote-getter in the district. He has a large family, and between his family and friends, his influence extends throughout the district. His immediate family consists of mother and father, three sisters and two brothers. He's inexperienced, but smart and will learn quickly. Foster enjoys smoking weed. He's a recreational doper, smokes when he's out partying with friends. He makes sure he has a designated driver or calls Uber when he's been smoking. He's a careful guy. I don't know if he has a girlfriend, but he could have any girl he wants. His looks are one reason he won so handily."

Phil looked up from the report and asked, "Is there any chance he's gay?"

"No, his younger brother is gay, but I saw no indication Foster is."

"Watch the brother, too. We may be able to blackmail Foster if the brother is into anything illegal or embarrassing." Phil handed the folder back to Eddie and said, "For now give me the short version. I'll read the report more carefully tonight."

"Sure Boss. The next one is Mary McMurray, age between sixty-five and seventy. So far, we can't find her exact date of birth. She's married to Mark McMurray, a businessman who works for a large financial institution. They have one daughter, Ellen, and one grandson. Her son-in-law works for the Federal Government and was transferred to New Jersey five years ago. So far, it is unclear just what he does. Mc Murray retired this year from Everything Foods as Special Assistant to the CEO."

"What is a special assistant? Is it a glorified secretary?"

"I'm not sure what her duties consisted of, but it seems the job carried a great deal of weight with her boss, the CEO.

"Number four. Lettie Grimes, code name, Lolita, married to a drunk, has three children we know of, takes care of a sickly mother whose husband left her with nothing. Lettie Grimes is a flirt and seems to be on the prowl all the time. She may be having a thing with one of the board members, Vince Miller.

"There's Ted Kowalski, married with two boys and a wife, Martha. Ted's a retired accountant for the IRS and the vice-chairman of the school board.

"Vince Miller, code name Slick, is a self-proclaimed entrepreneur. We haven't been able to figure out what he does, but I know he's up to something. I don't know what it is. His background's sketchy. He lives with his wife and three kids, two boys and a girl. The two boys have a type of muscle disease. The rest of Miller's story you know already. I reported to you about his name change and criminal record last month.

"Lastly, Father Grant is a Catholic Priest stationed in St. Pancras Parish in the northern tier of the district, elected by a parochial inter-faith group and usually is the top vote-getter except for this last election. Tom Foster blew everyone away. He got twice as many votes as Father Grant who came in second. Foster probably took more votes from the priest than any other candidate."

"Good Job. Just don't forget, you're still keeping an eye on Mrs. Krouse. Oh, and don't forget, Lou wants you to do something about the Thompson kid. He wants him out of his daughter's life.'

"Don't worry, Boss. I got it covered. One call and Lou's daughter dumps the black kid."

§

"Every person has a right," said Reverend Bright, "Regardless of race, religion or color, to expect they won't be punched, kicked or arrested for doing nothing."

"Also," said the Reverend Tucker," "A man has the right to go out for the evening with his girlfriend, and not have his girlfriend manhandled by police officers. She shouldn't be strapped to a gurney, rushed to the hospital, put on a bed, and have her dress pulled up to her neck. Someone removed her panties, and exposed her lady parts."

A gasp went up from those present.

'And lastly, a female shouldn't be examined while six strangers stand around her bedside all because she is white and her boyfriend is brown,' finished Reverend Tucker.

"This is not the way to end an evening," added Reverend Thompson. "But this did happen last week to my son, Jeremy."

All three ministers listening to Reverend Tucker this Wednesday afternoon planned to repeat the story to their congregations next Sunday morning.

§

Most people in Church this morning had heard bits and pieces of what happened to Jeremy, but now they would get the whole gory story. The congregants barely breathed as the Reverend Tucker spoke. Jeremy sat on the altar, and as Reverend Tucker mesmerized the congregation with the story, Jeremy replayed the events of the evening in his mind.

Jeremy remembered exiting the banquet hall, happy for all the recipients of this year's winners of the Outstanding African-Americans in Public Service Award. He was flattered several people commented they expected him to be on next year's list of honorees.

Jeremy remembered holding Theresa's hand as they left the banquet and headed to the curb to hail a cab. Jeremy tried to hail ten cabs with no luck. Finally, Theresa pointed to a bus stop on the next corner. Both were relieved the dark streets brightened as they approached the lighted bus stop.

Jeremy's soul, energized by the speeches at the awards dinner, soared with confidence the black community would see real change in its schools. Jeremy was on top of the world, a song in his heart and the woman he loved on his arm. Life couldn't be better.

Jeremy continued to try hailing a cab, but each taxi that passed was full. Theresa sat on the bench under the bus stop canopy thankful the Q47 ran at this time of night. Theresa felt the two glasses of wine she sipped throughout the evening. Jeremy drank ginger ale. Theresa sat at the bus stop while Jeremy watched for an empty cab.

"What a great night I had."

"Me too."

"There's a police car coming down Seventh Avenue; maybe, I can ask for a lift," joked Jeremy.

Before Theresa responded, the patrol car pulled up beside Jeremy. Two uniformed cops jumped out.

"What's the matter, officer?" asked Jeremy.

"We received a report of a domestic violence incident. The call described a man and a woman who fit your descriptions. Can I see some identification?" The other officer went directly over to Theresa and asked if she needed help.

Theresa responded, "No officer. Why do you ask?"

"We received a report that a female fitting your description needed help."

"Thank you for asking, but it's not me."

Jeremy gave his ID to the officer and explained to the cop he and his girlfriend just left the annual dinner honoring Outstanding African-Americans in Public Service. The officer snickered.

Jeremy explained, "We were trying to grab a cab but had no luck, so we figured we'd wait for the bus."

A second patrol car pulled up and out popped two more cops. Both officers went over to Theresa. "She looks like she's intoxicated," said the heavyset cop.

Another patrol car pulled up, and three more cops went over to Theresa. Jeremy saw two of the officers grab her arms and look at her wrists, hands, and arms. He watched Theresa attempt to pull away, but the cops were too strong for her to resist.

Jeremy heard his fiancé scream, "You're hurting me."

Jeremy started for Theresa, but the cop held his arm and said, "Stay put."

Seconds later an ambulance roared down Seventh Avenue and pulled up to the bus stop. The EMS team ran to Theresa still standing by the bench. "Please sit down, Ms. We want to check to see if you're alright."

"Get your hands off me. I'm fine. Why wouldn't I be?"

"We want to look at your arms and legs. You have to let us examine you." One of the EMS men pulled Theresa's arms around her back. Theresa tried to free herself. "Help," she screamed, again and again.

Another cop came over and took hold of Theresa's hands while the EMS pushed up the sleeves of her dress. The second EMS knelt on the sidewalk and tried to examine Theresa's legs, pushing up the hem of her dress a foot above the knee. Theresa twisted wildly and increased the volume of her screams.

"She's hysterical," yelled the cop. "Can't you give her something to quiet her. We'll draw a crowd."

Jeremy watched as the cops picked Theresa up, placed her on a stretcher and put her in the ambulance.

The EMS guy checked to see if she was drunk. "Fellows, it looks like the lady had a drink or two, but she's not intoxicated."

"We want her brought to the hospital, and we want her checked," said one officer. "We may have to charge her with public intoxication."

"But she isn't intoxicated."

"We want to make sure."

The cops slammed the ambulance door shut, then hurried to their patrol cars.

"Where are they taking my girlfriend?"

"Gotham General Hospital, it's on fifty-seventh and eighth. I suggest you calm down before you go there." The cop took off on foot down the street.

Jeremy didn't know who to call, so he ran toward the hospital ten blocks away. When he arrived, he charged into the emergency room and went from bed to bed pulling curtain after curtain open. Finally, he saw a group of cops at the end of the hall.

As Jeremy approached one cop recognized him and gave an ominous look. The cop pointed to his sergeant who moved Jeremy a few feet away from everyone.

"What are they doing to my girlfriend?"

"We are just checking to make sure she is okay. We received a report, and we have to follow up."

"Who reported what?"

"He didn't give his name. He just said there's a guy with your description beating the shit out of a white girl at the bus stop where we found you."

Jeremy looked over the sergeant's shoulder, and two police officers were holding Theresa's hands over her head while two male nurses pulled her legs apart. Five policemen stood there looking on as a male doctor examined Theresa's vagina.

Theresa continued struggling with all her might, but her captors would not be thwarted. Jeremy pushed past the sergeant and got five feet away from Theresa when a big, strapping officer tackled him to the ground and cuffed him. The Sergeant ordered two of the cops to arrest Jeremy and take him to Central Booking.

Jeremy fought off the cops trying to help Theresa. The cops dragged Jeremy down the hall while the medical team continued to invade her body.

§

Reverend Tucker finished relating Jeremy's nightmare by telling the congregation, "Jeremy Thompson now faces the criminal charges of resisting arrest for struggling with the police while they were violating his girlfriend."

The churchgoers called out charges of their own, police brutality, racism, and many others. One man rose to his feet outraged, "We should go right down to city hall and protest this abomination."

"There will be plenty of time. We have learned from Brother Darrel; we must organize a well-planned agenda before acting. But be assured we will act."

§

Lou's secretary heard her boss banging on his office desk. "Listen, Vince, yours is my only sure vote, and I'm not sure I trust you."

Ignoring Lou, Vince said, "I'm pretty certain we have Lettie's vote. I spoke to her yesterday. She promised to vote for you for chairman if you give her a good committee to chair. I spoke with Ted Kowalski, and he's on board if he can remain the vice-chairman."

"Last term, Father voted with you most of the time. That's five votes, and you need four. You'll win the board chairmanship."

"I'm worried. The crazy McMurray lady isn't one to take lightly. She's been around the block more than once. She's not new to the game, and I think she has made in-roads with Father. He's beginning to see things he didn't see before."

"You mean, you hiring all your friends?"

CHAPTER 16

"CONGRATULATIONS ON YOUR ELECTION TO THE SCHOOL board," said Rocco Pinzon, the district superintendent, "And welcome to your first official school board meeting. We have four new members on the board, and I would like to explain a few procedures."

Rocco looked around to see if any incumbents objected. No one said a word, so he continued. "This first meeting is an executive meeting," continued Pinzon. "It's closed to the general public. This meeting prepares us for our monthly public meeting. At this meeting, we review the agenda for the public meeting and take preliminary votes on resolutions. The official vote for all matters is at the public meeting. Nothing passes until you vote in public."

Lou gave Rocco a signal to move along.

"The first thing on the agenda tonight is the election of the chairman for the next year. The board member who receives four votes for that office wins. After you choose the chairman, he appoints the other three officers: vice-President, treasurer, and secretary. State law says I must conduct the election. Are there any questions?"

No one uttered a word.

"In which case, I'll begin. Are there any nominations for chairman?"

Vince Miller called out, "I nominate Lou Marinara for chairman.

Mary looked at Tom and the priest. "I nominate Father Grant for chairman."

"Are there any more nominations for chairman before I begin to call the roll?" The superintendent waited a few seconds then told the board members, "When I call your name, please state your vote. Lou Marinara?"

"I vote for myself."

"Vince Miller?"

"I vote for Lou Marinara."

"Mrs. Grimes?"

"I vote for Lou."

"Mrs. McMurray?"

"I vote for Father Grant."

"Father Grant?'

"I vote for myself."

"Mr. Foster?"

"Father Grant"

All eyes were now on Ted, but he sat quietly in his seat. The superintendent asked," Mr. Kowalski, who do you vote for?"

Ted responded, "Lou."

The superintendent counted the votes and announced, "Lou, you're our new chairman for the coming school year. Congratulations."

"Thank you, Superintendent Pinzone, and for the first order of business as the chairman of this school board, I will appoint the other offices. I appoint Theodore Kowalski as vice-chairman, Lettie Grimes as secretary and Vince Miller as treasurer."

Mary McMurray turned to Tom and whispered, "We better get another vote on our side quickly, or this will be the result for every vote we take all year."

Superintendent Pinzone suggested they take a bathroom break of ten minutes. All agreed.

On the way out of the boardroom, Mary leaned toward Father and said, "Vince Miller, treasurer, so Mr. Fox is in charge of the henhouse." Lettie overheard Mary and couldn't stifle a chuckle.

§

After the break, Lou Marinara took the chairman's gavel firmly in hand and announced, "Tonight, the first problem we have is what to do with the French, German and Italian teachers in the district."

The rest of the board looked at him bewildered. The superintendent jumped in and explained, "For the past few years, fewer students are opting to take French, German or Italian for their foreign language. Student enrollment in these foreign language classes has dropped eighty percent during the past four years. Most students want to take Spanish, so many people speak it in this city. These students have their parents' support."

"The tide doesn't look like it's going to change anytime soon," said the superintendent. So, the school board faces a dilemma: what to do with the foreign language teachers who don't teach Spanish."

Lettie suggested. "As much as I hate the idea, I guess we'll have to lay them off."

The superintendent looked tolerantly at Mrs. Grimes. "You'll learn after you have been on the board for a while those teachers who have tenure are like rocks around our necks. We have contractual obligations, and laying-off over a hundred teachers all at once would cost us more in lawyers' fees than the cost of their salaries. What we have to do is figure out is how we can keep these teachers, and we better do it quickly. The public meeting is three days away, and school opens in another week."

Mrs. McMurray suggested, "Maybe the language teachers can teach a class or two in a non-related area."

The superintendent explained, "Teachers need to teach at least two out of six of their classes in their licensed area in the language department."

"Why don't we have the students take a little of each of the languages," suggested Lettie.

Lou laughed and Lettie sunk in her chair.

Mary spat, "Listen, jerk, we're not any of your slutty girlfriends, so don't give us any of your attitude. Some of us have forgotten more than you ever knew."

"Do you realize, I'm the chairman of this board, Mrs. McMurray? You can't address me like that."

"Oh, excuse me, Chairman Ass Hole."

The rest of the board sat there not knowing where to look. They waited, hoping Lou would not react. The silence was deafening.

Finally, the superintendent asked, "Does anyone else want to say anything?"

"I believe Lettie is on to something," agreed Vince. "I always wanted to try different languages before I signed up for one. Maybe, we can have a grace period where each student could try out a language.

"Yeah, like when you go looking for cars. You go for a test ride," joked Ted.

Everyone now had something to say on the subject. Everyone was talking at once. The first closed meeting turned into the prototype of what every meeting would be like for the next several years.

The chairman called the meeting back to order with, "We should come up with a new program which can begin at the beginning of this school year."

"The junior high," said Rocco, "Is where the kids are asking to take Spanish. We can mandate a program where each kid entering seventh grade will take six weeks of German, then six weeks of French, Italian and Spanish. Afterward, they can choose the language they like best. We'll tell the parents their kids will taste the flavor of each language. Parents love the word 'flavor.'"

Lou added, "They do love that crap."

The superintendent tried to hide his thoughts, "Lou, you're a piece of garbage."

"Let me give this to my curriculum chief, Ms. Trainor, and see what she can do with it."

"Rocco, I'll meet with Mrs. Trainor also," said Vince Miller. "I want to give her some insight into this matter."

Mary leaned over to Tom and whispered, "That's not all Miller will try to give Ms. Trainor."

Tom tried not to laugh. He succeeded except for a slight smile. Tom knew he must develop tons of self-control if he planned to sit next to his new friend at meetings.

The superintendent continued, "Of course, I must tell you, this may be a good financial and political decision, but it's a terrible educational one."

Lettie asked, "Rocco, won't this great opportunity expose the kids to other cultures through language?"

"Yes, Lettie and luckily it's what the overwhelming majority of the parents will think. It's also why this plan will save us from fighting a losing battle with the Teacher's Union but don't kid yourself; it's a terrible idea."

"Convincing junior high school students to learn a foreign language is hard enough," said Father Grant. "Convincing them to start learning another one every six weeks is almost impossible."

Lou suggested, "Why don't we take a break for a few minutes and stretch our legs. Mr. Kowalski sometimes has a kidney problem and tonight seems to be one of those nights."

Ted's face turned bright red as he scurried out of the room.

The majority board members sat in their seats and batted around the incredible scam presented to them a few minutes ago.

After about ten minutes when Ted didn't return, the superintendent said, "I think I will go and check on Mr. Kowalski."

The rest of the board took the opportunity to stretch their legs and use the facilities.

§

During the break the board members broke into small groups in the corridor, already forming alliances. These alliances would shift, often from month to month during their time on the board, depending on the personal agendas of each member. Mary McMurray and Tom Foster knew they would always work together. They rode the same track.

Twenty minutes into the break, Superintendent Pinzon came into the hall and asked everyone to return to the conference table. He wanted to present a few additional items before it got any later. Everyone sat down except for Lou and Vince. The board members looked at them wondering what trick they had up their sleeve.

"Vince and I talked during the break. We discussed the foreign language problem in the district and we're in agreement, offering six weeks of each foreign language to the kids is how to go."

Lou paused, and Mary asked, "Sooooo?"

Lou looked over at Miller who took up where Lou left off. "We recommend the program should be district-wide. If one part of the district gets wind they are receiving less of something, the other part will be up in arms. We have a chance to fix this problem, and if we don't, everyone will hate us, especially the teachers."

Superintendent Pinzon interrupted their thoughts, "Ladies and Gentleman, we'll have to come to a decision tonight. There's a great deal involved in putting this program in place. I ask the chairman to take a vote on the matter, and after the vote, I'll quickly go on to the remaining items on tonight's agenda."

The chairman made the motion and called for a vote. "The proposed program will be approved, and it will be district-wide. We'll go around the table and as the secretary calls your name, please, say 'Yes' or 'No.' Mr. Miller, how do you vote?"

Vince responded, "Yes."

"Lou?"

"Yes."

"Mrs. McMurray?"

"No." responded Mary. Tom Foster and Father Grant joined her. Lettie and Ted voted with Lou.

"Motion carried," announced the superintendent.

§

After the meeting, Vince grabbed the priest in the parking lot. "Father, can I have a minute?"

Skeptically, Father walked over to Vince. He was in no mood to rehash the events of tonight's meeting. "Vince, I'm tired. I don't want to discuss what happened inside, and I don't want to be lobbied anymore tonight."

"Father, it has nothing to do with the school board. I wanted to discuss a problem I have. Can I make an appointment to see you at the rectory?"

"Fine. How is Wednesday, at eight o'clock in the evening?"

"Thanks, Father, I appreciate it."

§

Vince Miller arrived at the rectory not sure his decision to come was the right one. "What if Father doesn't understand what I'm saying? What if he tells the rest of the board?" Vince was relieved when he recalled priests take a confidentiality oath.

Vince rang the doorbell, musing over his decision to see Father Grant. The rectory door opened, and Miller's deliberation was interrupted. "Good to see you, Vince. Come in."

"Thank you, Father, for seeing me. I know how busy your schedule is."

"It's no problem. I'm glad to help. What did you want to discuss? You told me it had nothing to do with the school board."

"It doesn't. What I need is guidance concerning a personal matter." Vince paused, and Father assured him, "Go ahead this conversation won't go outside this room."

"Thank you, Father. Well, here goes. I have three children, two boys, and a girl. My daughter is healthy, but my two sons have Muscular Dystrophy."

"I'm familiar with MD. I have a cousin with it."

"My wife, Linda and I have been able to handle my sons' illnesses well. I have the money to hire the help needed to take care of my boys' needs. My wife and I love our sons and believe it or not; they give us great joy.

"Nice, Vince. I'm happy for you."

"Father, my wife and I want to have another child. We're hoping for another girl, but if we have a boy, the odds are high he'll also have Duchenne Muscular Dystrophy."

Father waited for Vince to continue.

"Before you say anything, Father, I want to explain to you, my wife and I are people who take chances. If we have another child and it's a boy, we'll enjoy the child as we have our other children. If we have a girl, she'll be healthy, and we'll enjoy her.

"Vince, I'm not sure what you want me to say."

"Father, I'd like to tell you a story few people know. Although this marriage is my first, it's Linda's second. Linda had two children, a boy, and a girl. Her son had MD, and her daughter was fine. Linda was six months pregnant with her third child and tests revealed the child was a boy. More test showed he had MD."

Vince caught his breath and continued. "One night Linda fell asleep on the couch watching TV. When she woke up, she was in the hospital clinging to life. After a few days passed and she was out of danger, Linda wanted to know how her husband and two children were doing. The doctor told her there was a gas leak in her house and her husband and children were dead including the baby she was carrying."

Vince looked over to see Father Grant's reaction.

"Linda was grief-stricken, and immediately she was put under a suicide watch for a week. When the doctors saw her begin to cope with the loss, they released her and sent her home with around the clock nurses. Linda was strong, and helped by her local priest; she accepted what had happened.

I met my wife a year after the tragedy. We fell in love, married and soon after, Linda became pregnant. We had a baby boy born with MD. She conceived soon after and gave birth to a healthy baby girl. A year later she gave birth to our third child, a boy who also had MD."

Father stared at Vince not believing what he had just heard. At first, he hesitated to say anything. Then, he realized he could not speak.

"What do you think, Father?"

Father Grant remained silent, and Vince stared at him until Father said "Vince, I'll have to digest what you told me, but right off the bat, I believe postponing your decision might be wise. Wait until you have given this more thought. Speak to some more medical professionals and see what they say. Try to speak with a good psychologist and a marriage counselor. Make sure you and your wife are really on the same page."

Vince said nothing.

Father wasn't able to read his visitor's expression. He hoped Vince wasn't disappointed with the limited answer he gave, but it was difficult to speak with a person he considered irrational.

Vince interrupted Father's discomfort. "Linda is already pregnant."

More stunned than confused, Father replied, "Congratulations."

"Thanks, Father."

"Do you plan to have the baby tested for gender and MD if it's a boy?"

"I don't know. We don't believe in abortion, but who knows what we'll do when the time comes."

"Vince, I have an appointment in a few minutes. I may have mentioned it when I said I'd squeeze you in today. My prayers are with you and your wife, but as of now, it looks like only you can decide what path you'll take. You have my prayers, whatever road you choose."

"Father, I feel much better after our talk. I can't thank you enough."

Father found himself headed to the liquor cabinet for a drink before his next parishioner arrived.

§

"Tom saw the agenda for Thursday's executive school board meeting. On it was a motion proposing to rename Chestnut Elementary School to The Robert Ryan Elementary School named for the school's recently deceased principal. Tom looked to see who put this motion on for

Thursday's meeting. Renaming schools was new to Tom, so he called Lou Marinara for guidance.

Tom caught the chairman running out to court. Lou's was in a rush, but politely answered Tom's questions. "We're responsible for naming schools in the district. When someone puts a motion on the agenda requesting a school's name change, the board votes on it. Lettie put Robert Ryan's name on the agenda probably at the request of the PTA President at the school. Tom, I apologize for cutting you short, but I'm late for court."

"Go ahead, Lou. Thanks for the information."

Tom called Mary to see if she knew anything. Mary's phone rang at least ten times and went to voicemail, usually meaning Mary was on the line with someone else. She picked up as he was leaving a message. "Sorry, Tom, I was just on the line with the district office. I want to find out who was behind the motion to change the name of Chestnut School. I like the name, and I am not inclined to vote for the change."

"It's why I called. Who's this guy, Ryan?"

§

Lou held the gavel with his stubby fingers and banged the table three times. "We all know why I called tonight's meeting. We have all been bombarded this week with calls from across the district."

"It used to be simple," said Vince. "Boys peed in the boy's room and girls tinkled in the girl's room."

"Hey, Vince, where have you been." chimed Lettie.

"This isn't Kansas, Dorothy," joked Mary.

Lou asked the superintendent to give his report before any discussion began. "Go ahead. Everybody, please give Superintendent Pinzone your full attention."

"Thank you, Mr. Marinara. As you already know, the district is buzzing about a certain student in the district's northern tier. This young girl decided she was going to use both the boys' and the girls' bathrooms at Oakwood Junior High. The principal will allow this to continue until the board gives him some guidance."

"What guidance does he want? He can't let this continue," said Ted. "I've received fifty calls from screaming parents. It has to stop. This young lady has to use only one bathroom, and it has to be the girls' bathroom."

"Why is this girl using the boys' toilet?" asked Lettie

The superintendent answered, "The young girl in question wants to use whatever bathroom she feels comfortable with that day."

"That's convenient," remarked Mary. "Everyone knows the line for the girls' room is always a lot longer than the men's line. Maybe, she has something there."

"Mary, can we be a little more serious," said Lou condescendingly. "Please, let the superintendent continue with his report,"

Mary wanted to give Lou the back of her hand but held her tongue out of respect for the superintendent.

"The principal called the girl's parents to school yesterday, and they were cooperative. They're beside themselves with embarrassment. They're also worried about their daughter's safety. There have been threats on their home phone and their daughter's Facebook and Twitter pages. The climate has heated up since she first used both bathrooms."

"When did this start," asked Mary.

"It began two weeks ago, but it only happened twice the first week. This past week the student did it every day. The boys make offensive remarks, mostly of a sexual nature. The girls make them too, and from what I hear, the girls' remarks are much crueler and more threatening."

"Why weren't we informed immediately?"

"The principal thought this was a joke at first. He even considered the same thing Mary brought up, the line for the girls' bathroom was too long, and the student had to go."

"But the next time she pulled it," said Vince, "A hundred irate parents called demanding the principal's and our resignations."

"Let's hear the rest of what Rocco has to say," suggested Mary.

"The latest Federal Government Bulletin seems to lean toward allowing each student to choose which bathroom they want to use depending on the student's preference that day."

"What percentage of the student body is transgender?" asked Father.

"The figures are pretty sketchy, but in New York City over the last year there were over 700 hundred people who submitted applications to the Health Department to have their birth certificates changed to indicate gender neutrality," said Superintendent Pinzon.

"That is hard to believe," interjected Ted.

Rocco ignored Kowalski and continued. "And to complicate matters further, for the first time the New York City Health Department has issued a birth certificate with a new designation for gender called INTERSEX for individuals born with both male and female genitalia."

"So, what happens to the boys who feel uncomfortable with a girl in the boy's bathroom or a girl who is nervous about a boy in her bathroom?" asked Vince.

"It's where the controversy is now," said Pinzon. "We have an obligation to all the students to respect their rights, but defining those rights is going to be the challenge."

"The right of the overwhelming majority of kids versus a small percentage of the population is the monumental questions before us," added Father.

"When I ran for the school board, I never imagined, I'd have to deal with this sort of stuff," said Lettie.

The Chairman cleared his voice, "I'd like to go around the table and see what your feelings are. The superintendent and his administrators need direction from the board. I'd like to have as much solidarity among the members as possible. If we all go off in different directions, we could have a tough road ahead."

Vince was first to speak, "I don't like this at all. Girls should use the girl's room, period."

Mary followed, "I don't know what to say. You throw this at us, and you expect us to give an intelligent opinion. I need time to consider it."

Father Grant added, "I'm thinking of the majority of both boys and girls in our schools. Everyone has rights. We're a country where the majority makes the rules and as long as the minority's rights are not trampled the majority rules. At least for now, I'm for separate facilities."

"We're in a new era," said Ted. "Some of our schools have two front entrances. Over one entrance it says 'Boys' and the other it reads, 'Girls.' At one time, the boys entered on one side; the girls entered on the other. We're a long way from the Dark Ages. We have to be at least open to some accommodation for these unfortunate children."

Mary added, "My friend in New Jersey told his mother how aggressive the girls are today. They come right up to the boys and ask them if they want to have sex, and this is in junior high."

Not to be outdone, Lettie joined in, "An assistant principal in one of the middle schools told this PTA friend of mine, he caught some girl on her knees pleasuring a boy. When they saw the principal coming, neither of them jumped up and ran down the hallway. They stopped and casually sauntered off."

"My neighbor told me last month some girl in her son's class sent him a picture of herself with no top on," said Vince. "The boy is in ninth grade. And the following week the same girl sent a picture of herself nude. My neighbor told me her son wasn't the only one who received those kinds of pictures. The boys send these types of pictures too. What's going on in our society today?"

"My nephew attended his fifth-year college reunion last year," said Father. "And admitted he was surprised to see the clothes the freshman girls wore on campus. He's no prude, but he commented the girls looked like sluts. And this was at an "Ivy.""

"Last week Mark and I entered the pizza shop on Main Street. In walks this yuppie couple, he with his sweater wrapped around the shoulders, the wife in a nice tennis outfit and sunglasses on top of her head. They had their thirteen-year-old daughter with them. I swear, I never saw shorts so short. There was nothing left to the imagination. The pants were cut so short, you could look up her 'address.' The blouse was cut very low but showed nothing. She was so young; there was nothing to show."

"The kids today have seen everything by the time they reach junior high school," said Lettie. "Seeing lady parts and male equipment isn't what it was like even ten years ago."

Father Grant asked, "What do the school board attorneys say?"

"The school board has attorneys?" Mary asked in a surprised tone.

"Yes, we do. All school boards in the state have their attorneys, either in-house or on retainer. This district has always had a firm on retainer."

Tom inquired, "What firm is it?"

"Bologna, Blatt, Campanelli & Associates," said Lou. "They're the best around."

"How long have these people represented the board?"

"Twelve years," answered Pinzon."

"And how long have you been on the board, Lou?" asked Tom

"Let me think for a second."

"Twelve years," chimed in Ted.

Mary rolled her eyes.

"We haven't spoken with the lawyers yet," said Pinzon. He looked at Lou and added, "At least, I haven't."

The superintendent continued his report. The seven board members sat uncomfortably as the superintendent gave specific remarks made to the transgender student by her classmates. The report ended, and Lou called for a fifteen-minute bathroom break.

Lettie glanced over her shoulder, "I'm using the ladies' room, but I may wander over to the men's' room depending on how I feel."

Mary fought the urge to say something back. Unfazed, Father and Tom continued to talk. Vince looked ready to follow Lettie into whatever bathroom she went. Ted raised an eyebrow, and Superintendent Pinzon shrugged.

Vince, Ted, and Lou huddled at the end of the hall. They called Lettie over when she exited the ladies' room. The four yapped away as the superintendent waved everyone back into the boardroom.

Mary, Father, and Tom had a few minutes to discuss the girls' and boys' bathroom issue, but Mary spent most of the break asking Father

Grant, "Who is this law firm, Bologna, Blatt, Campanelli and where did we get them?"

"Every school district has one," said Father. "Lou knew them from a business acquaintance."

The three looked over at Pinzon signaling them with both hands to return to the table.

§

"Now, that we're back," said Lou, "I would like to take a vote to stop this transgender creature, I mean girl, from using the boys' toilet facilities."

The superintendent said, "Madam Secretary, please, call the roll."

Father stood up and objected. "Wait a second, here. You want to call a vote. I thought we'd discuss this subject more."

"What's more to say? A majority of us want to nip this ridiculousness in the bud. What would happen if everyone used whatever bathroom they wanted to use?"

"What would happen? I don't know, but shouldn't we at least discuss it some more."

"I want to vote," said Vince. 'Please call the roll, Madam Secretary."

Lettie proceeded with the vote and announced, "The vote is four to three to stop this district from becoming Sodom and Gomora."

"You're an ass, Lettie," Mary grumbled. "So this is how it will be. The four of you will run roughshod over us three."

"No, Mary, but we do live in a democracy," said Vince. "And the majority wins."

"Five-minute break," said Lou.

"Why another break? We just had one," said Father Grant.

"For all of you to calm down," said Lou getting up and leaving the board office.

§

When the board returned after the short break, Tom was still pissed off at the transgender vote and figured he'd let off steam on something bothering him for a long time.

"Lou, I want to ask you whatever happened to the lady with the daughter in one of our special education programs."

Lou looked at Tom blankly.

"You must remember the mother who spoke at a public meeting right before Christmas. She was upset concerning her daughter's placement. You remember the meeting where Emily Cusack announced her intention not to run again."

Lou still looked puzzled, but the superintendent's mouth clenched, his body stiffened.

Lou continued to look puzzled.

The superintendent cleared his throat, "Lou, Mr. Foster is referring to Cathy O'Brien. Her daughter is in Polk Memorial. She's in a tenth-grade special education program."

Lou was befuddled.

The superintendent continued, "The girl's name is Susan. She's doing fine."

"I'm glad because her mother wasn't doing so fine when she tried to tell her story to the board last December. I don't know who was ruder, Lou, some of the other school board members or Lou's gang of loudmouths who tried to 'boo' her off the podium."

A light bulb blinked in Lou's brain, and his face turned mean. He banged the gavel and screamed, "You're out of order, Foster."

"What was out of order Marinara was your treatment of that lady. It was the first school board meeting I ever attended, but after I saw how you and the other board members treated the lady, I decided to run for the board."

Ted suggested sarcastically, "So, Mrs. O'Brien is the one we can thank?"

"Ted, you were no better. You and Emily Cusack chatted while the lady tried to tell you about her daughter's autism."

"What nerve you have. You're on the board for barely two months, and you speak to Lou and me that way."

"I'm speaking a lot nicer than Lou did to Mrs. O'Brien, and further-more, if I ever hear anyone speak to any parent at any meeting like you spoke to Mrs. O'Brien, I'll publicly demand your resignation from this board."

Lou felt the acid rise in his esophagus and barely whispered, "We'll see."

"And tell your big mouth friends, if they try 'booing' again, I'll look into how and from whom they received their jobs."

Lou reached in his pocket for an antacid. His throat burned, his temper raged, his hatred apparent.

Tom didn't back down.

"It's time for a break, ladies, and gentlemen. Let's meet back here in ten minutes." No one minded the superintendent had taken the liberty to call a recess.

Ted charged from the room holding himself, with Lou and Vince hot on his heels. Father commented, "Well, that was something."

"We better work on a fourth vote," suggested Mary. They looked over at Lettie in the corner arguing with someone on her cell phone.

"Tom, do you know what autism is?" asked Father

"Yes, I do."

"Please give us a quick course before the others come back," pleaded Mary.

"The term autism is an umbrella word covering a spectrum of learning conditions. The range of conditions runs from severe to slight. The American Psychiatric Association lists the subtypes as Asperger Syndrome, autistic spectrum disorder, and pervasive develop-ment disorder-not otherwise specified (PDD-NOS). With Asperger Syndrome, the kids function at a high academic level. You know the kid is smart, but he asks inappropriate questions which causes him to get punched in the face.

Both Mary and Father nodded their heads. Most everyone has met such a child or adult.

Mary couldn't help herself. "Do you believe Ted has Asperger Syndrome?"

"He sure has problems, but autism isn't one of them."

Father asked, "I have a child in my parish who hardly speaks. Does he have autism?"

Mary gave Tom the eye. Lou, Vince, and Ted had walked back into the office as Lettie ended her phone call.

Lou sat at the head of the conference table and began. "Now, that we've gotten some things off our chest, I hope we can get back to tonight's agenda."

Lou paused and then said, "Tom, during the break, I asked the superintendent to have a full report done on Mrs. O'Brien's daughter to make sure she's receiving all the attention she needs, including putting her in another school, public or private at the district's expense." Lou turned to the superintendent, "We want the report ready for our next meeting in two weeks."

Tom nodded his approval.

Lou continued, "I apologize, but I have to excuse myself. I have an important personal matter to address. But I ask you, before you adjourn for the evening, to let Lettie speak to you about something of a sensitive nature."

The remaining board members looked around at each other surprised Lettie had anything serious to say.

"Lettie, you have the floor."

§

"Thank you, Mr. Chairman. It has come to my attention there's this new teacher at The Garden School who is a nut job."

The superintendent interrupted. "Mrs. Grimes, I must object. I feel uncomfortable with name calling and…"

"Please, shut the fuck up and let me finish. If you had kept a closer eye on what's happening in our schools, maybe I wouldn't have to bring this before the board."

"Lettie, if you wouldn't mind, could we put your report off until the next meeting. I want to give it my full attention, but I have an early train to catch. I'm going to Connecticut for the day tomorrow," explained Mary.

"Me too. I have to go," said Ted

Everyone got up to leave, and Lettie said, "As a favor to Mary I will postpone my report."

The superintendent sat back in his chair, a big grin on his face.

§

Vince had been looking across the table at Tom all night and thinking what a lucky guy young Foster is. He has so much going for him, a supportive family, close friends, good looks, personality and something else I can't put my finger on. After a few minutes more observing Tom, Miller realized what it was. Tom had an inner calmness. "I would be unbeatable if I had it."

On the way out the door, Rocco said to Vince, "Tonight was the closest the kid has come to losing his cool." Vince thought, "I can't blame Foster; the O'Brien matter infuriated me too."

Driving home, Miller continued to obsess about Tom. He drove down the highway with the radio off, cruise control on and Tom Foster front and center on the windshield. "Foster has friends who'd carry him home if he drank too much on a Friday night. If Foster found himself in a pickle, he had parents and siblings to share his problem, people to help him solve them.

"I bet Foster never felt the loneliness I experience every day. If I don't take care of something, no one will do it for me. I never had a real friend. How can people expect a person like me to turn out like Tom Foster?" Vince asked himself aloud.

Vince Miller's mother didn't have the skills, either emotional or intellectual, to give him a sense of comfort. His whole life he had to have bravado, moxie, and brass knuckles.

Vince felt the dull pain in his stomach, the same one he'd lived with his whole life; the same stabbing pain he felt back in Jersey when he was five. Vince moved his body to another position hoping to curb the pain beginning in his lower abdomen, but he knew from experience this ache took awhile to shake.

Vince found if he didn't shake the pain within a certain amount of time, loneliness turned into depression, a black hole he didn't want to go near. Vince fought the pain his usual way; he hoped the pill he just swallowed wouldn't make him too high before he arrived home.

CHAPTER 17

JEMMA REDDA, SECRETARY TO THE SCHOOL BOARD, RESEM-
BLED a garden gnome. She was curt with people who called the
school board office, a gatekeeper who selected which calls would make
it through to board members. Doctors have office staffs from hell.
Well, school boards have office staff that could train people to work in
doctors' offices.

Jemma made sure complaints never reached certain board members
like Father, Tom and, especially, Mary McMurray. Lou Marinara,
however, was informed of all calls to every board member.

Efficient and unpleasant, Jemma was a Marinara gal all the way. Lou
gave her the job, gave her raises he snuck past the board and a monthly
stipend from his private account.

§

Lettie Grimes called the school board office to tell Jemma, "I walked
into the kitchen at seven-thirty this morning to make a cup of coffee.
My mother's head lay on the kitchen table. I couldn't see her face. I
assumed she was asleep. I tiptoed around the kitchen to make coffee.
I didn't want to wake her. I finished my coffee and thought I'd wake
her and offer her a cup. I walked to the other side of the table, and as
I came closer, I saw her eyes were open. I screamed; my daughter came
running. She screamed and ran to call 911. My mother was eighty-three.

I'm sorry, Mrs. Grimes." Jemma sympathized.

"She's been through a lot in her life especially with my brother."

Jemma waited to see if there was more. There was.

"My mother was the head of every group at our church. She was 'Queen Bee' until my drug addicted brother robbed the priest's house one Sunday afternoon and stole the weekly collection."

"Your mother must have been mortified?"

"She certainly was, but she held her head up and continued as if it wasn't any of her business. She didn't do it, and that was that."

"Unbelievable, I wouldn't show my face in the church again. What a strong person your mom was."

"She sure was, but it wasn't the end. My brother went to jail for six months, got out and continued taking dope. One night he fell asleep in his bed smoking a joint and burned the house down. The firemen got to my brother in time, and except for a little smoke in his lungs he was fine."

"What about your mom?"

"They found my mother in the bathroom with no pulse. Two firemen dragged her onto the front lawn and performed CPR, but they couldn't get her heart going. Finally, after twenty minutes they gave up. They started packing up their gear when one of the firemen passed and heard my mother give out a gasp of air. One of the firemen quickly knelt and felt her pulse. He signaled the crowd a thumbs up. The crowd roared with approval. The medics brought mom to the hospital and released her three days later."

"Is that when she came to live with you?"

"Yes, but she insisted my brother come also."

"At first I said no, but what was I going to do? Luckily, he found a little chippie to move in with and comes here to stay when he fights with her. Then he leaves again, but the next time he shows up he's not getting in the house."

Did you tell him about your mom?"

"No, I don't know where to reach him. Anyway, here are the particulars, wake tomorrow 2 to 4 and 7 to 9 at Connolly Funeral Home.

Requiem Mass at 10, the following day at St. Hyacinth Church, interment in Holy Rood Cemetery. Please tell people instead of flowers the family requests a donation to the Maltese Rescue Mission, Speonk, Long Island."

Jemma thought how lucky people are who have their mothers for so many years. Jemma was four-years-old when her abused mother fell or was pushed, down the cellar stairs by Jemma's father. The nightly beatings her mother received at the hands of her father still gave Jemma nightmares. Jemma remembered little else about her mother.

Jemma wondered what her life would have been with her mother by her side. Her mother would have protected her from her classmates' taunts in grammar school, being ostracized by her fellow high school students, being the object of pity by all her teachers and feeling the disdain of past and present employers.

§

As mourners exited their limousines for the Theodora Grimes funeral, gusts of freezing arctic air blasted them in the face.

Theodora's final resting place sat atop a small knoll, shaded in summer by a large oak tree. Today, no shade was needed, only a warm fur coat.

Lettie Grimes led the parade on the arm of Vince Miller. Lettie's face is only slightly visible behind a black veil attached to a large black hat.

Mary McMurray, five feet behind Lettie, whispered to Tom, "Look at Lettie, veil over her face, ready to collapse, Vince Miller holding her up. She thinks this is an audition for Godfather Four."

Sculptures of beautiful angels, precious cherubs, and beloved saints adorned the tops headstones. The cold temperature dipped into the teens as the mourners prayed one last time for Lettie's dear mother. The cold wind cut the service short.

Headed back to the car, Mary said to Tom, "Vince has Lettie's vote, at least for the next month. We better go after Ted, or we'll be out in the cold."

Tom responded, "Like we are now?"

Both chuckled unceremoniously.

Vince caught Mary and Tom's amusement and immediately informed Lettie.

§

Tom found it difficult to contact Mary McMurray from Friday afternoon through Sunday evening. It took a while for him to notice a pattern because he was usually busy with friends and family on the weekends. Tom enjoyed partying and made sure the weekends jumped with action.

He tried never to mix business with pleasure, so he made a real effort not to call Mary, his partner in crime, on the weekends unless it was important. Unfortunately, things came up more often than he liked. He would call Mary, but she never returned his call until Monday.

One Saturday afternoon, Tom wanted to have the tires rotated and the oil changed in his car. The auto garage was a block from the McMurray house and he'd stop by Mary's and say hello.

He walked the one block to Mary's house and rang the bell. No answer. Both her car and Mark's sat in the driveway. Tom stood on the top step, leaned over and peaked in the living room window.

"Can I help you?" Tom turned around and recognized Ernie Spikes who appeared out of nowhere. "Hi, Ernie, I'm looking for Mary. Do you know if she's around this weekend?"

"Sorry, Tom, but Mark and Mary are away for the weekend."

Tom knew from experience not ask where they went. Ernie protected the McMurray's privacy like a guard dog.

"Will they be back tonight?"

"I'm not sure, but I'll tell Mary you came by when she comes home."

Tom knew it was time to leave, "Thanks, Ernie."

"Goodbye, Tom. Nice to see you."

Tom walked back to the auto shop puzzled.

On another Saturday night, Tom drove past the Mc Murray's house on his way to a party. Lights were out, mail still on the stoop. He pulled over to the side of the road and called the McMurray house phone.

When no one answered, he left a message he'd called. On Monday when Mary called him back, Tom said, "Mary, I tried to contact you over the weekend.'

"I'm sorry, Tom I didn't listen to your message until Mark and I arrived home this morning."

Tom was a polite guy, and he waited to see if his friend mentioned where she and Mark were over the weekend. Tom wasn't a nosey guy, but he had to admit he was now interested to know where the Mc Murrays went on the weekends."

"Tom, if I don't answer your call, it's because we go up to the country most weekends. We have a small bungalow upstate."

"To be truthful," said Tom, "I was curious because you never seem to call me back on the weekends."

"Well, now you know the reason. I never call to access my messages or bring my cell phone with me, a habit I fell into when I worked for Everything Foods. Maybe you can come up for a weekend this summer. Even if you have another girlfriend by then," kidded Mary.

"I'm pretty sure I have a steady in Jen."

"Great bring her, too, but you don't have to wait until the warmer weather. We have a place in the city. It's easier to get to."

"That's impressive. Where is it?"

"Central Park South, right next to the New York Athletic Club. When I worked for Everything Foods, my boss couldn't give me the title I deserved, so he rewarded me with a big salary and even bigger bonuses. It made up for not receiving the public recognition I deserved.

"Some people need the recognition for their self-esteem, and I respect and understand their need, but even as a child, I never needed it to feel good. I guess my reward was the knowledge I did something successfully."

Tom listened and as usual, was impressed by his friend.

"I hope you'll forgive me for not confiding in you, but only a few people know I have a place in Manhattan."

"On Central Park South, no less."

"We bought it the year both Mark and I received our top bonuses. We paid cash, so we got a great deal. I was able to use it when I had to stay late at the office."

"Why didn't you give up the house in the borough?"

"Mark was made the head of his firm's suburban office right after we bought the apartment in Manhattan. He'd have to travel from Manhattan to Long Island. We lived in the borough during the week. We also weren't ready to give up a place we lived in for so many years. I was always so busy at work that I never had the time to clean out all our accumulated junk."

"Will you keep the three places now that you're retired?"

"Sure. The house upstate is all paid off. The taxes are a few hundred dollars a year. We own the apartment free and clear. The monthly maintenance is quite high on Central Park South, but we can afford it. My retirement package was unbelievably generous. I won't brag, but it was more than ten million. Mark and I aren't big spenders, and my pension alone covers all our expenses."

"Do you like living in Manhattan?"

"Yes and eventually we'll live there ninety percent of the time. As you age, you need to have people around you and apartment living is the answer. Our building allows dogs, so Marigold is safe. You can walk to your doctors, to the food store and the pharmacy and every store delivers.

"It sounds great."

"Come for dinner next week, Saturday or Sunday."

Tom looked at the appointment calendar on his phone, "I can't see next weekend, but I'm free both days the weekend after."

"It's a date. Come at five on Saturday for cocktails, and I'll make a seven o'clock reservation at Marea down the block."

§

Tom took the R Train to 57th Street and Seventh Avenue, walked two blocks up Seventh to Central Park South. There was Mary's building on the corner. The front of the building was a semi-circle, wrapping around the corner at Central Park South and Seventh Avenue, a circular driveway at the entrance.

As Tom approached the building, a uniformed doorman greeted him. "Good evening, who are you visiting today?"

"Mr. and Mrs. McMurray," answered Tom.

The doorman opened the door immediately. Once in the lobby, Tom faced the deskman who asked the same question as the doorman.

"Oh, the McMurray's. They told me to expect you. Welcome." The deskman picked up the intercom, pressed a button and waited for someone to answer. Tom hoped the desk man wasn't dialing 911.

"Surely, Mrs. Mc Murray, I'll send Mr. Foster up immediately." The deskman called his assistant over and said, "Justin, please escort Mr. Foster to the correct elevator bank."

Tom turned to follow when his new leather shoe slipped on the highly polished cream-colored marble floor. He was glad no one appeared to notice. Three elevator banks were each staffed by a uniformed operator. The assistant deskman handed Tom over to the correct elevator operator who greeted Tom with a big smile and welcoming hello.

The elevator operator stood ramrod straight in an elaborate uniform. The gold braiding on the operator's hat was impressive without being gaudy.

Upon reaching the twentieth floor, the operator stepped into the corridor and pointed to one of the four apartments on the floor. "The McMurray's are two doors down on the left." He waited while Tom walked to Mary's door and stood in the corridor until Mark McMurray waved to him.

As soon as Tom entered the apartment and looked straight ahead, he saw the entire length of Central Park. The sun hadn't set, but lights appeared on the east and west side of beautiful Central Park.

A view of the Park from Fifth Avenue is lovely, but it doesn't compare with the view from Central Park South. The eyes stretch for over two miles, the Great Lawn, the Pond, the Boathouse, the Carousel, and the Reservoir.

Mary and Mark watched Tom stare out the window. He reacted with awe, the same as everyone did who visited for the first time.

§

Tom walked into the school board office a half hour early for the monthly closed meeting. Jemma Redda, the board's secretary, had called Tom this morning, snidely mentioning she could not stuff anymore in his mailbox.

Board members disliked Jemma, even Tom. He'd heard Jemma worked at the school board office since the county combined the twenty school districts. The first board elected Lou as chairman and Lou immediately hired his wife's cousin, Jemma.

"Apparently," thought Tom, "The first set of school board members didn't consider hygiene an important job requirement."

Jemma's hygiene problems originated in her rear and traveled to her feet. Skin irritations often appeared on her legs and arms, requiring an assortment of greasy ointments.

Tom saw Ted at the far end of the room reading his mail. Ted detested Jemma more than most and sat as far away from her as possible. Tom greeted his fellow board member. "How's it going, Ted?" Tom was in no mood to deal with Ted's inane chatter but knew he was in for at least some of Ted's nonsense.

Ted called over, "Tom, did you read this garbage? They want to close the schools for another holiday."

Patiently, Tom took the bait. "For whom?"

"Rosa Parks."

Ted told everyone he always voted for the most liberal candidate on any election ballot. Tom believed him until he saw Ted continually oppose any person of color who came up for a supervisory position in the district. A candidate of color had a better chance of flying to the moon than snagging Ted's support, and Lou had no person of color in his family or any friend who wasn't white. The result was the district had not a single minority in any administrative position in any northern tier school, and a smattering of non-Europeans in the southern tier schools.

Tom pushed the conversation toward what he considered a neutral topic. "Is your wife cooking for Thanksgiving?"

"Yes."

"It's a lot of work for Martha."

"Not this year. It's only the two of us."

"Are your sons away?"

"They are. One's going to New Jersey to his girlfriend's house; my other son is going with his girlfriend to her fancy house on Long Island. Martha and I will sit at home eating our turkey dinner on paper plates in front of the TV."

Tom didn't know what to say.

Ted began a soliloquy which ended with, "My wife and I are devastated."

Tom still didn't know what to say.

"When your kid is born," Ted said, "You go to the hospital and hold him for the first time. You never imagine this baby will grow up to be such a shit."

Tom felt very incompetent. He wanted to say something to console Ted, but what could he say. Ted's kids are little shits.

"Can you believe those brats are leaving us alone on Thanksgiving. We'll sit at an empty table and give thanks for two kids who don't give a damn what happens to us."

Tom waited for more, but Ted sat silently at the conference table, eyes wet, his head on the table. The room was silent until loud-mouthed Lettie Grimes arrived.

"What's going on? Is this a funeral or something?"

Ted ignored her. Tom walked to his mailbox.

Jemma called from the outer office, "I need help. My dress is stuck in the desk." Lettie headed out to help.

Left alone with Ted, Tom offered, "If you can stand the crowd and noise, you and Martha are more than welcome to come to our house for Thanksgiving. Mom cooks for thirty on Thanksgiving. My family would love to have you and Martha join us for dinner."

Ted looked at Tom and waited a second before he said anything. Anticipating, Ted's answer, Tom was ready with, 'But, if you change your mind.'

"Tom, we'd be delighted to come. What time should we arrive?"

Tom stuttered, "I'll call you."

Loud-mouthed Lettie's ended any more talk. Tom wanted to say, "Shut up, Lettie," But knew there wasn't a chance in hell she'd listen.

§

Soon after Tom's election, his friend, Ed McNally asked, "What is it like to be on a school board? You are an elected official and have the right to be called Honorable. I think the next time we're out in a bar, and we're trying to meet girls; I'll introduce you as the Honorable Thomas Foster, alright?"

Tom looked at Ed and saw he wanted his question answered. "The first week after we took office I tiptoed around the district office. I feared disturbing anyone, but that changed quickly. Everyone bowed and scraped and asked if they could fill my slightest request. It didn't take the other new board members and me long to believe we were important."

"I can't believe you would be anything but polite with people under you."

"Well, I was. I caught myself being curt with the office personnel who approached me. I noticed some of my colleagues on the board developing a haughty manner toward the staff. I heard one or two board member use the royal 'We.'"

"You're joking," said Ed.

"I'm not, and after a while, I began suspecting these members used the royal 'We' once too often at home and were told by their spouses to 'go fuck themselves,' because after a few months everyone's voice had lost most of its haughty tone and curt manner. Every so often the Noblesse Oblige attitude toward underlings returns, but only for a moment."

Ed laughed heartily.

"Kowalski's wife told me that Ted became so insufferable his first six months on the board, she refused to talk to him until he completely dropped the affected British accent he'd developed." She reminded him, "Ted, you're Polish for God's sake."

Ed bent over with laughter.

"Martha told me Ted would drop a piece of paper on the floor and wait for her to pick it up. It stopped real quick after she went to live at her mother's for a few days."

Ed said "I can picture Kowalski doing this, and it's hilarious, but at the same time, it gives me an insight into what people in public office become if they don't have a Martha Kowalski at home to keep them on the straight and narrow.

§

"Father Grant demanded Chairman Marinara call a special school board meeting to discuss a potential lawsuit the district might face.

"Thanks for meeting on such short notice. Father Grant gave me a heads up on the matter, and we'd be wise to listen to him and his guests carefully."

"What guests?" asked Ted. "No one mentioned any guests. We don't usually have guests at closed meetings."

Lou responded, "This is a special occasion." "Father, please begin."

"Thanks, Lou, and thanks to my fellow board members for coming out on such short notice. I wanted to speak to you on a matter which needs our immediate attention. The incident occurred last week at Maple Elementary School, a block from my parish church. I'm the board representative for Maple, and Superintendent Pinzon called me concerning this sensitive situation."

Father had everyone's attention. The board was aware Father was an attorney and knew his apples.

"Three teachers called me at my rectory and asked if they could come to see me right away. I was free, and I told them to come over immediately."

Superintendent Pinzon politely interrupted Father, "I called Father before the teachers arrived and gave him the gist of what happened, then I had called the principal of Maple to the district office."

"Rocco, are you telling us what happened," asked Lettie, "Or is Father Grant?"

"I'm telling it," said Father. "You all know Penny Mertz. Her two children attend Maple Elementary; Matt's in kindergarten and Karen's in third grade. Both kids have reputations as the brattiest kids in the school. The teachers know how active Mrs. Mertz is in their school and her cousin, Emily Cusack, was on the previous board. Everyone treats her with kid gloves. The teachers watch to see what parents the principal favors and they act accordingly."

"Father's right," said Lettie

"Now, who's telling the story?" said Ted.

"Two days ago Matt Mertz's kindergarten teacher, Peg Reilly, told little Matt to give back a crayon he took from Robby Smith's desk. Matt refused, and Mrs. Reilly took it from his hand."

"I can imagine what Penny Mertz had to say," laughed Lettie. "Sorry Father, go on."

"Peg Reilly thought the problem was resolved. She returned to her desk and turned on a short instructional video for the children. The tape played for no more than five minutes when the principal appeared at the door, and Peg invited her into the classroom. Right out of the box the principal barked, 'Did you raise your voice to Matthew Mertz a few minutes ago?'

"The principal stunned Peg with her demand for an answer. Only five minutes had passed since the crayon incident. Peg Reilly was sure there had to be a secret nanny cam in the classroom."

Father looked around the conference table to see if he had everyone's attention then continued. "Mrs. Reilly responded, 'All I did was head off a potential fight.' The principal just raised her voice and screamed, 'Well, it's not what Matt told his mother!'

"The principal continued to wait for a response. Peg Reilly was dumbfounded. She told me, 'In all her years of teaching, no principal had ever come to my class to chastise me as if I was an undisciplined student.'

"The principal waited longer for a response. Finally, Peg mumbled, 'I'm sorry.' The principal responded, 'Well, this isn't over. I'll see you at the monthly faculty meeting this afternoon.' Peg miraculously finished the school day, although she had no idea how."

Father stopped to look at his notes before he said, "At this point, I want to ask Ms. Sophie Marco and Ms. Ellen Trumble to tell you what they witnessed at the faculty meeting the same afternoon."

When Jemma brought the two teachers into the boardroom, Father pulled two more chairs up to the conference table.

"Ladies and gentleman, I want to introduce Ms. Marco and Ms. Trumble, teachers at our Maple Street Elementary School."

All the board members smiled and politely, replied, "Hello."

The two teachers nervously waited for their cue to begin.

"Please, tell the board what happened to Ms. Reilly."

Ms. Marco took charge and began a detailed description of what occurred at the faculty meeting. "We have a mandatory teachers' meeting every month, beginning fifteen minutes after dismissal. Teachers rush around before the meeting, filing into the bathrooms to freshen up. It's when a bunch of us first noticed Peg Reilly. We could see right away something was bothering her."

Ms. Trumble took over the narrative. "We asked Peg if there was anything we could do for her. Peg shook her head no and headed for the auditorium."

Tom looked across the table at Vince Miller and saw him wink at Ms. Trumble. Tom turned back to the speaker.

"At precisely three fifteen, the principal walked onto the stage and stood at the lectern. The crowd quieted immediately. With no explanation, the principal instructed us to disregard the agenda placed in our mailboxes this morning.

"The principal seemed to enjoy her teachers' curiosity and seemed to relish her authority. The principal said, 'Right after lunch, a disturbing occurrence interrupted my administrative duties. A call from a parent alerted me to a situation in Ms. Reilly's kindergarten class.'"

Lettie whispered to Mary, "Can you believe this shit." Mary ignored Lettie; Ms. Trumble had her full attention.

"The principal continued, informing the faculty of Mrs. Reilly's outrageous breach of professional behavior," said Ms. Trumble. "The whole faculty sat in silence unable to believe their principal was discussing such a personal matter in front of them. The entire faculty, including the assistant principal, slumped deeper their seats. Mortified, no one knew where to look or what to say."

"One question, Ms. Trumble," interrupted Ted.

Lou quickly said, "Ted, please shut up until Ms. Trumble finishes. There'll be plenty of time for questions.

Lou looked at Ms. Trumble and said, "Please continue."

Flustered, Ms. Trumble continued, "The principal droned on. The teachers stopped listening until their boss said, 'Mrs. Reilly, please come up on the stage.' Our eyes were fixated on Peg as she sat paralyzed on the hard auditorium chair. Seconds passed. No one in the room stirred.

"Finally, Peg Reilly got up and walked down the aisle. She climbed the four steps and went to the center of the stage. Peg looked out at the audience filled with friends and colleagues. She turned to her tormentor, their faces inches apart.

"The principal began, 'So, Mrs. Reilly, what do you have to say to your fellow teachers and, of course, to me?'

"Peg Reilly was silent. Everyone one in the auditorium, except the principal, was on the edge of their seat. Seconds passed slowly. The principal tapped her toe to show her impatience. The silence was deafening.

"Peg opened her mouth, 'I've nothing to say to my wonderful co-workers, but to you, I say fuck you. Go screw yourself, you hypocrite, you moron...'

"We all knew Peg's words were on target and each teacher mentally added new names to describe this awful person, our abhorrent principal."

Now Ms. Marco chimed in, "Rage burned in Peg's eyes. She blurted out, 'I correct a student so he won't grow up to be a person like you, and what happens? What happens is a stupid, ass-kissing twit who obtained her job by sucking up to every person she thought influenced the school board, comes rushing into my classroom as if the school is on fire and you come to my classroom and demand an explanation of why I spoke to a student. You wouldn't even wait to listen to an explanation. All you wanted was to please Penny Mertz.'"

Ms. Marco took a breath and began again. "Peg Reilly stopped talking trying to fight off tears, and said, 'You disgust me. You're a fraud. You hide your true concerns behind the overused slogan, 'My main concern is what's good for the children.' What you more accurately mean is your sole concern is what's good for you.'

"Finally, Peg broke into tears. One half of the audience cried, the other half held back tears. A teacher called out to the principal 'I want to know how you knew what happened in Mrs. Reilly's class?'

"Another teacher in the back row yelled, 'Don't you remember, the principal instituted the policy, at the recommendation of the PTA, students in kindergarten through second grade may call their parents from the classroom if they have the teacher's permission.'

"At which point, we all realized what had happened after Peg dared raise her voice to the PTA President's son. As soon as Peg turned off the classroom lights to show a video, Matt took out his phone and called his mother. The kindergartener informed his mother of the terrible abuse he had experienced at the hands of his teacher.

"Mrs. Mertz hung up with her darling Matthew, called the principal and demanded an explanation for Mrs. Reilly's abusive behavior. The principal, a weasel of the first order, ran down to save the boy."

When Ms. Trumble and Mrs. Marco finished, Father thanked them on behalf of the school board. The other members gave expressions of appreciation.

Father asked Jemma to escort the women from the room. As soon as the door closed and before anyone asked nonsensical questions, Father explained the legal ramifications. "If I may, I want to tell you the rest of the story."

All were eager to hear Father's expertise. "After Peg Reilly finished destroying her boss, the teachers cheered. The principal responded to the audience with, 'You're fired, Mrs. Reilly.'

"You can't fire me. I have a contract," said Peg as she stormed off the stage.

"The principal hurried after her and called Superintendent Pinzon."

Father looked over at the superintendent, and Rocco started where Father left off. "The principal demanded I bring Mrs. Reilly up on charges. I told the principal to go home and be in my office at nine the next morning."

"It turns out," continued Father, "Mrs. Reilly plans to sue the principal and the district for emotional distress. If she files a personal injury suit, it won't succeed for a few reasons. It happened on the job, so technically it's a workers' compensation case. Her suit has a better chance as a tort case like intentional infliction of emotional distress. A jury might find the principal went too far in her capacity as principal.

"The district would have a good case contractually for insubordination against Mrs. Reilly. One of the teachers took a phone video of the meeting. Thank goodness no one posted it on YouTube."

"So, what do you suggest we do, Father?"

"Well, we have to discuss this with our attorneys and with the union representatives. But in my opinion, we should try to come to a settlement, one which would be sealed. The principal is obviously in need of retraining."

"Retraining, are you kidding? She's a sadistic bitch," yelled Lettie.

"For once, I agree with Mrs. Grimes. How did you hire her, Rocco?" asked Vince. The superintendent turned and looked at Lou.

Mary mocked, "I understand. Someone had another relative to keep off the unemployment line. But, Lou, did you have to make her a principal? Weren't there any toilets that needed cleaning?"

Lou sat there, beet red. He had to say something. "Listen, she was as qualified as any of the candidates."

"Yeah, qualified as any of the candidate applying for a job at a state prison," snarled Mary.

"Excuse me," Father interjected, "Let's come back to the legal aspects of this."

The others quieted down, content they'd gotten their digs in.

The superintendent took the floor, "This situation means a public relations disaster for our district and the board. I suggest we forget bringing charges against Mrs. Reilly and we transfer the principal to a position at the district office. In June, we should insist the principal retire; she's old enough."

Father added, "And in the future, we hire individuals who have a little more sense than to put the district in such jeopardy."

"No," screeched Lettie. "We have to hire people with a lot more sense."

Ted added, "What scares me is the parent of this little kindergarten kid."

"Me, too, Ted," said Mary. "We all know how this kid will turn out."

Everyone at the table shook their heads in agreement.

The school board members sat quietly for a second before superintendent cleared his throat, "I suggest we speak to the school district's attorneys."

Lou asked, "If there are any objections, raise your hand." No hands went up. Lou directed Superintendent Pinzon to proceed.

Softly, but loud enough for everyone to hear, Mary said. "We're in good hands with the Law Firm of Bottom, Feeda, and Associates."

§

After the meeting, Mary had to use the ladies room before she started home. When she walked into the parking lot, she noticed her car was the only one in the lot; then she saw Lettie Grimes by the parking lot entrance. Mary started her car and drove toward Lettie.

Mary rolled down her window, "Are you alright?"

Lettie turned and cried.

"Get in the car, Lettie," demanded Mary.

Lettie wiped her eyes on her sleeve and got in the car. "Thanks, I appreciate it."

"Do you have a ride home?"

"I came out, and my ride took off."

Mary wanted to go home, take her girdle off and go to bed, but she couldn't leave Lettie on the street.

On the drive to Lettie's, both women remained silent. Mary would not ask Lettie what happened. After five minutes, Lettie opened up, "He left me standing on the curb. What a jerk I am."

"Who left you on the curb?"

Lettie didn't answer right away then cursed, "Vince Miller, the bastard."

Mary held her tongue.

Lettie wept. Mary continued to drive offering nothing except, "Tissues are in the glove compartment."

They reached Lettie's house, and Mary assumed Lettie would hop out. Instead, Lettie sat next to Mary crying.

"See you next week at the committee meeting, Lettie."

Lettie ignored Mary.

"Mary, I'm a fool. I always fall for jerks, the guys who are selfish, the guys who are only after one thing from me, sex."

"Lettie, maybe you should see someone, a professional may help."

"I have, and it helps for a while, but I fall back into the same routine."

"Did therapy give you any insight into why you choose these wrong paths?"

"Yes. The therapist explained it's common for abused children to mistake sex for love."

"Who abused you?"

"My step-father."

"Did you tell your mother?"

"I did, and she didn't believe me. She accused me of lying." Lettie cried again. She opened the car door and ran up the path to her front door.

Mary watched as Lettie fiddled with her keys. Mary pulled away when she saw Lettie was inside. Mary no longer just wanted to go home and take off her girdle. Now, she wanted to take off her girdle and have a stiff drink.

§

Vince Miller met Gerald Gentile in a bar on the Lower East side of Manhattan. Gentile handed Miller a small case with cash in it. The two talked about Forrest Elementary School, and Vince told Gentile everything he needed to know to perform well in his interview.

Gentile asked Miller, "Are these the exact questions?"

Vince gave a very helpful tip. "There are three types of questions asked at interviews for jobs in the school district. The first type of question asked by school board members is a question an applicant can't answer satisfactorily to the whole board. The reason for this is each group of board members has a favorite candidate.

"At your candidate's interview, everyone expects the candidate has received the questions in advance. A board member's candidate will answer the question in a way which will show his great command of the material. His answers will be viewed as superior in all ways, at least by his side. The next applicant goes through the same drill. In the end, the only thing that counts is which side can bring four votes to the table."

Are you sure you can get the votes for me? And if you can't, will I get my money back."

"Gerald, you worry too much. The deal is done."

§

Vince woke up in a panic. He overslept again. I'm exhausted trying to get Lou to vote for Gerald Gentile. Gentile paid Vince thirty thousand dollars for the job of an elementary school principal in the northern tier of the district. The pay and benefits totaled far more than Gerald Gentile was making as an adjunct lecturer at the local community college. Principal jobs gave an individual the security few positions in private industry did.

Emboldened by his success with Gentile, Vince looked forward to more supervisory positions to become available.

"This is easy." And it was. After Lou agreed to vote for Gentile, Ted followed as did Tom and Mary. Lettie abstained, still hurt by Vince's behavior.

Gentile had a great deal on the ball. He was personable, well-spoken, well-dressed and good-looking. As chairman of the personnel committee, Vince made sure the other finalists were drab, ruffled and obnoxious. "Being on the school board was all I thought it would be." Vince mused.

His position as personnel chairman would allow him to augment his yearly income, tax exempt. Vince viewed his fellow board members as rubes who just fell off a pumpkin truck.

§

A few weeks later Vince was at it again. Everyone except Lou wondered why Miller was so desperate to make sure Dick Price became the principal of the worst high school in the district. Day and night Vince lobbied for Dick Price to become principal of Elmhurst Memorial High School.

After his easy win with Gerald Gentile, he figured he'd be able to push through anyone for a job. Vince thought he'd have little trouble with Price, but so far his efforts were without success.

Lou was entirely on board with the selection of Price, but Vince failed to nail down Lettie or Ted's commitment as easily, but he was optimistic. McMurray, Foster and Father Grant were long shots.

Lou knew what Miller was up to with Price because two months ago, Lou invited Miller to a party at a beautiful beachfront venue on the south shore of Long Island. At the party, Lou introduced Miller to

Bennie Singh. "Bennie owns twelve cellphone stores in New York City and fifteen on Long Island."

After Lou left Bennie and Vince alone, he went off to speak with a young chippie from the city. Bennie and Vince hit it off right away. They had a lot in common. Both men were entrepreneurs who had no trouble telling the other how brilliant they were. The conversation finally landed on the subject of marketing strategies. Bennie told Vince, "All the marketing strategies in the world won't do any good unless you can find the right personnel. In my case, I need people to run my stores."

"What kind of personnel?"

"First, I need numbers. Turn-over is unbelievable. I find it difficult to get good workers who'll work hard for minimum wage."

"What about illegals? They'll work for minimum wage and be happy for a job."

"Yes, but they're an enterprising group. Illegals soon learn they can make more money doing landscaping, carpentry, construction. Illegals save all the money they make, build their businesses and leave without notice."

"What do you do?"

"I don't pay them the money I owe them. I keep the first week's salary and tell each worker I will give it to them after six months. When they squawk I tell them I will pay them twenty percent interest on the money I hold back. If they leave before the six months, I keep their money. If they stay more than six months, I give them the money I owe them with three percent interest and tell them they misunderstood me because of the language barrier."

Bennie checked to make sure Vince was keeping up. Bennie continued, "Sometimes if I have someone ready to fill a job, I fire the one in place and keep the money I owe them. It's the best. The ideal thing is to hire, fire, and keep their money then hire and fire again."

Bennie laughed at Miller's shocked expression.

"Do the illegals complain?" asked Miller.

"Yes, and I tell them to go screw themselves. I say they are illegal and have no rights."

"What do they do?"

"Nothing. The illegals are afraid I'll report them to ICE, you know the Immigration, and Customs Enforcement."

"Vince asked, "In the long run, wouldn't you be better off paying your workers a decent salary and maybe they'll stay longer. The way you're doing it now, you're constantly training new people?"

"You're half right. I need to figure a way to hire workers who'll stay with me, learn the products and work hard for little or no money."

Vince laughed, "Good Luck."

"I shouldn't admit this, but I get a kick out of the fact an immigrant like me hires other immigrants, and I make them modern-day-slaves. I'm in this country the same amount of time as the workers I hire, and already I'm their master. I control them and have power over them. I want to open thirty more stores throughout the five boroughs and Long Island. I have the capital. But I need more slaves; I mean workers."

"Sounds ambitious," said Vince, ignoring Singh's 'slave' reference."

"You came here legally?"

"Yes, but I came with money."

"Where did you get the money to open these stores?"

"Originally, I received funding from India, from friends and family. My family is relatively wealthy, and I have many rich friends in India. The U.S. allows individuals to enter the U.S. if they bring in half a million dollars and open a business. It comes with a promise of a green card. The one string is I must hire five workers in the U.S.

"Do the five workers have to be U.S. citizens?"

"No. So, I apply to have a relative enter the U.S. to work for our company. The government gives my relative a work visa with a path to a green card. I open a store, put a relative in charge, and hire locals or illegals.

"You accomplish two things at once. You receive a green card, and so do your relatives."

Bennie shook his head yes.

"You hire mostly indigent illegals from Central America?" said Vince. "You exploit their ignorance by not paying them or paying them below the minimum wage. You try to pay them very little, so they have to work overtime to survive. You cheat them on the amount of overtime they say they worked and if they complain you tell them you'll report them to ICE, and there's nothing they can do." Vince looked squarely at Singh and said, "You're my kind of guy, Bennie."

"The problem is serious. I need workers to operate the new stores I want to open."

For the next few days, Bennie's conversation stuck in Vince's mind. He had to admit he was initially shocked by how casually Bennie discussed the treatment of his workers, but when Miller saw the cash generated by Bennie's business practices a wide smile appeared on his face.

Vince spent a great deal of time during the next few days thinking of ways how he could help Bennie get the workers he needed.

§

Preparation for Vince's monthly Human Resource Committee meeting pushed Bennie's interesting personnel problems to the back burner because preparation for committee meetings required far more work than Vince ever imagined.

Lou gave him the prized chairmanship anticipating Vince's ability to facilitate Lou's choices for administrative positions, assistant principal, principals, and district office positions. In return for such cooperation, Lou promised to throw Vince a bone, like Gentile, if he wanted a crony placed in a school. Vince wanted far more than the occasional bone, and he planned the committee was his first step.

"I can't believe the number of resumes we receive for each position," he told Sue, a district staff secretary assigned by the superintendent to help him review the applications. Sue scanned the applications as they arrived in the mail and discarded those applications lacking the basic state qualifications, licenses, degrees and experience for a position.

Sue culled candidates with extraordinary credentials, candidates whose resumes jumped off the page. These applications usually accounted for twenty-five percent of those submitted. The law requires the district office to keep the other seventy-five percent on file for six months.

Sue gave Vince and his committee these top twenty-five percent to review. Sometimes she wanted to say why do I bother? No applicant has ever gotten a job in the district unless they were a relative and friend of Chairman Marinara.

Miller and his committee of parents met and plodded through the applications, a challenging and time-consuming effort, taken seriously by everyone except Vince.

After three months of sitting in the board office with unattractive mothers, Vince brilliantly discovered a way to save himself time. He'd arrange for the parents on the committee to come to the office one or more afternoons to review the applications. Hours later, he'd show up. "Thank you so much for your help. I have reviewed the applications at home during the past week, and I must say we have some outstanding prospective candidates."

The thought of spending hours in a room sifting through boring applications with some of the most irritating women on the planet was more than Vince wanted to do. And besides, he knew who he or Lou wanted for each job.

The present applications were for a principal's position in the only all Latino high school in the district. Students scored far below the national average in reading and math. "I don't care who gets the job. I wouldn't wish this school on my worst enemy," said one mother on the committee from the northern part of the district."

A mother from this Latino high school chatted with her fellow committee members during a break. The mother explained, "We need to find the best candidate. We need a strong administrator who speaks Spanish. Very few of the parents speak English. Poverty is deep, and school supplies are scarce. Please help me find the right person to turn our school around," she implored the other members.

The woman looked at the other mothers on the committee and realized they weren't listening to her. So, when everyone returned to the conference table and before Vince was about to excuse himself, she raised her voice and said, "Parents in this school can barely provide food for their children. Many parents are undocumented. Most students were born in the US, so they're citizens, but their parents aren't. Parents are desperate for jobs and often take work where the employers take advantage of them."

Like a thunderbolt, the conversation Vince had with Bennie Singh hit him. This was the answer to Bennie's personnel problem. Miller had found the solution. Vince figured he and Bennie could work out an arrangement where both made money.

Suddenly this principal's position became very important to Vince. He called Bennie Singh when he reached the parking lot, and Bennie picked up on the first ring.

"Bennie, it's Vince Miller. I enjoyed our talk the other day, and I've been thinking about how I can help you with your human resource problem.

"I'm free tomorrow. Drop by my office around twelve-thirty? I'll order lunch, and we can talk."

"Great. What's your address?"

"I'm two blocks from the district office, 410 Oakwood Drive."

CHAPTER 18

BENNIE SEEMED GENUINELY HAPPY TO SEE VINCE. THEY IMME-diately felt comfortable in each other's company. After finishing their corned beef on ryes, Bennie became serious. "It's coincidental you called because right afterward four of my workers told me they were leaving to start their furniture refinishing business. All four guys worked at the same store. They left me high and dry. Business is booming, but I don't have enough people to maintain my stores. I mentioned to you I want to expand, but without reliable workers, no more stores."

"That's a problem," said Vince. He was now positive Bennie would be receptive to his plan.

"I train people,' moaned Singh, "And they leave as soon as they can. No loyalty."

"Bennie, I have a possible solution. I figured out a way to maintain a steady flow of men and women who'll work hard for low pay, and more importantly, will stay for longer than any of the workers you've had in the past."

Vince had Bennie's full attention. The rest of the afternoon the two discussed Vince's proposal. "There are a lot of questions, but first, how much will you pay me for my services?"

Bennie quickly answered, "For each person you get me, I'll give you a thousand dollars. I take half out of their first month's salary. I tell them it's a fee for getting the job. I'll chip in the other five hundred dollars." Bennie paused then said, "Do you think you can do it?"

"I'm sure I can. I'll find a cooperative principal at an all Latino speaking high school, and we're in business. It'll take me a month to place the right principal at the right school." Vince didn't tell Bennie he had the school already picked out, Elmhurst Memorial High School.

"Of course, Lou will have to get a piece," said Bennie.

"We'll need his cooperation to accomplish what we want to do," said Vince.

"Absolutely."

Vince took out his cell phone and dialed Lou. Luckily Lou was available to talk right away. "Lou, I'm on my way over."

Miller told Bennie he'd be back and rushed out the door. "I don't want to waste time getting this off the ground. There's plenty of money to be made for all of us."

When Vince arrived, Lou's office door was closed. The secretary informed him, "Mr. Marinara will be another fifteen minutes. Please, take a seat. Would you care for a cup of coffee or a bottled-water?" Vince winked at the twenty-year-old, "No, I'm good."

Vince picked up a *People Magazine*, but before he started an article about Pamela Anderson, a woman of fifty walked into the office, gave a hello to the secretary, went into the adjourning office and closed the door. Vince asked the secretary who the lady was.

"That's Pena. She's our bookkeeper."

Before Vince read anything about Pamela Anderson, Lou's door opened and out came Lou and an impeccably dressed older man in a blue serge double-breasted suit.

"I appreciate you coming in Don Luigi. Be assured I'll find out."

"I know you will Louis. I depend on you. Call me soon with the answer."

Don Luigi limped slowly out the door into the corridor.

"Hold all calls," Lou barked at the young secretary.

"Come in, Vince." Lou pointed to the only chair not piled with papers. "So, what's so important you had to run over here today?"

Vince related his conversation with Bennie Singh.

Lou listened, more interested than Vince imagined.

When Vince arrived at the part which addressed Lou's approval fee, Lou said, "Don't give me anything. All I want Bennie to do is clean some money for me each month."

Vince didn't know what to say. People accused him of laundering money, but the truth was, he knew nothing about it, but he would learn. "Sure, Lou, Bennie will help."

"Good, tell Bennie I'll stop by his office around five to talk. But for now Vince, I have to get back to work."

"Sure, Lou, I'll call you tomorrow and check if everything went well with Bennie."

On his way out, Vince eyed the young secretary bending over to file correspondence.

§

Lou stopped by to see Bennie Singh at five.

"Lou, thanks for coming. Vince told you of our little project. Of course, I insisted your approval was essential before I would proceed."

"Thank you, Bennie. You're a friend."

"Vince tells me you don't want any remuneration. Instead, you want my help in some laundry work."

Lou smiled. "I need your help. I have an important client with money who finds himself unable to explain where he got it. He'll pay you a premium for your services,"

"How does your friend want me to do the cleaning?"

"He'll deliver you cash. You'll report higher income from your businesses, pay the taxes and return his money all refreshed and clean."

"I'll return the money to him through fictitious services like garbage removal, office supplies, and cleaning services, building supplies and construction services.

And I don't have to pay you anything?"

"Not up front, use my legal services. With the large number of stores, you plan to open you'll need a lot of legal counseling. I also represent the man in need of laundering. He keeps me quite busy and quite rich."

Both men laughed, then Bennie asked, "So, do we have a deal?"

"We do."

§

Vince's plan to solve Bennie's personnel problem was predicated on placing the right principal in the right school, and that school was Elmhurst Memorial High School. Vince would put Dick Price in as principal of Elmhurst with its overwhelming Latino student population.

There were two more days before the application deadline for Elmhurst was due. He called Dick Price that evening. "Dick, I want you to apply for the position as principal of Elmhurst Memorial High School."

"I thought you told me to hold off and wait for a better school?"

"Something came up and all of a sudden this school is far more attractive than we thought. This school has greater money-making potential than any of us imagined. You want to make as much money as you can, right?"

"Right."

"Let's meet for dinner tomorrow around seven at Ruggerio's, and I'll explain everything."

§

Located off the beaten path, Restaurante Ruggerio was a favorite eating place for those who liked their privacy, soft lighting, plush dark red seats and matching velvety red drapes. The atmosphere struck the right tone for the people who patronized the place.

When Miller walked through the front door, Dick Price was drinking a martini at the bar. He jumped up and greeted his benefactor with a man hug. Antonio, the maître d' ushered Vince and Price to a table in the far corner away from the bar.

After some polite conversation, Miller got right to the point. "Dick, there's a lot of money to be made in the school I mentioned on the phone."

"How?"

"The school is ninety-nine percent Spanish speaking. Sixty percent of the students and parents are illegal. The other forty percent are citizens, but they're poor and illiterate. An overwhelming number of the students are underachievers. Teachers are worn-out and are going through the motions. Nobody cares what happens in the school."

"Okay, but where's the big money opportunity?"

"Everyone is below the poverty level. It isn't exactly a place where people worry about how their 401K is doing. But it's a place where people discuss money daily. The people discuss how they're going to get money to eat each day, how they'll pay the rent at the end of the month, and how to get a job."

Still, Price didn't get it.

"I have a business contact, and he needs lots of workers."

"So, we're starting an employment agency?" asked Price sarcastically.

"Yes, as a matter of fact, we are. We'll be headhunters for the poor."

"It sounds noble."

"Well, I don't know if it's noble, but it's a way to make a great deal of money."

Vince spent a good part of an hour going over the specifics. Price listened as Miller explained most of Bennie Singh's stores are in low-income neighborhoods. "Bennie would open forty more stores tomorrow if he had the workforce. Money isn't the problem, operating the stores is. Cellphones and internet services sell themselves. Bennie Singh needs plenty of people who speak Spanish, a few who speak Korean and Chinese, to wait on customers.

"Bennie needs at least two hundred and fifty new hires. He averages seven employees per store. He wants the stores ready in three months. He'll pay a fee to us of a thousand dollars for every one he hires through us. That's two hundred and fifty thousand dollars."

Vince looked at Price. Price's eyes were rotating faster than a washing machine on spin cycle.

"Bennie has friends and relatives in other businesses who are in the same boat. They have the capital to expand their businesses, but can't find workers. Parents in Elmhurst Memorial have trade skills like carpentry, plumbing, masonry. We can recruit parents to build the new stores and maintain them. All the stores need repairs and updates. The possibilities are endless. You'll receive your regular salary plus commission on each person you recruit and another fee for being the district coordinator. Sound good to you, Dick?"

Price found it difficult to answer with a mouth full of greed.

§

"Father, it's Mary. Did I catch you at a bad time?"

"Not at all, Mary. How are you?"

"I'm fine, Father. The reason I called is to speak with you concerning the principalship at Elmhurst Memorial. Vince and Lou have been pushing Dick Price. At the last meeting, Vince seemed desperate to convince us how good this Dick Price is. Tom Foster and I don't want Price to get the position. There are so many more qualified candidates, most of them speak Spanish, unlike Price. We hope you're not voting for him."

"Mary, I'm embarrassed to say I haven't reviewed any of the applications yet. The school is on the opposite side of the district. Usually, people call me lobbying for their favorite candidate weeks in advance of a vote on a principalship. So, I start off knowing more about candidates than you can imagine. Then I read over the resumes of the top seven candidates the committee recommends."

"Not many applied for the job. The school is rough, and there weren't many applicants, but all who applied seemed outstanding except Dick Price. Tom and I felt it peculiar Vince and Lou were so interested in Price getting the job. Father, this position is important to the minority community in our district. The right person can hopefully turn the school around. We need someone who reflects the community ethnically or at least someone who speaks Spanish."

"That makes sense."

"I hear no one on the faculty, or even the staff speaks Spanish. How it happened is a real puzzle. I've asked around, and people believe it didn't happen by accident. There is no way in today's world the superintendent couldn't find any teachers, aides, or supervisors who speak Spanish."

"Mary, I promise to go into the board office tomorrow and look at the applications. I'll call you right after I return to the rectory."

"As you know, Father, the thing that counts when we vote is the number four. We'd be disappointed if you don't vote with us."

"You, Tom and I are usually on the same page. I see Lou and Vince's shenanigans."

"They're up to more than shenanigans this time, Father."

"How many votes do we have?"

"With you, we have three, you Tom and me. We need one more."

"It leaves Lettie or Ted. Maybe we can convince both?"

"Ted always tries to make it look as if no one influences him, but when it comes down to the actual vote, he goes with Lou."

"What about Lettie."

"She's fooling around with Vince, so who knows? She's a loose cannon."

"But, she's usually interested in the kids."

"Lettie also has an interest in men. Excuse me, Father, but I don't trust her when it comes to a good time or a good choice for principal. I'll call her this afternoon and feel her out. I'll see how she's leaning."

"Mary, we'll speak tomorrow after I read the applications and after you speak with Lettie."

"One more thing Father. When you're at the district office tomorrow could you ask the superintendent if he has found some job for Esther Portnoy? I know you mentioned it to him before. Her grand-kids aren't doing too well with her working long hours."

"Mary, I'm glad you reminded me. She would be a great addition to the district. I've worked with her for years on the inter-district ecumenical council. She is amazing. I will remind the superintendent."

"Again, Father, please vote with us on this one."

"Speak tomorrow."

Mary sat at her desk and tried to come up with a plan to convince Lettie, or maybe Ted, to vote with her.

"I'll call Ted, first."

§

Lettie looked all over the house and couldn't find her cell phone. "I'll look one more place, and if it's not there, I don't know where else to look."

She headed for the laundry room in the basement when the house phone rang.

Lettie saw it was Vince.

"Vince, I can't talk now. I have to put some clothes on and go outside. There are cops all over the side of my house."

"Are they on your property, Lettie?"

"No, they're on the street."

"What happened?"

"It's what I want to find out. The doorbell is ringing. I have to go. I'll call you later. But, I'll tell you now I'm not inclined to vote for your friend, Price."

"I'll hold on."

Lettie ran to answer the door.

"Are you all right, Lettie?" asked her next door neighbor.

"I'm fine. What happened?

"An explosion, either a gas pipe or a water main."

"Lettie, I have to go to work. We'll talk tonight."

"Thanks for stopping by."

Lettie returned to the phone determined to close any door Vince thought was open about her voting for a moron like Dick Price.

"Listen, Vince, before this conversation goes any further, I want you to know I'm not voting for your friend, Price. He's a sleazeball, and he creeps me out even to look at him." Before Vince responded, Lettie said, "Have to go," and hung up the phone.

Miller looked at Lettie's phone in his hand. Last night was the second time she had left it in his car. He was sure he had convinced her to vote for Price, especially after last night. "That bitch." He threw Lettie's phone on the floor and stamped his right foot squarely on top. "Next time, Lettie, it may be your head."

CHAPTER 19

MARY'S CAR AMBLED ALONG BELOW THE SPEED LIMIT. TOM was pleased Mary wasn't tempted to speed in the pouring rain. Her driving usually was erratic and caused him more than a little anxiety. It was bad enough the school board meetings were wired to electrify even Mother Teresa, but combine that with Mary's stopping at what seemed every corner except for those corners with a stop sign, made Tom promise himself he'd insist on driving to the next meeting.

"I hear a lot of people plan to come tonight," said Tom trying to keep his mind off the road.

Mary responded by looking over at him instead of watching the road. "I've heard it before. Everyone says they're coming, but when the time arrives, they don't show. We decided on the principal's job at Elmhurst Memorial last week at the executive board meeting. Vince and Lou's guy, Dick Price, didn't have the votes."

"Even Ted decided to go along with us, but only after you promised to embarrass him at the public meeting. Lettie didn't like Price from the start."

"Dick Price is the worst damn candidate out of the bunch," said Mary.

"When we didn't go along with him, Lou threatened the public would tear the auditorium apart if the board didn't vote for Price."

"You know who the public is, don't you?"

"Sure, the 'public' is all his friends. You know the ones he snagged jobs for over the past six years. What a blowhard. If the SOB imagines he can intimidate me, he's crazy."

The idea riled Mary up. Her already dangerous driving maneuvers made Tom want to hop out of the car at the next red light, that's if she stopped for the light."

Out of the blue, Mary hit the brake. She hit it so hard she banged her head on the steering wheel. Tom's whole body jerked forward as far as the seat belt stretched. This time it wasn't Mary's fault. Some jerk in a black Chevy pickup pulled in front of her. The Chevy came out of the blue and pulled off at top speed.

"He tried to push us off the road," yelled Tom.

They sat there for a minute and took turns cursing the guy. The driver was long gone, but both felt better after their rant.

"Do you think someone did it on purpose?" asked Tom.

"If they did, they failed, and now they'd better pray I don't find them."

This was the difference between Mary and Tom. Her immediate reaction was to fight back; Tom's reaction was to step back.

Mary stepped on the gas, drove off and picked up right where she left off.

"Lou's 'gang of thieves' better not cause trouble tonight or I swear I'll reach over and whip that mop off his head and toss his stupid toupee into the audience like a Frisbee."

"Let's see which of his people scrambles to catch it first," laughed Tom. "We'll watch his flunkies retrieve it, and we can give a prize to the lapdog who brings it onto the stage first and lays it at our illustrious chairman's feet."

"Do any of his gang have educational credentials, other than being friends or relatives?"

Mary rolled her eyes, "What do you think?"

Mary never minced words. Tom always enjoyed his friend's quick wit, and tonight her sense of humor eased the butterflies in his stomach. Still frazzled by their near collision and the possibility someone tried to run them off the road, Tom was a mix of apprehension and anticipation as they pulled into the parking lot of Elmhurst Memorial.

§

The smell of wet clothes made Tom want to take a deep breath of fresh air.

Wet umbrellas thrown under the auditorium seats made the floor slippery. The water from the umbrellas ran down the aisles leading to the stage. More than one person in attendance wished one of the board members would slip and break their neck. This group wanted blood. Some of the craziest people on earth find their way into schools, often through friendships with local school board members. A good number of those worms had been called into service tonight.

Elmhurst Memorial shook with the sounds of eight hundred people. All the auditorium seats were taken, and people lined the sides of the room. The place rocked. Mary and Tom worked their way to the stage. On the way, they heard derisive words directed at them.

"I don't recognize many of these people," remarked Mary.

"Maybe they're some of Lou's people just starting to look for jobs? For some reason, the noise and the people all over the auditorium don't alarm me even though I know the next few hours aren't going to be pleasant. These people didn't come here tonight to offer us help with future re-election campaigns."

Tom glanced at one woman with a black jacket just as she turned her back to him. Written on the jacket in white letters was ACADEMY OF BOXING. "You could tell she was as proud of her jacket as if it read Harvard College," he thought.

The threatening expressions on many faces in the crowd gave the room an uncomfortable air. Being around Mary had given Tom the experience to see how to beat these people is by standing tall.

"When you know you're right, you must let people know you're not taking any of their shit. Public officials must draw a fine line between individuals who come to these meeting to seek help and those who come only to intimidate. That fine line appeared thick tonight.

Mary and Tom climbed the five steps to the stage. Tom sat on one side of Mary, Lou on her other side. Mary and Tom made it a point not to sit together at public meetings, but tonight was different.

"What a night. It'll be fun, Mary," snickered Ted. "There's still time to escape."

"Shut up, Ted. And breathe in the other direction."

The meeting began with Lou banging his gavel. The audience quieted, but a din was still present. "There must be eight hundred people here tonight," Lou commented with a grin.

After the board members gave their committee reports, Chairman Marinara told the rabble there were only a few items on tonight's agenda, the vote on Dick Price for principal of Elmhurst Memorial High School was the main one. The crowd cheered loudly.

"Ladies and Gentleman, there will be a slight delay in starting tonight's meeting. Vince Miller, one of our board members, is delayed in traffic and will be a few minutes longer. At this time we do not have enough people on the board who plan to vote for Dick Price for principal of Elmhurst. We'll take a short break and return as soon as Mr. Miller arrives."

The crowd softly chanted, "We want Dick Price." The chant quickly ratcheted to a roar. "We want Dick. We want Dick. We want Dick."

Tom looked over at Marinara hoping he'd quell the thugs. Instead, Tom saw a huge smile on the chairman's face.

Mary leaned over to Tom and said, "What's Lou trying to pull. We voted Price down at the executive meeting."

"Nothing is carved in stone until we vote in public," said Tom.

The crowd alternated, "We want Dick," with "Chain the doors, chain the doors until we get Dick."

In an attempt intended to be unsuccessful, Lou softly called for quiet and banged the gavel limply.

Embolden by their numbers, the leaders yelled, "Firebomb them. Chain the doors." Tom noticed a few burly men with chains in their hands rushing up the aisle toward the auditorium doors.

Tom whispered to Mary, "Bunny Krouse told me Lou's cronies use this threat of chaining the doors if board members don't vote the way Lou wants them to vote."

Tom saw Mary getting angrier and angrier. Fortunately, in walked Vince to a thunderous round of applause.

Chairman Marinara picked the microphone. "This meeting is called to order and welcome Vince." The audience began another round of applause and Lou pretended to bang the gavel vigorously. Finally, Marinara said, "I know Mr. Miller appreciates your enthusiasm, but we must take care of tonight's business, finding a new principal for Elmhurst Memorial."

Mary turned to Lou sitting to her left. "That's not on the agenda? We weren't voting tonight on a principal and specifically not on Richard Price."

"I put it on the agenda a few hours ago. As chairman, I can put anything I want on the agenda."

Mary looked over and saw Lettie pointing at what was a very expensive cellphone and throwing a kiss at Miller and mouthing the words, "Thank you."

"Well, I'll be a son-of-a-bitch," said Mary.

Lou began, "I nominate Dick Price for the position of principal of Elmhurst Memorial High School." Vince seconded the nomination. "Madam Secretary, please call the roll."

In a low voice, Lettie Grimes called Lou, Vince and herself. All voted yes. Lettie called Father Grant, Mary, and Tom. All voted, no. The crowd booed them so loudly Tom thought his eardrums would burst. "Chain the doors. Firebomb them," screamed the crowd."

After a minute Lou attempted to quiet the crowd, not for the board members who voted no, but so Ted Kowalski could cast the deciding vote.

All eyes focused on Ted.

Lettie called for Kowalski's vote. Ted hesitated, and the room fell silent. Ted appeared to decide how to cast his vote, but Lou suspected Ted wanted all the attention a little longer. Finally, he muttered, "Yes."

Chairman Marinara announced, "Ladies and Gentlemen, we have a new principal of Elmhurst Memorial High School."

When Mary heard this, she had enough. She reached over to Lou and ripped the microphone from his hand, rose from her chair, walked to the center of the stage and put her hand in the air for quiet. The rabble decreased their screaming. A huge, fat man with jeans hanging down below his waist continued yelling.

"Speak, Asshole" Mary demanded.

"Do you know who I am?" the man asked.

"Yeah, you're the idiot who got Ds in high school."

The whole auditorium erupted in laughter. The crowd howled. They guffawed. No one stopped laughing, no matter how much Lou Marinara banged his little gavel.

"Listen carefully, idiot." Mary waited to see who dared make a peep and repeated, "Listen carefully. You're all thugs. Those of you who are screaming are animals, and those of you who sit in silence and let these thugs take over your schools are despicable. I'm telling you right now; I'll never listen to you animals while I'm on this school board. Now, those three idiots who chained the doors better go and remove them because if the chains aren't off in sixty seconds, I'm calling the cops and I'm having you arrested."

No one in the audience moved except the three guys who had chained the doors. They tore up the middle aisle and removed the chains. Mary waited at the center of the stage until the doors were wide open.

"This meeting is over," yelled Mary. "Now get the hell out of this school." The crowd rose and immediately filed from the auditorium.

Mary waited a few minutes and returned to her seat. When the room was empty, Mary rose, put on her coat and marched out to her car.

§

The day after the school board meeting Vince was ecstatic. He won. The cost may have been high, but he succeeded. He put Dick Price in the worst school in the district. Last night the high school auditorium shook with the roars of the crowd, his crowd. What an accomplishment.

Miller had to admit Mary McMurray and her posse put up a good defense, but he had the votes, four to three. Kowalski came over at the last minute. Ted almost shit in his pants when the crowd yelled, "Lock the doors and firebomb the place." He chuckled at how Lou's friends' intimidation tactics were like a bullet headed straight for Ted's head, but had to admit, tonight Mary Mc Murray caught that bullet in her teeth and spat it back at the crowd.

The audience turned from intimidators to the intimidated by an old lady. Vince saw this was not McMurray's first trip to the rodeo. He suspected Mary McMurray had stood up often to far more reckless people than last night's crowd. When Mrs. McMurray said, "…those doors better open now…," the ringleaders knew they'd better get those doors open.

In the back of Miller's mind, he realized future votes would be far more difficult. Father Grant, Mary McMurray, and Tom Foster were forever bound. They held the moral high ground and McMurray planned to use it to beat Lettie or Ted into voting with them.

All McMurray and her posse needed was one more vote. Ted and Lettie saw how Mary stood up to the crowd. Those thugs won't be threatening Mary McMurray again. Lettie and Ted will have no one protecting them after last night unless they join forces with Mary.

Vince put the future votes out of his mind and concentrated on his present victory. Price starts at the school this morning, recruitment begins as early as next month and, "Payday is just around the corner."

Vince picked up his phone and called Dick. "It's never too early to plan how to make money."

§

Dick Price answered his phone in his spacious principal's office with a private bathroom. "Principal Price, here."

"Dick, it's Vince.

"Vince who?" responded Principal Price.

"Do I have to come over there and kick your ass?"

"I'm messing with you, Vince."

"Listen, it's time. Bennie called me at eight this morning, telling me he needs people right away. At yesterday's meeting, you mentioned your school has Parent-Teacher Conferences tomorrow night, and you plan to troll the halls looking for potential workers for Bennie."

"I got to go; there's a fire alarm going off. I have to see what's happening. Call me the day after tomorrow." The phone went dead.

Pissed off, Vince screamed into the dead phone, "You better not screw up."

Vince waited two days and called Price. Dick had good news. "I have four parents interested. I told them I'd get back to them with particulars."

"Have them call, Bennie. I'll text you his number. He'll tell them what to do. We're cooking with gas. Good job, Dick."

"These parents told me they had people they knew who'd also be interested."

"Keep up the momentum. I'll call tomorrow and see what's next. Have some of your teachers ask around. Tell them they'll be doing a good deed. Those do-gooders love it when they think they're helping people."

"The turnover in personnel at this school is so high; those teachers will be gone by next year. A new group of bleeding hearts will take their place. The project is working out, Vince."

"It's just the beginning, Dick."

§

Vince waited outside the office watching Lou's twenty-year-old secretary sashaying around the office in four-inch heels. Vince had good news to tell Lou, and he thought it better to tell him in person.

Miller's eyes diverted to Don Luigi exiting Lou's office again. One day Vince planned to ask Lou what the story was with Luigi, but for today the big news is the recruitment project was in full gear. Business was great. Bennie asked Vince to tell Lou, "Send a double load of the cleaning-starting next week."

When Don Luigi left the office, Lou said. "Come in. What's the good news?"

§

Mary entered the school board office. "Hello, Ted. How was Thanksgiving?"

"Great. I spent it with Tom Foster and his family. Martha and I had a wonderful day."

"That's good; the Fosters are such nice people."

"Yeah, they were kind enough to invite us when they heard we'd be alone for the holiday."

Mary didn't feel she should comment. Ted continued, "My two pieces of you know what took off with their girlfriends and spent Thanksgiving with their parents. Those ungrateful SOBs."

Now, Mary was sure she didn't want to comment, and Ted went on and on complaining how ungrateful his kids were.

When Ted stopped railing, Mary remained silent. She realized Ted expected her to say something, but she didn't know where to begin. Ted gave her an opening, "Mary, what would you do if this happened to you?"

Mary had learned over the years when people ask for advice, they don't want the truth. Ted continued to press Mary for an answer, but Mary chose the easier road, "I don't know what to say, Ted."

"My kids still live with us, eat us out of house and home, plus pay no rent. Their mother does their laundry. They use our cars."

Mary saw Ted fill up, so she took over. "How old are your boys, Ted?"

"They're 24 and 26." Ted sobbed quietly. "What should I do?"

Mary threw caution to the wind, "First of all, I'd throw their sorry asses out the door as soon as they step in the house tonight. If you don't do something, you'll be housing them, feeding them and doing their laundry until they're a hundred."

"But they don't have any money to rent a place for themselves."

"Fine, tell them their cruel behavior devastated you and Martha. Tell them they have one hell of a nerve going off to some stranger's family to spend Thanksgiving, while you sit home alone. Tell them as it turned out you had a wonderful Thanksgiving in spite of their thoughtlessness. Tell them they are selfish, no-good bastards."

"I don't know if I could say all of that."

"Then be prepared to have them around until you die. You know Ted, it isn't all their fault. We think kids know things intuitively. Well, surprise, they don't. Many things are counter-intuitive. It's probably more exciting to spend time with their Hoochie Coochie than with you and Martha. If we don't say anything, they assume mom and pop don't mind if you treat them like crap. Parenting is a tricky thing, but one thing is for sure, if we as parents don't teach them, no one will."

The office door opened. Father Grant bounded into the room. He saw the expression on Mary's face and looked at Ted. "I'm sorry. Did I interrupt something?"

"No, Father, I just discussed my failure as a parent with Mary."

"Ted, I can leave and work down the hall."

"No, stay. Maybe you can give me insight on how I screwed up as a parent."

"Ted, as you know, my first-hand experience with kids isn't that extensive."

Mary offered. "You don't have to be a parent to know how to handle people, Father. To bring you up to speed, Ted's kids took off to spend Thanksgiving with their girlfriends' families and left Ted and Martha high and dry for the holiday."

"Well, Ted, it's never too late to try and fix it," said Father.

"Mary just told me how, but I'm not sure I can do it."

"Maybe Mary will come over and do it for you," joked Father."

Father's remark lightened the air and Ted, Tom and Mary chuckled.

Jemma entered the board office and saw the three board members having a harmonious conversation.

She immediately left the room and called Lou.

"Hi, Angie, is Lou there? I have to speak to him."

"What's it about Jemma?"

"Tell Lou, Ted, Father and the Mc Murray woman looked a little too cozy. They were laughing and enjoying some story about Ted."

"OK, Jemma, I'll tell Lou as soon as he comes home."

§

Ted took Mary Mc Murray's advice seriously. He went home and used his slight knowledge of the internet to look up 'Tough Love.' Numerous articles provided Ted with food for thought. Ted scribbled notes on a pad and went downstairs to speak with Martha. "What do you suppose we should do?"

"I had no idea we didn't have to put up with some of this stuff," said Ted sarcastically. "I've been reading articles on the internet, and it seems a parent can tell their children what they think of their behavior even after the kids are over twenty-one. "

"Especially, when those grown kids still live with their parents. I thought all we had the right to do was wash their laundry, provide their food…"

Martha interrupted, "Their car insurance, their health insurance, their beer and their friends' beer." Ted's tone of voice had fired Martha up. She became angrier with each second. Ted knew his wife had been suppressing her feelings for a long time. "Ted, this is what we'll do."

Ted watched the anger in his wife's eyes; fire fed by the fuel of many hurts. Martha's eyes screamed, "I've had enough of their shit."

Ted shared his wife's anger. He was finished playing the part of a doormat.

"First, we throw all their clothes out the window. We tell them to take their shit and find a new place to put it."

"I agree, but why don't we put their things in black plastic bags, so they can take them and leave quicker. If we throw them out the window, they'll have to gather them up. It will take more time."

Husband and wife smiled at each other. Finally, they were on the same track, and they planned to ride that rail for peace and satisfaction.

Ted, with leg problems and Martha with joint problems, sprinted up the stairs to their kids' rooms.

§

Mary entered the school board office with a flurry. "This is ridiculous. Now we are meeting in the afternoons. We've been averaging a closed meeting a week. We were supposed to have one a month?"

"We are unless something urgent comes up," answered Lettie.

"A closed meeting every month, a week before a monthly public meeting, and an individual committee meeting in the middle of the month, that's what I signed up for when I ran for this board."

"The superintendent's secretary sounded upset when she called," said Tom. "Something about a lawsuit filed under Title IX, a tenth-grade girl wants to play football on the boy's football team."

"Title IX is a federal law, isn't it?" asked Mary.

Ted muttered something, but Mary interrupted, "I was speaking to Tom. He's the one with the Master's Degree in this sort of thing."

Hesitantly, Tom answered, always conscious not to sound like the big expert on education. "Yes, it's Federal, and the Justice Department fights these cases vigorously."

"Has our esteemed law firm, Bottom, Feeda and Associates weighed in on this? We pay them enough," bristled Mary

Ted chuckled, "You mean Bologna, Blatt, and Campanelli? Did you see the last bill they sent? They charge four hundred dollars an hour."

Mary raised her voice, "We better find out what's up with these lawyers."

Lou banged his annoying gavel, "Let's get started Ladies and Gents. Superintendent Pinzon, please begin."

"The problem before us today is whether girls should be permitted to try out for teams traditionally restricted to boys."

"In my day, few girls played any sport," said Mary. "And if they did, often the stigma of being unfeminine accompanied any participation in an activity meant for boys."

The superintendent explained this young girl played better than at least two of the guys on the football team.

Lou asked, "But, what if she injures herself? Are we liable?"

"Yes, but no more than if one of the boys breaks something. Our insurance policy is gender blind."

Ted said, "That's good, but what bothers me is the touching involved in football. Suppose the girl accuses one of the other players of inappropriately touching? Does the insurance policy speak to that?"

"It says the same as it does if the girl touches one of the guys. It's as simple as that."

"Now, we're being ridiculous," snapped Mary. "Girls shouldn't be on the same team as boys because girls can't compete with boys in size or strength and that's it. Let's vote."

"Mrs. McMurray, please give me another minute to finish my report."

Reluctantly, Mary nodded, "Go ahead. Wait a second. Have you checked with our attorneys?"

"Yes, our attorneys investigated this matter and spoke to everyone involved, and they're certain we can't win a lawsuit if we don't let her at least try out. The law is clearly on the girl's side. For the past twenty years, federal case law has piled up with decisions that give girls equal opportunities in sports. Money spent on boys athletics must be the same as for girls. When there's no girls' team in a certain sport at a school, and there's a boys' team for that same sport, the girls have a right to try out for that team. If they're as good as or better than the boys, they receive a slot on the team roster."

The whole board fought to put their two cents into the discussion, but Mary half listened to the chatter. Her mind drifted back thirty years to all the discussion of whether women should be on the Police and

Fire Departments. She thought the idea was ridiculous until someone burglarized her next door neighbor's home.

Mary sat with her neighbor until the cops arrived and in walked a six foot three, two hundred pound female cop. Her manner was polite but commanding. Her partner, not a small man, looked like Peewee Herman next to this lady cop. When Mary saw how this lady cop took charge, she realized some women could be cops and firefighters and others cannot, and this goes for male applicants also.

Mary's attention came back to the meeting by Lou's gavel banging. "I change my mind. This high school girl should at least be able to try out for the team. If she's as good as the guys, the coaches should let her play. And Rocco, if she does make the team, please, tell me when and where she plays her first game."

The board voted six to one to allow the female athlete to try out for a position on the boys' football team.

This was the first time since Lou sat on the board, he found himself on the losing side of a vote.

§

Eddie Fisher had a problem. The gas company notified him they needed to enter his basement to replace a pipe. His basement held the remains of his Grandmother under the concrete floor. Five years ago, Eddie buried his Grandmother with all the dignity she deserved.

At the time of her last sickness, Grandmother Fisher, at ninety-six, made her grandson, Eddie, promise not to put her into a cold cemetery, miles away from where she'd lived for the past sixty-four years.

Eddie would have preferred the more traditional funeral, with cemetery internment, rather than the arrangement his Grandmother begged him to make. She asked Eddie to wrap her body in a white sheet, place her in a large plastic bag, preferably transparent, place her in a hole in the basement, and seal it with concrete.

If the utility company entered his basement Monday morning and excavated the basement floor to fix the gas pipe, they would find Grandmother Fisher resting in peace. The cops would arrest him, the prosecutor would charge him, and the judge would throw him in jail. Eddie couldn't let this happen.

By Sunday, the usually cool and competent Eddie Fisher was jumping out of his skin trying to figure out what to do. He frantically ran to the basement, lifted a huge sledgehammer and broke up a portion of the cement floor.

After a half hour, Eddie was exhausted, but there was still no sign of Grandma. He sat on the cellar steps and gave his arms a rest. Eddie heard the front door bell, Ring! Ring! "Who the hell is that?"

Fisher ran up the wooden stairs and slipped on the top step. Legs first, he slid to the bottom of the stairs. Ring! Ring! Ring! Ring! Ring! Ring! The ringing in his ears hurt worse than the pain from the fall.

Eddie forced himself up the stairs, pain shooting down both legs. He staggered to the door and pulled it open. "Good afternoon, Sir. I'm from the Gas Company. We're going house to house telling our customers we won't be coming tomorrow to replace your gas line. We won't need to enter your house. We were able to fix the leak from the street. We're sorry for any inconvenience we may have caused."

Before Eddie responded, the man was off his steps and on to the Cassidy house next door. Eddie closed the door and slid down to the floor.

§

Mary was in the school board office by ten o'clock in the morning catching up on a boatload of work for her committee. She called the committee meeting early so they could work all day.

Jemma, the board secretary, came in and said, "There's a call for you Mrs. McMurray. It's your husband."

"Ok, Jemma. Tell him I'll be right there."

Mary wondered why Mark didn't call her cell.

"Hi, Mark."

"Mary, I tried your cell, and it went right to voicemail."

"Sorry Mark, it was in my bag, and I must have put it on silent. What's up?"

"I wanted the number of Doctor Reems."

"Why? Are you alright?"

"I have this indigestion for the past few days. I'm due for a good check-up. I'll call today and see if Doctor Reems can take me tomorrow."

"Look in the top drawer of my desk. My address book is on the right side. Listen, I'm in a meeting. I have to go. See you tonight."

Mary returned to her committee meeting. Felicia Estes continued to talk after Mary began explaining the need for major infrastructure repair in at least ten schools. Mrs. McMurray stopped talking and stared at Estes. The rest of the ten people squeezed around the large conference table watched. When Estes realized she was the center of attention, she clammed up quickly.

My report indicates the Finley School has four functional toilets out of eight in the boy's bathrooms, five non-operational urinals, no towel holders and no doors on the stalls in any bathroom. Many of the high schools and junior highs aren't in much better shape."

"Mrs. McMurray, where are these schools?" asked one mother.

"They're all in the southern tier of the district. By a show of hands how many of you send their kids to schools in the southern tier?" asked Mary.

Everyone looked around the crowded table to see if anyone raised their hands.

"Not a one," said Mary sarcastically.

The rest of the meeting continued with a war of wills between Mary and the PTA parents from the northern tier schools. These parents were determined not to allow any money to be allocated to fix the ten schools targeted by Mary for rejuvenation.

The sides were about equal, Mary on one side, all the mothers on the other side. The school board ultimately votes on the matter and decides the schools marked for major repair. Mary had a vote; the parents didn't. The problem was Mary needed three more votes on the board to have the money go to the right schools.

The meeting ended around noon. Everyone left with strained smiles on their faces. Mary knew these mothers were going home to call one or more of the board members to lobby their viewpoint. Lou, Vince and Lettie's phones will ring non-stop in about an hour. Tom and Father may receive a call or two, as would Ted.

Determined to win this battle, Mary would fight for improved toilets, stalls, and towel holders and she would not relent until everyone's can was covered. Mary laughed, "It's a long way from Wall Street and Everything Foods. I wonder what my old friend J.P. Stanford would think of me now?"

Mary left the district office after her committee meeting and headed for a late lunch with Tom Foster. She pulled into the diner and saw Tom walking in the door. She was pleased she wasn't late.

Mary slid into the booth across from Tom, "What a day." She explained to Tom how the committee members fought against any funding that would go to repair basic accommodations in the schools in the southern tier.

"Those mothers wanted the money to buy dazzlingly decorated bathing suits for the synchronized swimming team and new computers. The suits and the computers they have are only a year old."

"The problem is," said Tom, "There are no parents to fight for the schools that need the basics."

"Like toilets."

"Who should we work on first?"

"I'll call Father," said Mary. "You call Ted. You have more patience with him. I'll wind up telling him to shut up." Mary heard her cell phone buzz in her bag. "Mark, how are you feeling? Did you reach the doctor?"

Tom watched Mary speak with Mark and thought how great it must be to have a partner for so many years.

"Alright, Mark. Lie down for a while and see how you feel. I'm having lunch with Tom. We're planning maneuvers, see you later."

"How is Mark?"

"He's been having indigestion problems since yesterday."

"I hope he'll be alright."

"He will be. He has an appointment with the doctor tomorrow. Now let's order."

§

After lunch, Mary returned to the district office determined to finish her work. As she walked down the corridor, she saw the deputy superintendent leaving her office.

"Mrs. Mc Murray, how are you today," said Regina Moriarity.

"Busy, very busy, Regina. How are you? I heard you had a birthday last week. Happy Belated Birthday"

"Thank you for the good wishes. Another day, another dollar, the years go by so fast."

"Tell me about it."

"Do you have a minute?" asked Regina. "I wanted to discuss something with you."

Mary looked at her watch. "I don't, but I'll make time."

Mary followed Regina into her office. Only Eddie, standing at the far end of the hall, saw the two go into Regina's office.

"Thank you, Mrs. McMurray, for giving me a few minutes of your time."

"My pleasure, Regina and I told you before to call me, Mary. Is there something up? Tell me what's on your mind."

"I want you to know I work hard for the district and I love my job."

"The board knows how hard you work, Regina."

"Lately, the superintendent is trying to undermine my work. He's sabotaging my projects by pouring every little duty on me so I can't finish my real work. He's added responsibilities to my office staff, and it prevents them from doing my work. I wanted you to know this if he tells the board I'm not doing my job."

"Why is he doing this to you?"

"He thinks I'm after his job."

"Do you want to be superintendent?

"Not now. I would apply for the position if Rocco leaves or retires."

"When will he be eligible for retirement?"

"In two years, but if the board gives him a new contract, he could stay longer."

"Regina, be assured I'll keep what you said in mind if Pinzon starts bad mouthing you."

"I can't tell you how much I appreciate it. I want to do the best job I can for the district."

"I'll start the board thinking of hiring more personnel for your office."

When Regina didn't comment on Mary's offer to hire more people, Mary said, "Are you afraid you'd have Lou's spies right here in your office?"

"It crossed my mind."

"This may be a blessing in disguise. It's a chance for the board to hire competent workers not related to the school board chairman."

"It would certainly be nice for a change."

"Regina, I'll keep in touch and update you on what's happening."

"Again, Mary, I appreciate your help."

Mary walked back to the school board office feeling the board was now headed in a new direction.

§

By the time she finished with Regina Moriarity, Mary was so far behind schedule she called her husband and asked him to order a pizza, half mushrooms, half onions and peppers, and have it delivered to the house at 5:30.

Mary called Mark's cell, no answer; then on the house phone, no answer.

Mary walked down the hall to the school board office to retrieve her mail and dictate correspondence to Jemma.

While trying to explain to Jemma what she wanted, Mary heard her phone beep.

Mary excused herself to Jemma, "Hello? Mark, I tried to get you an hour ago, but there was no answer."

"I was asleep."

"How do you feel?"

"Not much better."

"Try to fall back to sleep. I'll pick up a pizza on my way home."

Turning to Jemma, "I need these letters to go out tomorrow."

Jemma protested. "I have to do some reports for Mr. Marinara. I don't know if I have the time. Over the years, many of the board members have done their own typing, especially the women."

"Listen, Jemma; I don't ask for your help often. You don't seem to realize you aren't here as Mr. Marinara's private secretary. You and I have had this conversation before. If these letters don't go out tomorrow by the end of the workday, there will be trouble. Do you understand?"

Jemma said nothing, but she shook her head up and down.

"Good. Now, where is the file on new federally funded programs?"

§

The chill in the air whipped through Regina Moriarity's hair. She turned and faced the façade of the Art Deco school building that housed the district office. The wind refreshed her cheeks. An hour ago she spoke to Mary McMurray and now Regina Moriarity, a fifty-one-year-old, single woman felt she was twenty-two again and just beginning her career.

Regina felt the way she did when she began her teaching career, full of life and ambition. Regina took a deep breath and whispered to no one "I'll be the educational leader of this school district come hell or high water. I'll help transform this place into the finest district in the state."

Had Regina been wearing a hat she'd have thrown it in the air, but she never wore hats, so instead she continued down the steep slate stairs and drove home.

That night during dinner, Regina told her sister, "Marge, a few hours ago I announced my intention to become the next superintendent of my school district."

Marge asked, "To whom?"

"To myself," roared Regina.

§

Jemma returned with the files Mary had requested and sat down next to Mrs. McMurray dreading the grilling she knew was coming. Lou had convinced the board Jemma needed a raise due to her taking on some responsibilities of the school district's funded programs office. In reality, Jemma did little more than some typing for the funded program's director.

Today was Jemma's day of reckoning. Mrs. McMurray had a million questions, and Jemma knew she could answer none.

"Jemma, this file has English as a Second Language..." Mary stopped mid-sentence when she saw her phone light up on the table next to her. It was Mark. 'Hello," Mary said with a slight hint of annoyance. "Yes, Mark."

"Mary, I can't find my medicine. I don't feel well. My chest feels tight and I ..."

Mary heard the phone drop to the floor and the thud that followed.

"Mark? Mark, are you there? Are you alright? Call 911."

Getting no answer on the other end of the phone, Mary frantically called 911. When she hung up, she had the same sunken feeling she had forty years ago when she dialed for help for her ten-year-old daughter, Veronica.

CHAPTER 20

TOM FOSTER HAD GOTTEN TO KNOW MARK MURRAY WELL IN a short time and was deeply saddened by his new friend's death. After Mark's funeral, Mary stayed with her daughter, Ellen in New Jersey to recuperate from the devastating loss of her husband of almost fifty years.

Mary did not attend tonight's meeting, and Tom missed her. She was still in New Jersey with her daughter. Tom left the school board office at 10:00 p.m. The monthly executive board meeting wouldn't end for another hour. It was boring and nonsensical, except for the Vince Miller's budget report informing the board of the financial restraints affecting the ability to fill certain supervisory positions. Vince neglected to say how this job-filling constraint affected him personally.

The budget restraints thrilled Tom. Those restraints stopped any hiring for six months, and by that time Mary, and he hoped they could attract one or two more votes to their side.

Tom arrived at the meeting four hours ago. The jammed parking lot filled with the cars of people attending a student concert forced Tom to park at the far end of the lot over by the tall bushes. Now, the lot was almost empty, and Tom walked quickly toward his car because he was in a hurry to meet Jen and because the dark, vacant lot posed possible dangers.

Tom walked a few steps and out of the bushes stepped a young guy with a baseball bat in his right hand. Tom stopped and watched the young hood walk to the center of the lot. He stared straight at Tom and waved the bat from side to side as if he was swinging at a baseball. Tom stood in place trying to decide if he'd charge back toward the school, or wait until the hoodlum came for him.

After an endless two minutes, the bat wheeling hood turned and walked out the side exit onto the street. Tom waited another minute looking to see if the gangbanger had any more friends that might appear out of the bushes. None appeared, and Tom sprinted to his car safely.

Tom drove to the exit closest to the school building. Ted Kowalski came running out of the building waving his hands in the air. "Tom. Tom, I've something to ask you. Tom stopped his car and rolled down the window.

"What is it, Ted? Is everything all right?

Ted caught his breath and told Tom what was on his mind.

As Tom rode to meet Jen, he laughed thinking what Jen would say to Ted's request they join them at City Winery in Manhattan to see the '80's disco star Buster Poindexter in concert. "Jen, he's the one who sang the song *Hot, Hot, Hot*. It could be a blast."

Tom avoided telling Jen about the thug with the bat.

§

Tom had a million things he had to do, but tonight he was looking forward to seeing an aging hipster from the eighties in a club in downtown Manhattan with of all people, Ted and Martha Kowalski.

Tom was happy Jen was coming. It would be a hoot.

A trip to Manhattan on a Friday night with everyone trying to enter and exit the city was a potential nightmare. "Tom, I'm grateful you offered to drive."

Tom turned to Ted in the back seat of the car and smiled.

"Tom is glad to do it. Your car drives beautifully" said Jen.

Martha, Ted's long-suffering wife, said, "It's great you two joined us tonight. When our son gave us the four tickets he'd won to see Buster Poindexter, I didn't know how we'd get to the concert…

"It's not a concert, Martha. The tickets call it a lounge act."

"Tom, what is it?"

Trying to be his diplomatic self, Tom answered, "It's a combination lounge act and concert."

Tom asked, "Ted you never told me how you snagged the tickets?"

"My son, Stanley, was the fourth caller to dial a radio station. It was a contest or something," said Martha. "Have you ever seen Buster Poindexter?"

"Only in pictures," answered Jen.

His most famous song is Hot! Hot! Hot! We used to dance to it at a bar in our old neighborhood."

Tom and Jen almost burst out laughing at the image of Ted and Martha stomping around the dance floor. Luckily, both had a good handle on their self-control.

"Ted, what made Stanley connect you and Buster Poindexter," said Tom.

"We must have mentioned Buster Poindexter once to our oldest son. He was listening to the radio when they announced they were giving out free tickets to see Poindexter to the first five people who called into the station. Stanley called, and sure enough, he was the fourth caller. The station sent the tickets right out, and our son surprised us with them. My son never saw Buster, but he remembered the funny name and figured it was another joke on us."

"Ted what did I tell you? If you bore Tom and Jen one more time with our family problems, I'm getting out of the car and going home?"

Ignoring his wife's threat, Ted continued. "We tried to look enthusiastic when he gave us the tickets which wasn't hard because we weren't used to him even thinking about us, never mind ..."

"Will you stop it, Ted."

"Sorry," said Ted.

"We have to go down Seventh Avenue," said Jen. "It runs into Varick Street. The Club is right before you reach the entrance to the Holland Tunnel. The trick is, you can't stay in the right lane, or you'll wind up in New Jersey."

Eddie Fisher found it difficult following Kowalski's car, but with Tom Foster behind the wheel, it made it harder. Tom was young and observant and would notice someone following him if Eddie followed too closely. Driving became almost impossible when they turned onto Seventh Avenue.

Eddie Fisher couldn't imagine where the four were going. Why were Tom and Ted even in Manhattan together? Why were they headed downtown toward the Meat Packing District? Eddie could understand Tom and his girlfriend heading for some trendy bar, but going there with Ted and his wife was hard to imagine.

Ted's white Subaru continued down Seventh, each block getting closer to the Holland Tunnel.

The last block before the tunnel, Foster made a left on to King Street. Halfway down King, he pulled into a parking space on the street. Eddie, in his dark brown Honda, became frantic. He passed Ted's Subaru and tried to turn away from the passenger window hoping Ted or Tom wouldn't recognize him.

Eddie stopped for a red light at the corner and watched Tom and Jen and Ted and Martha exit the car and walk back toward Varick Street.

The car behind Eddie beeped its horn, but Eddie didn't move until Tom, and the rest were out of sight. "If that guy beeps once more I'll get out of this car and shoot him."

Eddie made a quick right, another right and came to a stop on Varick in time to see the group enter a place called City Winery. "What the hell are they doing?" Eddie said out loud.

Eddie drove around until he found a parking space. There was no rush now; he knew where they were. Now, it was time to discover why they were there. Eddie sat in the car and thought about what to do next.

Eddie googled City Winery, "The only Winery in the City;" "Has Cabaret Atmosphere;" "Tonight, Buster Poindexter, in person;" "Sold out."

"What is Ted doing in a cabaret lounge waiting to see a show featuring an 80's pop-rock singer and his band? And why are Foster and his girlfriend riding around with those old farts?"

He took a stroll past the City Winery to discover more. Eddie pulled his coat collar over his neck and looked into the winery through his dark glasses. The bar was dark, and his dark glasses made it impossible to see the inside of the cabaret. Frustrated, Eddie figured he'd no choice, but to take a chance and go into the bar. Ted and his posse were probably at one of the fifty small tables in the audience. With the music blasting and strobe lights flashing, the group would not spot him. The problem was, he might not see 'Downtown Ted,' either.

Eddie scanned the room and glimpsed Tom and his girlfriend. He strained his eyes to focus on the rest of the table. He saw Ted's wife, but no Ted. "Where the hell is that jerk?"

Ted came down the aisle knocking into tables along the way. No one said anything. By this time the smell of weed permeated the room. Drinks arrived, a bottle of red and a bottle of white. The waiter cleared the table of the old glasses. Ted gave a tip to the server. Ted and his gang drank wine and enjoyed Buster's songs and comments on everything from politics to sports.

Eddie looked over and watched 'Downtown Ted' calling over the waiter, again. A few minutes later four more bottles of wine appeared. The crowd sang with Poindexter. The place rocked. The room shook with frantic energy. Ted and Martha hopped up and down, waved their hands and went wild. The line to get in the club was around the corner. Everyone wanted in.

Finally, the band played the song everyone was waiting for, the song most associated with Buster Poindexter - Hot! Hot! Hot! The crowd jumped up and danced to the song's staccato beat. The band upped the volume and Eddie's ears were ready to pop. "Good, this will get Ted out of here real quick."

The crowded room, with everyone on their feet, made keeping an eye on the group difficult. Eddie didn't want to miss them if they up and left. The band continued to play the popular song again and again. The crowd loved it. Eddie looked over and saw Ted Kowalski standing on the table wiggling his hips with his wife trying to join him. "Holy Shit, if she climbs on the table, it'll break, and they'll both find themselves in the hospital. Ted won't make the meeting next week, and Lou won't have his fourth vote."

"I've got to get Ted out of here."

Eddie's mind raced to think of a plan to get Ted out of the club, but the noise slowed his usually agile brain. He reached in his pocket to make sure he had the burner phone he always kept with him.

Eddie charged for the front door and walked quickly to his car. He passed Ted's car and saw there were some spaces open. He drove quickly around the block and pulled into a space fifty feet from Ted's Subaru. Eddie turned the engine off and pulled out the burner phone. His finger hit 911 and when the 911dispatcher asked, "Is this an emergency?" Eddie answered, "Yes, there's a fire in the City Winery Bar. It's on Varick off King Street. The place has a few hundred people. The fire was near the front door. People might have a hard time exiting."

Eddie hung up and waited. Six minutes later, the sound of police sirens filled the downtown air, followed by the blasting horns of the Fire Department. Eddie thought how incredible these city departments are, a six-minute response time.

§

Tom saw the call was from Ted Kowalski. He was curious to hear how Ted felt this morning after drinking bottle after bottle of wine last night. "Good afternoon Ted. We had a big night last night."

"Tom, Martha and I want to thank you and Jen for last night, and we want to apologize for our behavior."

"Don't be silly, Ted. You and Martha were having a good time."

"We sure did. Our heads hurt today, but it was worth it. The music took us back thirty years."

"You two must have been quite the dancers."

"When you're young, you never imagine what old farts you'll become. We were never the coolest people on the block, but we thought we were part of the in-crowd. Of course, we weren't."

"I've learned, Ted, the only place the in-crowd hangs out is in a person's mind."

"Tom, I'm sure you've always been a part of the 'A Group' with your looks and personality."

"You'd think so, but there was always a doubt in my mind that people just saw me as a nerd."

"One of the big reasons I ran for school board was I hoped to make a difference in helping young people by hiring teachers with the ability to explain life lessons to them," explained Ted. "We need programs in the junior and senior schools which help kids navigate those difficult, emotional years."

Tom wanted to say, "Ted, you've been on the board for so long. Why aren't any of these programs in our schools?"

Ted sensed Tom's thought, and said, "I never had the votes to fund these programs. Lou always had another relative or friend to put on the payroll."

Tom waited for more, but Ted clammed up.

"Life is complicated. You and Jen allowed us to go back and feel how we did when we still had a future before the kids came along and made us feel inadequate, stupid and even awkward in their company."

"Don't say that Ted. You and Martha are…"

"Please, let me finish. When you're young, you have this sense of inadequacy, but you keep it in the back of your mind. When you are older, and the kids are grown, they pull that feeling from the back of your mind and drag it to center stage. Last night that feeling wasn't there. Thank you again, Tom."

Tom didn't know what to say to Ted. The conversation had suddenly gone above Tom's pay grade.

Thankfully, Ted had to leave for a doctor's appointment.

"Please, don't forget to thank Jen for putting up with two old hippies." Tom chuckled, and Ted responded. "Don't laugh. We were hippies. Well, sort of."

"Take care, Ted. See you at the next meeting."

§

Before Ted Kowalski knew it, he was sitting in another meeting bored to death and asking himself why he was here today and not out with Martha at some exciting place having fun. Since going with Tom and Jen to Manhattan, Ted and Martha tried to keep up their newfound social momentum by going to a local bar a block away from their house on Saturday nights. They'd sit at the bar, have something off the bar menu and have a few glasses of red wine.

But for now, there he was with six other board members trying to cure the district of all its evils. He resented having to take a few hours off from work to be here. Who calls a meeting in the afternoon?" he thought.

Frustration dripping from his lips, Lou quickly responded "I called this executive board meeting for this afternoon because none of you could make our required monthly meeting in the evening. We are required by law to meet in executive session at least once a month."

Mary sat quietly until the chairman finished and asked if there was any new business. Mary said, "I have a few questions. Did any of you read in last week's paper about the school district on Long Island with one school building housing Grades K to 12? They approved a twenty-five million dollar expansion. The voters approved the twenty-five million dollars by a vote of 160 to 131. Obviously, the 160 votes were cast by parents in the school. The district enrollment is two hundred students."

"That's a great deal of money," said Father Grant. "For one hundred and sixty people to have the power to spend twenty-five million dollars in taxpayer money is criminal."

"I read the same article," said Tom. "The piece caught my attention because my cousin lives in that district. The article said the district superintendent is part-time. It makes sense. What doesn't make sense is he receives a salary of two-hundred thousand dollars. And if that's not outrageous enough, the district has an assistant superintendent for finance. His salary is three hundred thousand because his position is full-time. The district office is in the same building as the Kindergarten to Grade 12 and has a staff of fifteen. Salaries range from thirty thousand dollars a year to one-hundred and twenty-thousand, not including a janitorial staff of six."

"And by the way," said Mary, "I want to ask you something. Is there anyone working for the district either retired from this district or any other district?"

Pinzon looked sheepishly at the chairman. Pinzon hoped Lou would address the question. The whole board stared at Lou.

"Let me address this, Superintendent Pinzon," said Lou reluctantly.

"It's all yours," a relieved Pinzon replied.

"Presently, we have three people in this category."

Mary resisted saying, "Spit it out, you pompous windbag."

"To fully address Mrs. McMurray's question, I will explain why we have these people on the payroll."

Now Tom had to control himself from screaming, "We know why they're on the payroll. They're all relatives or friends of yours, Mr. Chairman."

"Mr. Clark, head of Pupil Personnel, retired from our District five years ago in June. We were unable to find a suitable replacement by September. We imposed upon Mr. Clark to return temporarily until we find a replacement. He kindly agreed to return to help us out."

"How much did his kindness cost the district?" inquired Mary.

Lou ignored Mary and continued, "Mr. Clark returned to the district at the same salary he earned when he left."

Lettie interrupted, "Are you saying this guy Clark collects a pension and an additional paycheck from our district?"

"How long did Clark work for the district."

"Thirty-one years."

Tom interjected, "That means he receives a pension of approximately eighty percent of the salary he made when he worked here."

"Yes, and he comes to work presently and receives the same salary for the work he does now," said Superintendent Pinzone.

Father Grant said, "The district cut music programs. Was that to pay for Clark's double dipping?"

Mary called Tom last night, and the two developed the script playing out now. Mary had spent the past few days researching a personnel issue she wanted to be explained. She politely raised her hand, and the chairman recognized her. "I'd like to ask the superintendent a few questions concerning district office positions."

Pinzone looked over at Lou for possible guidance.

"I want to know about the other two retired people who work full time in our district," pushed Lettie.

"Mr. Salerno and Mr. Koch are retired and work for us also."

"For how long?" Mary asked"

"Mr. Salerno retired seven years ago from our school district and is in charge of all supply grants for the district. His salary is ninety-thousand dollars. Mr. Koch has been retired for three years and earns one-hundred and ten thousand dollars. He came to us from a neighboring school district. Mr. Koch is an expert in curriculum development."

"In seven years you couldn't find anyone else who is knowledgeable about supplies?"

"Mr. Salerno is worth his weight in gold. He makes sure the district gets every penny it deserves from the federal government."

"I hope he finds enough pennies to pay himself his ninety-thousand dollar salary."

"Mr. Koch. Wasn't he on a neighboring school board a few years back?" asked Ted.

Lou replied, "Now that you say it, he was."

"I'm new on the board, and I don't want to jump to conclusions, but can't we find permanent people for these three jobs," asked Tom.

Mary didn't wait for the superintendent to answer. "I make a motion to instruct the superintendent to advertise for these positions immediately."

"Are we moving too fast?" said Lou. "You may find that these three men are the best individuals for the jobs."

"Okay, Lou, let them apply and be interviewed," said Tom. "We'll make our decisions accordingly."

"Lou, I want you to call for a vote," said Lettie. "I have to get the hell out of here."

"By a show of hands, do we authorize Mr. Pinzon to advertise?"

Five hands immediately rose. Lou slowly put up his hand. Vince saw Lou and did the same.

Mary laughed. "Lou, we'll make an honest man out of you yet."

Mary ended. "I want to revisit this topic at the next meeting, but now I have had enough of your garbage. I'm leaving."

For once the whole board agreed with Mary McMurray.

§

Mary came home disgusted with today's early meeting, and she longed for a hot cup of tea. She walked to the kitchen, threw her hat, coat, and bag on the table and filled the kettle. She collapsed onto a kitchen chair. BANG! A loud noise came from the master bedroom directly above the kitchen. Mary's heart pounded so hard her ears hurt. A dread sped through her veins and fear paralyzed her for a moment.

Memories poured into Mary's mind of when she was ten. She returned home to an empty house after school one afternoon, a man hot on her heels. Mary remembered the feeling of helplessness she experienced sixty years ago.

She sat silently and waited for another sound. The hall stairs creaked. Each step down from the second floor became louder and louder. Mary knew every loose floorboard in the house. She knew the intruder was getting closer. Mary couldn't tell if the footsteps headed for the kitchen or the front door.

In a shaky voice, Mary foolishly called, "Is that you, Mark? You mentioned you were coming home early." She immediately regretted her words because the intruder seemed to accelerate speed across the floor. Without moving off her chair, she reached for a shillelagh in the corner of the kitchen. Mark had shown her how and where to strategically jam the walking stick if a person tried to attack her.

Mary held her breath as the footsteps came closer. She was sure the intruder was steps from the kitchen. The intruder tried to be quiet, but the old wooden floors didn't cooperate. He was a few feet away from the entrance to the kitchen and Mary was sure he wasn't coming for some milk and cookies.

A loud knock on the back door made her jump off the chair. "Knock, knock." Mary looked at the glass door and saw Ernie Spikes. He held up some papers for Mary to see. She unlocked the door. Simultaneously she heard someone run to the front door.

Mary jerked the back door open and fell into Ernie's arms. He felt Mary's body shaking. She looked up at him and gasped, "You saved my life. Someone was here. He ran out the front door when you knocked." Ernie grabbed Mary's hand and pulled her to the front of the house. A green car sped down the street toward the highway.

Ernie brought Mary back into the house and settled her at the kitchen table. Ernie turned off the stove. The kettle continued to whistle for a few more seconds while Ernie poured Mary the cup of tea she wanted so badly when she first arrived home.

"Mary, was the guy upstairs when you came home?"

"Yes, I heard a bang. The bastard must have dropped something on the floor." Mary paused for a second, her hands still trembled. Ernie worried; it wasn't like his long-time friend.

Mary knew Ernie didn't know what she was thinking and told him. "When I was a little girl a man followed me home from school. That year, my father worked in the next county and came home on weekends. My mother took a part-time job for three afternoons a week. She wanted to save some money to take me to Disneyland in California. So, I was, a latch-key kid for a year."

Mary stopped to take a deep breath, and Ernie patiently waited for her to continue. "For a few weeks, I noticed a strange man walking in the neighborhood as I walked home from school. I thought he might be trouble, but he always kept a half a block or so away from me. One day he came a lot closer than usual. I hurried toward my house. He quickened his pace, and by the time I reached my walkway, he was barely twenty-five feet away. I ran up to my door, key in hand. I frantically put the key in the lock. It opened on the first try. The man ran the last ten feet to my door. He lunged at the door as I tried to close it. The door slammed closed, and I pushed my shoulder into the door as hard as possible. The lock held and I crunched down on the floor. I heard a curse of exasperation on the other side of the door. Few things have ever upset me, but when I think of that day, I still become emotional."

Ernie said, "That experience would make anyone uncomfortable, Mary."

"I never felt like that again until today. It took sixty years for the terror of that day to return."

Ernie watched Mary's color return. He saw Mary transform into her old self. She seemed even stronger and more determined than he'd ever seen her. There was fire in her eyes. She looked at the shillelagh and mumbled more to herself than to Ernie. "The next time, he'll find this stick up his ass."

Ernie suggested he go upstairs and see what made the big bang. "You stay here Mary. I'll go look."

"I'm coming. I want to see what the son of a bitch touched."

"Let me look first."

"Ernie, I appreciate your big brother attempt to protect me, and you probably saved my life, but shrinking violet isn't my style."

"Mary, maybe you should consider having someone come live with you for a while."

"What I'll do is call an alarm company and have a security system installed. I may hire someone to watch the house and take some suggestions from a security professional. Among my other duties at Everything Foods, I oversaw Security Operations. When I go into the city for the weekend, I'll speak with the House Detective in my building. You know the protection we have there."

"I sure do. The first time you invited me over I thought it was probably easier entering Fort Knox than your building."

Mary chuckled. "If this guy comes back, we'll surprise him and fix him good. The bastard doesn't realize who he's dealing with."

§

Ernie Spikes left. Mary sat at the kitchen table and shivered again. She tried to control her movements with little success. After five minutes, she went to the cabinet under the sink and took out a bottle of Jack Daniels Bourbon.

Mary drank socially, never alone and never straight bourbon. She poured two ounces into a milk glass from the drain board. She swallowed the bourbon in two gulps. The brown liquid burned her throat, but immediately her shaking subsided. As Mary felt her body and brain relax, she felt her anger billow. She was angry with herself for allowing her emotions to paralyze her. "I'm getting old. Nothing used to scare me."

Mary sat at the kitchen table and became angrier by the minute. Mary McMurray decided never to be fearful again, occasionally with help from Jack Daniels and his friends Glen Levitt, Johnnie Walker, and Jim Beam." Mary laughed at her joke. "Whatever it takes, I'm ready. I'll never let any son of a bitch make me shake in my boots again." Mary sat right at the kitchen table until she had a plan.

Sitting quietly in her empty house, it dawned on Mary what was upstairs in the guest bedroom. She went upstairs to the bedroom next to hers. No one touched that room. Mary doubted the intruder would have found the loose floorboard in the clothes closet.

Mary knelt on the floor, pressed the one short floorboard and it popped out revealing the shiny black pistol Mark had brought home fifteen years ago. Mark worked in the field. The gun came to him when visiting a client. When Mark arrived at the client's home, the man was babbling about suicide.

The man had a gun on the coffee table, and Mark realized the client planned to kill himself. The client rambled for about twenty minutes, then jumped up and went into the bathroom. Mark grabbed the gun off the table and quickly let himself out the door. As soon as Mark was in the hallway, he called 911 and informed the police of what happened.

By the time the cops arrived, the client had jumped from his terrace, down fourteen floors.

Later that night, Mark looked in his briefcase. "Now, what the hell do I do with this?" He wasn't sure where to bring the gun, so he put it up in the attic for safe keeping. That evening Mark and Mary received a call from Michigan that Mark's aunt had died. They rushed to Michigan minutes before they buried Aunt Lydia. By the time they returned, Mark had forgotten about the gun.

A few weeks later Mark remembered the gun and was determined to return it to someone. He went to the attic to get the gun, but couldn't find it. He and Mary looked all over the attic, but could not locate the pistol.

Five years later, when Mark was patching the roof on the house, he stuffed his hand into one soffit, and his hand hit something hard. He tugged at the object and pulled the forgotten gun from its hiding place. Neither Mary nor Mark knew what to do, so they put it under a floorboard in the guest bedroom, and it lived there ever since. Every so often Mary took it out and handled it for old time's sake.

Mary's father was a New York City police officer. He carried a gun even after retirement. In summer when the family went up to the Irish Alps in upstate New York, he took Mary out to the fields and let her watch him shoot cans off a fence. When Mary's hands grew larger, her father allowed her to hold an unloaded pistol. At age fourteen, she pulled the trigger of a loaded gun. Young Mary was hooked.

From that moment, every time Mary and her father went to the country, they spent hours target shooting. At sixteen Mary's father gave Mary her own gun. By this time, she was a sharpshooter. After she grew up and went to work, Mary and her boss, an avid marksman, often went to the shooting range during lunch.

A loud knock on the front door brought Mary back to the present. She ignored who was knocking and rose from the closet floor with the gun. The cold metal felt good in her hand. She had no doubts she could shoot the pistol with no difficulty. "It's like riding a bike."

From that moment, Mary kept her gun in a place close to wherever she was. She took it with her when she went to late night meetings, to early meetings, and afternoon meetings. Determined not to be at the mercy of anyone, Mary kept the gun on her even though it was illegal. She'd have to buy large handbags from now on.

§

Rocco Pinzon began the monthly executive meeting with, "I have some disturbing news to tell you. One of our assistant principals took a stroke in school yesterday."

"Where did it happen," asked Father Grant

"He was in his office, sitting at his desk."

"Is he in the hospital?"

"Yes, and that will be followed by rehab. The poor guy will be there for a while. He won't be back to school for the rest of the school year."

"It would be nice if the board sent him something, like flowers," suggested Lettie.

"Flowers would be good," added Ted.

"Do I have the authorization to spend the money," asked Lettie. "If so, let me see a show of hands?"

"All seven raised their hands.

"Wait. There's more. A parent was present when it happened, and she called me and related an unbelievable story. The parent was sitting waiting to speak to the assistant principal when his secretary came out of the office and said she thought Mr. Bridges had taken a stroke."

"How terrible," said Father Grant.

"The secretary went back to her desk and sat down. The parent waited for the secretary to call 911. Instead, she opened her computer and started typing something. The parent said, "Aren't you calling 911?"

"No," replied the secretary. "I'm looking up the number for Fairview Hospital. My boss needs to go to the hospital."

The parent became frantic and screamed, "You need to call 911." When the secretary ignored her, the parent went behind the desk and called 911 herself.

"What an idiot." groaned Mary.

"I guess secretarial school doesn't teach a class in common sense," said Ted.

"The woman should not be working in a school or anywhere else," said Vince "What a moron."

"How in hell was she ever hired?"

Everyone froze. All knew Mary wasn't letting that softball pitch pass without a swing. Each secretly enjoyed Mary's quips, as long as she directed them at someone else. The price of this fun was a sometimes painful tension around the table.

As expected, Mary broke the silence with, "Hey, Lou, which side of your family is this one from?"

Lou looked around the table and saw he was alone on this one. He rose from his seat, "I have to piss."

When Lou returned from doing his business, he said, "I just received an important call, and I have to leave immediately. Mrs. Grimes asked me before the meeting if she could have time to tell you about a recent incident she thinks you should know. So, I will turn the gavel over to Lettie."

Lou handed the gavel to Lettie and left the room.

"There are a lot of crazy people in the world, and many of them, unfortunately, work in our school district. I attended a committee meeting last Wednesday and Molly, the guidance counselor at Garden Avenue School, told me a new teacher came to the principal the first week of classes suggesting the parents put one of her first-graders on Ritalin, a drug that helps kids calm down and concentrate. The principal told the teacher he'd instruct the guidance counselor to call the parents."

"First grade?" said Tom. "Seems so young to put a kid on medicine."

"Wait until you hear the rest. The second week of school, this same teacher came back to see to the principal. 'I've two more children in my class who need to be on Ritalin.' This time the principal referred the teacher directly to the guidance counselor. The counselor dutifully called the parents."

"Does her husband work for a pharmaceutical company?" Vince wisecracked.

"The problem didn't end there. During the next two months, this teacher skipped the middlemen, the principal and guidance counselor. She made five calls directly to the parents to advise them their children needed to take Ritalin. When the principal inquired why she went directly to the parents, she responded, 'Why should I bother you or the guidance counselor? I know what my students need.'"

"The guidance counselor," said Lettie, "Told me by Christmas, practically every kid in this teacher's class was on Ritalin or Aderol. The teacher claimed they all needed medication for concentration, stress or behavior. The parents dutifully brought their kids to doctors who then prescribed the meds based on this teacher's recommendation."

"Did the principal step in?" wondered Vince.

"Apparently, the parents talked to each other and complained to the principal. He investigated and discovered that twenty-four of the twenty-five kids in this teacher's class were on medication, all on the recommendation of this unprofessional nut job."

"I can't believe a person like this was allowed in a classroom," said Mary.

"The principal looked into this teacher's personnel file and remembered he'd asked about her family during her interview. She had three children, no husband. The principal called the teacher into his office and asked, 'How is it you're so knowledgeable about Ritalin and the other drugs you recommend so freely?' This nut job admitted all three of her kids were on these drugs, and she was delighted with the results."

"It sure took the principal a long time to intervene," said Mary.

"The principal dug further," said Lettie. "And asked her how she came to our school district. "

"Oh, Lou Marinara is a friend of mine. He called Superintendent Pinzon and told him he wanted a job for me. First grade isn't my specialty, but it's all that was available."

"What is your specialty, Mrs. Gibbs?" She replied, 'Gym.'"

"The principal quickly ended the interview. The guidance counselor told me the principal was afraid of Mr. Marinara, so he ignored the whole thing, and at the end of the year he told the superintendent to transfer her."

"Where did she go?" asked Ted.

"She went to some other unsuspecting principal who'll have the same problem with her. She'll have a job somewhere in the district as long as she has Marinara in her corner."

"Is this true Rocco?" asked Mary.

Reluctantly, the superintendent shook his head yes.

CHAPTER 21

THE MEETING ENDED LATE, AND TED WAS IN SUCH A RUSH TO leave, he forgot his brand new scarf on the chair in the school board office. He was annoyed he'd agreed to keep those double-dipping retired friends of Lou on the districts' payroll for so long. He was halfway home when he realized his loss.

The scarf was a Christmas gift from Martha. He enjoyed the soft cashmere fabric around his neck. Ted owned few things which gave him as much pleasure as that scarf.

Ted dreaded the ride back to the school board office. "I'm tired, but I'm not taking any chances some SOB will find it and take it." Previously, Ted wore the rough woolen scarf his mother had made for him fifteen years ago. "The damn thing never wears out." It now hung in his bedroom closet, and that's where it would stay. "I'm never putting that scouring pad around my neck again," Ted swore as he made a U-turn.

By the time Ted returned to the school, most lights in the building were off. Luckily, the custodian hadn't locked the front door. Ted hurried down the dimly lit first-floor corridor and saw the school board office was dark. He remembered the light switch was on the wall to the right when you entered the room. He'd see if the door was locked, and was relieved when he turned the doorknob, and the door opened.

Ted flipped on the lights, the ones with the bulbs that take a few seconds to go on. When the lights illuminated the room, Ted jumped. Two naked people, a man, and a woman hopped off the conference table and headed for the superintendent's bathroom right off the board office.

Ted saw his cashmere scarf on the floor. He scurried over to pick it up and ran out of the office. Ted didn't know the identity of the woman, but the identity of the other reveler was Vince Miller, and that's what Ted Kowalski reported to his fellow board members as they sat around the new conference table discussing a possible sexual harassment suit.

"Vince, you should pay for this brand new table," said Mary. "You ruined it, and you should pay for it," repeated Mary, enjoying every minute of Vince Miller's discomfort.

"Theoretically, he didn't ruin the table, Mary," interjected Lou.

"Maybe to you Lou, but I hear your boy here sprayed his Pledge all over the table."

"Vince, are you going to tell us?" asked Lettie, "You were just helping the cleaning lady polish the conference table, and instead of using a chamois cloth, you used your butt."

Lou banged his gavel at Lettie, and she responded, "Lou, you're as disgusting as he is."

Vince Miller sat slumped in his chair, red-faced and embarrassed beyond belief.

Mary turned her attention back to Vince. "Since your arrival on the scene last year, you've pulled more than a few capers with the ladies of this school district, but you went too far this time. Do you realize how much this might cost the district? For months, the notoriety alone will divert our attention away from the reasons why we're on this school board."

"What about me?" Ted said, "My heart rate doubled since I walked into this room a week ago. My cardiologist put me on beta blockers to slow my heart down. I should sue. I saw this coming. For over a month, Clara and Vince have been eyeing each other from a distance."

"Well, Ted, the distance became a lot closer," said Mary."

"Now," said Father, "We have to decide what we'll do about this lady."

"I'm not voting to give that lady a dime," said Ted. "You're all crazy. Vince should settle this by himself and not involve the board."

"Father, are we liable for anything?" asked Tom.

"Clara is an employee of the district. Technically, the school board is her supervisor. Since Mr. Miller is on the board, he is her boss. Off the top of my head, I see a sexual harassment suit for starters."

Vince sat silently in his chair.

Lou broke in, "We have some other items on the agenda to talk about before we adjourn. Let's talk to the lawyers from the insurance company. For now, let's table it."

"Table it?" thought Tom. "Did he say table it? What an ass," thought Tom disgustedly.

§

Theresa Marinara turned to her mother, Angie, and said, "Mom, thanks for finding my birth certificate. My flight's at seven in the morning. I want to leave by five at the latest. I'm swinging by Jeremy's to pick him up so we can go to the airport together." Angie had to admit she was happy that Theresa was getting away for a few days. Lou's screaming every day about Jeremy was driving everyone crazy.

Theresa needed her birth certificate. Angie kept copies of her daughter's document somewhere in the attic, but it would take hours to rummage through all the crap up there to find it. Angie remembered her husband kept a folder for each member of the family at the office. Lou wanted to be sure there was one place everyone could go when they needed important papers instead of frantically searching all over the house.

Angie called upstairs to Theresa "I'll be back in a second I have to run up to the store."

"All the stores are closed."

"Don't worry; I'll find one open."

Angie threw on her coat and grabbed her bag. The ride to the office was fifteen minutes at rush hour, but there was no traffic at ten o'clock at night. She pulled right up in front of the office. The lights were on.

"Good," she thought. "I wasn't looking forward to going into a dark office at this time of night."

As she put her hand on the doorknob it hit Angie, Lou was at a retirement dinner, and the staff leaves at five, sometimes six o'clock. Apprehensive to go in by herself, the fact there was never a burglary here in the thirty years, and Lou owned the building encouraged her.

Angie put the key in the front door of the office and found it was unlocked. "Strange," she thought. Angie entered the front office. She walked further into the reception area and heard someone talking in the back, near the copy machine. She tiptoed further into the office, and she recognized the voices. Angie strained her ears to hear. She moved almost to the entrance of the copy room and stopped. Lou was talking softly to Pena. Angie's heart beat fast but relieved the voices were ones she knew.

Before Angie entered the copy room, she heard Pena say, "Angie will find out about us unless we cool it for a while."

"Pena, I don't want to cool anything. We did it under her nose for twenty-five years, and she never suspected. Why is she all of a sudden going to find out anything?"

"But Lou, I have a feeling since I'm back from Florida. Angie has something on her mind when I talk to her. I feel she's hesitant to speak with me on anything personal. I don't know what it is, but I feel she's suspicious?"

"No, if Angie did hear something, she's not one to hold anything back. That's why she's so easy to read."

"Why do I get this feeling something is wrong?"

"I know what's bothering her, but you can't tell anyone."

"Do I ever tell anything we talk about to anyone else?"

"Okay, what's wrong is Theresa's boyfriend. He's black. All Angie can think of is Theresa is with a *mulignan*. You know how prejudice she is."

Angie silently turned around and left the office. On the way home, she almost killed herself and another driver. Angie's eyes swelled with tears until they ran down her cheeks. She pulled over to the side of the road and cried for ten minutes. She reached into the glove compartment and took out a small box of tissues. She whipped her eyes dry, blew her nose and thankfully drove home without an accident. When Angie walked in the front door, Theresa was sitting on the couch.

"Was the store open?"

Theresa saw her mother's eyes were beet red. Theresa yelled hysterically. "What's the matter? Mom, what happened? Were you in an accident? Are you alright?"

Angie went over to the sofa and sat next to her daughter. Theresa waited for her mother to say something. Finally, Angie said, "I went to your father's office to find your birth certificate. I'd forgotten all about having to get it until you thanked me. When I arrived at the office, the lights were on, and the door was unlocked. I heard voices in the back. Pena and your father were having a serious discussion. It became apparent right away they were having an affair, and your father admitted it has gone on for the last twenty-five years. "

"That's why he didn't object to Pena coming back from Florida. I'm a fool. I helped her come back. Mom, I'm so sorry I helped her. Please forgive me."

"He told Pena I was out of control over your boyfriend. Me! As if he wasn't against Jeremy? My sin was going along with your father. I certainly wasn't crazy over you going out with a black boy, but I saw right off the bat he was a nice person. I'm a product of my age and upbringing. From the time I was born my parents taught me whites don't marry blacks. As I became older and worked with different people, I realized if a person has the same values as you, differences don't amount to that much. Living with your father, I didn't dare say anything. Your father is a violent man, and I'm afraid of him."

Theresa hugged her mother as she sobbed on her daughter's shoulder.

"Mom, what should we do?"

"First, we'll find either your birth certificate or your passport, and you'll go on your little vacation."

"I can't leave you here."

"Listen, Theresa. Your father doesn't know I overheard him and Pena tonight, so, he and I won't be having any scenes. I plan to make believe everything is alright. By the time you return, I'll have a plan. But it's a blessing you won't be here for the next few days. I don't know if I could hide my feelings if you were around looking at me."

"But mom…"

"Go upstairs and finish packing. I'm going up to the attic, and I'm not coming down without one of the proofs you were born."

Angie wasn't up in the attic fifteen minutes when she called down to Theresa, "I found both your passport and your birth certificate. Come up here I found some other things I want you to help me figure out."

Theresa climbed up to the attic. Angie heard a car and looked out the crescent-shaped window. "Your father just pulled up. We better go downstairs. As you know, your father wants no one up here without him. I rarely needed anything up here so I never thought about why he didn't want me up here. Now I know why."

"Let's hurry down before he sees us."

"Make sure you don't show any sign of what happened tonight," said Angie.

"I'm sure I can do it, but I worry about you."

"Don't worry. I can be quite an actress when I want," said Angie

Both women heard, "I'm home. Where is everybody?"

When Angie reached the second-floor landing she called out, "We're upstairs. I'm helping Theresa pack." Angie winked at her daughter. Theresa knew her mother would be fine while she was gone.

§

The superintendent was on the phone with Eddie Fisher when Mrs. McMurray called. The superintendent quickly hung up and took Mary's call. "Mrs. McMurray, it's good to hear from you. How can I help you?"

"Rocco, when I ran for the school board I promised I would visit all our district schools. I want to go around touring as many schools as possible. I need your help."

"Of course, you'll have all the help you need. Is there a particular school you want to begin with?'

"Yes, I want to start at the most northern tier school and work my way down through the southern tier."

"What about the Rhododendron Middle School?"

"Fine."

"When do you want to start?"

"I'm free the day after tomorrow. How is your schedule?"

"Let me look. I have my appointment book right here. The day after tomorrow is perfect. I have some things in the morning, but I'll push them to the afternoon. Come to my office, and I'll drive."

"No, I can meet you outside the school at about nine-thirty."

"See you then."

Two days later, Rocco waited on the school steps of the Rhododendron Middle School until Mary arrived. He had arranged with the principal to prepare for a visit from Mary McMurray.

Mary pulled up in front of the school just missing the superintendent's Buick. Rocco held his breath until Mrs. McMurray turned off the ignition and exited her car. As they walked in the front door, Mary said, "I have heard mixed reviews about the district's sex education curriculum during the past week."

Superintendent Pinzon asked, "More good reviews than bad I hope?"

"I was being kind. I heard only bad. I'd like to see for myself, and I think I would like to go into the classroom with just an assistant principal. If the teacher sees you, the teacher will get nervous."

"Fine. I can tour the school with the principal while you are in the classroom."

Mary and the assistant principal quietly slipped into the seventh-grade classroom of Hattie Rosenberg. Mrs. Rosenberg, a seventy-one-year-old woman with long grey hair and forty pounds overweight, was seated at a large desk in front of the room. On top of the desk sat a cucumber and a latex condom.

Mary took a seat in the back of the classroom, extracted a pen and pad from her large purse and listened intently to the sex education lesson already in progress. Mrs. Rosenberg fidgeted with the large vegetable and the rather small latex condom. Her continuous narration of how students should use a condom, voiced in a matter-fact-of-fact tone, emphasized the importance of a good lubricant."

Mary watched with concern as Hattie opened her desk drawer and pulled out a tube of cream. The teacher squeezed a generous amount into her left hand while holding the cucumber firmly in her right hand.

Mary and the assistant principal's eyes popped as Hattie doused the vegetable with lubricating cream, spreading the cream all over the veggie. Satisfied with her lube job, Hattie continued her efforts to fit her two props together.

The sight of Mrs. Rosenberg creaming the cucumber started the seventh graders giggling.

Mary's concern turned to horror. The nine-inch cucumber slipped out of Hattie's hand, flew into the air, and landed on the floor next to a student in the front row. Giggling turned to laughter as Hattie ran to retrieve her vegetable. Hattie slipped on the greasy cucumber lubricant and fell to the floor.

The seventh-grade students howled at the sight of Mrs. Rosenberg diving across the floor trying to recover her prop and slipping on the yellow linoleum floor. Each student turned into an instant comedian, cracking jokes.

Within seconds mayhem erupted. Poor Hattie picked herself up and returned to her desk, trying desperately to continue the lesson. Mercifully, the bell rang signaling the end of class.

The assistant principal ushered Mary into the corridor. Before the assistant principal opened his mouth, Mary warned, "Don't say a word," and hurried to her car. She made it in time before a bout of uncontrollable, hysterical laughter hit. Mary roared, "I wish Mark were here. What a hoot!"

§

The following week, Frank Fontaine, Bunny Krouse's new love, stood by his school's main entrance and greeted parents and school board members. The lobby of the high school sparkled with highly polished waxed floors. The bright white walls smelled of fresh paint.

When Mary walked in the door, Frank headed over to greet her. "Good to see you, Mrs. McMurray."

"Hi Frank, you're just the one I wanted to see. I have something I hope you can explain.

"Glad to Mrs. McMurray, if I can."

"You heard about my visit to the junior high last week.

"Everyone has."

"Between you and me, it was one of the funniest things I have ever seen."

"Everyone is talking about it. I'm surprised it's not on YouTube."

"After I laughed till my body hurt, I thought, "How in the world did this old woman wind up in a classroom with thirty-seventh graders, a cucumber in one hand and a prophylactic in the other."

"I can answer that for you."

"Teachers who teach sex education fall into two categories: Those who are old and should retire and those who very young and inexperienced."

"I can see an older teacher doing it because of knowledge and experience, and a young one because they have the real-time experience to share."

"I wish it were the reasoning, but it couldn't be further from the truth. The young teacher gets the assignment because no one with any seniority wants to teach sex education. The kids laugh either at you or with you. In either case, it's not a good assignment. The older teacher is given the class as a punishment for not retiring."

"That's why poor Mrs. Rosenberg landed in the job?"

"There's very little training. So, Mrs. Rosenberg, or someone like her, goes in with a cucumber and a condom and a recipe for disaster."

Frank Fontaine looked over at the entrance door. "Excuse me, Mrs. McMurray. I see something I don't like."

Fontaine flew across the lobby toward three guys with gang written all over them. Fontaine's assistants, all former college linebackers, followed right behind him. The crowd moved toward the auditorium and blocked Mary's view. When she looked again, the principal and the hoods were gone.

The buzzer went off for the start of the meeting. Mary hurried into the auditorium and took her seat on the stage.

§

After the meeting, Tom and Mary walked to their cars. Mary said, 'Tom, you might try visiting a classroom or two to see what's happening. You know about my little visit to the junior high school."

Tom said, "Quite an experience you had," and laughed.

"It's not funny. We have to address the sex education curriculum. If we're serious about the subject, then we have to give adequate funding to the schools for training in such a delicate area."

"I had planned to visit my local elementary school last week, but a bunch of things came up. I'll call Pinzon and tell him to contact the principal and set up a time for me to observe."

"You'll know a lot more than the rest when you go. You should sit on the district's curriculum committee."

§

Tom's mother dropped him off at the Rockingham Elementary School on her way to work. Alice had to clock into work before nine-thirty. So, Tom stood outside the elementary school by himself at nine o'clock in the morning.

The misty air spraying his face was uncomfortable. The realization he was a young man standing in front of a kindergarten through fifth-grade school in a raincoat, even if it was from Brooks Brothers, made him feel creepy especially after a mother arriving late with her first-grade child gave him a look. "I better go in, or someone's going to call the police."

Tom walked quickly up the ten steps to the front entrance of the school. As soon as he stepped into the vestibule, a guard stopped him. "Good morning. Who are you here to see?"

"I have an appointment with Assistant Principal Benson. My name is Tom Foster from the school board."

"Oh, Mr. Foster, Mr. Benson told me to expect you. Please sign your name in this book."

"I'm forty-five minutes early. Is there a place I could sit and wait for Mr. Benson? I don't want to interrupt him ahead of time. I'm sure he's very busy with morning routines."

"He certainly is. We had the state standardized tests the past two days, and Mr. Benson is the supervisor in charge of testing."

Tom told the guard about his mother dropping him off so early, but realized that was too much information.

"I think it'll be alright if you go sit in the teacher's room. It's usually empty at this time of the morning. It's the third door on the left." The guard pointed Tom in the right direction.

"Thanks a lot," said Tom.

"I'll call you when it's time," said the guard. "Again, welcome Mr. Foster from the school board."

Tom walked seventy-five feet down the corridor and counted, "Door one, door two, and door three." Tom missed the first small utility door on his left.

The doorknob turned easily, and the door opened widely. The lights were off, and no one was in the room. A more extensive look around the room revealed desks and chairs piled along the perimeter. Tom had entered an unused classroom. Tom had heard this school had a declining enrollment with some empty rooms.

Tom flipped on the light. A large hairy rat crossed the room four feet in front of him. The rat ran into the wall, dazed, the rat turned and headed in Tom's direction. Tom quickly exited the room, his heart pounding, his stomach churning.

When Tom stepped back into the hallway, the guard called to him. Tom couldn't make out what the guard said so he walked closer. The guard yelled, "You were on the wrong side of the hallway. I hope I told you the right side. Tom responded, "You told me the left side. I'll give it another try. Thanks."

Tom went down the hallway feeling out of place. His eyes counted three doors, one with a storage sign on it. "Here, we go again. Is it three doors including the storage room?" Tom decided, "I'm going one more door."

Foster entered the fourth room startling a man and two women. The three people sat around a single desk with number two pencils in their hands; erasers pointed at the test grids before them.

The two young women jumped up. The older man gathered the papers and hurriedly put them in the top drawer of the desk.

"I'm very sorry to interrupt you, but the guard told me I could wait for Mr. Benson in the teachers' room."

"Mr. Foster, welcome to Rockingham Elementary School. I'm Mr. Benson. The guard should have told me you were here."

"It's not his fault. I told him not to call you. I'm early."

The two young and attractive teachers stood nervously next to the assistant principal not knowing what to do. Mr. Benson introduced the girls as two first-year teachers.

"If you can give me a minute, I'll be ready to take you around our school. In the meantime, Amber would you bring Mr. Foster to the teachers' lounge and get him a cup of coffee. We'll meet in my office in ten minutes. And Amber, please take good care of Mr. Foster."

The taller, slimmer teacher immediately relaxed, more comfortable in her role of caretaker than as school teacher. "If you follow me, Mr. Foster, I'll show you the way."

Tom thought sarcastically, "I bet you will." He watched Amber walk ahead, her tight dress clinging to her shapely butt.

After Tom's new babysitter poured him coffee, she brought him to Mr. Benson's office on the second floor. As Tom followed Amber up the stairs, he wished the assistant principal's office was on the sixth floor.

When Mr. Benson saw Tom approaching his office, he got up from his desk and ran to greet him. Benson's office door was wide open. Every inch of the office was visible. Tom thought it was possibly the assistant principal's way of saying, "Look, I have nothing to hide."

"Again, Mr. Foster, welcome to Rockingham Elementary."

"Thank you for having me, Mr. Benson. I've been looking forward to this visit."

"You're the board member representative to our school, are you not?"

"Yes, the chairman of the school board usually assigns a board member to several schools close to their home, and another eight scattered around the district."

"Today I've arranged for you to visit a fifth-grade classroom. I told the teacher to expect us and to prepare a lesson. He wants to teach a lesson in 'Young People's Survival Guide for Everyday Life.' After the lesson, I asked Amber to give you a thorough tour of every nook and cranny of the school."

"Great."

"The classroom is right here on the first floor. The teacher's name is Mr. Samuels."

The teacher looked up from his desk and smiled and Tom and the principal entered the room and took a seat. Mr. Samuels called the class to order and began his lesson.

Mr. Samuels asked the class, "I'd like to ask a question. How many of you live on a street without sidewalks?" About half the room raised their hands. "How many of you have ever ridden your bike at night on the side of the road?" Every hand in the room went up.

"What would you think if I told you you're crazy walking in the street at night?" One student called out, "I'd say you were crazy for saying that." Everyone laughed, including the teacher.

"Thanks, James. How many of you agree with James?" Everyone raised their hands.

"What would you say if I said you're crazy if you ride your bike either in the middle of the road or on the side of the road at night, and probably even in the day?"

Robin called out, "We'd think you're crazy." Everyone laughed, again. Obviously, Mr. Samuel had developed a good rapport with the students in his class.

"What if I told you that a million people are hit by a car while walking or riding their bikes by the side of the road each year in the United States?"

The class made no response, but their expressions showed surprise. Pete, a student in the back of the room, raised his hand, "Are you saying we shouldn't ride our bikes except on the sidewalk."

Another student in a center seat asked, "Suppose we don't have sidewalks?"

Another said, "I go bike riding with my father on Saturday mornings, and we ride in the road. Should I tell my father I'm not going with him anymore?"

The assistant principal leaned over to Tom. "I'm getting a lot of complaint calls tomorrow."

Tom responded, "I bet you will."

The students were engaged in the lesson, and a spirited dialogue continued until the end of the period.

The teacher wrapped up the lesson with, "I'm not telling you anything except the facts. I'm not saying don't ride your bike in the street. I'm saying you should think about where you walk and where you ride your bikes. I'm presenting you with questions you'll answer yourself with the information I've given you. When you go home and speak to your parents, remember to tell them I'm not recommending either path to take. I'm giving you information which will help you survive as a young person in today's world."

"What a lesson, thought-provoking, interesting," said Tom softly. "The teacher encouraged the students to become involved and to think critically."

"And they sure did. I picked Mr. Samuels because he's one of our best teachers. Anything he teaches, he teaches well."

The assistant principal reminded Tom that Amber would be down in a few minutes to give him the complete tour of the building. "If you'll wait here, I'll go get her."

Tom wasn't sure if Benson winked at him as he took off to get Amber.

As soon as the assistant principal turned the hall corner, Tom hurried past the guard. "Please," said Tom, "Tell Mr. Benson, I had to leave. I'll see him again."

Tom wanted to call Mary with a full report of his visit. He wanted to know if she knew what Amber, Benson and the other girl were doing with the erasers when he walked in on them.

Tom also didn't want to forget to tell her about the terrific teacher he observed. Both he and Mary wanted to find the bright lights in the district and expand their numbers in more schools during their term on the board.

CHAPTER 22

AFTER EACH MEETING, MARY SWORE SHE WOULD STEAL LOU Marinara's annoying gavel, but by the time each meeting ended all she and the others could think of was getting the hell out of the district office.

After the banging stopped, Mary didn't wait for recognition from the Chair and said, "Rocco, I have meant to ask you about this Rubber Room I hear about on TV? Does it exist?"

"Yes, Mary, it does. It's a room where we assign individuals we remove from a school. Usually, they're waiting for a hearing on a complaint made about them by their school principal. Yes, indeed, Rubber Rooms do exist."

"Do we have one in our district, and if so, where is it located?"

"We do have one, and it's located right here in this building."

"How appropriate," laughed Lettie, "That it's in the same building as we're in."

"Is it a coincidence?" joked Father.

"So, if Lettie becomes disruptive at one of our meetings, we can send her there?" asked Mary innocently.

Rocco ignored Mary's comment.

Mary continued, "I'm going to visit the Rubber Room and speak to some of its denizens."

The superintendent reluctantly addressed Mary's request, but Lou interrupted. "Mary, you don't understand. You haven't been around long enough to understand the no-nos in this business."

Tom and the board members waited for Mary's reaction to Lou's dripping, patronizing statement.

Lettie had a big smile on her face. Lettie was the kid in the school who stood up on the lunch table and chanted "FIGHT, FIGHT" when any cafeteria disturbance occurred.

Vince and Father stared down at the tabletop.

But, Mary was silent. Lou continued imagining he had obtained Mary's attention.

The rest of the board saw Mary as a leopard quietly waiting to attack her prey.

"The union in this district," continued Lou, "Would be upset if you visited the Rubber Room, and God forbid you engaged any of its inhabitants in conversation."

Still, there was nothing from Mary.

"Mrs. McMurray, don't go visiting these people. You might get hurt."

Tension ate at everyone's stomach. The smile on Lettie's face vanished. Each knew the explosion was seconds away. Still, Mary showed an immutable face, a better poker player never lived.

Embolden by Mary's silence, Lou continued with a haughty, "Mrs. Mc Murray, I must insist that you promise to stay away from the Rubber Room."

Everyone at the table imagined Mary's response to Lou.

Lettie almost heard Mary answering Lou's 'You don't understand,' comment.

Ted waited to hear what Mary had to say about 'You haven't been around.'

Vince and Father cringed at the fireball Mary would throw in response to Lou's, 'I must insist you promise to stay away...'

But all Mary ordered was, "Make the arrangements, Rocco. I'm going to see this Rubber Room. If Marinara here doesn't want me to go see the place, there must be plenty to see."

By this time Lou realized Mrs. McMurray didn't plan to take his crap, he was happy her response was as measured as it was.

Mary stood up and said, "This meeting is over."

The board members did not saunter from the room, they ran. No one wanted to engage in small talk.

Lou and the superintendent sat at the table stunned that Mary ended the meeting.

Lou said, "She can't end the meeting like that."

The superintendent said, "Right Lou, but she just did."

§

Out in the parking lot, which was becoming the second home of the school board, Mary said to Tom and Father, "That was quite something."

Tom responded, "Before I forget, I want to tell you both about my visit to the Rockingham Elementary School. I called you when I left, but you weren't home, and then I haven't had a chance…"

"Tom, I don't mean to be rude, but spit it out. I have to stop by to see a parishioner before I go home."

"Sorry, Father. Just give me a second."

Tom told Mary and Father Grant about his visit to the Rockingham School and the incident of the two teachers and the assistant principal huddled around a table intensely working on test grids with erasers in their hands."

Mary looked at Father Grant and said, "Any idea, Father. Nothing comes to my mind."

Mary and Tom could see Father was thinking of something.

"Okay, Father now it's your turn to spit it out."

"There is always talk about how the principals change the answers on the state reading and math tests before they send them to Albany, but no one has ever come up with any proof."

"Yes, and no one has ever proven Lou wears a cheap toupee, but our eyes tell us he caught it in a rat trap under the sink."

"Got to go," said Father.

'Speak tomorrow, Tom," said Mary heading for home thinking only of her tight girdle.

§

Bright and early the morning after the Rubber Room discussion, Mary McMurray called the school board office and instructed Jemma about a research project she wanted to be done. "I want the names of the people residing with full pay in the district's Rubber Room, and the reasons the district placed them there, and I want it ASAP."

"Mrs. McMurray, I don't know when I can have that information to you. I'm busy."

"Doing Lou Mariana's work?" shot back Mary. "Listen, Jemma. Drop his crap and have the information for me by this afternoon." Mary slammed the phone down.

Jemma immediately called Lou and related Mary's request. "Lou, she wasn't at all pleasant."

"Tell me about it. Get the information McMurray wants and make sure you give it to her by this afternoon, and Jemma, don't give her any attitude. I'll handle her."

"Don't worry; I won't. That lady isn't a nice person."

Lou hung up, "Talk about the kettle calling the pot black."

§

Jemma had the information Mary requested by four o'clock that afternoon. Mary came to the board office and reviewed the notes Jemma gave her. Jemma's research was enlightening.

The next morning Mary entered the Rubber Room clutching her handbag tighter than usual. She was taking no chances with this group.

The room was the size of a classroom. Large windows allowed for plenty of light, even on a cloudy day like today. When Tulia, assistant Rubber Room director of security, saw Mrs. McMurray close the door, she stopped filling out forms and walked over to greet her.

Tulia had explicit instructions to handle this board member with kid gloves. "Make sure you stay with her at all times," said Phil Turner. He and his lapdog, Eddie Fisher, were in charge of problem teachers.

The two introduced themselves quietly not to disturb six people, two women and four men sitting at desk corrals reading books, watching videos and writing letters. Mary remembered from her notes these six individuals were awaiting disciplinary hearings for disobeying an order of a supervisor, for speaking to a supervisor in a manner considered unprofessional, for inappropriate fraternizing with a student outside the school, or for hitting a supervisor or fellow teacher.

Although Mary had carefully read the complaints made by the principals, her task now was to put faces with the accused. Two of the complaints emphasized the volatility of one man and one woman. Mary didn't scare easily, but she was no fool either. Her plan included a great deal of caution, at least initially.

Tulia politely ushered Mary into a small conference room in the rear of the large classroom.

"Mrs. McMurray, if you have any questions, I'm here to answer them as best I can."

"Thanks, I need your help in identifying the individuals. I received some information on each one. Now, I need to know who is who."

"No problem." Tulia discreetly pointed out each person.

"I want to speak to them.

"Separately, or as a group?"

"Individually and I want you to introduce me, and I can take it from there."

Tulia looked befuddled. She didn't know what this old lady meant by, "I'll take it from there." Tulia's instructions from Phil Turner did not include what to do if Mrs. McMurray requested to speak with the six teachers.

An alarm rang. "That's an emergency signal for an intruder in the building," said Tulia. "All security personnel must respond. Mrs. McMurray, please stay in this conference room."

"Do the six remain here?"

"They stay, but please don't engage them in any conversation until I return. I have to leave now." With that, Tulia hurried out the door.

Like a bat out of hell, Mary headed for the young teacher in the corral closest to the conference room. Mary pulled a chair up to the corral and introduced herself to Genevieve Gallion, the girl accused of insubordination. Mary had read the report. Genevieve was a twenty-three-year-old teacher at the Cosgrove Junior High School in the center of the district.

"Hello, my name is Mary McMurray. Can you spare a minute to talk?"

The young woman stared at Mary not knowing how to respond. Mary quickly followed up with, "I came here today to find out your side of the story. I'm on the school board, and I'm interested in all the people working for our district."

The young girl continued to stare and say nothing. Mary continued, "I read the complaint against you. Would you mind if I asked you some questions?"

Although Genevieve did not know what to expect, she said, "Okay."

Through the classroom window, Mary saw Tula returning from her emergency. Mary whispered, "Can I call you at home?"

"Yes."

"Write your cell on this sheet of paper, I'll call you tonight."

When Tulia saw Mary speaking to Genevieve, she quickened her pace. "Sorry for my abrupt departure, but when the alarm goes off, all security personnel better move or else." Tulia wanted to say to the old lady, "I thought I asked you not to speak to anyone," but she thought better of it. She is sure as shit didn't want this old lady after her.

Mary thanked Tulia, "I have to leave for another appointment, but I'll be back soon. Thanks for your time. I won't forget to tell the superintendent how helpful you have been."

"Thank you, Mrs. McMurray; it's a pleasure meeting you. I have heard so much about you."

"I'll bet you have."

As Mary passed Genevieve's corral, she leaned in and took the young woman's number. "I'll call you around six." Mary waved to Tulia as she closed the Rubber Room door.

§

For the next few days after Theresa and Jeremy took off for their vacation, Angie played the role of content and obedient housewife. She cooked Lou's favorite dishes, stroked his ego and didn't give him the slightest inkling she would cut his throat when she got the chance.

The third night Theresa was away, Lou asked, "When does Theresa come home?"

"She'll be back the day after tomorrow.

"I forgot. Who did Theresa go away with again?"

"She went with two of her college friends." Angie was dying to tell him, "She went away with the black boy you think I'm so hysterical about, you son of a bitch."

The last few days when Lou left the house, Angie crept up to the attic and read Lou's papers. She made extensive notes on his business activities for the past twenty-five years. Angie didn't know her husband was involved in illegal activities. She knew Lou skirted the law more than she would like, but the number of schemes, the paybacks, and the people he associated with who caused both physical and psychological pain were far more than she ever imagined.

On her last trip to the attic she saw something about Jeremy, but Lou came home unexpectedly for lunch and worked at home for the afternoon. Late in the afternoon, her husband got a call, and he hurried back to the office. As soon as her husband turned the corner, Angie climbed to the attic. She was halfway up the steep attic stairs when she heard the doorbell ring. "Lou probably forgot his keys." She answered the door. Standing in front of her was Pena.

Angie, ever the consummate actress, greeted her sister-in-law with a peck on the cheek and a big hug. "What a nice surprise, Pena. Come in and have a cup of espresso and a biscotti."

Angie saw Pena was taken back by such a welcome. "I can't stay. I have to go back to the office. I stopped by with your scarf. I found it in the office a few days ago, and I have meant to bring it over. You must have dropped it when you were in last week."

Angie tried with all her strength to keep her cool. Pena didn't seem to be pulling anything and she didn't appear to suspect Angie dropped the scarf the night she caught Pena and Lou at the office.

Pena handed Angie the scarf and turned to leave. Angie reached for her arm to pull her closer to say good-bye. Pena didn't realize Angie's intention and went down a step. When Pena grasped Angie's intention was to hug her again, it was too late, the awkwardness of the moment overshadowed the goodbye. Angie hoped this wouldn't make Pena suspicious.

Angie waved to her sister-in-law as she pulled away, then hurried back to the attic. Angie didn't have time to dwell on Pena's visit. Jeremy's name was on the front of a folder. The folder read, 'Mulignan Kid.'

Angie slipped on the top step to the attic and hurt her knee on the unfinished, dirty wood. Blood appeared on her skin. Ordinarily, she'd go to the medicine chest and wash the scrape with peroxide and bandage the exposed skin fearing infection, but today she put her fear of infection out of her mind and continued her mission. Angie had a strong intuition the folder labeled 'Mulignan Kid' contained no recipe for eggplant.

The blood continued to drip down to the floor. Angie didn't care. "I have to find out what's in the folder before Lou gets home."

Angie found a small chair, sat on it and opened the folder. The first page gave a biography of Jeremy, date of birth, schools attended, parents' names, address and phone number. The next three pages were notes from telephone conversations with Eddie Fisher and some person Eddie found to help neutralize the mulignan. There were three money figures written throughout the notes, $10,000, $5,000 before, $5,000 after.

Angie's hands shook so hard the pages were hard to read. Frustrated, Angie placed the pages on her lap and they read much easier. She scribbled notes on a pad. The fourth page spelled out the answer: "Chop mulignan soon before the relationship goes further, EF to pass money to a friend by the 22nd."

Noise in the driveway alerted Angie that Lou was home. She put the papers back in the folder as neatly as her shaking hands permitted and climbed down the stairs. She made it to the bathroom before her husband called, "Anyone home?"

"I'm in the bathroom, dear. I fell and scraped my knee on the rug."

"Are you alright?"

"Yes, dear." Angie delivered an Academy Award-winning performance. She had all to do to keep from throwing up. The thought of the man she lived with much of her adult life hiring someone to kill a young boy, no matter what color he was, made her sick. Angie forced herself downstairs. She needed to keep up her pretense until Friday when her daughter and Jeremy flew back from the Bahamas.

§

Theresa had given her mother the name of the airline and the flight number of the plane she was returning on Friday night. Angie made sure Lou ordered no car for Theresa. She wanted to pick her daughter up at the airport. She had to warn Jeremy Lou had hired someone to kill him.

Lou's attic folder stated 'by Friday the 22nd,' and for all Angie knew, Lou was pretending not to know his daughter went to the Bahamas with Jeremy. Lou may have hired a killer to eliminate Jeremy right in the airport terminal, or on the way to the parking lot, or maybe on the ride home and do it right in front of Theresa to teach her a lesson.

Waiting frantically in the airport lounge, Angie had the urge to jump on a flight to Italy and leave her son of a bitch husband to do what he wanted with that slut, Pena, but she had far more important things to do before she even thought about leaving Lou Marinara.

Angie looked at the information board on the wall and saw Theresa's flight was on time, arriving in eleven minutes at Gate 12. She proceeded as far as security allowed and sat down to wait.

The minutes went by slowly. Angie busied herself by looking at the people waiting for loved ones to arrive. Her eye stopped at a middle-aged man with a red cap on his head. He stood about thirty feet from the entrance to Gate 12. His head bobbed from reading the newspaper to nervously looking everywhere. Angie inspected the guy up and down. Was this the killer or was her imagination getting the best of her?

The schedule board continued to indicate Theresa's flight was expected to arrive on time. By two minutes to arrival time, the crowd thickened, partially obstructing Angie view of the man wearing the red cap. Angie held her breath. Anyone in the crowd may have a loaded gun, a sharp knife, or a poisonous needle. There were no metal detectors to pass through to enter this part of the terminal. Anyone in the crowd could be the killer.

Theresa and Jeremy appeared out of nowhere. "We had a great time, mom, and thanks so much for picking us up."

"We could have grabbed a cab, Mrs. Marinara. But it's nice to have someone meet us."

"No, you couldn't have," said Angie.

Theresa and Jeremy looked at Angie, not catching her meaning.

"Come on. Let's go to the car quickly."

"Mom, we didn't eat on the plane. Can we buy a hamburger over there at Wendy's?"

Angie's response scared Theresa. "No, it's too dangerous. Let's go to the car."

On the ride from the airport, Angie broke the frightening news to Theresa and Jeremy.

"I can't believe the man I called my father for twenty-four years would even consider killing another person."

"Jeremy wouldn't be the first person your father either killed or had someone kill. "

Theresa's eyes filled with tears.

"I don't know what to say Mrs. Marinara. I can't thank you enough for tipping me off."

"You better call your father and tell him to meet you somewhere away from your house. I thought I saw a strange guy sitting at the gate just before you both came off the plane. I lost sight of him when the people came swarming off the plane."

Jeremy took his phone out and saw the battery was dead. Theresa handed him hers. As Jeremy dialed, he prayed his father would answer. He didn't want to leave the message, "Please, call back. Someone wants to kill me."

"Hello, Pop, glad you answered."

Theresa only heard her boyfriend's words but knew Reverend Thompson was worried. He gave Jeremy instructions to go to someone's house, Theresa couldn't tell who. "Thanks, Pop, I'll see you there."

Theresa waited for Jeremy to catch his breath. "Mrs. Marinara, can you drive me to 213 Hensley Drive over by the shopping center?"

"Of course, Jeremy, I'll put the address in my GPS. Who is on Hensley Drive?"

"Pastor Bright, my father's best friend. He'll meet us there. My father is calling him now to say we're on our way."

"I'll drop you off, then Theresa and I will go home. We have a lot to do. We have to make sure we don't let my husband destroy evidence before we get copies to bring to the authorities."

"My father didn't know I went away with your daughter. Please, drop me off at the end of the block, and I'll walk from there."

Theresa looked at Jeremy. "Jeremy I thought you told me your father knew."

"I lied. I'm sorry."

Angie said, "There's no sense getting into that now. You can save that for another day. For now, we have to keep Jeremy safe." The young couple looked gratefully at Angie Marinara.

§

After dropping Jeremy off, Angie drove to a coffee shop in the adjacent town. They sat in a comfortable booth, and Angie explained to her daughter about the four pages in the attic that explained the arrangements made by Lou to have Jeremy killed.

Over coffee, Angie detailed the other documents in the attic. Angie explained how many documents showed the lifetime of corruption her father had participated in since she was born.

"How do I look at my father after this?" asked Theresa.

"You have to convince him you don't suspect anything. If you don't, you put your boyfriend in even more danger. We need time to copy the papers in the attic and convince the police to arrest your father and the district attorney to prosecute him."

"Stop calling him my father. He isn't my father anymore."

"Fine, but don't let Lou Marinara know how you feel until this is over."

Mother and daughter finished their coffee in silence, each wondering how they would pull off the destruction of Lou Marinara. From that moment on, Lou Marinara wasn't husband or father to either.

§

On the way home from the coffee shop, Angie and Theresa decided it was too late to do anything more tonight. They were too exhausted to plan anything. They needed a good night's rest. "We'll develop a plan in the morning as soon as your father leaves for the office."

Thankfully, Lou was asleep when Angie and Theresa arrived home. They quickly went to their rooms and beds. Angie lay awake next to a man she now hated more than anyone alive. Theresa mercifully fell asleep when her head hit the pillow.

Both Theresa and her mother were up and dressed early the next morning. As soon as Lou pulled out of the driveway, Angie scrambled up to the attic. Her daughter followed right behind her. Angie found the folder labeled 'Mulignan Kid' and, for starters, told Theresa to go down to the den to copy the four most important pages.

Theresa hurried down the steep attic steps. On the last step, she fell and twisted her ankle. When she tried to get up the pain was too intense. "Mom," she cried, "I can't get up."

Carefully, Angie climbed down the stairs. Her knee still hurt from the scrape yesterday.

Angie helped her daughter into the bedroom and onto her bed.

The doorbell rang. Angie ran to the bedroom window. She looked down, and there was Pena.

"Shit, it's your Aunt Pena."

"Tell her I'm asleep. Tell her I'm exhausted from my trip."

Angie ran to the door and greeted her sister–in–law with, "What a nice surprise,"

"I hope I didn't wake anyone. I wanted to see how Theresa's trip was. She's my favorite niece as you know. I owe her a lot. I'm on my way to the office, and I know once I start work, I won't have a chance to call her."

"Pena, how nice of you to stop by, but Theresa's asleep. She was exhausted when I picked her up at the airport. I'm sure she'll sleep until noon."

"Then, I won't even come in. We might wake Theresa with our chattering. Tell her I stopped by and I'll give her a call tonight." Pena hugged Angie.

Angie waited until Pena pulled away before she went up to see her daughter.

"Where are the papers I had when I fell?"

Angie ran into the hall and saw the papers scattered on the floor. Three of the four pages lay on the landing. Angie panicked.

"Mom, did you find them?"

Angie whispered, "One's missing."

Theresa asked a million questions Angie couldn't answer. She saw the missing page down on the first floor. "I found it. The page must have blown downstairs when I opened the door for Pena."

Angie headed down the stairs, but her two-inch heel caught on the runner and she fell the next five steps. "I broke it."

Theresa heard her mother moan and knew she was hurt. She forced herself off the bed, surprised the pain had lessened since she laid down.

She limped to the top of the stairs and looked down at her mother. Theresa knew Angie had to go to the hospital.

Before Theresa spoke, Angie said, "Take the four pages and copy them now. Put the originals back in the folder upstairs and arrange them, so no one will realize they were touched."

"What about the copies?"

"Put them in your underwear drawer under your panties. Your father will never look there. Strange he'll do every disgusting thing under the sun, but he'd never go into an underwear drawer."

Theresa carefully descended the stairs to the first floor holding the wooden banister tightly. She picked up the paper off the floor and the other three from her mother's hand and limped into the den. It took minutes to copy the papers. The climb up the stairs was painful, but Theresa had to do it, and quickly. Her father could come home at any moment.

Theresa reached the second-floor landing out of breath. The much steeper flight of stairs to the third-floor attic would be painful, but it had to be done. Theresa pulled herself up by holding the railing, painfully lifting herself step by step. She made it to the top step and rested before standing up.

"Enough resting, I have to get downstairs and call 911 for my mother." She rummaged through the papers and found the folder with Jeremy's codename 'Mulignan Kid' on it. She slipped the four pages into the folder and neatly put it among the other documents.

On her way down from the attic she heard her mother moaning. Theresa went right to the house phone and called 911. The EMS arrived so quickly she barely had time to get down the stairs and open the door.

The medics put Angie on a stretcher. They were exiting the door when one of the female medics noticed Theresa's ankle was swollen twice the size of her other one.

The medic told her partner to bring in another stretcher. Mother and daughter barely fit in the ambulance together. On the way to the hospital, Angie whispered to Theresa, "Let me do the talking. You play dumb."

Theresa replied, "That won't be hard."

The male Medic asked, "Can you tell us what happened?"

Angie explained, "I tripped on the stairs coming down from my bedroom. My heel caught on the rug. I called for help, and my daughter came running and tumbled down on top of me. It would be hilarious if my leg didn't hurt so badly. Is the leg broken?"

"I'm not sure if the bone broke."

Theresa asked, "What about me?"

"I'm pretty sure it's only a sprain, but don't quote me."

When the ambulance arrived at the hospital, both mother and daughter answered no to the question, "Is there anyone you wish us to call?" Five hours later the hospital released Theresa with a sprain and some bruised muscles. An hour after, the hospital released Angie with a hairline fracture of the tibia.

When they were ready to leave, Theresa asked one nurse if she could use her cell to make a quick call. Jeremy was frantic when he answered. "I've been trying to get you all day."

Theresa explained what happened and Jeremey yelled into the phone. "I'll be right there." He hung up.

Forty-five minutes later Jeremy ran into the emergency room. He was beside himself. "What happened? How are you? Are you alright?"

"Calm down, Jeremy. Everything will be alright. Let's get out of here. I'll explain everything."

"Jeremy, you won't believe it," said Angie. "They're remaking one of the old Abbott and Costello movies, and the producers want your girlfriend and me to star."

Theresa laughed, "Poor Jeremy, he has no idea what's going on, except that I'm alright."

§

At six sharp, Mary dialed Genevieve, the girl from the Rubber Room. The teacher felt more comfortable talking on the phone. Genevieve told Mary her side of the story. "The principal of my school approached me after school. The school had emptied out an hour before, and I was decorating my classroom for Halloween."

Mary listened to the young teacher tell her story. She didn't rush or interrupt Genevieve. Mary tried to take notes, but her shorthand skills were old. Finally, Genevieve stopped, and Mary stepped in.

"So, he tried to compromise you by insinuating he'd help you by giving you the best class in the school next year, and in return, you would allow him liberties."

Mary McMurray knew she sounded like an old lady using the word liberties. Although Mary knew what went on in the world, she must work on using the descriptive words of the younger generation.

Mary said, "I'm offended by the name Rubber Room."

"To tell you the truth Mrs. McMurray, I don't even know what the name means."

Mary debated if she should explain to the young teacher that in crazy houses of years ago they put severely mentally ill people in rooms surrounded with rubber so patients wouldn't hurt themselves when they banged their heads on the walls. Mary decided she'd skip the explanation. The young girl was upset enough she was in this room.

"It doesn't matter Genevieve. But, let's go back to my original request. Can I ask you about the others in the room? What are they like? Are they nice? Are they dangerous? Do you speak with them?"

"I talk to one of the guys. I know him pretty well now. He's the tall one, late thirties, dark brown hair, sits next to me. His name is Eldred Moore."

"He's the good looking one. What's his story?"

"He spoke out too many times for his own good. He'd report things to the principal not knowing the principal was the one encouraging the situations."

Genevieve felt herself becoming more comfortable with this lady from the school board each moment they talked. For months more than a few people in the school district tried to trick her, but she had a hunch Mrs. McMurray was different.

"What school is Eldred Moore from?"

"Locust Swamp Junior High, it's in the southern tier of the district, a tough school, a lot goes on there."

"Genevieve, I'll do some investigating for you. I may be able to help you with some of your problems. Would you do a favor for me and ask Eldred if he'd mind if I called him?"

"Sure, Mrs. McMurray, I'll call you tomorrow with his number. And I can't thank you enough for your interest in me."

After speaking with Genevieve, Mary called Tom to make a date for him to join her on her next visit to the Rubber Room.

§

Mary dropped into the superintendent's office unannounced.

"Good to see you, Mary? What a nice surprise."

Ordinarily, Mary would have bristled at the 'what a nice surprise' comment, but Rocco, if nothing else, was a gentleman. He treated everyone, board member, parent, student, and underlings respectfully.

"I won't take up too much of your time, Rocco. I know you must have a million things to do." Mary heard herself saying what usually irritated her in others. "I want to speak to you about one of the teachers, Genevieve Gallion, assigned to the Rubber Room."

"I know her. What did you want to say?"

"I spoke to her for quite a while when I visited the Rubber Room."

Rocco had received a full oral report from the guard in the room about who Mrs. McMurray talked to and for how long. He knew Mary had talked to Genevieve but was unsure of the others.

"Rocco, I thought Ms. Gallion was a substantial individual, and maybe she's receiving a raw deal from her principal."

"Why do you think that?"

Mary explained she thought the principal was trying to remove Genevieve for reasons he isn't telling you." Mary was careful not to say too much more.

"Let me review her file so that I can speak to you more intelligently."

Mary wanted Rocco to cooperate. She had to give him a chance. He had his good qualities. She also knew he'd try and discover what Lou Marinara thought of this teacher and her principal. Pinzon didn't want to step on Lou's foot unnecessarily.

Mary didn't know that Pinzon would not share Mary's interest in Ms. Gallion with Lou. He wanted to court Mary's vote for his contract renewal next year.

"How about we speak in a few days? I have my committee meeting early next week. What if I come in early that day and we can meet before my meeting."

"Fine, Mary. That would be great."

"One more thing before I go. Think about this. If you see this girl has a good case, I want her taken out of the Rubber Room and assigned to one of the district offices. The Rubber Room is in the same building. You could say you have been looking into cost-cutting, and there's no reason not to put Ms. Gallion in a job she can do and save money at the same time."

Mary's request was a chance for him to score points with her. Mary and her posse were on the rise, and Lou Marinara was on the decline, but Rocco knew when dealing with old dogs like Marinara, you had to be careful. This dog might be dying, but he could bite hard even when he sees his end in sight."

"Mary, you know I value your input. You have gone out of your way to look into this, and I promise I won't disregard your opinion."

"Thanks, Rocco, I'll see you early next Tuesday."

Pinzon wanted to ask how Father and Tom Foster felt about Mary's idea, but he knew already. "Mrs. McMurray wouldn't have come in to speak with me unless she was sure of at least three members.

If Ms. Gallion's case came up for a vote, she could browbeat Ted, and maybe Lettie, into voting with her. Mary McMurray was always a force to be reckoned. Now, she was also a force to be feared."

§

The following Tuesday Mary returned to Superintendent Pinzon's office to see what he had to say about Genevieve Gallion. Mary walked past his secretary with a "Good afternoon, Claire." Pinzon was sitting at his desk and immediately rose to greet his visitor.

Mary came to the point after a few pleasantries. "Well, Rocco what will you do on the matter we discussed last week?"

"Mary, after I went through Ms. Gallion's file and reread the formal complaint filed by her principal, I came to the same conclusion as you. I also asked some of the teachers in her school what they thought. Ms. Gallion may well be the victim in this case. The problem is I don't control the complaint process. "

Pinzon saw Mary wasn't happy with his last sentence and he quickly added, "But I do control the management of the district staff, and that means I decide where individuals are assigned and to which offices."

A smile appeared on Mary Mc Murray's face.

Rocco continued, "I assigned Ms. Gallion to the district office. She begins next week."

"You're a professional, and I commended you for your decision to save the district money. All departments are short-handed. I hear the budget office has been complaining the most," said Mary.

Great idea, I'll put her there. Now Mrs. McMurray, is there anything else I can help you with?" said Rocco with a conspiratorial grin which Mary immediately returned.

§

A few days after Mary's telephone conversation with Genevieve Gallion, Tom arrived at Mary's house in the district at 1:00 p.m. for lunch and a work session. Lunch at Mary's house in the district was a lot different than going to her Manhattan apartment, no horse-drawn carriages, no hordes of tourists, no Central Park.

Mary opened the door on the third knock. Absent was the doorman, the deskman, and the elevator operator, but the feeling was the same, a warm smile and an affectionate embrace. The two had lunch, grilled cheese on delicious rye bread with slices of crisp bacon. No wine, caviar or filet mignon.

"The county announced this morning it had contracted a computer firm right here in the city to use a newly developed software program to monitor conflicts of interest in the county. Mitchell Rose, county executive, announced his determination to ferret out corruption at every level of county government." Mary Mc Murray put the newspaper down on the table. "Maybe they have a software program to keep track of Lou Mariana's dirty deals."

"Thanks to Jeremy, we know many of Lou's schemes. He hires every relative and friend whether or not the person can even spell the job title."

"Now he wants to give that disgusting politician the key to our Human Resources office. If Troy Burns and Lou Marinara think they will destroy our district with more incompetent SOB's, they're wrong. Lou's milk train has made its last stop in this district."

"How long have Marinara and Burns been partnering?"

"Not too long. The two know each other for a few years. Lou and Troy circled each other for a year deciding how much they could trust each other. They look at the district as a source of jobs."

"We can't ask Elliot Rush to help with monitoring all the positions coming up."

"He'll be on the phone in two seconds with Lou," said Mary. "We need one of ours in his office so they can tip us off."

"They're all Lou appointees."

"If that's the case, we have to put someone in his office either by hiring a new person or transferring someone from another office."

"It'll look fishy."

"What about someone in a nearby office, a clerical position. These people know what's going on, not just in their office, but throughout this whole place."

"Your friend, Genevieve, she was put in the budget office as part of the compromise you brokered to help her out of the Rubber Room."

"I'm sure she'd help. She's grateful for my assistance. Genevieve's a fine person. Rocco hasn't put her in the budget office yet. I'll call him and ask if he'd put her in Rush's department, then she can see firsthand what's what. It's a great idea, Tom. You're on the ball, young man."

"I learned from the master."

Mary smiled at her friend. Mary knew how lucky she was to have Tom working with her. Tom was like a son, and she knew Tom was there for her if she needed anything.

Tom came from a large family, so he naturally brought his dishes to the sink.

"Leave everything right where it is. I'll take care of it later."

Tom followed Mary into a small office off the hall. He sat in a comfortable orange upholstered wing chair. Mary sat opposite him behind a cherry wood desk. "I've asked Father Grant if he could join us by telephone this afternoon. He said he would be in his office all afternoon. I'll ring him, and the three of us can talk."

Mary dialed Father; he picked up on the second ring.

"Don't worry boys. I'll hold your hands through this, but now the first thing we have to do is figure out a way to get Ted or Lettie into our camp."

After the three board members discussed ideas on how to recruit Lettie and Ted, Father asked, "I meant to ask you what's the story with Troy Burns?"

"The story is a short one. Burns and Lou trade favors at the district's expense," said Mary.

"It's funny you mention Burns," said Tom. "My mother was in church last Wednesday. She doesn't usually go to church during the week, but she recognized him kneeling in a front pew praying. Last week wasn't the first time she saw him at church on a weekday. She sees him on Sundays and holydays."

"He's the one always sneaking out of Elliot Rush's office," replied Mary.

"To tell you the truth," continued Tom, "I was surprised to hear he even knew what a church was."

"That guy is bad," said Mary.

"Don't judge, unless you want to be judged," warned Father. "But with that advice, I say you'd be surprised who does and who doesn't attend church. I could tell you some dandy stories, but I won't say another thing."

"Mom said she thought he went to impress people to try and show how good he is, but she has changed her mind. He dresses so as not to bring any attention to himself. He uses a side door to enter the church and mom says he doesn't talk to anybody after church. He doesn't go around campaigning."

"Does he belong to any organizations at the church?" asked Father.

"I'm not sure. Mom says he's really serious. He puts his head down engrossed in prayer."

"We have some people in my church," said Father. "People you have read about in the paper. They're accused of stealing, taking bribes, everything under the sun. It is widely known they make money on the backs of suffering people. You see them on Sunday prancing up to the altar."

"But that doesn't seem to be Troy Burns. He avoids people. He goes to church during the week, wears clothes which aren't exactly a disguise, but his clothes bring no attention to him, older clothes, glasses, and a hat."

"Well, whatever he's up to, we'll have to address the rumor Lou and he swap favors for jobs and money."

"It's why we need someone we can trust in Elliot Rush's office."

Mary lowered her voice. "I'm going to ask the superintendent to put Genevieve Gallion in Rush's office.

"Won't Elliot suspect something?"

"No. Rush is desperate for help. He's been down one secretary for a few months, and he's way behind. Despite the budgetary constraints the district is under, Lou has been on his back to push the positions along, particularly the supervisory ones. We have to hire five assistant principals, four elementary school principals, two junior high principals and two high school principals. The acting principals have been in place for longer than the state law permits."

"I heard Rocco took another secretary out of his office last week," said Tom, "Because of an emergency in one of the schools. I guess Rush won't have time to figure out why the superintendent assigned Genevieve to his office. He'll be happy to get another pair of hands."

"Does Ms. Gallion know what to look for?"

"I'll prep her."

"I guess we're in business."

"Tom, here's a pad and pen. We have to be able to recognize the good guys from the monsters. Some of these people play havoc with the lives of so many unsuspecting people."

"Let's first start with the non-board members and work our way up to the seven of us on the board. Now, who is good and who is a piece of garbage?"

"Let's start with the parents. There's Bunny. She's good. Then there's Felicia Estes and Betty Kramer. They're bad. The PTA parents, some are good, and some are awful. There are the parents who got their jobs through Lou Marinara…"

"Enough of the non-board members, let's start with our esteemed colleagues

"Our initial criteria for bad must be board members who make money from their position on the board."

"I agree. Certainly, Father, you and I gain no money from this. That leaves Vince, Lettie, Lou, and Ted.

"For now, let's put Lettie on the good side. And by good, I don't mean she isn't a terrible person, all it means is she isn't a criminal."

"I lean toward putting Ted on the good side, but I'm not positive yet."

"I wouldn't trust Vince Miller as far as I could throw him and that isn't far. Vince's so greasy, he'd slip right out of my grip."

"This leaves Lou, put him on the bad side. He's into many things, some criminal, both in and out of the district. I believe he's also dangerous."

"Lou should be in jail."

"Before I hang up I want to tell you some good news. The superintendent grabbed me when I was at the district yesterday and told me he thinks he may have something for Mrs. Portnoy in a week or so. He heard a rumor one of the people in the budget department is retiring and handing in her papers next week."

"That's great. It comes just in time. That poor lady is getting it from all over. Bunny told me her boss is about a hundred and a dirty old man to boot. He stares at her bosom all day long. She is a good lady, but she is anything but a teeny bopper."

"Terrible," chimed both Tom and Father.

"Wait there's more. She works across town and the neighborhood is seedy. When she leaves work lately, some young thugs are hanging around the bus stop. A couple of weeks ago they started calling after her, 'Hey Jew lady, go back to your part of town. Bunny said each day these guys are becoming more aggressive."

"Those fucking bastards," said Tom. Then realizing who he was speaking with quickly apologized to Father and Mary.

"Don't worry Tom. You saved me from saying it, said Father. "Hopefully, the person in the budget department will leave soon and the superintendent can get Mrs. Portnoy into the district offices in a couple of weeks."

§

When Genevieve Gallion arrived in Rush's office, Eddie told him to keep an eye on her. Eddie wanted to know how she got the job. Elliot was so busy dealing with human resource problems between principals and teachers, principals and assistant principals, school aides and para-professionals, he didn't have the luxury of playing part-time private eye. Rush was just glad to have another set of hands to keep him from drowning.

Rush only saw a young girl who caught on quickly to work he needed her to do. Rush hadn't even had time to make a move on Ms. Gallion, and she'd been in his office for a few weeks.

Elliot only knew what Superintendent Pinzon told him. "Take good care of this young lady. I pulled her out of the Rubber Room. This morning her principal came into my office and confessed he was trying to put the make on her and she rebuffed him. This principal retaliated by claiming Genevieve was incompetent. This idiot principal just got religion, and now he wants to repent for his sins by admitting his grave errors in judgment. The problem is the jerk's new born-again religion could cost our school district a lot of money. I convinced the asshole to keep his mouth shut, and we'll take care of Ms. Gallion by offering her a cushy job in the district office."

Two days after his talk with the superintendent this attractive woman came to work in the human resource office. Elliot was so busy with his work, he pawned Genevieve off to his secretary to train. The secretary showed the new arrival the ropes.

Within a few days, Genevieve became an invaluable asset to the office. Ms. Gallion dove into the district's personnel records with fierce determination to do the job. Mary and Tom asked Genevieve, "Try and find the names of the individuals hired in the past two years, both supervisory and teaching staffs. Look up the names of the people hired as school aides, teaching assistants, lunchroom workers, and after-school personnel."

"We'll give these names to Roy Baker," said Mary, "And he'll have a clerk down at the police station put them through the computer. Let's see what we find."

Tom warned, "Make sure you don't take any chances. Be careful no one sees you doing anything suspicious." Genevieve knew Tom put her safety above finding any information.

§

Phil Turner enjoyed Troy Burns' company and looked forward to Troy's visits to the district office. Phil would tell Troy what positions he could offer his campaign workers each month and Troy would hand Phil a list of construction projects up for bid. On the list was an amount which had the best chance of winning the bid. This information allowed

Lou Marinara's people to prepare a prospectus for his cronies which would beat any other bids.

Phil also looked forward to the wonderful lunch which always followed Troy's visits. Today, Phil planned to eat lightly. Jeannie, his secretary, joked about his love handles and their increasing size. Yes, today Phil Turner would eat lightly, but expensively, on Troy's dime.

§

Eddie knocked softly on Phil's office door. Turner had warned him not to bang on the glass like a police officer ready to break down the door. "It startles Jeannie."

Eddie was familiar with his boss's secretary. Eddie helped arrange her transfer from one of the district's elementary schools to Phil's office.

"Eddie, come in."

Eddie poked his head into the office, looked around, no Jeannie.

"Come in. What do you want," said Turner?

"I have the Kowalski report you wanted." Eddie handed Turner the two-page report.

"Summarize it for me."

Eddie replied, "He's with us."

"It's all I have to know. I'll call Lou this afternoon. I need the list of positions coming up by lunchtime. I'm meeting with Troy Burns today."

"I'll put a fire under Elliot."

"If that's all," said Turner. "I'm expecting someone."

Eddie knew the expected visitor. She was waiting outside the door. On his way out, Eddie politely said, "Hi, Jeannie."

§

Fisher charged into Elliot Rush's office. "Where is the list of jobs I told you we wanted? Phil needs it by lunchtime," screamed Fisher.

Elliot was happy he had the list ready. He handed Eddie the list and the son of a bitch grabbed it out of his hand. Elliot held his tongue and said, "I was dialing your number. You told me to keep an eye on this new girl Pinzon stuck in my office and, of course, I followed your instructions." Eddie didn't miss the sarcasm in Elliot's voice.

"I've watched her carefully since day one," Rush lied.

Eddie sat forward in his chair all ears. "Go on."

"Yesterday, I left my office a few minutes early. I wanted to get a haircut. I forgot my wallet in my desk drawer and went back to the office to get it. "

"Get to the point," interrupted Eddie.

"I opened the office door and the new girl had the personnel files of the school aides open on her desk. She furiously wrote down the names of the aides."

"So what's wrong? She was put there to help you."

"Yes, but we are only on the teacher and supervisory personnel files this quarter. I specifically told her not to start with the aides' files until we finish the others."

"Maybe, she wanted to get a head start on next month."

"It doesn't matter to me, but you told me to keep my eyes open. I don't always know what you consider important."

Eddie got up to leave and said, "Thanks for nothing, Shithead. The glass in Elliot Rush's door survived another bang.

§

Yesterday, Genevieve Gallion arrived home after work shaken. She dialed Mrs. McMurray's number when she took off her coat and poured herself a glass of red wine.

Mary answered on the second ring. "Genevieve, it's good to hear your voice. I planned to call you this weekend to see how you were doing and ask if you've been able to get any more names. The last batch you gave us told a great deal."

"I was able to get some more names. I finished the names of the supervisory positions in the district and all the teachers hired in the past two years. Today I started with the names of the school aides."

Mary heard the lovely young woman choke up. "What's the matter, Genevieve?"

"Elliot caught me going through the aides' files. He had explicitly told me to wait until next month before starting the school aides."

"What did he say?"

"Not much. Elliot asked me why I had those files out. I told him I wanted to get a head start on the work and I had the time. I couldn't tell if he was suspicious, but he's no fool, and he'll watch me more carefully, now."

"So, do you feel everything is alright?"

"No, I don't. After I left the office, Elliot remained and didn't leave to get the haircut he mentioned. I stopped by a friend's office down the hall to say hi. I was in my friend's office about a half hour. As she and I left the building, we glimpsed the creepy guy, Eddie Fisher, go into Elliot's office. I told my friend to go on ahead. I said I wanted to go to the ladies' room and when I was in the bathroom, I heard Fisher slam Elliot's door. I thought the door would fly off its hinges."

Mary immediately said, "Genevieve, I don't want you to take any chances with those people. They're dangerous. Stop snooping until I have a chance to talk to some people."

"I'm alright. I was startled when Elliot came in and caught me going through the files. I'll be okay."

"I wish you had someone to pick you up from work?'

"I'll be fine. I can take care of myself."

§

Tom and Roy walked down the main corridor of the district office past the superintendent's office, past Regina Moriarity's office, headed for the after-school program's office.

Roy hoped to meet some of the district office personnel he had heard about but never met. Today no one was in the long hallway. All office doors were shut. As they reached their destination, Tom and Roy were about to enter the after-school program's office when they heard a door open opposite them.

Out came the most beautiful girl Roy Baker had ever seen.

Tom nodded to Genevieve Gallion not wanting anyone to see he knew her. Genevieve's success in tipping Mary off about job applications was paying off. Tom didn't want to screw it up. He feared Elliot Rush would come out to the hall and become suspicious. But Roy was blocking Tom from entering the office. Roy continued to stare at Genevieve. The moment was awkward. Tom thought he'd quietly introduce Genevieve to Roy, and then elbow Roy into the office.

Roy was speechless during the introduction. Genevieve smiled at Roy, enchanted by his lack of guise. "It's great seeing you, Mr. Foster and nice to meet you, Roy."

Roy was in heaven as he stood still watching Genevieve walk down the hall. Tom thought he noticed a little more wiggle in Genevieve's step than he'd remembered.

Tom called Mary in the evening. "Hi, Mary is it convenient…"

"Perfect timing, I just finished the dishes." Both Tom and Mary had agreed to be honest about telling the other if they were busy when the other called.

"I brought Roy Baker to the district office this morning. He wanted to find out some information about an after-school program. He's a coach for a baseball team, and they rent one of the district's fields for little league. We were also hoping to meet some people he'd only heard about but never met."

"Sure, he's had to listen to us blab on about these people. I'm sure he was curious to get a gander at them. Who did you meet?"

"No one, except Genevieve. I was careful to make sure no one was around when I introduced her to Roy."

"Remember, Tom, we never mention Genevieve around anyone."

"I know."

"What did he think of her?"

"He was thunderstruck. I never saw anything like it. He was speechless. I quickly introduced him and ushered him into the after-school office. No one saw us."

Mary was relieved. "I'm glad; we don't want to blow her cover. Did I say that? I've been watching too much NCIS."

"On the way home, after he recovered from seeing Genevieve, Roy asked me if I would arrange another introduction. He wants to take her out on a date."

Mary was silent on the other side of the phone and Tom waited for Mary's reaction. He had learned he was better off waiting until Mary gave things some thought. When she was ready to speak, she said, "Tom, it's a good idea. That's if she isn't going with someone already."

Tom knew there was more to Mary's words than an older woman trying to play match-maker. "I'll call her right now and test the waters. Roy is a good looking guy; she might be interested. I'll call you back later."

Mary didn't have to rise from the kitchen chair to look up Genevieve Gallion's phone number. Mary knew it by heart.

"Hello, Genevieve."

"Hi, Mrs. McMurray."

"Is this a good time? If not, I can call back later."

"It's fine."

"Great, I'm calling on a matter that has nothing to do with the district office."

"It sounds interesting."

"I don't usually get involved in people's personal affairs, but I received a call from Tom Foster."

"I saw him today. He's a good-looking guy."

"Yes, he certainly is, but what about the guy he was with today. Before you answer let me tell you, the fellow Tom was with, thought you were truly something, and he wants Tom to introduce you more formally." Mary forged ahead before Genevieve said anything. "I know him, and he's the real deal."

"He was nice, a little shy but cute. I would be happy to be introduced."

"I'm glad to hear it because if you aren't going with someone, he's someone to consider dating. Genevieve, I never play matchmaker, but I'd love to see you with a guy like Roy. You work with some pretty creepy people, and I'd feel much better if you had a friend like Roy."

"Mrs. McMurray, I liked him a lot when I saw him. I spent the better part of the afternoon thinking about him."

"Are you free on Sunday afternoon around three?"

"Yes, I'll make sure I am."

"Well come to my house at three for drinks and snacks."

"Terrific. What can I bring?"

§

Roy Baker was thrilled that his introduction to Genevieve Gallion went wonderfully. They hit it off, and now he was picking her up after work for their first official date. Roy waited in his car for Genevieve to appear at the front doors of the district office. At the stroke of five, Genevieve came bouncing down the front stairs. She was a Princess running toward her Prince Charming.

Roy loved the way Genevieve Gallion held her body. Genevieve's carriage was all-royalty, and he hoped by the end of the evening she wouldn't see him as a toad she didn't want to kiss.

Roy's plans for the evening included a boat taxi ride across the East River to Manhattan and dinner at the legendary Water Club.

Roy hopped out of the car to open the door as she approached, but Genevieve's nimble frame beat him to it. She was in the car and seated before he even got to her side of the car.

The smell of Genevieve's shampoo drifted into his nostrils, and Roy was in paradise. He hardly got the words, "Hi Genevieve," out of his mouth. Genevieve smiled at her date's distress, and she was determined to ease Roy's anxiety right off the bat. "Hi, Roy. Would you do me a favor and call me, Gen?"

"Sure. I...I could do that."

Roy immediately relaxed. The short boat ride across the East River further relaxed him, and by the time the waiter sat them at a table over-looking the water, he was back to his confident self, no butterflies in his stomach. Roy was overwhelmed by his attraction to the woman seated across the table from him.

CHAPTER 23

THE VIEW FROM THE PICTURE WINDOW OF REGINA MORIAR-ity's summer cottage took your breath away. The bright sun, the cloudless blue sky and the shimmering turquoise waters of Long Island's Great South Bay were sights to behold.

Regina prepared all morning for her guests. Now, she sat at the window with a stiff drink in hand. The school board members weren't due for an hour, plenty of time to brace herself for some heavy-duty ass kissing.

Manuel had done a beautiful job on the lawn. The fertilizer he used this spring resulted in a green carpet rivaling any golf course. The Moriarity's cabin cruiser tied at the dock was ready to rock and roll.

Regina's sister, Marge, called from the kitchen. "The caterer will deliver the food at five o'clock. I made hors d'oeuvres, and we can start serving them after everyone has a 'drink in hand.'"

"You made hors-d'oeuvres?"

"Well, I defrosted them. What do you want from me, Regina?"

Marge Moriarity was in charge of the food. She was the cook in the family. She made restaurant reservations, brought home take out or had food delivered. Marge and Regina had always been working girls with no time and little interest in learning to cook.

Regina finished her neat bourbon and went to the bar to pour another. Marge joined her. Regina filled her sister's glass more than halfway. Marge pounded the sauce with the best.

Marge Moriarity's position as director of human resource for the entire city school system gave her a great deal of power. The rumor around town was if you pissed off Marge Moriarity, she'd go to the IT room, press a button and you and your personnel records disappeared. People gave her wide berth.

Marge was accustomed to having people curry favor with her, unlike her sister who seemed always doing the reverse with school board members.

"Who exactly is coming today?"

"I expect the Priest, Mary McMurray, Tom Foster, Ted Kowalski, his wife Martha, and Lettie Grimes."

"How far do I go in pushing you for superintendent?"

"As far as you wish. I'm sick and tired of pussyfooting around. I need four votes, and five votes are coming today. It would be nice to have five on my side, but four is all I need."

"Do you have any definites?"

I'm sure I have Mary, Tom, and Father. Ted is leaning toward me, but he's had years of being tied to Lou Marinara."

"If Ted's wife is coming, I'll give her special attention. What about the Grimes woman?"

"If I were a man, I'd have a big advantage with Lettie Grimes, but you can handle her. She's down to earth, and she likes you. You have a way of playing the 'best friend' type. Keep feeding her drinks and talking plenty of girl talk."

Regina heard a car pull into the driveway. "Shit. They're early."

"Don't worry Regina; we're ready."

"I wanted to have another drink before anyone arrived."

"It's Ted."

"What an ass. Kowalski doesn't know what it means to arrive on time. He's either late or early."

Marge put her arm around her sister's shoulders. "Don't worry Sis, we can handle anything, just like we did when Daddy used to come to see us in bed."

§

The dark roads from Regina's summer cottage to the Expressway made the ride home tense, but Mary made any ride enjoyable. While Tom drove, Mary commented, "Those two old babes know how to throw a party."

"Regina and Marge Moriarity know how to make a person feel good. There's nothing they won't do for you if they like you."

"Or want something from you."

"Sure, I know. But it's still nice. No one treats me like this."

"Not even your mom?"

"Especially, my mom, I'll never get a big head while she's around."

"Who can't help appreciating the flattery, even though you know there's a purpose behind it?"

"Mary, I was in Regina's office last week, and the head of one of the funded programs knocked on her door. Regina ignored it once, twice, then the third time she went to the door and flung it open. Mrs. Flores, the director of drug programs, saw the expression on Regina's face, and it scared the color right out of her face. She spoke, but Regina cut her off with, 'Ms. Flores, I can't possibly speak to you now. Do you realize who I have in my office? Do you realize I'm speaking with a school board member? You will have to come back later.'"

Mary could picture Regina doing it.

"Regina came back to her desk and apologized for the nerve of one of her staff. I knew Regina was flattering me, and she wanted to make me see how important I was to her, but I have to admit it felt good. I left Regina's office feeling pretty satisfied with myself."

"We should keep her here for that skill alone," said Mary.

"Unfortunately, when I came out of her office I was assailed by some mother who didn't care for the way I voted on the same-sex bathrooms."

"Tom, you have to learn to let it run off your back. Every vote we make will displease someone."

"I am beginning to see that. Getting back to Ms. Moriarity, does she have your vote for superintendent when Rocco leaves?"

"I haven't decided yet."

"Is this the turn ..."

Bang! Bang! Bang!

"Those are gunshots," said Tom.

"It sure sounded like it."

"Crap, my tire is flat."

The rear left tire made the sound everyone knows and dreads, especially when you're out in the boondocks. Tom pulled to the side of the narrow road as a black Buick drove around them.

Tom exited the car and checked the tire. "It's pretty torn up. Someone put a bullet into the rubber."

This tire wasn't Tom's first trip to the rodeo. He had many flats with his first car; he became an expert on changing tires. He took the jack out of the trunk and changed the tire in the dark.

A car approached, and Tom recognized it as the Buick that passed a few minutes ago. The sedan drove by slowly but passed without an offer of help. The darkened windows prevented Tom or Mary from seeing the driver.

The Buick pulled away, and Tom quickly finished changing the tire. Mary and Tom hopped back in the car and sped off toward the Expressway with its lights and other cars. After riding a few miles on the Expressway, Mary said, "What happened back there was no random flat tire."

"Tomorrow, I'll bring the tire to the repair shop, and I'll give it a good inspection. If it were a gunshot that did it, we'd have to talk to someone about it."

Both Mary and Tom rode the rest of the way home silently, too absorbed in their thoughts to speak.

§

Tom called Mary the day after he returned from the repair shop. "Mary, it was a bullet that tore up the tire. We have a problem. I'm calling Roy to find out what he thinks we should do."

"I have someone who I'll ask also."

"Let's speak tomorrow."

Tom hung up, and Mary immediately called her son-in-law, Todd. Mary never knew where Todd would be when he was at work, but she knew he wouldn't mind her call. Todd told her a long time ago to call him for anything. If he couldn't answer, he'd call her back shortly.

Mary usually called her daughter first, but she didn't want Ellen to worry.

Todd picked up on the fifth ring. "Hi, Mom, what's up?"

"Sorry, Todd, for bothering you at work, but…"

"Mom I told you to never worry about calling me. First of all, I know if you call it's important. Now, what's up?"

Mary told her son-in-law what happened on their way home from Regina's. She also gave him some of the background why she was concerned.

"I'll call you tonight? We'll get to the bottom of it." Mary thanked Todd and hung up. She knew the resources her son-in-law had available, and she was never so glad her daughter married an FBI agent.

§

Sometimes being on the school board made Tom feel he was back in junior high school, calls back and forth at night to your friends, gossiping about who did what to whom, looking for weaknesses in your enemies armor you could exploit.

Tom laughed at what a conversation with Mary would sound like to an outsider. "Did you hear what he said about what she said, and what she said about somebody else?" Maybe junior high is the real preparation a kid needs for life, Tom thought.

Tom was learning that information is real power, and that dirt on someone is the best information you can have. Tom hoped he'd learn information about Ted that would help him win Ted's vote on some important matters, a principalship, a program, a construction project. It's the way the game is played. "It would be nice if people acted for the good of their neighbors, but frankly, they don't."

§

Tom waited in the living room for his mother to finish doing the dishes. Right after dinner, everyone ran out to some engagement. Tom was glad he would have his mom's full attention tonight.

Tom wanted to tell his mother he was ready. "Jen is the girl for me."

In Tom's eyes, Jen had it all, personality, looks, brains, a good heart, everything. When Tom told his mother he planned to get engaged to Jen, she was thrilled. Alice Foster said, "Wait here a minute." She ran up to her bedroom and opened a small safe in her closet.

Alice came downstairs and sat next to her son on the couch. She opened a small box and showed Tom a ring. "This is your great-grandmother's engagement ring. The jeweler said the ring has an exceptionally brilliant and flawless diamond, emerald cut with a platinum band."

Tom didn't know what to say.

"Your great-grandfather was a prominent investor in the nineteen twenties. He lost most of his money in the stock market crash of nineteen-twenty-nine. This ring was one of the few things he was able to save. Great-grandfather couldn't bear to ask your great-grandmother to sell this beautiful piece of jewelry.

"Tom, I saved the ring for you and your two brothers. It's large enough to cut into smaller pieces. The way it is, a woman would be afraid to wear it in public. It's yours if you want it." Alice saw Tom eyes saying he didn't.

"Mom, I already bought a ring for Jen. Great-grandmother's ring is beautiful, but Jen always said she wanted a sapphire ring instead of the traditional diamond. Maybe it would be better if you didn't split it. You could sell it and put it into your retirement fund. It must be worth at least a hundred thousand dollars."

Tom saw the sadness in his mom's eyes, but he also saw a woman who understood his feelings.

"Mom, I'm late, but I wanted to tell you I'm asking Jen to marry me tonight."

"Jen is a lovely girl. I'm so happy she'll be part of our family. Go and do it and I wish you both all the happiness in the world."

"I'll call you later to tell you the details."

§

Tom pulled up to Jen's house. Only a light in the living room was on. Her parents were in the Bahama's for a week on business.

"What time is the movie?"

"The movie is at eight," said Jen. "We have a few minutes before we have to leave. Do you want a beer?"

"No, not really. Come sit over here with me on the couch."

"I'll be right there. I want to get a bottle of water to take to the movie."

Tom waited for Jen to come over and sit next to him. He reached for her hand and held it softly.

"You seem so serious, Tom."

"I want to ask you something."

"And what might that be?"

Tom looked into her eyes and said, "Will you marry me, Jen?"

Jen looked surprised and more than a little shaken.

"So, is it a yes or no?"

Jen said nothing and Tom wasn't sure if surprise accounted for her silence or something else.

Finally, Jen said. "Tom, I love you, I do, but I can't marry you." Her eyes filled with tears. "I've been waiting for the right time all week to tell you I'm going to Paris next month to live for the next few years." Now it was Tom's turn to be shocked.

Jen waited for her words to sink in. More tears appeared in her eyes. She couldn't believe she was giving up the opportunity to be with a wonderful man like Tom. She kept asking herself, "Am I making a big mistake?"

Before she changed her mind, she continued. "Tom, I've seen you begin to walk down a path that will be your life's work, a career in public service. I want to be on the same road, but…" Jen paused, wiped a tear with her hand, and continued, "But it's a path I don't want to go down. It makes me uncomfortable. I don't like the people public service attracts. You and Mrs. McMurray are the exceptions."

Tom tried to interrupt. However, Jen pleaded, "Please let me finish. I want you to understand my decision and how I feel about you. I'm a lucky girl to have had you in my life for the past year."

Jen cried, and Tom put his arm around her and pulled her close. He held back tears, trying not to make things worse. After a few minutes Jen pulled away knowing if she didn't, she might change her mind. The two faced each other with tears in their eyes. Jen looked at Tom, afraid she was making a mistake. Jen loved Tom and wanted to be with him, but she didn't love him enough to share a lifestyle she abhorred.

In the past few months, Jen watched Tom drifting more and more in what she considered a dangerous direction, a direction her father warned her about since she was a young girl. "Don't become romantically involved with a man who supports himself at the public trough. If you decide to marry, make sure he earns his money in the private sector."

Jen listened carefully to her father's little adages, even the ones she didn't understand. She heard replays of her father's voice, "Make sure you can earn your own money. I'll pay for all the education you want. It will be more difficult to do as a woman. Pay inequities between men and women are real. Augment your income in the private sector with the earnings of a man who knows how to make money in good economic times and in bad."

Tom sat on the couch, stunned. His stomach ached. He loved this girl, but all he felt was emptiness.

Jen stopped and looked at the guy she was about to walk away from and said, "I'm trying to explain why I won't marry you, Tom. I need you to know it's not you. There are times in your life you can't have what your heart wants."

"But, Jen I…"

Jen was determined not to let Tom talk, afraid he'd try to change her mind. "Tom, you have to let me finish. I want to go to Paris and complete my degree in fine arts. I started my masters here at Fashion Institute as a lark. As you know, my undergraduate degree is in economics with a minor in education. The minor in education was supposed to be a hedge against not finding a job in finance. I have decided I want to pursue a Master's Degree in Art Education.

"Have you applied anywhere?"

"My father said he'd pay for my courses at the Sorbonne. After the Admissions Director reviewed some of my sketches, he said after a year of basic coursework he'd consider admitting me as a full-time student. My father promised he'd help me open a gallery in Chelsea. I like the idea of meeting people who are interesting and creative. I can't see myself dealing with politicians and those who work for the government. They seem like greedy little bastards."

Jen's words made Tom rethink the direction his life was taking. Some people he met so far in the local school board world were more than sleazy. He remembered what Mary McMurray once said after leaving a public meeting. "Tom, did you see these people? Can you believe we're in the same room with people like that?"

Tom knew Mary was no snob, but she was calling it the way she saw it. The people were greedy, grubby and interested only in their own benefit and they didn't care if it was at the expense of someone else's kid.

§

The bleak night made all the board members want to call in sick for tonight's monthly executive board meeting, but all showed up right on time. Mrs. McMurray was the only one who looked wide awake.

"Before we begin tonight's scheduled agenda, I want to add a topic," said Mary. "After reading an article in yesterday's paper concerning salaries of superintendents in neighboring districts, a discussion of our superintendent's salary is warranted."

The topic caught everyone's attention; all eyes were glued to Mary. Each thought one thing, "What's she up to now?"

Mary loved seeing her colleagues puzzled expressions. "The salary of Robin Turner, in one contiguous district, is five-hundred thousand dollars. Harvey Stein's over in Calverton County is three hundred and seventy-five thousand dollars. I've met both of them. Robin looks like she hasn't taken a bath in a month and Stein acts like he doesn't know his ass from his elbow. He can't speak without going off on some dumbass tangent."

Mary read off four more superintendents' salaries. "Every one of the salaries is more than three hundred thousand dollars; add pension contributions, vacation and sick time, and you have another hundred thousand."

Although the board members had read about these ridiculous expenditures, no one knew where Mary was going with this speech. She continued, "I'd like to discuss an increase in Rocco's salary. What we pay him is far below the compensation he should be receiving for the work he does. I propose an increase of forty thousand immediately."

Mary's six other colleagues looked stunned. Most thought she wanted to fire him when his contract was up.

Mary asked, "Rocco, how many years do you have left on your contract?"

"A year and a half," replied a surprised superintendent.

"Fine, I propose a similar increase next year."

"I second Mary's request to put the matter on the agenda for discussion," voiced Father.

Ted commented, "I guess Christmas is coming a little early, Rocco?" Rocco Pinzon smiled, bewildered by the events of the past few minutes.

CHAPTER 24

LUIS GOMEZ AND HIS GIRLFRIEND, ROSA DROVE DOWN MAIN Street to meet Elmer and his girlfriend, Carmen. Luis gently held Rosa's hand. He loved Rosa's soft skin against his rough hand. Rosa meant the world to Luis. Her loving approach to everything made Luis remember there's another side to life besides cruelty, hatred, and killing. Luis had changed since Rosa came into his life.

Luis pulled into the parking lot of Pancho Villa Restaurant. Carmen and Elmer were waiting at the door. "Amigo," said Elmer. The two men embraced. Carmen and Rosa hugged each other also.

Luis said, "I'm hungry."

"Let's eat," Elmer replied.

Luis held the door while the other three entered the restaurant.

The candlelit dining room added to the festive mood the couples were already enjoying. Being in each other's company was a treat for all four. Luis came tonight with a heart filled with more happiness than he had since arriving in the United States.

The maître'd showed them to a spacious booth, and all four settled into the comfortable leather seats.

When the waiter came over, he asked if they would care for some drinks before eating. Luis said, "Yes, we want a bottle of your best

Champagne." Rosa smiled widely. Elmer and Carmen looked surprised. Luis wasn't one to spend money frivolously.

Luis looked at his friends with a grin Elmer rarely saw on Luis.

"Okay," said Elmer. "What's up?"

Luis and Rosa looked at Elmer. Their smiles became wider and wider.

The solicitous waiter returned with a bottle of champagne, uncorked the bubbly and poured a small amount for Luis to taste. With great flourish, he drank the champagne and nodded his approval. The waiter filled the glasses and disappeared.

Luis lifted his glass and asked Carmen and Elmer to join him in toasting his new bride. "We were married this morning at City Hall."

A loud roar broke the quiet atmosphere as Carmen and Elmer congratulated their friends. "And there's more," said Luis. "Rosa is pregnant, and we want you both to be the child's godparents."

Luckily, it was a Tuesday night, and the restaurant was almost empty. The joy of the four friends overflowed with the sounds of great jubilation.

§

Mary McMurray did not look forward to making the call she was about to make, but Mary knew she must. Although Tom had the best personal relationship with Ted Kowalski, he would beat around the bush and that slippery pig, Ted, would slip out of her young friend's hands.

Ted picked up the phone. "Ted, this is Mary McMurray. Am I catching you at a bad time?"

"No, Mary, it's good."

"I'll get right to the point. Tom and I want to team up with you and form a coalition to vote together to make the district the finest in the state."

"A tall order indeed," chuckled Ted.

"If we have four votes we can do it. With your experience, we can accomplish a great deal."

"Are there any particular votes you're referring to?"

"Yes, some supervisory positions are coming up, and if we fill them with competent people, we can begin to change the direction of our schools."

"What else?"

"There's a lot of dead wood in the district office. It's time for a change in more than one office."

"Like which ones?"

"There's pupil personnel which supervises everyone who works in the district including after-school activities."

"Why pupil personnel?"

"Lou's right-hand man is sitting in that office. Mr. Rush received the position after the tragic death of the little girl in his old school. Elliot Rush had no qualifications for the job. Lou brought Rush to our district because he was a relative and because Lou wanted someone in that position to make sure all jobs went to his cronies."

"Do you know about the after-school jobs?"

"Yes, Rush gives Burns almost a hundred after-school jobs for his campaign workers, paying fifty dollars an hour."

"Let me think about your proposal. I'll get back to you."

"Father, Tom and I are going to fix this district, and I hope you will be with us. We won't give up until we succeed."

Kowalski knew times were changing and he didn't know if he had it in him to change with it.

§

Angie Marinara heard Lou scream down from the attic, "I can't find…" Angie froze as she waited for her husband to finish his scream. Fear paralyzed her mind as she tried to think of a reason to give for one of Lou's files being out of order. Angie tried to make sure she left all of Lou's papers in the exact place they were.

Just the sound of her husband's voice made her sick to her stomach. She hated every part of Lou Marinara. Angie couldn't think of one reason she'd ever lived a day in the same house as that son of a bitch.

Lou repeated his cry, "Where the hell are my golf clubs?"

A deep sense of relief spread through Angie's body. She yelled back, "They're in the garage where you left them last year when you went to your yearly golf outing at the club."

Angie remembered encouraging her husband to get more physical exercise. "Play more golf, Lou. It's good for you." Now, Angie was glad her husband had ignored her pleas. Lou was even in worse shape than he was last year, probably added another fifteen pounds to his already two hundred and fifteen-pound disgusting body.

Angie heard him bounding down the stairs from the attic. She prayed this man whom she once called her husband would fall down the stairs and break his neck. She stopped and remembered this wasn't a matter for prayer, so she settled for cursing the day Lou Marinara was born.

Lou came into the kitchen. "Angie, do me a favor and straighten up the attic today. I can't find anything. Move my papers to the back of the attic. Don't go messing with them. I'll do it next week when I don't have so much work. Just pick them up and put them in the back corner."

Angie couldn't believe her ears; she'd been given the keys to the kingdom. She'd go through all her husband's papers, and if one or two were out of place when he looked, he'd assume anything out of order resulted from her cleaning.

Angie rushed breakfast and had Lou out of the house in record time. She watched until her husband pulled out of the driveway, waited five minutes, turned off the flame under her scrambled eggs and hobbled up to the attic.

Angie's body was tense; she hurt all over. Then, it hit her. "Relax. The jerk asked you to come up here and touch his papers." A Cheshire cat smile appeared on her face. "The bastard gave me the biggest gift possible, and I'll return his kindness by sending him to prison. These papers will do the job."

Angie carefully rummaged through the files, culling out papers she hadn't copied before. She limped down to the copy machine on the first floor and made a few sets of each. She'd give them to Jeremy. He'd know what to do with them.

§

"Listen to this Bunny, the other day I was standing in the lobby of one of our schools talking with the principal and in came a kid with a black eye, bruises on his arms, and cuts on his cheek. This fifth-grade kid passed us with a huge smile on his face.

"'Come back here Jimmy,'" said the principal. "'I want you to meet Mrs. McMurray; she's on our school board.'"

"The boy said, 'It's nice to meet you, Mam.'"

"The principal explained, "Jimmy is new to our school Mrs. McMurray. Jimmy, where did you receive the black eye? I hope you weren't fighting in school.'"

"He answered, "Oh no, sir, I got the black eye and the cuts at home. I didn't get them in school.'"

"Bunny, my heart sank. What kind of place did he live in?"

"What did the principal say?"

"He said, 'Tommy, would you go to the main office and tell my secretary to let you sit in my office. I'll be right there.'"

"The boy looked at the principal and said, 'Am I in trouble, sir?'"

"The principal assured him, 'Not at all, I want to ask you a few things.'"

"The boy went off to the office, unconvinced he wasn't in trouble. I asked the principal, 'What's going on?'"

"He said, "I don't know, but I plan to find out.'"

"I asked, 'Do you mind if I sit in on your talk with the boy?'"

"'No. It might help. I find a young child in these cases is more relaxed when an older woman is listening to what he has to say.'"

"'Can I meet you in a second? I have to use the lavatory.'"

"No problem, I'll tell him you'll be joining the conversation."

"The principal told his secretary to, 'Hold all calls.'"

"I finished in the bathroom and hurried to the principal's office, as Jimmy began his story. 'I live in a church house. Four blocks from here.'"

"What's a church house?" asked Bunny.

"That's what the principal asked. I knew, but I didn't want to interrupt and explain. It is a house left to the church by a parishioner in a will. The church doesn't want to sell it, so they let a family in need live there. Jimmy explained why his family was living there. 'My father left us last year and hasn't come back. My mother, me and my two sisters had no place to live. Our church had an extra house, and they let us live there.'"

"'Is the house nice?'" asked the principal.

"'Yes, except for the neighbors. They didn't want poor people living near them. They say mean things to us when we pass on the street, and their kids tease us all the time about living free in a church house.'"

"Bunny I didn't hold back. 'Tommy, how did you wind up with the cut face and black eye?'"

"'The other day the teasing got worse. One of the boys poked my little sister and I told him he better be careful or I'd do more than poke him.'"

"I asked, 'Did the kid leave your sister alone?'"

"Tommy replied, 'I thought so, but yesterday after school, about ten mothers and about twenty kids came to our house. The mothers and kids gathered on the sidewalk and in the road in front of our house. The mothers had signs saying Go back to where you came from.'"

"How terrible, Jimmy." I asked, 'Did you or your mother say anything?'"

"Tommy explained, 'No, but I wanted to say that we are home. This is the only home we have'."

"What happened next?" the principal asked.

"The people yelled, 'Get Out! Get Out! Get Out, now!'"

"Jimmy stopped to catch his breath and continued, 'I couldn't take it anymore. My two sisters were balling, and my mother stood in the middle of the living room frozen stiff. I ran out the front door and screamed, Get off my property.'"

"I asked Jimmy what the crowd did."

"Tommy went on, "One lady, the leader, laughed and then everyone laughed. I knew I had two choices either cry or hit someone. I ran up to the leader's kid, Cal Estes, and punched him in the stomach.'" Jimmy cleared his throat, and the principal asked if he wanted a glass of water."

"Jimmy didn't answer right away. He waited and continued. 'Cal's mother told the other boys to help her son, and they all circled me. I stood there and said, "Come on. I'll take you on one at a time. One of the bigger boys came at me and punched me a few times, but I kicked him in the…

"I told the boy, 'This isn't the time to worry about your language. Please continue.' Jimmy looked at the principal for his OK and the principal nodded his approval.

"Tommy spoke very quickly, "I kicked him in the balls. He went down. No one came near me after that. They thought I was crazy or something." The principal asked Jimmy if any of the mothers said anything."

"'No, they all seemed to walk away. When the last one left our property, I went back in to the house. My mother seemed to be coming out of her cloud. She took me to the bathroom and put peroxide on my cuts and a bandage on the biggest one.'"

"Bunny, the principal and I sat there and wondered what to say or do next. Jimmy saved the day. He asked to go back to his class."

"The principal told him, of course, he could. Then he added, 'Let me write a quick note to your teacher to tell her you were helping me with something.'"

Jimmy left saying, "Thanks, and nice meeting you mam.'"

"I wanted to give this brave little boy the biggest hug," Mary told Bunny. "But all I did was wish Jimmy a nice day."

"I know Felicia Estes," said Bunny in a voice filled with rage. "She's a bitch."

"I do too. I had a run in with Estes during the campaign."

"I'll take care of her, but good," said Bunny. "But I have to wait."

"Well, I don't."

"Why don't we make Felicia Estes a joint project?"

"You have a deal, Bunny Krouse."

§

"Frank, I want to tell you something, and I hope you'll believe me."

Frank looked worried. He was afraid Bunny would say, "We can't see each other anymore."

"The story of my escapades with my kids' principals," Bunny stopped for a moment, "Is only a story?"

"Bunny, I told you it doesn't matter."

"Please, let me finish. You can say what you want after I finish."

Frank shook his head and looked straight ahead at the woman he cared for so deeply.

"The whole thing began ten years ago," said Bunny, "When Felicia Estes and I waited outside the school to pick up our kids. The principal came out, saw me and came over to congratulate me on Norris winning the school math contest. After he walked away, Felicia, jealous as ever of any kid's success except her own, made one of her usual disgusting remarks, 'Who did you blow?' Me being me, quickly replied, 'Him,' pointing to the principal. Then, to give it to Felicia, I added, 'But, Felicia, please don't tell anyone.'"

"And, of course, Felicia kept your secret."

'She told everyone in the school. The next day I came to school, and as soon as I approached a group of mothers, they scattered."

"It must have been terrible?"

"Yes, especially in the beginning. It was four months after I lost Sal. It was hard. The one I confided my feelings to was my old grandmother. She was a smart woman. When I told her I was the talk of the neighborhood, she smiled. "I told you when you were a little girl your quick lip would cause you trouble someday."

Frank couldn't help chuckle. "And you haven't changed a bit."

"Yes, but I learned to use it to my advantage with the advice of my grandmother."

"'Bunny,' Grandma said, 'There's no way you'll convince anyone you aren't giving 'relief' to the principal. So be ahead of the story and frame it your way.'"

"I was young and didn't understand. My Grandmother predicted, "All the mothers will watch to see if your kids receive special treatment. Whether in fact they do or not, won't matter. People will think about it. So, you might as well obtain credit for it. The other parents may indeed give you wide berth, but they'll also give your children an even wider berth. They'll leave them alone. With Sal gone, you need someone or something to keep the wolves at bay with the kids. These simpleton mothers will assume you have a great deal of power due to your activities. Eventually, they'll come to fear you. Be aloof to everyone, but a small group of friends."

"What did you do to Mrs. Estes? Knowing you, you did something."

"I did nothing, but I was always ready to strike. Mrs. Estes practically pees in her pants when she sees me. I give her a sly smile and walk past. And I make sure I give a very public visit to each of my kids' principals at the beginning of each school year."

"And it certainly worked. Everyone watches themselves carefully when you're around. I see it all the time. All the mothers are scared shitless of you."

Again, Bunny smiled coyly at Frank.

"But I suspect when Norris graduates this year, Felicia Estes is in for quite a shock. I'm anxious to see what it is."

"There's a bone I plan to pick with that witch, and I could use your help."

"Anything, my love."

§

Bunny and Mary planned their little retribution crusade against Felicia Estes with stealth precision. After what happened with little Jimmy at the church house, Bunny and Mary decided they couldn't wait to blast this horrible person out of commission. Felicia Estes was too dangerous, too destructive, to let her run free within the school community.

Both Bunny and Mary had their axes to grind with Felicia Estes, Mary for the LuLu Belle episode, and Bunny for Felicia spreading the BJ legend.

Bunny's imagination combined with Mary's fearlessness would lead to a final solution to Felicia Estes.

"Bunny, I'll pay for all expenses. Let me give you five hundred for seed money."

"I have a pretty good video camera. The biggest expense will be for a little party after the shooting. We have to have something for the kids and the mothers. Hold off on the money. I'll tell you the cost after we finish."

Bunny handed the money back to Mary, but Mary insisted Bunny keep two hundred.

Within days, Bunny contacted Mary. "I have all the people ready. We have the house picked. We shoot the day after tomorrow right after school."

"Can you make it?"

"I'll be there with bells on."

§

Frank Fontaine operated the video camera, Bunny organized the participants, and Mary McMurray watched with an enormous smile on her face.

Bunny placed the children in a semi-circle around the front of the house. Bunny gave the ten mothers placards to hold. She placed the mothers behind the children. When everything was perfect, Bunny said to Frank, "Roll It."

Frank hit the record button and on cue the kids, and their mothers cried out, "Get out! Get Out!" The mothers held up the placards, jerking them up and down like Bunny had shown them at rehearsal.

Out came a young boy screaming at the intruders, a fight ensued, and the camera continued to roll capturing a re-enactment of the horrible demonstration organized by Felicia Estes against little Jimmy and his family.

After the video ended, one in the group put the entire video on YouTube and Facebook.

§

The reaction to Bunny and Mary's film project was a disaster for Felicia Estes. She was scorned in the schoolyard and at PTA meetings, but the most devastating consequence of the video was her husband's insurance business.

In a week, Mr. Estes' business went from boom to bust. The notoriety mortified Felicia's husband and children. Mr. Estes filed for divorce and took himself and the kids to his parents' home in Nebraska.

Felicia was left with no means of support while waiting for the final divorce decree. Her husband said, "I'm not giving her a cent until I have to."

Felicia had no money of her own. She could not make the mortgage payments, and she had no money for rent. She fell out of sight for a few months. Eventually, someone saw her coming out of a building next to the Episcopal Church on Dakota Street. Everyone soon discovered the building was a church house for people who have no place to live.

When Bunny and Mary heard about Felicia, they were both surprised they didn't feel happier.

§

Mary had invited Father Grant to a sold-out matinee of Figaro at the Metropolitan Opera in Lincoln Center, and they were on their way to have dinner at Jean Georges a block from Mary's apartment.

"I hope Regina and her sister enjoy their retirement," said Mary.

"They will," said Father. "The Bahamas are beautiful."

Mary added, Regina confided she looked forward to some rest and recuperation after the last few years of trying to become the superintendent. Regina was so tired, and she didn't know what she'd do if she finally got the job. She was so worn out. She almost didn't care what happened.

"She'll be receiving a good pension. Regina will receive almost as much as if she did go up to superintendent's pay. With the last raise we gave her, she makes almost as much as Rocco. For all the years they were working, neither Regina nor her sister had 'chick nor child to worry about."

"The district payroll clerk told me the tax-deferred annuity reserved for people working in education allows them to put away twenty percent of their salary tax-free each year," said Father. "Each of the Moriarity sisters worked nearly thirty-five years. They'll have more money than they can spend."

"I hope they both cut down on the booze," said Mary. "Regina told me she and Marge have been attending AA meetings for the last few months, and they'll continue when they set up house on the islands."

"I'm glad to hear it," said Father. "I'm fond of both of them."

"I wonder," said Mary, "If they'll keep in touch when they come back each summer to Long Island."

"I'm sure they will, but they won't have the big parties they used to throw, not after giving up Demon Rum."

"You know," said Mary. "I would have voted to make her superintendent if Rocco was ready to retire."

"Rocco has done a pretty good job compared to many of the superintendents I've seen."

"Okay, Father, let's get down to business. Do you have a sister who needs a job or a niece..."

Before Mary could finish Father said, "I don't have a sister or a niece, but I do have a cousin."

Mary gave him a look, and they both laughed heartily.

Father's cell phone rang and he saw who was calling. "It's Esther Portnoy. I left her a message and told her to call me. "Hello, Esther. I am with Mary McMurray and I am going to put you on speaker phone. I want Mary to hear why I called you before."

"Hi, Mary. I hope you are well."

"Thanks, Esther I am fine. The question is how are you doing with those hoodlums who harass you on your way home from work?"

"Those horrible people are still calling me 'Jew lady' and last week they started throwing garbage at me. I get home and smell awful."

"Did you call the police?" asked Mary.

"I did but by the time the police get there the hoodlums are gone. Yesterday I started taking a car home. It cost me more than an hour's pay. So, I am working a day a week just for transportation. I need that money for my granddaughter's tuition. I was hoping the job in the district office is coming up soon."

Father looked at Mary and cringed. "Esther, that's what I called you about. The position in the budget department fell through. The person decided not to retire at this time."

There was deafening silence. Mary heard muffled sobs and said, "I'm so sorry, Esther."

There was no response on the other side of the phone. Mary and Father waited a minute until Esther gathered herself, "Thank you both for trying. I know you've done what you could. I'll work it out some way." Mary heard Esther trying to keep her composure.

Father said. "I am going to keep after the superintendent, Esther. Be assured of that."

"Thank you, Father and you too, Mary."

Esther hung up and Mary said, "It's that son of a bitch Marinara. No one gets a job in this district unless they know Lou Marinara and aren't Jewish.

§

Mary sat in her kitchen trying to digest Lettie Grimes death. Lettie left home at seven o'clock on Thursday evening and was dead an hour later.

Mary rang Tom. He answered on the first ring. "Mary, can you believe it?"

"No, I can't. Lettie was a pain in the ass, but the way she died…"

Tom heard Mary's voice crack and he waited a moment before he said, "I didn't hear the details. I didn't hear anything except she was dead. Who will fill the vacancy?"

"The one with the majority vote."

"Who would be good?"

"I haven't had a chance to think," Mary paused. "What about Jeremy Thompson?"

"That would be fantastic. Can we get Jeremy the votes?"

§

The day after Lettie Grimes' death, the entire board plus Superintendent Pinzone sat solemnly around the table in the school board office. They were joined by PI Eddie Fisher listening from down the hall to their every word.

Eddie had installed a recording system in the school board office six months ago. He listened to the board members surmising what happened to their dead colleague. Eddie knew what happened. He was there for the whole thing. Eddie turned up the volume and listened.

"I warned her about dating men online," said Ted.

"Online had nothing to do with it," said Father. "Someone pushed her onto the subway tracks as a train pulled into the station."

"That's what I mean," said Ted. "She was probably going to meet some guy she met online."

Mary saw Father Grant's frustration and said, "What do we do now?"

"I'll call the florist on Metropolitan Ave," said Tom, "And send a floral piece. Can I spend up to a hundred?"

"Yes, if Lou doesn't want to pay," said Mary, "I'll reimburse the district."

"When are the wake and funeral?" asked Vince.

"The wake is today and tomorrow, six to nine," offered Jemma, "At Connell Funeral Home on Main Street, burial the following day in Honeycomb Cemetery,"

"Before we leave, can anyone give us any information on what happened?" asked Vince.

"It seems Lettie left home about seven o'clock and hopped on the subway," explained Superintendent Pinzon. "She probably changed trains at Forty-Second Street, and while she waited for an uptown local, a crazy man pushed her onto the tracks."

"I hope the family opts for a closed coffin," added Ted. "I heard on the radio the train cut her up pretty badly. When they tried to put her on a stretcher …."

"Alright, Ted. That's enough," yelled Mary.

No one said a word. Most were visibly upset. Although Lettie was annoying, she was also funny and had a vulnerability that belied her attempts to appear tough.

"I plan to go to the wake and attend the funeral. Do we want to go as a group, as a school board?"

"We should go separately," said Lou. "I have to work around my schedule. It's full this week."

"Mary rolled her eyes. "Fine, you go separately. I think as many of us as possible should go as a group. It will be a nice tribute to a fellow traveler. It will be good for Lettie's children to see their mother honored. I'll hire and pay for one or two limousines to take us to the cemetery. We can go separately to the wake. Who wants to ride with me?"

Ted, Tom and Father said, "We'll ride with you."

Lou said, "Angie and I'll take my car." Vince said nothing.

Mary asked Ted, "Will Martha be coming?"

"I'll get back to you."

"I'll ride with you, Mary," said Vince. "My wife can't make it."

"Fine, we'll meet at the Church, park our cars and the limo will take us to the cemetery. Lettie would be happy with this arrangement."

Lou adjourned the meeting. He and Vince hurried out the door. The rest of the board stayed in their seats.

The intercom dropped dead when Lou and Vince left. Eddie frantically tried to fix it. When the voices of the board members went dead, Eddie panicked. He knew the good stuff he wanted to hear would start now.

The wires were connected to the hearing device on Eddie's desk five doors down the hall. He rushed to his door and saw the cleaner he'd hired last month. "Get down to the board office, stand outside and listen to what they're talking about."

Mary remained seated and took a chance while Father and Ted were still there to bring up the delicate subject of who would fill the seat on the board vacated by Lettie.

"While the four of us are here, does anyone have an idea who we'll vote for to replace Lettie?"

"I haven't thought of anyone," said Ted. "Lettie is only gone a day."

"I know, and I hesitate to bring it up, but I thought since we're here I'd ask your advice on the matter. Ted, you've done this before. What do you think?"

"It's too soon to discuss this matter. Lettie's body isn't cold yet, and we're talking about who should replace her. I'm going home; I'm tired." Ted got up and left.

Father, Tom, and Mary remained seated.

"I guess we'll have to wait for a while now. We need Ted's vote. Four votes spark the magic moment."

Mary asked Father what he thought about Jeremy Thompson becoming the next school board member.

"I have nothing against him. I've met Jeremy a few times at our Inter-Faith Coalition Counsel. He's a bright guy and likable. I want to see who will apply from the community before I commit to voting for him."

Mary and Tom looked disappointed at Father's unwillingness to commit to Jeremy, but happy Father was considering it.

Tom interjected, "This is a good time to see if we can work as a team. Whoever we vote for, we have to have a fourth vote, and Ted is it. There's no way Lou or Vince will vote for Jeremy Thompson."

"Vince or Lou certainly wouldn't vote for a black man or for that matter, anyone who they thought we wanted."

While Mary spoke, Tom signaled Father and Mary by putting his finger to his lips while quickly heading for the door. Mary continued. "We have to make sure…"

Tom was out the door in a flash. Father and Mary heard him speaking to someone in the hall. "May I ask who you are? I don't recognize you."

"I'm the new night cleaner."

"I've never seen you before. My name is Tom. Are we holding you up?"

"No, Mr. Foster, not at all. I'll come back later."

"You know my name. Why?"

The flustered cleaner began, "I…my boss told me he wants all the workers to know peoples' names."

"Who is your boss?"

The cleaner stuttered, "Ed, Eddie Fisher."

"I didn't catch your name."

"I'm Larry."

Tom put out his hand, "Nice to meet you." Then, turned and walked back into the boardroom.

Mary whispered, "That was strange. We have to be careful. Lou has his people all over this place."

"Do you think Lou told him to spy on us?" asked Father.

"What do you think?" said Mary sarcastically.

Tom responded, "Let's get out of here."

In the parking lot, all three watched to see each other leave.

§

Fisher hoped he had only missed more conjecture of what happened to Lettie Grimes. "Boy, were they off. They weren't even close. Those idiots have no inkling of what happened."

Eddie still pictured the scene. "Lettie was standing on the subway platform waiting for an uptown local when one of her classmates at Sex Addicts Anonymous pushed her onto to the tracks just as the train roared into the station."

Having followed Lettie Grimes to her meetings in the basement of a private school on the Upper West Side, Eddie knew most of the crowd. "I saw the guy's face when Lettie speaks to some of the other men in the group. His face reddens." Eddie observed how pissed off this guy got when Lettie Grimes let other guys walk her to the subway station. Fisher noticed this man was the only person Lettie never spoke to in the sex addiction group.

After each meeting, Lettie's murderer would follow her to the station to make sure she was safe. He always remained a reasonable distance behind. So, tonight when Lettie's stalker waited until the train was coming, then sprinted toward Lettie, reaching her in time to push her off the platform into the path of the subway train, Eddie Fisher almost wet himself.

Eddie remembered feeling sick and was afraid he'd throw up and draw attention to himself."

Eddie was brought back to the present by Larry, the cleaner. "What did you hear?"

"Nothing, Foster asked what I was doing. I said I was sweeping." He left out he told Foster, "Eddie wanted me to know all the board members names."

§

Tom called Jeremy to tell him of Lettie Grimes death.

"Hey, Tom, what's up?"

"Jeremy, you won't believe it, but …"

Tom waited for his friend to digest the news before he surprised him with the possibility the board could choose him to replace Lettie. "We might be able to get you a seat on the school board."

"Tom, what have you been smoking?"

"No kidding, Jeremy. By state law, we have to fill Lettie Grimes' seat within a month. Father, Mary, and I spoke last night. You need four votes. You have mine and Mary's and a good chance of Father's vote. If we convince Ted Kowalski to vote for you, you're on the board."

Jeremy said nothing. So Tom asked, "Are you there, Jeremy?"

"Tom, please, let me have a minute to…"

"Well, you don't have a minute. We have to get to Ted before Marinara or Miller do. You're going to have to meet with Ted Kowalski to get his vote. He's our sole option. Surely, Marinara is a hopeless case, and so is Miller. Ted's the one we have to convince."

"When should I meet him?"

"Right away."

When is right away?"

"Now. Mary made arrangements for you to meet with Kowalski for lunch at her house."

CHAPTER 25

THE TENSION IN THE SCHOOL BOARD OFFICE MADE SMALL talk impossible. Ted sat straight in his chair. Mary fidgeted with the papers in front of her. Tom read a magazine about fishing. Father Grant looked calm, but his shaking left hand belied his feelings.

As planned, all four board members present had arrived at the board office an hour before time to prepare for this critical vote. Mary wanted to make sure Tom, Ted, Father and she all agreed. Mary wanted no last minute surprises. Tonight, Jeremy Thompson would be voted to replace Lettie Grimes on the board.

If all went as planned, Mary would leave tonight's meeting with a solid majority of the votes on the board which would allow her to fulfill the promises she made to the voters to improve schools.

"I'm surprised," said Tom. "Neither Lou nor Vince got word of what we're doing,"

"Don't be so sure," said Ted. "Little gets past Lou, especially with Jemma here all day. He called me this morning and told me there was an investigation into the possibility Lettie was killed by a member of the black clergy in the district so that they could get Jeremy Thompson on the board."

Father Grant looked at Ted as if he was from another planet, then at his watch, "They're five minutes late. Maybe they did get wind of it and won't show up."

Tom asked, "What happens, next?"

"We vote to put Jeremy on the board to replace Lettie."

"But Lou's the chairman. Can we do it without him?"

"The by-laws of this board and New York State say in the absence of the chairman, the vice–chair conducts the meeting. You're the vice-chairman."

The appearance of Vince and Lou interrupted Mary. "Sorry, we're late. Lou had to stop for this plate of delicious sandwiches." Vince put the colorfully wrapped sandwiches on the conference table.

Mary asked, "Can we begin, please?" The urgency in her voice prompted Vince to sit down.

"Lou! Please let's get started. We don't want to be here all night."

"Sure, Mary, but we won't get much done."

Mary and the others immediately realized from Lou's remark he didn't know Ted planned to vote for Jeremy Thompson. Lou thought he deadlocked the board, three against, three for Thompson. Miraculously, Lou and Vince, with all their spies listening, didn't know Jeremy had Ted's vote. "You know there's a possible investigation…"

"Holy shit," thought Tom. "Wait till Lou finds out his future son-in-law will be sitting next to him at the next school board meeting."

"Cut the shit, Lou. We've already heard your fairy tale."

"No one has four votes."

"Call the vote, Lou," yelled Mary, "And stop playing fortune-teller."

Lou looked over at Vince, slightly puzzled. He picked up his pen to record the votes, "Okay, here goes. We're here for this special meeting to fill a vacancy on our school board," said Lou. "The New York State Education Law dictates when a vacancy on a school board exists, the vote to fill the vacancy must take place within one month. Are there any nominations?"

"I nominate Jeremy Thompson to fill the vacancy of our late colleague Lettie Grimes. May she rest in peace," said Father Grant.

"Are there any other nomination?"

"If there are no other names…"

"We should at least discuss this matter before we jump to a vote," said Lou.

Tom tried to control his impatience. "Lou, the majority of the board has the same person they would like to see in Mrs. Grimes' seat."

"Tom, it's all well and good but…"

"I told you to cut the crap, Lou, let's vote, and the majority wins. Remember, you taught me that at the first meeting I ever attended," said Mary.

Lou tried to stall the vote. He figured he'd stall filling the position by forcing a tie vote: He, Ted, Vince against Foster, McMurray and Father Grant.

"Call the roll, Lou."

"Okay, okay. Again, does anyone else want to put a name up for a vote?"

Vince complained, "I haven't had a chance to think of anyone."

"One more time, Lou, call the vote," said Mary this time louder.

"Remember," said Lou in a solemn voice, "A candidate has to receive a majority of the board's votes which is four votes. I abstain."

"Father Grant, how do you vote?"

"I vote for Jeremy Thompson to fill the vacant seat left by Mrs. Grimes."

Lou wasn't surprised. He didn't count on Father's vote. That ship sailed months ago.

Mr. Miller, how do you vote?"

"Our search for a new candidate to sit on this board hasn't been wide enough," said Vince gravely,

Mary interjected, "The only thing not wide enough was your scrounging around for enough votes to put your stooge on this board. Stop with the commentary and VOTE!"

I abstain. We should not ….”

“No speeches, Vince,” interrupted Mary.

“Mr. Foster?”

“I vote for Jeremy Thompson.”

“Mrs. McMurray?”

“Jeremy Thompson.”

“It’s three votes for Thompson and two abstentions,” said Lou with a smirk on his face. “And lastly, my long-time friend...”

Ted Kowalski didn’t wait for his Lou to say his name. He burst out, “I vote for Jeremy Thompson.”

Lou threw the voting sheet tally on the table and said, “Fuck you all.”

As he ran from the room, he heard Mary McMurray say, “As always, Lou is a class act!”

§

Mary sent Jemma to look for something in the basement. Mary waited in the school board office, her anger about to reach volcano level. She placed both hands on the conference table, the fingers of her left hand tapped nonstop. Mary had a score to settle with Elliot Rush.

At eleven o’clock Elliot Rush walked into the board office. He approached Mary and sat down across from her.

“There’s no reason to sit Mr. Rush. Our chat will only take a minute.”

Elliot Rush, nervous and intimidated, waited for the knife to be plunged into his chest.

“Mr. Rush, this district saved your scalp four years ago,” said Mary. “You came to this district, a person in need of solace. This district provided you with a job, a job when no one wanted to touch you. Instead of keeping your nose clean, you fraternized with every skirt in the district, had an affair with a PTA president, a liaison with a staff member who you supervise, and finally, an affair with a board member.”

“Mrs. McMurray, can I explain?”

“No, you can’t. The board has given me the authority to inform you that at the end of this school year your contract will not be renewed.

That's all I have to say. Please return to your office and try and not to pick up any chippies on the way."

Dumbfounded, Rush turned and left the board office.

The superintendent entered the office and said, "How did it go?"

"No problem. You know, Rocco, I'm no prude. I worked for thirty years in private industry. I've seen everything. Rush's conduct was commonplace. Screwing was an industry sport, but for some reason, I naively thought the public sector maintained a higher standard."

"Mrs. McMurray, the carryings on of people in the educational systems of this country would surprise parents more than anything else would. If you want, I could make sure this conduct lessens considerably. I would need the strong support of the board. I tried to correct those incidents that came to my attention when I first arrived in the district. I abruptly stopped when I realized much of the power structure in the district wasn't pleased with my efforts."

"Like who?"

"Like the principals, the unions, PTA and some board members."

Mary sat there trying to absorb the superintendent's accusation of bureaucratic support for philandering.

"The students must have an inkling of what's going on, especially at the high school level."

The superintendent reluctantly answered, "I have no way of really knowing for sure."

Rocco Pinzon's secretary came into the room and informed him his ride was waiting outside to take him to his meeting downtown with the Chancellor.

"Mrs. Mc Murray, would you excuse me?"

"Of course, Rocco."

Mary was annoyed with herself for not asking the superintendent the follow-up question, "Have you seen much fraternizing on the school board?" Next time.

§

Elliot Rush went back to his office and sat there not knowing what he would do with the rest of his life. He knew his educational career was probably over forever, but deep down he knew he'd find something to do. He'd overcome a lot since he took life's first shot to the groin twenty years ago.

He remembered it like it was yesterday. He had looked forward to his high school prom from the first day in senior year. He joined the prom committee and worked hard to make prom night the best night of the graduation activities.

June came, and he asked a girl to go with him. Elliot had been eyeing her for six months. Nervous and scared he approached his class-mate as they came out of chemistry class. The words came out of his mouth smoothly and, low and behold, this wonderful, terrific, superb, fellow senior answered, "Yes," I'd love to go to the prom with you."

The school held the prom at the local Hilton Hotel. A parent of a student in the graduating class catered the affair for free as a gift to his daughter's class. This great gesture lowered the price of the prom allowing more seniors to attend.

The girls, dressed in beautiful ball gowns, swooned over the boys dressed in black tuxedoes, white shirts, black bow ties and matching cummerbunds. Each couple kicked off their shoes when they entered the ballroom.

The lights dimmed as the evening started. Romance was in the air, but there were plenty of chaperones to ensure the romance didn't spill over into any other part of the Hilton Hotel.

"What a night," Elliot whispered in his date's ear. The young lady responded by laying her head on his shoulder. The beat of the music from a live band alternated from fast and hard to slow and smooth.

Elliot never remembered being as happy as he was that day. The senior class intended to cap this perfect night off with a breakfast at the biggest diner in town. The school rented the diner months ago to prevent any after-hours drinking and driving. The night was perfect, a full moon in the sky, a warm temperature and June floral smells in the air. Elliot was in love with life that evening.

Elliot loved his date more than anyone could imagine. He dreamed of taking her home and giving her a good night kiss on her porch, but the school insisted the parents pick up their daughters. The boys went home any way they wanted.

Elliot watched his princess drive away in the back seat of her parent's car. She turned and blew a kiss out the back window. He and two other boys walked home. Conversation was limited, each boy dreaming of what could have been if parents didn't drive the girls' home.

The last of Elliot's companions turned into their driveways, and Elliot continued another block alone. Elliot was excited to tell his mother about the prom. As he turned on to his block, he saw someone sitting on his porch steps. It was probably his mother waiting to hear about his night.

When Elliot walked closer to his house, he saw his step-father on the bottom step, his face in his hands. Elliott wanted to tell the world about tonight. He'd start with his step-father. The light in the upstairs bedroom meant his mother was awake, too. Ten feet from his step-father Elliot yelled, "What a time I had."

His step-father lifted his head out of his hands, his face swollen from crying.

"What's the matter, Len?" Elliot screamed.

Len tried to speak, but instead, he let out choking whimpers. Elliot ran up and put his hand on his step-father's shoulder.

Len rose and balled again. "Your mother is dead. She had a heart attack about an hour ago. The EMS just left. I'm waiting for the funeral director to come and take her away.

Elliot immediately ran into the house and up to the bedroom. The door swung open and there on the bed lay his mother. As he approached the bed, Elliot saw his mother's face, lifeless and pale. He knelt beside the bed and cried. Minutes later the funeral director and his assistant barged in, "Please leave son. We have to remove the body."

Elliot backed away, tears dripping down his cheeks. He ran to his room at the end of the hall and slammed the door.

CHAPTER 26

THE LAST FEW MONTHS TROY HATED SITTING ON THE STAGE in town hall listening to one local contractor after another flattering him and the rest of the town council.

Recently, when Troy sat on the dais during a meeting, he found himself examining the coffered ceiling of the historic town hall. The intricate plaster moldings on the walls seemed more interesting than the speakers coming before the council plying their wares.

Often, Troy returned to his office after a meeting and instead of reviewing upcoming legislation or calling Phil Turner for another favor for a supporter, he looked up architectural sites to find the name of particular ornamentation in the council chamber.

One day he realized how much of his time his new interest in architectural art consumed. He smiled remembering his old friend, George, who had passed away last year. George had struggled with colon cancer for years. He was a tough, irascible guy who took a great deal of chemotherapy before he died. During the last two years of his treatment, the oncologist had experimented with estrogen shots as part of George's therapy.

Troy saw George six months after he started estrogen treatments. The two were at a mutual friend's birthday party. Both had a Jack

429

Daniels in hand when George asked Troy to hold his drink for a second. George walked over to the living room wall to examine something. "Troy, do you see how deep this yellow is? You never see yellow so deep on a living room wall. But it works. It works."

Troy watched in amazement. George took his drink back and said, "Did you ever imagine I would notice something like that?"

Troy didn't know what to say, so he nodded his agreement. George laughed and lowered his voice. "To be truthful Troy, with the medicine I'm on, I notice and appreciate stuff I never knew existed. I notice styles of clothes on both men and women and a whole bunch of other stuff." All Troy remembered over the years was George making fun of anything which wouldn't go in a Man Cave.

On the way home, Troy thought George's experience wasn't far from his own. In the past months, he snuck into church and sat quietly in a pew. He enjoyed the peaceful solitude church provided. A month ago, Troy volunteered one night a week in the church food pantry. Last week, a middle-aged woman walked into the pantry to help stock the shelves.

Troy's stare was interrupted by the minister who ran the pantry. "Troy, I'd like you to meet someone." The Reverend called over to the woman Troy was staring at just moments ago. A big smile appeared on the lady's face as the minister said, "Troy, I'd like to introduce our newest volunteer."

The woman said. "Hi."

The Reverend then gave instructions on tonight's goals. "If we can at least organize the canned foods into groups, it would be great."

The woman said, "A pleasure to meet you, Troy," and returned to work.

The minister returned in two hours and said, "That's it for the night. Thanks very much for your help. Hope to see you next week."

The woman put on her coat and left. Troy turned to the minister when the woman was out the door and said, "She seems nice. Does she live around here?"

"Yes," smiled the minister. "She lives very close. The minister's face turned serious. "She has been through some rough times recently."

§

Troy Burns arrived the following week at the church food pantry eager to see the new volunteer he met the previous week.

The minister thanked Troy for coming and instructed him and three other volunteers on what needed to be done.

The woman Troy was waiting for hadn't arrived by 9 p.m. Troy prayed she'd appear. By 10 o'clock, he gave up hope.

On the walk home, he couldn't believe he prayed for something. "Those visits to church have affected me." He couldn't remember when he last prayed for anything.

Troy was pleased he had pushed for more information about the missing volunteer before leaving tonight.

"She went to a meeting," said the minister. "She'll be here next week, and by the way, she asked me about you a few days ago when I met her on the street."

The news put a big smile on Troy Burns' face.

The minister again warned, "She has had a real hard time these past few months. She's vulnerable. Please be careful, for your sake and hers."

Troy assured him he'd tread lightly.

Troy knew there had been a change deep within him this past year. "Little by little, I'm more dissatisfied with my life," he said as he continued down the dark street. A young fellow saw Troy talking to himself and crossed the road.

Troy laughed at the young fellow's reaction and called across to the teen, "A year ago you'd have been smart to cross the street, now you have nothing to worry about young man."

§

Troy showed up at the church pantry, hair newly cut and styled, ready to ask the new volunteer out for coffee after their work.

Troy planned to casually say, "Hey, do you want to go for a cup of coffee and a bite to eat?" He practiced this line walking to the pantry, but on the way, Troy realized he didn't even know this woman's name. I'll ask the minister before I say anything about coffee.

He walked into the food pantry and there she was, dressed more carefully than when he met her two weeks ago. The touch of lipstick was new, and so was the redness in her cheeks.

Troy was a happy man.

§

After Troy asked his fellow volunteer out for coffee, he realized a more appropriate invitation might be to go for a drink.

"Coffee would be great," replied the lady.

The two went to the small diner down the street and talked for over an hour enjoying each other's company when Troy's new friend excused herself and said, "I have to go. I have an early meeting tomorrow."

Troy asked, "Can we meet again?" His new friend agreed, and Troy asked, "How about dinner Saturday night?"

"I'd like that."

Another Saturday night dinner followed a Wednesday night movie which followed a Friday night concert and a Sunday church service. The pattern continued for the next few weeks.

Both Troy and his new girl found the time they were apart unbearable. Finally, Troy asked, "Would you move in with me. I love you, Felicia Estes."

Felicia responded with the saddest look. "I'm not ready, Troy. I need more time to think. I need to finish my therapy before I make such an important move."

The look of heartache on Troy's face forced Felicia to add, "I can tell you one thing, Troy. I haven't felt like this since high school, and I'm sure we have a future together, but give me some time to get myself together."

"But living in the church house must be embarrassing. Come live with me, Felicia."

"Where I live isn't important to me anymore. Who I am is."

"Alright, for now, we'll continue the way we've been going, but we'll revisit this soon."

"Good night, Troy, and thank you. Remember, I love you."

§

Mary's Manhattan apartment overlooked Central Park and her building employed ninety-five percent men. The elevators operators, the front desk, and the front door men were born in the Dominican Republic, or their parents were born there. The building management chooses these men for their dignity and their trustworthiness.

The workers receive a salary higher than the average Manhattan apartment employees, but they paid a price for the extra money. The men must stand while on duty, except during breaks.

When Mary discovered this was a requirement, she promptly attempted to change the rule. She had little success convincing the co-op board to moderate this harsh regulation.

So, Mary came up with a way to make life easier for at least one shift of workers during the week. These men had become Mary's friends over the years. They were extended family. Mary told her daughter Ellen kiddingly one Christmas not to expect too much from her for Christmas. Ellen looked quizzically at her mother.

Mary saw her daughter's look and said, "I have to be very generous with these fellows. No one else greets me with such enthusiasm each day as they do. No one else opens the doors for me like they do or comes running to help me when they see I have heavy packages."

Ellen laughed, "I couldn't agree more."

The Saturday night shift was Mary's favorite. The co-op was always quiet on Saturday night because unlike Mary who came to stay in the city on the weekends, the overwhelming percentage of the tenants ran to their country homes on the weekend. She was glad she had sold her house upstate. She hardly used it in the past few years.

Every Saturday evening that she was in residence at the co-op, Mary brought a bottle of wine to each elevator operator and a small tray of cheese and crackers. This gesture alone would have made Mary the most well-liked tenant in the building, even if she wasn't already. Mary treated everyone at the co-op with the respect they deserved, unlike many of the other tenants.

§

Roy Baker dropped Genevieve at her door by eleven o'clock. Both had enjoyed the evening with friends who had finally received approval as potential adoptive parents. When Genevieve and the happy couple raised their wine glasses in a toast, Roy joined them with a glass of flavored seltzer. He was the evening's designated driver.

Driving down Elm Street, a soft rain fell on the dark pavement. Roy's warm car felt good. Roy loved Genevieve and was ready to settle down. He pictured himself proudly pushing a baby carriage down the street with Genevieve Gallion Baker walking beside him. Tears of joy appeared on his cheeks.

Out of the corner of his eye, Roy saw a figure dart into the street. He jammed on his brakes. His car skidded, and Roy saw a young woman fly five feet in the air. The bang he heard as his car hit the young woman was a sound he would hear for the rest of his life.

Roy pulled to the curb and raced to the young woman. She wasn't conscious. He pulled out his phone and called 911. He told the dispatcher he was 'on the job.' "My name is Roy Baker, Badge number 76521. Please come right away. I hit a young girl with my car."

A crowd formed. Roy looked closely at the woman and saw her extended belly. Roy realized the woman was pregnant. Without warning the young girl's body shook. Roy recognized an epileptic fit from his EMS training. He looked around and grabbed a four-inch stick from a near-by Elm tree.

The young woman violently bit down on the stick. Roy's quick thinking prevented the young girl from biting her tongue to pieces. The girl's shaking increased. The medics arrived and quickly put the girl in the ambulance. Roy's tears of joy a few minutes ago had quickly dried and had turned to a heartache so strong Roy considered telling the medics he needed to go to the hospital with them.

A young Latino boy saw his friend Rosa Gomez placed in the ambulance and ran to tell her husband, Luis.

§

The Giordano Funeral Parlor, built in the 1920's was adorned with over the top Baroque flourishes inside and out. Visitors stared at the plaster columns and marble balusters. Cherubs hovered on the ceilings, and gold leaf accents covered the walls. Marble floors and wood inlay tables finished the décor.

The same family ran the place for generations. During the past sixty years, the Giordano Funeral Parlor buried many a Mafia Chief. The Giordano family knew how to give a proper sendoff, but by the 1990's, the Italian neighborhood of the past was non-existent. No more Mafia Chiefs needed burying. Business dwindled to burying an occasional Irishman or Pole. Things were bad for this generation of Giordanos, and the family sold their long-time-family business lock, stock, and barrel to a young couple from Central America.

The Latino community was thrilled to have a place of their own to bury their dead, to mourn without Anglo owners peering over their shoulders making sure they didn't steal the ashtrays.

Luis picked this funeral home to take care of the funeral arrangements for his beloved Rosa and their unborn child. Luis picked a highly polished mahogany casket for Rosa's body. All white flowers filled every wall in the room. Rosa's white wedding suit fit tightly around her waist and mourners were reminded two people lay in the coffin. Luis rarely left Rosa's side during the three-day wake.

A constant line of friends and acquaintances passed the casket offering condolences. His friends feared Luis' collapse, and by the end of the second day, the undertaker placed a chair next to the coffin for him. Visitors saw the pain in Luis' face. His loss was palpable.

Outside Giordano's, a white rental car pulled into the lighted parking lot. Roy Baker exited the car and walked to the entrance of the funeral home. He'd dreaded this moment for the past four days.

Every time Roy thought about the tragic accident his car caused, he threw up. Roy's head hurt, and his stomach churned constantly. The vomiting only stopped a few hours ago. But Roy knew he had to be here and try to explain to Luis Gomez how sorry he was for what happened.

Roy inched past twenty young Latino men standing at the entrance to the funeral parlor. He went another ten feet once he was in the vestibule. A sign pointed to the room where Rosa Gomez lay in rest. Young men and women jammed the lobby waiting to offer Rosa's husband their condolences.

Each mourner stepped aside when they saw Roy Baker. They left a clear path to Rosa's casket. Once in the room, Roy saw Luis standing over Rosa. He headed to Luis, but a young Latino man named Elmer blocked his path.

Elmer bent over Roy's shoulder and quietly said, "Please leave now, you aren't welcome here."

Roy felt his stomach roll and knew he'd better leave. Before Roy turned to leave, he caught Luis' stare. The Latino's cold eyes held a hatred for Roy that made everyone in the room shiver. Roy turned and headed for the exit and felt all eyes on him. It felt like knives were piercing every part of his body. Roy made it to the bushes near his car before throwing up, again and again.

§

Mary's daughter, Ellen, called to tell her mother some exciting news. The FBI reassigned Todd to Paris for three months. For social reasons, the government required Ellen to accompany her husband. Living in an apartment on the Seine, the FBI expected Ellen to entertain a great deal.

"What does Harry think of going to Paris? I bet he's thrilled."

There was quiet on the other end of the phone.

"What's the matter, Ellen?"

"Mom, that's the rub. We can't take Harry."

"And why not?"

"There's a certain amount of risk in Europe right now, and the government fears shootings, kidnappings and worse. They won't take the chance with a youngster."

Mary didn't know what dumfounded her more, Ellen's willingness to put herself in a vulnerable position in a possibly dangerous city, or her willingness to leave her son behind for three months.

"Who will Harry stay with, one of his school chum's families?"

Again silence.

"Ellen, are you there?"

"Yes, Mom I'm here."

"What's the matter?"

"We wanted to ask if Harry could spend the three months with you?"

Mary's first reaction was one of joy. She'd love to have her grandson stay with her, but her second thought was, "Can he miss so much school time? What about his music."

"We thought you might find a music teacher in the area. There are some music practice studios on Fifty-seventh Street people can rent by the hour near you. This way no one in your building will complain about the noise."

"Sounds good to me. I'm thrilled."

"We spoke with his school district, and they said they would give him the material he'd miss during the three months, but he'd also have to be enrolled in some school as well. We figured with you being on the school board this would be no problem."

"There won't be a problem. I know the local principal, and I'm sure he'd arrange anything I ask. If I register Harry from my address and he really lives at this address, the school must accept him for as little or as much time as he lives here."

"Harry's present principal will also call the principal to explain the situation."

"I'd love for Harry to stay. I'm over the moon."

"Mom, I'll call you next week with details. I'm so relieved you want Harry to come and stay."

"Harry and I will have such fun. I can't wait. Harry's at a perfect age. I'll make sure your son has a ball."

"Great mom, but I don't want to come home to a spoiled brat."

"That will be yours and Todd's problem. I plan to have plenty of fun with my grandson."

Mary chuckled as she hung up the phone. Her mind raced, "I can show Harry New York like no one else. We can go to a new part of the city every week, Upper East Side, Museums, Chinatown, Little Italy, the Financial District, Theatre District, Lincoln Center, SoHo, NoHo, Tribeca, Upper West Side. What fun it will be."

§

Ellen McMurray Taylor prepared to leave for the airport. Todd left for Paris three days ago. The past two nights she and Harry slept at her mother's Manhattan apartment. Ellen wanted to make sure Harry settled in before she left for Paris. She had such mixed emotions about leaving Harry with anyone, but her mother was an exception. Mary would make sure everything would go right for Harry.

Ellen had a checklist, and everything had a check next to it, favorite foods, doctors' phone numbers, and homework for the next three months. The list went on and on.

The one thing left to say was goodbye and it was by far the hardest one to check off. "Mom, if you or Harry need anything, phone us immediately. I can be home in a matter of hours. Todd's bosses assured me they would be here in a flash if you needed them, and they'd have me on a plane immediately if something important happened here."

"You've told me everything, Ellen. I know how resourceful the FBI is. If I have any trouble, I'll have no hesitation to call them."

"We'll be fine," said Harry. "Don't worry. I'll call right away if Grandma has any problems."

Ellen hugged Harry and her mother one last time. Tears ran down her cheeks. "I know I'm being silly." She looked at her ten-year-old son and ran out the door. Ellen didn't turn to wave. She feared she wouldn't go.

§

Eddie watched Ellen McMurray Taylor pull away from her mother's apartment. He knew she was on her way to the airport. Eddie could feel Ellen McMurray Taylor was a gentle person, nothing like her bitch of a mother.

Ellen's car was about to pass where Eddie was parked. He was prepared to pull out and follow her, but he misjudged and accelerated just as Ellen's car was parallel to his. Eddie jammed on the brakes just in time not to hit her side panel. Ellen stomped on her brakes.

Eddie was in the wrong, but Ellen looked over and gave a quick wave and a no problem smile and took off. Eddie sat in the car composing his thoughts and picturing Ellen's smile.

The McMurray lady told everyone at the school board how happy she was to have her grandson staying with her for three months. "Now, let's see how tough the old lady is, alone with a kid for three months."

Eddie would soon discover how tough Mary McMurray was.

§

Fisher rode back to the district office to report to Phil Turner he saw McMurray's daughter get into her car and leave for the airport. When he arrived at the district office, Turner was in a meeting with Lou Marinara and Superintendent Pinzon. Eddie waited in the hall for ten minutes then took a walk around the first floor.

Eddie enjoyed the uneasiness he caused the office staff, everyone except the new girl, Genevieve Gallion. Whenever he passed her in the hall, Genevieve always greeted him with a smile and a hello. The rest of the female staff scurried back to their office and closed the doors when they saw Eddie coming. Even Regina Moriarity seemed intimidated by Eddie's sudden appearances.

Eddie watched Chairman Marinara and Superintendent Pinzon leaving his boss's office and walked back. Eddie was twenty feet from Phil's office when one of the young secretaries slipped into Phil's office before him.

Eddie waited in the hall, but the secretary didn't come out of the office for twenty minutes. Eddie was getting pissed waiting. Finally, the young woman walked out of the office, her red lipstick smudged, her expression coy.

"Does the guy ever work?" Eddie mumbled. He answered his own question with a resounding, "No, not when he has me to do all his dirty work."

Determined to get into Phil's office before anyone else appeared, Eddie charged in and stood in front of his boss's desk ready to report on Mary McMurray's daughter, but before he had a chance, Phil peppered him questions.

"Did you see the lady leave for Paris?"

"Yes, she left the house forty-five minutes ago. She's gone for three months."

"Did we ever find out why she went to Paris?"

"Her husband had to go there on business."

"By the way, what does the husband do for a living?"

"I couldn't find out exactly, something to do with the government, a scientist of some kind. Google didn't come up with anything. He's probably a 'nobody.'"

"Okay, now get back to your office, and I don't want to see you for the rest of the day. I have things to so."

Eddie turned and left, but for the first time, he felt resentful of Phil's constant disrespect.

§

Eddie Fisher was back in his office and took a bite of his fish taco when the phone rang. It was Phil. Eddie was tempted to ignore his boss's call, but he picked the call up despite himself and was sorry he had. "Get down to my office right away. I need you to go somewhere."

Eddie took two more bites of the fish taco and went down to see Turner.

"The Gomez kid just called me directly and wanted me to meet in an hour to talk about product. He wants to sell in more schools. He wants to expand into a school in the northern tier, just over the southern border."

"Where does he want you to meet him?"

"The Starbucks on Main Street, but I am not going, you are and make sure he knows expansion into the northern tier isn't on the table. It's non-negotiable. Tell him his suppliers are friends of ours and he'll be out in the cold if he tries anything. Tell Gomez his supply might be cut along with his throat. Tell him I said that and tell him never to call me directly again."

Eddie left not sure how hotheaded Gomez would take Turner's threats.

§

Eddie knew Gomez would be at the back table in Starbucks. Since Rosa's death, Luis drowned himself in work in hopes it would help relieve the pain he felt 24/7. Eddie greeted Luis with a knuckle bump, sat down and waited for Gomez to speak. "I knew that fuck Turner wouldn't show up."

Eddie said nothing, and Gomez continued, 'I want more customers, and I always need more product."

"What in particular?"

"Everything man! Every day I run out of something, either weed, heroin, cocaine, or meth. If my supply increased, we could go into the first few blocks of the northern tier."

"It's not happening. "Phil doesn't want you selling in the north, just in the south."

"Why?"

"Because he doesn't want you to," said Eddie. "There would be too much commotion. The cops would be all over you."

"So, Phil is worried about me?"

"Yes."

"Bullshit. Phil doesn't want to sell it to the white children, only the black and brown kids."

Eddie didn't know what to say. Gomez was right, and they both knew it.

"From now on I deal with Turner." Luis jumped up and headed out the door leaving Eddie unsure of what he meant. Eddie took his phone out and called his boss. He repeated what Gomez said.

Phil went crazy, "What the fuck did he mean, that dirty Mexican."

"He's not Mexican," said Eddie. "He's from El Salvador." When Eddie returned to the district office, Turner's secretary said, "Phil's gone for the day."

§

A few days later, Turner announced, "Eddie, I have to go to Mexico to see a sick friend. I'm leaving you in charge."

Eddie knew these sick friends his boss went off to see several times a year were twenty- year old prostitutes hired by Lou Marinara through Don Luigi Costa.

"I'm leaving right after work. I'll be back in three days. Hold down the fort. Call Chairman Marinara if there's an emergency. Sorry for the short notice, but when my friends get sick, I have to go help them."

"Sure, Boss. I'll handle everything." Turner didn't hear Eddie say under his breath, "I hope you catch the same thing you caught during your last bedside visit."

Eddie discovered Phil's itinerary weeks ago, but he played the game with Turner. Eddie would continue his surveillance activity and meet with the G&R Gang to make sure they were following the rules.

§

When Phil Turner returned from his nursing duties in Mexico, he told Eddie about a great new enterprise he wanted to investigate. "Eddie, there might be some decent money in it."

"This will be our little activity. I'll ask Lou if he minds if we start this project separate from anything of his. I know he doesn't like my new idea. Someone approached him years ago about it, and he turned the idea down flat."

Eddie thought, "Okay, spit it out. Stop going on and on. Get to the point." But he didn't dare speak to his boss that way. Eddie waited impatiently for Phil to tell him about the new enterprise.

"A friend and I were relieved for a few hours from sitting with my sick friend," said Phil. "We went to a type of sporting event I'd never been to before yesterday. My friend and I walked in and took our seats. The savagery of the people was almost more than the two ferocious dogs in the ring. People didn't stop betting until one of the dogs mauled the other dog to pieces."

Eddie's eyes popped, and he intently listened as Phil become more excited with each word.

"I never experienced anything more thrilling. I said to myself, this is something Eddie Fisher would love."

Eddie was sickened by Turner's idea, and even more at the enjoyment his boss felt relating what the two dogs did to each other. Before Eddie could ask a question, Turner went on. "I want you to start talking to Gomez about finding a venue for our little project and ask him if he could get a supply of dogs for us."

Eddie became more dumbfounded by the minute.

"These spics know all about this. They have these dog rings all over their country. Every town has one. Gomez probably has been going to these fights since he was a kid."

"Boss, I don't...."

"I don't have any more time for you, Eddie. You've been chewing my ear off since you got here. You won't let me get a word in edgewise. Call Gomez and let's get started. You're going to love it, Eddie. The money we'll make will be phenomenal. Now get out of here. I have things to do."

CHAPTER 27

EDDIE THOUGHT PHIL TURNER'S IDEA OF GOING INTO THE DOG fighting business was abhorrent. Although Eddie never had a dog for a pet and had little interest in walking, feeding or picking up after a dog, he found no enjoyment in mistreating animals.

Eddie dragged his feet about asking Luis Gomez to help set up a dog fighting business, but finally, Turner said, "I received Marinara's approval. I want to go full speed ahead."

Eddie had no choice but to speak with Gomez. Later that day Eddie took a ride to Luis' neighborhood. Eddie parked the car and waited patiently outside the park where Gomez sometimes held court. Sure enough after an hour, along came Luis with his two captains, Enrique and Jose. Luis walked past without noticing Eddie sitting there.

"Luis," called Eddie, "Over here."

Luis told his two pals to go on without him and stayed outside Eddie's car.

"What brings Big Ed to our neighborhood? Thursday is delivery day. You're two days early. Are you catching 'old-timers' disease?"

"Get in. I have something to talk to you about." Luis climbed in without a word.

"What do you know about dog fighting? You have it all over your country, right?"

444

"We do, and I hate it."

"Well Phil wants you to find a venue to start holding the fights, and he wants you to see about supplying the dogs."

"Turner can go fuck himself. I'm not going anywhere near that disgusting ..."

"Luis, I am just the messenger, but I checked into it, and there is a lot of money to be made if we get the right people to come."

"You mean my kind of people."

Eddie ignored Luis and continued, "There are admission fees, percentages of the gambling and stud fees." Eddie stopped on this note. "I don't want to push Luis too quickly, or he'll tell me to go fuck myself, too."

"I'll call you in a few days. Think about it," said Eddie. "There's a lot of money involved." Eddie took off before Luis exploded.

§

After Eddie Fisher took off, Luis yelled, "Every time I'm tempted to think maybe these people are better than me, I realize they are the same as the garbage back home. The disgusting people who treat animals..."

Luis could get no more words out, but his mind rolled with the scene of his first dogfight. At nine he went to see his uncle in the next town. The town had a swimming pool, and Luis' father wanted him to learn to swim. The first night Luis was at his uncle's house, his uncle took him to a dogfight in a neighbor's barn. On the way over to the barn, Luis heard the words 'Blood Sport' for the first time. He was excited. It sounded like fun.

When Luis entered the barn with his uncle, the young boy saw a mad scene. Men yelled numbers and waved pieces of paper over their heads. The smell of sweating bodies, the odor of wet fur and the stench of blood filled Luis' nostrils.

The barn was dark, all lights shining on a twenty foot wide, five feet deep hole in the ground. Only a minute passed after Luis and his uncle were in their places when two cages were opened and out flew two ferocious pit bulls. The dogs ran for each other, crazed by the roar of the crowd. Biting and clawing, both animals soon ripped the skin off each other's faces and backs. When the blood flowed, the crowd roared louder. Young Luis tried unsuccessfully to cover his ears and his eyes simultaneously.

The young boy could stand no more and ran from the barn. Luis walked all the way home. The journey took three hours. When his mother and father asked why he left his uncle's place, Luis didn't answer; he went to bed and cried all night.

§

A year after Luis arrived in New York, a letter came from El Salvador with a note addressed to Luis from his Papi with the sad news Luis' dog, Ringo, had darted into the street and was hit by a speeding car. Luis was depressed for days. He needed his family around him for comfort. Luis' grand-aunt tried to comfort her grandnephew but knew only time would heal the open sore in the boy's heart. She encouraged Luis to buy a new dog, but Luis resisted the temptation because he knew how much attention a dog needed. Neither he nor his aunt could properly provide for an animal. He attempted to make up for this by taking great pleasure going to friends' homes and playing with their dogs. He laughed and played like he was a kid again. His friends saw him let his guard down, even willing to look silly, but no one dared comment. Luis could act however he wanted. He was already the boss.

The pet store owner in the neighborhood considered Luis his best customer. Luis spent a small fortune each week on treats and toys for all the dogs on his block and on the next and on the next. He'd always bring a toy and some treats to his friends' dogs. When Luis walked down the street, dogs waited hoping to see their pal. His friend Elmer said, "I don't know who goes wilder when you see a dog, you or the dog. You love them, don't you?"

Luis laughed, "No one greets me like my dogs. No girl wiggles her tail when she sees me or licks me as they do. They never complain. They love me just because I'm me. Elmer, it doesn't get any better."

§

Eddie hesitated to speak again with Luis about a dogfight venue, but Turner haunted him every day. "Did Gomez find a place? Did he find out where we can get dogs?" The questions never ended.

Fisher left the office and called Luis. "Gomez, any word on the how we'll set up the dogfights? Phil is becoming worried you're not on board with this."

The cellphone exploded with every English and Spanish curse word in both languages.

"I'll tell my boss you won't cooperate. I'll leave out what you wished him and his mother, and I'll get back to you." Eddie hung up, happy only to be the messenger between these two dangerous men.

§

Phil Turner hated looking at Eddie when his adult acne was acting up. So, before Eddie could come to his office, Phil left. He would speak to Gomez himself and straighten the spic out once and for all.

After Eddie called and told him what Gomez said, Turner phoned Luis directly and arranged a meeting with Gomez in an hour down by the river. No one would see him talking to the disgusting Latino. Turner would explain to Gomez he'd better not fuck with the guys who supplied the drugs, or he'd wind up dead.

When Turner pulled up, Gomez sat on a log by the water's edge. Gomez didn't turn around, even when Turner beeped the horn. Turner opened the window and called, "Gomez, come here." Turner didn't want to get out of the car. Turner repeated his words, but Gomez didn't move.

Phil stepped out of the car and walked over to the young Latino. Turner yelled, "Are you deaf, asshole?" Still no reaction from Gomez. Turner put a hand on Gomez's shoulder, but before Turner placed a second hand anywhere, Luis swung around and plunged a large knife into Phil's heart. Gomez twisted the knife violently to inflict the most damage.

Luis went to the water a few feet away and washed the knife clean, the same knife that twice saved his life on the long trip from Central America eight years ago.

§

The bell chimed, and Ted dragged himself to the door. He dreaded seeing anyone. His lethargy, so strong and powerful made every step an effort. Since throwing their two sons out of the house a month ago, Martha and Ted thought of nothing else. "Did we do the right thing?" Self-doubt consumed their days and nights. Both hoped their appointment next week with a therapist would give them some relief because their visits to the local tavern had come to a halt last weekend.

Ted pulled open the hollow pine door as if it were a heavy bronze door at a cathedral.

A young woman he'd never laid eyes on before stood on his top step. With great effort, Ted said, "How can I help you?"

"Hello," replied the young woman, hesitantly, "My name is Patricia, I, is this…"

Before she finished her sentence, Ted said, "You must have the wrong house. You probably want the family next door. They have children your age."

"I'm looking for the Kowalski family."

Confused, Ted said, "This is the Kowalski residence."

"Oh, Mr. Kowalski, I'm Patricia Reynolds, your son's girlfriend."

Still confused Ted said, "Which one?"

"Stanley."

Martha came to the door. She had heard everything from the couch. Ted hesitated, and Martha pushed her husband aside and gently escorted Patricia Reynolds into the house.

"It's nice finally to meet you, Mr. and Mrs. Kowalski."

"The same, dear."

Ted gained his composure, and said, "Please sit down."

Martha followed with, "Come here, Patricia. Sit here, next to me."

"Sorry for barging in unannounced, but Stanley only told me this morning about what happened between you. A month ago when your son showed up at my place, he asked if he could stay for a while. He said he fought with you."

Patricia stopped talking, unsure how to proceed.

"Go on, Patricia," said Martha.

"I let him stay because I didn't know what to do. He had this bag of clothes…" Patricia began to cry.

Martha reached for her hand and softly held it. It gave Patricia the strength to continue. "It wasn't until last night that he told me the rest of the story, why you threw him and his brother out. He told me about Thanksgiving and how you almost were alone on the holiday."

Now Martha cried. Ted held back any emotion to appear manly. His efforts didn't work. It only caused his face to turn beet red and looked like a balloon ready to burst.

Ms. Reynolds continued, "The thought I had any part in it horrified me. I can assure you, both me and my family were under the impression you were with relatives for the day. Stanley lied to me, and I'm angry with him. I told him to get out of my apartment and don't come back until he apologizes to you."

Smiles now accompanied Martha and Ted's tears. Patricia smiled, and the three broke into a laugh. "Stan seems to be getting the heave-ho from everyone."

The doorbell rang before Martha said how much she appreciated Patricia's visit. "Don't answer the door," said Ted. "It's probably the paperboy; he wants to get paid. This is more important."

"The boy needs to be paid." Martha went over to the chair, picked up her purse and headed for the door. She rummaged through her purse as she opened the door. "How are you, young man…"

Martha looked up from her purse and saw her son, Stan. He had tears in his eyes, and he threw his arms around his mother. Martha cried. Patricia went over to help, followed by Ted. Within seconds all four had their arms around each other, bawling their eyes out, for all the neighbors to see.

The Ted Kowalski didn't mind who saw them. Over the years, the whole neighborhood had seen the Kowalski's bad times. This afternoon, the neighbors were welcome to see the Kowalski's magnificent display of affection.

After the Kowalski family finally came inside, Martha and Ted's other son telephoned and apologized for his insensitive behavior during the past year. Martha suggested he come over and spend time with his brother and, Martha hoped, a new member of the Kowalski family, Patricia Reynolds. She added, "While you're coming over why not bring your clothes. "We miss you, Paul."

I miss you too, Mom." Martha tried to rush off the phone before she bawled.

The Kowalski's enjoyed each other's company for the rest of the afternoon. Patricia pulled Martha over by herself in the kitchen. "Mrs. Kowalski, I want you to know you and Mr. Kowalski are always welcome in our house, but especially on holidays. And when my parents have the holidays, you'll always be invited. You'll love my mother and father."

Martha grabbed this great girl and hugged her tightly. Both women had a good cry before they let each other go.

§

Ellen had only been gone an hour when Mary said to her grandson, "Harry if we want to grab a bite to eat before the movie, we'll have to leave soon. Why don't you go upstairs and wash up? We'll leave in a half hour." Harry charged up the flight of stairs like a wide receiver for the New York Giants.

Smartly, Mary planned something for her grandson to do immediately after his mother left for Paris. She hoped the next three months would be an enjoyable time for him. Harry would miss his parents, but Mary hoped not too much given all she had planned for him. Mary knew for certain she would have a ball. Mary understood how lucky she was to have this time with Harry and do all the things she'd planned.

Mary belonged to The New York Athletic club, right next door to her building. She joined the club for its restaurant and social events held each month. Mary had never stepped foot in the gym, and she planned to keep it that way, but her many male friends would offer to take Harry. Her grandson was about to have the time of his life with his grandma.

§

Harry settled in his grandmother's apartment, and two weeks later he asked his grandmother if she would take him to a New York Yankee baseball game.

Mary loved baseball, but for the past few years, she enjoyed watching the games from the comfort of her couch. For years Mark and she held season tickets to Yankee Stadium, but a few years ago they decided they would give them up. During the last few years, she found the steep stairways, the jostling crowds and the noise more than a little daunting.

Mary thought she'd give Harry a break and let him go to the Yankee game with someone other than his grandmother. "Maybe, I can ask one of the workers here to take Harry." Then she remembered Tom Foster was a huge Yankee fan. "I'll ask Tom to take Harry to a game. I could meet them afterward for dinner in Little Italy. Tom said it was one of his favorite places to eat in Manhattan."

Tom looked at his phone and saw Mary McMurray's number, "Hi, Mary. What's up?" Mary loved the breezy way Tom answered the phone. "Tom, Harry has been asking me to take him to a Yankee game since he's been here. I'm just not up to it, all the stairs and the noise. Do you think if I bought some really good seats and sent you both by car, you could find time to take Harry? I know it's an imposition, but…"

"I'd love to go. It would be fun. Besides, it would be nice to hang around with someone young for a change. It seems like I spend a lot of time with people a lot older than me."

"Tom, shut up."

Mary liked Tom's joking about their age differences. Both knew age never hindered their friendship.

"No kidding. I'd love to take Harry to a game. He seems like a terrific kid. We got along great when you brought him to the meeting last week. By the way, what did he think of the meeting?"

"He shrugged his shoulders and said, "They're all crazy, Grandma.""

"He's got that right," laughed Tom.

"What are you doing Saturday?"

"Not much. My new girlfriend is away, and my family is off to the Jersey shore. They rented a big house for the week. I have job interviews next week, so I couldn't go."

"How about I get tickets to the game and send a car for you. After the game, I could meet you both in Little Italy. I'll have a car pick you up at the stadium, and we'll meet at Angelo's on Mulberry Street in Little Italy at about six."

"Great, but don't send a car to my house. I'll meet Harry in your lobby."

"Tom, as usual, thanks."

"Saturday's game starts at 1:30. I'll be in your lobby by noon."

"Have the doorman ring me. I'll send Harry down. Thanks again, Tom. You're the best."

§

New York's Little Italy sang with the noise and exuberance of hungry people. Sights and smells bombarded visitors' senses and rewarded them for coming downtown. Mulberry Street radiated with aromas of oregano and garlic. Sweet basil streamed into Tom's nostrils.

Restaurants lined the streets, interspersed with souvenir shops. Shirts with sayings like 'IBM-Italian By Marriage,' 'Sicilians Are Sensational,' 'Nice People Have a Root in the Boot,' 'You No Lika My Cooking, I Breaka You Face.'" Stores sold gadgets, artifacts, and clothes, all claiming Italian heritage.

Harry's eyes looked everywhere. Both sides of the narrow street teemed with tourists and hometown New Yorkers. Everyone walked the length of Mulberry Street from Spring Street to Canal Street watching the action, smelling the marinara and the clam sauce, the calamari, and the mussels. Once you crossed Canal Street, you entered Chinatown.

Tom and Harry walked into a store on the corner of Kenmare and Mulberry Streets. Every inch of wall and floor overflowed with merchandise: Religious articles, patron saint figures, spaghetti makers, cappuccino machines and espresso cups. Statues of Liberty in a myriad of sizes lined one shelf. Green, white and red tassels perfect for hanging off car mirrors and hand-painted pasta dishes for kitchen tables filled another wall.

Tom bought a shirt that read, 'Made in the US, With Original Italian Parts' for one of his nieces.

Harry slipped his wallet from his back pocket, walked over to the cashier and told the shop girl he wanted the sculpture of a spaghetti bowl with a fork suspended three inches above a dish of linguine.

Tom smiled at the sculpture. The twirling fork lifting the pasta from the red bowl was quite a novelty. Harry pulled out a five dollar bill and handed it to the cashier. The girl said, "That will be forty dollars."

Harry looked at the girl in amazement. He held the five dollar bill in his hand. Tom quickly interceded taking the sculpture gently from Harry, "It's a wonderful gift for your mom, but why don't we postpone buying it till your grandma comes." Tom handed the cashier the twirling pasta sculpture, "Thank you very much." He turned to Harry and said "Let's go eat. I'm hungry."

Tom guided Harry out the door. The two continued on Mulberry Street past restaurant after restaurant until Tom decided on one he hadn't been to since he was ten, 'Amici II.'

Tom promised to meet Mary at Angelo's Restaurant, but he wanted to go to Amici for old time's sake. He knew Mary wouldn't care; so he'd text her about the change. They passed the red and white Campari umbrellas, a staple outside Angelo's, and continued another half block, leisurely taking in the flavor of the neighborhood: old metal garbage cans, four-way spigots, johnnie pumps, and wrought iron fire escapes.

The dinner crowd mushroomed since their arrival on Mulberry. Old and young poured into little Italy, swelling the streets to the point navigating down the block was tricky.

The maître d' led Tom and Harry to a back table against the right wall of the restaurant. Philodendron plants spilled leafy stems down from brown wooden rafters. Red and white checkered tablecloths covered each table. Empty Chianti bottles with candles sticking out, gave a glow to each table settings.

Mary was due any minute. Tom texted her the restaurant's name as he looked at the menu. As usual, he found it difficult to choose only one appetizer or one entre over another.

"Harry, what's your favorite Italian dish?"

"For sure, it's meatballs and spaghetti."

"I tasted your grandma's meatballs. Don't be disappointed if these aren't as good."

"I see pictures of superheroes on the walls."

"Yes, a lot of them come here for dinner or rather the actors who play them come and eat here."

"I want to go see them up close." Harry rose from his chair and headed for the pictures on the opposite wall close to the front of the restaurant.

"Harry, wait." But, Harry shot across the room.

Tom let him look, but kept a close eye on the boy.

The waiter came over and asked if they were ready to order. "In a few minutes. We are waiting for a friend." The waiter offered a beverage. Tom said, "I'll have a Bud Light."

The waiter left, and Tom returned his gaze toward Harry. Tom looked over at the pictures, but Harry wasn't there. Tom immediately tried to focus more clearly. He frantically scanned the whole restaurant.

§

Tom ran toward the door, knocking over chairs in his path. He pushed through ten people waiting for tables. When Tom reached the street, there was no sign of Harry, up or down the crowded sidewalk

"Did anyone see a boy dragged down the street?" Tom screamed.

A woman Tom's age, yelled: "I saw a man carrying a kid a minute ago." She pointed toward Canal Street. Thanks to the running shoes he wore by mistake, Tom reached Canal Street in a minute. He stood on the corner of Canal and Mulberry Street and looked across at all four corners, no sign of Harry.

Tom glimpsed someone running down Canal Street on the border of Chinatown headed toward the Manhattan Bridge. Running as fast as he could, Tom swung his head into every doorway he passed: Gold Corner Jewelry, Golden Gate Rings, and Golden Duck Noodle.

Tom reached the next corner which intersected with Mulberry. There was no street sign on the four corners, only two Chinese restaurants and two Chinese take-out stores on each corner. Tom looked down the cross-street and saw a young boy about Harry's height crossing Mott Street, but the boy has light brown skin. Tom flew to the next intersection, Mott Street and Mulberry.

Tom saw a man dragging a small boy. The man and the boy were too far away to be sure the boy was Harry. Tom took a chance it was. The boy and the man turned onto Elizabeth Street up toward Grand Street.

Tom tore down the sidewalk toward Grand. He prayed he wouldn't lose sight of the boy. He reached Grand, ripped around the corner, no boy, only adults window shopping for lamps.

Winded and ready to collapse, Tom headed back up Mott and caught sight of a man pulling a boy by the arm. Tom's legs cramped, his chest throbbed.

Tom reached Café Carmela at the corner of Grand and Elizabeth Street, turned and looked to see if anyone was in front or back of him. He took a deep breath, crossed the jammed intersection, and continued down Mulberry. As he sped past Benito's, La Bella and Pisano's, Tom focused on the faces inside. Back at the corner of Canal and Mulberry he paused for a second, caught his breath, and dashed across Canal on a yellow light. A BMW with Jersey plates missed hitting him by inches.

On the other side of Canal, faces immediately turned Chinese. This was the beginning of Chinatown, a densely populated area of the city, a place where foot traffic was light after dark, where street lights illuminated dark tenement facades, and where closed Chinese restaurants lined the narrow sidewalks. The iron-shuttered Chinese restaurants catered to a busy lunch trade.

Panting like a thirsty dog, and again ready to collapse, Tom headed up further into Chinatown. He saw a man pulling a boy by the arm outside the Wanton Noodle Factory. Tom's legs wobbled. Running was impossible. His eyes strained to keep his focus on the young boy. The man turned the corner dragging the boy behind him.

If this was the abductor, he was headed for Kenmore Street back toward where this nightmare began. Tom prayed someone outside Amici's would recognize Harry and help. Tom reached Mulberry, heart pounding. He turned the corner, no sign of the boy.

Another deep breath and the wind returned to Tom's lungs. He stopped and took two more deep breaths. His leg cramps gone, Tom jogged up Kenmore, headed for Mulberry. These streets were more residential with four-story red brick structures. The man could have dragged Harry into any of these buildings, and no one would ever know.

A yellow cab stopped for a light twenty feet from where Tom stood. Tom hopped in. The cabbie took one look at Tom. "Are you having a heart attack?"

"No, but I need your help. Drive up and down these streets. Someone took my son. Please, drive up and down these streets and circle the immediate blocks. I'm sure my son is around here somewhere."

The Pakistani cabbie pulled away from the curb. "Don't worry. I know these streets. We'll find your boy." Tom didn't explain Harry wasn't his son.

"I'll go two blocks over to Broadway, then, onto Canal and down Mulberry, then, up and down the side streets."

Tom watched from the cab window for any small figure walking on the sidewalks.

The cabbie screamed. "Look over there, across Broadway, a man with a tight grip on a kid."

Tom screamed, "Stop." He jumped out.

The cabbie called after, "I'll follow you in the cab."

Tom brooked the oncoming traffic and yelled, "Harry."

The boy turned, and Tom saw Harry's frightened face. The man turned, and Tom saw the man's face. The pain in Tom's chest worsened and prevented him from running faster. Tom tried to keep his eyes glued to Harry, but the traffic interfered with Tom's line of vision.

Tom looked up Broadway. Harry was gone again. The only store opened was a supermarket at the corner of Prince and Broadway. The huge blinking neon sign read FOOD ASSOCIATES. OPEN 24/7. The rest of the shops had iron gates pulled down.

The Pakistani cabbie pulled up directly across the street from Tom. He beeped his horn and called Tom. The traffic muffled the cabbie's voice. The cabbie signaled he'd continue looking up Broadway.

Shuttered stores narrowed the answers to the question, "What store did the man pull Harry into." The kidnapper may have dragged Harry into the food store or may have gone further uptown. Tom had a strong feeling he should at least take a quick look in FOOD ASSOCIATES.

The electronic doors opened to let Tom through. The store was empty. All fifteen check-out registers were quiet. The fluorescent fixtures blasted light from the ceiling and showed not a soul in sight.

The food aisles looked like an empty movie set. How could this store afford to stay open? Tom remembered hearing business was brisk in the mornings and afternoons down here, but after the office workers left downtown, the area was empty except a few blocks over in Little Italy.

Tom walked past cash register after cash register and turned into the vegetable aisle. At the end of the aisle, he turned right into the next aisle, up another aisle down one more. Tom heard noise a few aisles away. He couldn't tell how many aisles for sure, maybe two over, maybe more.

The rustling noise sounded louder but still low. Was the abductor holding a hand around Harry's mouth or was it a clerk talking on his cell while stocking shelves for tomorrow's customers.

Tom tiptoed to the end of the aisle. The noise came from the back of the store. Tom proceeded down the condiment aisle. He looked for something to use to fight the kidnapper. All he saw was bread crumbs, ketchup, and salad dressing, nothing he could use. More noises came from aisle six near the rear of the store. He proceeded up aisle seven looking for some product he could use: Diapers, baby food, tissues, nothing. At the end of aisle 7, he saw a clerk stocking shelves.

Tom asked, "Have you seen…?" Then he caught sight of a mirror hanging from the ceiling showing the next aisle. A man pushed a basket. "No, wait, it's not a basket. He isn't pushing a basket…"

Tom flew towards the front of the store, turning into aisle six without losing a step. He saw Harry for a second as he turned into aisle 7.

"Harry," Tom called out

"Tom, please help!"

Rejuvenated by seeing Harry and hearing his cry for help, Tom raced to save the boy. Harry's hand tried to hold on to the shelves, but instead, pulled down three large glass apple juice bottles and a glass bottle of Gatorade.

Tom saw the kidnapper dragging Harry along the floor. Tom jumped over the puddle of apple juice and Gatorade foaming in the aisle. The tiled floor caused Tom to slip, but not fall. A leap over some potato chip bags caught his heel and down he went.

Tom quickly jumped up and continued his pursuit. Tom headed down Aisle 9 and watched the kidnapper run out the front door. Tom followed him out of the store. He realized the man was alone and it meant Harry was still in the store. Hope and jubilation filled him with such intensity he wept.

Tom ran up and down aisles calling, "Harry, Harry. It's alright Harry come out. You're safe. It's over; the nightmare is over."

The stock boy watched the scene and ran to the manager's office, positive they had a crazy man in the store.

Tom continued to call out to Harry, "It's alright."

Harry did not appear, and Tom's stomach tightened into a knot. He looked, aisle after aisle, but Harry was nowhere. Tom looked on the wide bread shelves, under displays, everywhere. Tom arrived at the last aisle, and still no Harry.

Panic gripped Tom's entire being; legs wobbled again, stomach turned, heart pounded.

Tom heard soft knocking and looked over at the milk and egg refrigerator, and there was Harry. Through the door, Tom saw the young boy's beautiful face pressed against the glass. Tom grabbed the door handle and almost yanked it off its hinges. He pulled Harry out of the cooler, pulled the boy close, and hugged him tightly. The poor kid almost stopped breathing.

"Tom, Tom, I can't breathe." Tom loosened his grip, and Harry smiled bravely. "I'm alright, Tom. Don't worry. I'm alright."

The store manager approached Tom carefully, waited a moment and said, "Can I do anything, Mister."

Tom held Harry close to him. "Everything is fine, now," and walked out of the store carrying Harry in his arms. The two had walked twenty feet when the Pakistani cabbie pulled up to the curb. "Hop in. I'm driving you anywhere you want, no charge." Harry and Tom hopped in. They hadn't driven a mile when Harry fell sound asleep.

CHAPTER 28

THE DOOR TO SUPERINTENDENT PINZON'S OFFICE OPENED far enough to see the two men standing in his office dressed in black suits, white shirts, black ties, with high and tight haircuts.

Mary had a few questions for the superintendent before tonight's executive board meeting, but when she saw he had company she waited. Tom Foster walked by and also wondered about the two official-looking men.

One man looked out at Tom and went to the door and closed it. When Lou and Vince passed the door was closed, so they saw no one. Ted was still in a daze since his future daughter-in-law spoke so kindly to him and Martha.

As board members entered the conference room, they took their regular seats. Pleasantries exchanged, Mary commented, "Ted, you look like the cat that swallowed the canary."

"I feel great. Life's never been better."

"I'm happy for you," replied Mary sincerely.

"Some of my happiness I owe to you, Mary. Your advice on what to do with my sons helped a lot. Martha and I are very grateful."

"Vince, I meant to ask," said Tom, "Have you found out if Linda is having a boy or a girl?"

"We just found out yesterday, Tom. It's going to be a girl."

Everyone congratulated him.

Talking slowed until there wasn't a sound in the room.

The group was becoming impatient for the superintendent to arrive to begin the meeting. "What's taking Rocco so long," asked Vince.

Tom jumped up. "I'll go see."

Tom wasn't out of his seat when superintendent Pinzone walked in, the two men in black suits following.

Before Rocco could introduce the two men to the board, they walked over to Vince Miller and announced, "You're under arrest for money laundering and racketeering in violation of Federal Law 18 U.S. Code Sec. 1956. A court has ordered the Federal Receiver of Taxes to seize all your financial assets."

The other man said to Vince, "Please, stand up."

As soon as Vince rose from his chair, the man handcuffed him. "Now, please, lie on the floor, face down."

The board sat motionlessly. Ted seemed to have stopped breathing. Tom, Jeremy, and Mary focused on Vince's face as he obeyed the agent.

Tom couldn't figure out why the man ordered Miller to the floor until the taller agent turned to Lou and said, "Louis Marinara you are under arrest, charged with money laundering..."

To Mary, it sounded like Lou and Vince were charged with the same violations of the law.

"Please stand up. I'm going to handcuff your wrists."

"The smaller agent jerked Vince to a standing position.

"Sorry for the interruption," said the agents as they unceremoniously ushered Lou and Vince from the room."

Ted, Tom, Father, and Jeremy sat at the conference table stunned. Mary said, "I guess we have to find two more people to fill these vacancies on the board." She didn't tell the rest of the group she wasn't surprised by the arrests.

Mary didn't imagine she'd witness Lou and Vince being ushered out of the district office in handcuffs. She felt the hand of her son-in-law,

Todd, in the way law enforcement arrested Lou and Vince. "I suspect Todd wanted me to get some payback for all the two had done." To Mary's surprise, she felt only relief.

The superintendent called out, "Why don't we call it a night?"

No one responded. Everyone got up and left.

§

The board met the following week for a special meeting to replace the seats vacated by Lou Marinara and Vince Miller. After a week of telephone calls back and forth the school board members decided Roy Baker would fill the Miller vacancy and Angie Marinara would fill her estranged husband's seat. The new coalition of board members decided during the myriad of calls Mary McMurray would replace Lou as chairperson. Ted Kowalski was to remain vice-chairman. Ted accepted it. He knew he wasn't up to the challenges facing a chairperson.

The irony of Angie replacing her estranged husband on the school board wasn't lost on anyone. The choice wasn't illogical. Angie had been involved in school board politics for thirty years, even before Lou had any interest.

Not only did Angie Marinara run her husband's first successful school board campaign, but all subsequent ones. Angie enjoyed the challenge, but she never suspected the extent to which her husband had abused this position on the school board.

Ted called the meeting to order. By a show of hands, who votes for Mrs. McMurray for chairperson of this school board? All hands went up. "By a vote of five to zero, Mary McMurray becomes our new school board chairman. Congratulations." Ted handed the gavel to Mary. "Mrs. McMurray will now finish chairing this meeting."

"Thank you, Ted, and thank you all for your confidence. We've two important items on the agenda tonight, replacement of two board members, Lou Marinara and Vince Miller who have resigned as part of their proposed federal plea bargain agreement. Can I have nominations for both of these positions? Four votes are all we need for confirmation."

"I nominate Roy Baker," said Tom."

"I nominate Angela Marinara," said Father Grant.

Jeremy seconded both nominations.

"Are there any more nominations for these two seats? Mary heard silence, and she called the roll. Tom, Mary, Ted, Father, and Jeremy all voted for the two nominated candidates.

"Both Roy Baker and Angie Marinara are outside in Jemma's office," said Tom. "I want to call them in and congratulate them."

A chorus of applause went up for the newest board members.

Tom walked out to Jemma's office and brought in Roy and Angie. Another round of applause greeted them. No one present felt anything but jubilation, except Jemma. No one noticed the tears dripping down her face.

§

"Bunny looks beautiful. Frank looks handsome in his black tux.

"What a day for a wedding," said Mary. "We had some concerns whether or not the ceremony would be able to be held outdoors, but look the sun is shining and the sky couldn't be bluer."

Angie said, "Mary, it was generous of you to rent out the event space on the roof of your building. The venue impressed everyone when they arrived at your co-op. We met with more security than at the White House."

"It's only fifty people. This rooftop is used for a lot bigger parties than this."

"Maybe so," said Angie, "But this type of venue is new to ninety-nine percent of today's guests.

Tom saw the ceremony was about to start. "I better go over with the groom. Frank's probably looking for his best man."

As Tom headed over to the temporary altar overlooking Central Park, Mary turned to Tom's mother, "Alice, your Tom is something else. I'd like to see him run for higher office. He can do even more good than he has done on the school board."

"What higher office?"

"Whatever comes up first, Assembly, State Senate or even Congress. All three of the ones holding the office are old. Tom has developed quite a reputation. Once in a while, I meet politicos, and they always ask about your son. They ask me, 'How is he?' I tell them Tom Foster has the whole package. They're asking because they always look to the future, and Tom is the future."

"Don't you need a lot of money to run for office today?"

"I'll raise the money from my friends here in Manhattan. They're always looking to back a winner. And they'll see Tom as just that."

"Look who showed up."

Alice Foster looked over and saw Martha and Ted Kowalski shaking hands with Father Grant. "I'm so glad Martha and Ted finally came to terms with their two sons."

"Tom told me about it. The older son Stan is getting married in a couple of months, and the girl's parents gave them a house in Westchester, three acres of land, a pool and a guest house. Stan's fiancée, Patricia, offered Ted and Martha the guesthouse to live in when they're ready to move."

"The wedding planner is signaling for us to take our seats."

Up at the altar, the groom whispered to Tom, "Let's enjoy today. We're into some rough weather ahead back in the district. I received a text from my assistant principal."

Tom looked at Frank and warned, "Enough, Frank. Not another word. Think only of the wonderful woman you're about to marry.

The organ began, Bunny's children, three boys and two girls started down the makeshift aisle. The breathtaking view of Central Park didn't distract one eye from watching Bunny Krouse walk down the aisle.

Frank looked at Bunny dressed beautifully, hair and make-up perfect. "She's beautiful. I'm the luckiest guy in the world."

Tom thought, "Not the first time someone used those words, but they are sure true this time."

§

An hour after Lou and Vince were arrested at the district office, Elliot Rush called Pena Marinara and told her everything had collapsed.

Although Pena dreaded this day, she had prepared for it since her return to New York. Each week, Pena secretly sent money to an account in the Italian sector of Switzerland. She told Lou, "The account has your name on it." She left out there was also an account, a much bigger one, with her name on it, under her maiden name, Latanzio.

An hour after Pena received the call from Elliot Rush, she was packed and on her way to the airport. Two hours after the call, Pena Latanzio sat in first class on an Alitalia jet headed for the mountain village of her birth in Sicily. No one would ever find Pena Latanzio. She'd live well with people who would protect her.

Pena picked up a copy of Vanity Fair from the pouch in front of her. The magazine slipped from her hand. She reached down to get it. As she straightened up, she looked across the aisle and saw Lou's friend, Bennie Singh. Their eyes met. He looked away and said nothing.

Pena took Bennie's cue. She paged through her periodical. "That son of a bitch caused so much pain to so many people, and he gets off scot-free."

Bennie sat thinking about how Pena helped her fat ugly boyfriend try to destroy a community. "Pena is one smart lady. Lou goes to jail, and she goes to the beautiful Mediterranean. Before I board my connecting flight to India, I'll slip my new cell number to her. You never know, maybe we can do business sometime."

§

The police arrested Eddie Fisher at his house, the house he shared with his grandmother. As the cops escorted Eddie out of the house, he considered telling them about grandma, then thought better of it. "Let her rest in peace. She's not bothering anyone."

"The police picked Fisher up after Lou Marinara confessed to fifty criminal counts, a mix of felonies and misdemeanors. Marinara implicated Eddie in an attempt to cut a deal with prosecutors from the U.S. Attorney's Office and with the local DA."

"Eddie Fisher beat them all," laughed Mary.

"Well not exactly," replied Tom.

"He thwarted Lou's plan," said Jeremy. "Eddie gave the prosecutors nothing. The government hired the best psychiatrists who plied Eddie with every combination of drugs known to man in an attempt to control Fisher's batshit crazy mind."

"And after months of therapy and drugs," interjected Rocco. "The Court declared Eddie crazy, insane, bonkers."

"Where did they finally send him? Is it a secret?" asked Tom.

"Rocco, do you know?" Mary asked.

"They sent him to a facility for the criminally insane in upstate New York, near the Canadian border. Lou Marinara isn't far away in prison two miles from Saranac Lake.

Angie was the only one who knew how ironic it was Lou was sent to a minimum security prison upstate. Lou would be taken there on the railroad by a federal marshal. The prison had been converted fifty years ago from a TB clinic.

Although Angie hated her husband of forty years, she hoped he would be comforted knowing he would die in the same place as his mother.

§

The last public school board meeting of the year meant two months off from almost all school board activity. "Tonight's agenda showed nothing of importance," said Frank Fontaine.

"The meeting will be quick," responded Tom. "Mary McMurray doesn't waste time with nonsense."

"Frank, thank you for preparing your school on such short notice for tonight's public meeting," said Mary. "James Buchanan High School's water main break made it impossible to hold the meeting there."

"No problem, Mrs. McMurray. We're happy to have the school board meeting here."

Mary had long given up telling Frank Fontaine to call her Mary. "He's such a gentleman."

"I set up my office for your preparation meeting." Frank pointed the way.

The board members sat down, and Mary said to the board, "This'll take only be a few minutes."

Frank closed his office door, and it swung back open. Three hooded figures appeared in the doorway. They carried submachine guns. The board members stood up.

"Sit, down," said one gunman in faulty English. "We're here to punish you for destroying our children's lives with your deals and pay-offs. We will kill you one at a time. You'll watch each other die. You'll be a lesson for those who will follow you. Your deaths will make the people mindful of the evil they do to other people's children."

"We'll start with the person on the end." said the second gunman. "And we'll go across the room until you're all dead." When the gunman saw Roy's face, he smiled broadly.

Although the gunman's mask covered all but his eyes, Roy saw the same penetrating stare he first saw at Giordano's Funeral Home.

The gunman pointed their machine guns directly at Father Grant sitting on the far left of the conference table. "Everyone look at the Priest. I'll count to ten, and then he'll be dead."

While all eyes were on Father, Mary slipped her hand into her oversized bag and gripped the pistol which she carried everywhere. She pulled the pistol out smoothly and shot the first gunman in the face. The second gunman shot at Mary but missed. Mary took a shot at the second gunman and took out his Adams Apple. The third gunman shot Mary in the chest.

Frank Fontaine charged the third man, knocked the gun out of his hand and pulled him to the floor. Father dove for the gun and pointed it threateningly at the surviving gunman. Frank Fontaine held the gunman tightly.

The police charged in the door, guns drawn. A shot rang out, and blood poured from the chest of the remaining gunman. The gunman fell, and Frank immediately dropped to the floor to administer CPR.

Fontaine pulled the mask off the gunman, and Tom recognized Luis Gomez.

Tom looked away and continued cradling an unconscious Mary McMurray in his arms. Within seconds Tom felt his good friend's body go limp. Tom felt for a pulse in Mary's neck. There was none. Everyone watched, how Tom gently continued to hold Mary. Father Grant began the prayers for the dead. The police and EMS knew there was nothing else to do and joined in the prayer.

§

Mary's daughter, Ellen, pulled out all the stops for her mother's final hurrah. The parish church was decked out like a spring garden, smells of jasmine, rose, hyacinth and lily filled the air. There were flowers on the altar and at the end of each pew.

Ellen insisted Tom sit in the first pew with the immediate family. Three rows behind sat Jeremy, Theresa, and Angie, next to Jonas and Nora Thompson. Sitting next to the Thompsons were Ted and Martha Kowalski. Martha wanted to sit further back, but Ted insisted he belonged up front. The rest of the next thirty pews were full of friends and neighbors and the staff of 300 Central Park South.

Ushers helped the crowds settle into their seats.

Newlyweds Bunny and Frank Fontaine sat with Tom's parents, Alice and Pete Foster. Bunny smiled, convinced Mary would be happy to see everyone here today. Bunny looked around the beautiful church and saw quite a few smiles on the mourners' faces.

Lulu Belle, Mary's beautician, was across the aisle happy Ellen McMurray asked her to do Mary's hair one last time. Lulu came with a large group of regulars from the beauty parlor.

The parish choir, augmented by five professional vocalists and accompanied by eight musicians playing three trumpets, four violins and a piano, sang beautifully. The organist played all of Mary Mc Murray's favorite hymns. The heavenly music calmed the packed church, and the mood turned solemn. The people realized Mary McMurray was gone forever. The mourning became palpable.

Father Grant stood on the altar and faced the mourners. The pallbearers watched for a signal to bring the body of Mary McMurray down the long center aisle.

Father's eulogy touched everyone. There wasn't a dry eye in the church. After Father finished speaking, the local Congressman, State Senator and the Mayor of New York City addressed the gathering from the pulpit.

Each speaker described how Mary left the community a much better place. The Mayor emphasized Mary retired from her job after a successful career in business and instead of spending her retirement traveling to exotic ports for excitement, she chose the excitement of our streets, of our schools and our community.

The mourners caught the irony of the word excitement and smiled. The Mayor saw the reaction his words caused and took the opportunity to point out Mary McMurray's sense of humor. "I can picture Mary looking down this morning and being grateful for all of you being here. I can hear Mary say, 'If I had ducked when the gunman pointed the gun, I would be sitting with you today.' "But then Mary would look around and see Mark sitting next to her, and she'd say, 'No thanks. I'll stay right here with my Mark, and we'll both wait for you all to come up to visit."

The Mayor waited for the mourners' chuckles, then said, "I've one more thing to tell you. Mary McMurray donated a half million dollars for a new park to be built on a vacant lot which she also donated. It's on Talbot Place. The new park will be named the Lettie Grimes Children's Park, after a former school board colleague. Mary knew how important this recognition would be to Lettie Grimes. Mary also requested in the future no street, school or park be named after her. Mary felt she had all the recognition she needed while she was alive." The Mayor paused, tearing up. "May God, bless you, Mary McMurray, and may you and Mark rest in peace. "The pews were filled with people holding their handkerchiefs as they filed out of the Church. Beautiful organ music filled the church, accompanied by the brass and string instruments playing Mary's favorite, *How Great Thou Art*.

At the curb mourners filed into limousines, SUVs, sedans and pickup trucks. The line of cars driving to the cemetery extended as far as the eye could see. The cortege began its journey to the cemetery out in Nassau County. The ride along the North Shore country roads, through some of the wealthiest communities in the country, went solemnly.

No one minded the forty-five-minute drive. As car after car arrived at the tall black wrought iron gates of Brookville Cemetery, each vehicle glided slowly through the cemetery gates.

Tom thought, "I feel like I did when I smoked weed for the first time. Troubles were left behind. Peace and tranquility combined with brilliant sun, green grass, and floral bushes. Mary, are you trying to tell me something?"

Twenty minutes after the first limousine pulled into Brookville Cemetery, the funeral director signaled the mourners to exit their vehicles and follow him to the gravesite. This old North Shore burial ground differed from the usual cemetery. Originally, families bought plots for their whole family, twenty, thirty or more grave sites. The original inhabitants of the North Shore of Long Island purchased the plots near their summer palaces. The Jones family had a plot, next to the robber barons who built summer mansions on the North Shore overlooking the Long Island Sound, the Whitney, Astors, Phipps, and Vanderbilts.

Ellen, Harry, and Todd led the mourners to a beautiful grove shaded by mature maple trees. A large gravestone with the name Mark McMurray stood center stage in the grove. The grave had been dug, and a green rug covered the hole. The mourners circled the open grave, and the pallbearers placed Mary's casket on beams laid across the hole.

Usually, mourners in all cemeteries revisit their preference for burial or cremation. This group was no different. Ted whispered to Martha, "I want to be buried, not cremated." Bunny turned to Frank and said, "Cremate me," Jeremy to Theresa, "You decide for me when the time comes."

The undertaker said, "We'll now take a second to say our silent prayer for our dear friend and relative Mary McMurray." Tom wiped his eyes as did Father, Bunny, Alice, Jeremy, and Theresa.

At the family's request, Mary's casket was lowered into the grave while the mourners watched. The sight of a person lowered into the ground was an upsetting sight not easily forgotten.

Gravediggers took the boards off the grave and the undertaker invited each person to take a yellow carnation from the funeral director and his three assistants and throw it onto the casket as they passed to pay their last respects to a wonderful woman.

A few mourners headed for their cars too upset to go up to the grave and throw a flower on the lowered casket, but all Mary's fellow board members walked to the edge of the grave, paused and tossed a white rose on their friend's mahogany casket.

§

On the way to their car Bunny explained to Frank how Mary wound up in this cemetery. "Mary and Mark read an advertisement in the Times one Sunday; a burial plot was for sale by a prominent Long Island family who had only a few surviving members, and those left in this storied lineage had no wish to be buried at Brookville Cemetery. The ten-plot grave was unused.

Mary turned to Mark and said, "It would be fun to have a plot in one of the most beautiful cemeteries in the country."

"There might be one problem my dear.

"And what might it be?

"The other residents may not accept us."

Mary hit her husband on the arm with the newspaper.

"Mark, if you don't mind I'm trying to give us some class."

"Let's take a look first," said Mark. "Well, drive out and see what it looks like."

§

Father Grant returned from the cemetery and went to the rectory mailbox. One piece of mail jumped out because of the quality of the envelope and the Bishop's seal. The return address made his heart race. "Am I in trouble? What did I forget to do?" He tore the envelope open and scanned the page. He didn't see the words 'transferred to,' 'failed to do,' or 'in trouble,' and felt a sigh of relief.

He went back to the top of the page and read each line carefully. He couldn't believe his eyes. The bishop wanted him to come to his office and work closely with him on several projects.

The letter read, "The areas I want to work with you are outreach programs for schools, students, and curriculum development with special emphasis on the LGBTQ teen population."

Father couldn't believe what the bishop had written. "I have long been impressed with your work on your local school board. Your work and the work of some of your fellow board members have shown you have been at the forefront of some very progressive areas, gender-neutral bathroom, and gender-neutral sports teams. Your efforts to ensure equal treatment for schools in both minority and majority neighborhoods have also impressed me. I have received requests from rabbis and Protestant ministers all over the diocese requesting your help with their congregations." The bishop's letter requested Father Grant call the diocesan office right away.

Father sat down, caught his breath and immediately made the call. Father did not realize the bishop kept such close tabs on his priests. "I can't believe the special title assistant to the bishop. I will have a chance to have a real impact on the lives of the two million people in the diocese. I believe I actually can make a difference. "

After eight rings the operator picked up, "Diocesan office, how may I help you?"

"This is Father Grant from St Pancras Parish. I received a letter from the bishop requesting I call him."

"I will put you through to his secretary."

The phone rang another nine times before someone picked-up."

"Yes, Monsignor Douglas here."

"Monsignor, this is Father Grant from St Pancras Parish."

"Hello, Father. I'm happy to hear from you. The bishop wants you to come in sometime this week. Are you free on Friday at eleven?"

"I am."

"Father, I have to go. It's crazy here today. We'll talk on Friday."

Father Grant got off the phone invigorated at the prospect of working in an office with so much activity, new work, new friends, and new challenges. He could feel some of the loneliness leaving his soul.

§

Todd sat comfortably in his split-level home in New Jersey. Ellen's lasagna dinner put him in a relaxed mood. He re-read the report he wrote at work today describing the arrests of Vince Miller and Lou Marina. Now, he had to finish the report by explaining the intricate web of gang and mafia entanglement in his late mother-in-law's school district.

Ellen walked into the den and sat across from her husband. "Need any help?"

"I do. You know some of these people better than I do."

"Harry went to bed early so we won't have any interruptions. Let's get started."

"The first tip anything was going on was when your mom called about Tom's tire being blown out by a bullet on their drive home from Long Island. I called my New York office and asked if they had any active investigations of anyone connected with your mother's school district."

"And their answer was a resounding, 'Yes.'"

"They said they had been looking for years at this guy, Marinara, and his connection to a Mafia Don, Luigi Costa. They tried to see if the Costa Family was doing any funny business with the school district, but they always came up empty-handed."

"Mom bumped heads with Marinara from 'Day One,' and it never changed. I guess she was the first person to challenge his shenanigans."

"There was a lot more than shenanigans going on. Your mom was a threat to Marinara's money laundering and to his byzantine maze of providing jobs for people."

"The New York office also told me they were looking at this guy Bennie Singh. Immigration complaints began to trickle in, and we referred any questions or complaints to ICE. They kept us up to speed and the name Vince Miller appeared in some of the complaints."

Ellen asked, "Weren't most of the letters from organizations representing undocumented workers cheated out of their pay?"

"Yes, it became so bad they took the chance of being deported rather than take any more of his shit. This guy Singh employed hundreds of undocumented workers in his stores across the metropolitan area. He would withhold pay telling them he would give them the money at Christmas. He said it was like a savings account for them."

The phone rang, and Todd saw it was Tom Foster. "Hey, Tom, how are you?" We were just talking about Bennie Singh and Vince Miller."

"Ask Tom if he ever heard who might have been the intruder in his house or my mother's."

"I'll put the phone on speaker," said Todd, "Then we all can talk."

"Can you hear me, Tom," said Todd.

"Yes. How are you? We haven't spoken since the funeral. I apologize, Ellen, for not calling before this."

Ellen heard Tom's voice crack. "Tom I understand. It's been hard here too."

Todd broke the silence. " Ellen wanted me to ask, do you have any idea who the intruder was that day at Mary's house or yours?"

"This guy Eddie said something to Roy Baker about Lou Marinara getting one of Luigi Costa's thugs to go and snoop around. Ironically, the intruder made your mother decide to start carrying a gun. The person who came to my house was Elmer Rodriguez. I recognized him when the police tore his mask off."

Todd interjected, "An illegal gun."

"Always the cop," said Ellen.

"Your mother only told me she carried the gun a few days before the shooting. She saved all our lives."

Again, silence. "Ellen, I'm sorry…"

"Don't say anything, Tom. She saved the others, and it cost mom her life. I'm sure she'd do it over again, especially for you. Mom loved you a lot, Tom."

Three people who loved Mary McMurray ended their conversation for now.

§

When the phone rang, again, Todd and Ellen were tempted not even to look to see who it was. Ellen was the first to give in.

"It's Roy Baker," said Ellen.

"We better get it," said Todd, picking up the phone.

"Roy, how are you?"

"Fine, Todd. I hope I'm not interrupting anything."

"Don't worry, but give me a second to put you on speaker. Ellen is here, and she wants to say hi."

"Hi Ellen"

"Hi, Roy, how is Genevieve?"

"She's good and sends her regards."

"She is such a great girl. I hope it works out for you two. My mom liked her a lot."

"Okay Ellen, that's enough. Roy didn't call to talk about his love life," said Todd. "Roy I'm glad you called, I have a few questions for you."

"Perfect timing, I have some questions for you. The local district attorney's office asked if I could clear up some things for them."

"You first," said Todd.

"Where was Vince Miller getting his personal drug supply?"

"Eddie Fisher supplied him on orders from Lou Marinara. I hear Mr. Miller is having a tough time detoxing. I went to the prison he's temporarily in yesterday morning, and the guards say they haven't seen anyone go through such extended withdrawal. I feel bad. Vince wasn't the worse guy in the world, and he has those poor kids with MD. I heard when he was a kid; his childhood was no picnic. Fisher started giving Miller drugs before the election. Marinara wanted to make sure he had a hold on Vince right from the start. Before he got involved with Lou, all Vince did was score some weed and some serious prescription drugs. Eddie's the one who got him hooked on cocaine. Towards the end when the pressure built working with Bennie Singh, Eddie offered heroin."

"I hope they send him to a prison close to the city. His kids want to see him, and their wheelchairs make visits difficult. They love him and want to be in touch. It's sad," said Ellen.

"Todd, is there any chance the FBI will go after Singh?" asked Roy.

"They'd like to, but it would be too difficult. With recent budget cuts, we have to pick our battles carefully, but you can be sure Bennie Singh won't be coming back here anytime soon."

"I heard the DA won't need to indict any individuals in the school district office. The charges against Lou, Vince and Eddie cover it," said Roy.

"That Fisher guy was quite a character, crazy as a hoot owl and smart as a fox. In a way, Fisher was a part of the reason I got my promotion. My boss told me that a good deal of the information they got out of Fisher was because of me. Fisher told them I was the one responsible for breaking the case open. He kept repeating it until it became fact. I don't know why he did it."

Interestingly enough, Eddie did the same thing for me," said Roy. "That's why I got promoted to Detective, First Grade."

"But why did he do it?" asked Todd.

"I think I know. Eddie liked Genevieve, and he liked Ellen."

"That's creepy," said Todd.

"No. It's one of the few un-creepy things about Eddie. One day at the office, Eddie passed several women as they gossiped in the hall. The women saw Eddie coming, and they turned their backs. Genevieve turned and faced Eddie and said, 'Hi Eddie. How are you today?' Eddie didn't answer, but he never forgot Genevieve's kindness that day."

"What did he like about Ellen?"

"He told someone that he was following Ellen the day she took off for the airport to go to Paris. She pulled away from your mother-in-law's house, and as she did, she smiled at him. Eddie said the smile made him feel good about himself. Eddie said he never had the same heart for spying on her after that."

Ellen and Todd said nothing."

"It shows you one small thing can mean an awful lot to a person who has very little. I've got to go. I'm picking up Genevieve to go to a movie."

Ellen said, "When we move into the city, I want to have you and Genevieve over for dinner. We'll ask Tom also and whoever he's going out with at the time."

"Tom is a busy guy, but Genevieve and I will gladly come.

§

Todd looked at his wife as he hung up the phone with Roy. "So, you finally decided we are going to move to Manhattan."

"I was being selfish. With your new promotion, and your commute into the city and back every day, it only makes sense we move into Mom's apartment.

"But you were afraid the move would interrupt Harry's music studies."

"I was talking through my hat. Mom's apartment is a few blocks from Julliard. There are music teachers all over the city; the best ones are there. Mom set aside an ample amount of money for Harry's music education.

What about when he goes to high school?"

The apartment is a few blocks away from the High School for the Performing Arts; you know the one from the movie, *Fame*."

"We can put the house up for sale right away and move quickly. It will certainly be a lot easier commute."

"I'm sorry for not agreeing to move right away."

Todd went over to his wife and put his arms around her thin waist. "I love you."

§

Friday morning, Father Grant took the Brooklyn Queens Expressway to Brooklyn. The bishop expected him at eleven o'clock and Father wasn't taking any chances he'd be late. The traffic was light, and Father sat in the parking lot, after arriving thirty minutes early.

Father used the time to review the questions he planned to ask the bishop. The last two evenings he sat in his room at St. Pancras Rectory and thought of things he would need to begin the job.

Father knew he needed an assistant and hoped one was not already in place. He needed a person with a fresh outlook, not someone entrenched in the bureaucracy of the diocese.

§

On his way home from Brooklyn, Father wanted to stop the car and do a victory dance on the expressway. The bishop welcomed him with open arms. He agreed with Father that new blood was essential for ensuring this special program's success.

The bishop said," I am assigning you a private secretary. She knows everything there is to know about my office."

Father's heart fell. He tried to get the strength to object when the bishop continued, "But you have complete freedom to choose your assistant to help you do the job."

Father knew who he needed to help, especially in the areas the bishop expected him to succeed. "Your Excellency, thank you, and I have just the person for the job. He is only twenty- two, but he's wise beyond his years. I have a great relationship with him, and he is intimately aware of the LGBTQ community and its needs. His name is Randy Foster, the brother of my close friend and fellow school board member."

"It's your office, and you have my blessing to hire whomever you want. One more thing, you are going to need someone to keep track of your expenses and the program's expenses. Do you know someone you can trust to do that job?"

Father Grant smiled knowingly and said, "As a matter of fact I do. Her name is Esther Portnoy. She and I have worked on the inter-faith council in my school district for many years. She is a topnotch book-keeper and I happen to know she is available."

"That's fine. That position can be done from home to save valuable office space, but I would like you to get started right away. I would like you to move to a Rectory close to my office. Take your time in relocating, but don't take your time starting your job here. Try to start by next week.

"If it's possible it could take a year before I move to a closer Rectory."

The bishop looked curiously at his priest. Father told the bishop what had happened recently on his school board. Father explained, "I'm the only one the new board members can count on for guidance. The new members, all five of them, need my help for a few months to acclimate to their new responsibilities."

"No problem. I plan to have you by my side for many years. I applaud your loyalty to your community."

"Thank you for understanding," said Father.

"But make sure you're here bright and early next week, Father. We have a lot of work to do."

The bishop didn't mention the phone call a month ago from Mrs. Mc Murray whom the Bishop knew well through her old boss, J.P. Sanford. Nor did he volunteer the diocese received a substantial dona-tion for a special program Mary wanted to be implemented.

The bishop also didn't share Mary's suggestion Father Grant would be the perfect person to head these new programs.

CHAPTER 29

MARY MCMURRAY'S ESTATE ATTORNEYS SPECIALLY CARED FOR her. The first time Mary came in their door, they saw a person who was decisive. Mary knew what she wanted and would pay for the quality work they provided their clients. She was clear in whom she wanted her estate to benefit.

Mary gave the attorneys a list of charities she wanted to receive money.

Mary gave a list of individuals she wished to grace with bequests. Ellen and Todd would receive the bulk of her estate, and Mary explained to her daughter, Ellen, she expected Todd and her to make sure there was money left over for Harry.

Mary felt Ellen and Todd were responsible for Harry's rearing and she didn't want money to interfere with their task. Mary McMurray left a trust for Harry's education which would cover all possible expenses. Her estate lawyers would administer the trust.

Mary left money to the deskman, Jose, for his two children. Jose's local neighborhood schools were not the best, but with her gift, the children could attend private schools. Mary left ten thousand dollars to the two elevator operators for enough wine to last for a while and two thousand dollars to the other thirty-two workers who made Mary's daily life easier through their kindness.

Mrs. McMurray's last notable gift of a million dollars was a donation to the Campaign to Elect Thomas Foster to Public Office. Mary left out the specific office to allow any campaign to be flexible. Her estate attorneys would take care of the technicalities as they arose.

§

"No one can replace Mary McMurray on this school board, but I feel she would be pleased I nominate Bunny Krouse-Fontaine to fill the vacancy our dear Mary left."

Tom held back tears, and Jeremy came to his rescue and finished for Tom. "Bunny has been involved in this district for many years. She has served as PTA president and has been on every committee this district ever had. Bunny has shown her determination to fight for all the children of the district, and I would ask the new chairman, Roy Baker, to call the roll.

Roy wasted no time making sure Bunny was on the board.

EPILOGUE

ELLEN, TODD, AND HARRY WALKED INTO THE LOBBY OF THEIR new home on Central Park South to a loud round of applause from a usually formal staff. Ellen knew the applause was not for them, but for her mother.

"We're all so happy you're here," said the doorman. The deskman and the elevator operators echoed the same greeting and added, "We miss your mom a lot." Ellen winked and said, "Especially on Saturday nights." Those that heard Ellen laughed loudly. Ellen leaned over to the deskman, "Tell the elevator operators, I intend to continue the Saturday night tradition."

The President of the co-op took out a piece of paper and said in a loud voice, "May I have everyone's attention. On behalf of all your mother's friends and neighbors in the building, we would like to offer our condolences on her passing. Mary was a great friend who helped me many times in my role as president of the tenants association. We will all miss her a great deal.

The president wiped a tear from his eye. "Mary wouldn't like it if I said another word. So, I'll welcome you to the building, Ellen, Todd, and Harry. May you give us even half the joy Mary did."

There was no formality in the roar of applause echoing off the marble walls of 300 Central Park South.

§

Tom and Jeremy walked down Main Street happy with their decision to resign from the school board simultaneously. Both young men were headed to new pastures. "Timing is everything in life," waxed Jeremy.

"Agreed," said Tom. "You have to know when it's time to leave. If you don't, it's like staying in high school one more year after you graduated. No matter how much you loved your school, it feels weird. I wish I could have given more notice before leaving."

"You had no choice, Tom. You can't be on the ballot for Congress and be on the school board at the same time. Do you realize you'll be the youngest congressman in the United States House of Representatives? You barely made the age requirement of twenty-five."

"That's if I win in November."

"You're the only one on the ballot."

"No, there are two other candidates."

"Sure, they're on the ballot, but no one ever heard of their parties. You have the endorsement of the two major parties."

"Thanks to Mary," said Tom. "She worked behind my back for the past year, talking me up to all the politicians in the county. Mary knew there was no one to replace old Jim Ryan. No one knew for sure when he would retire, but it was obvious it would be soon."

Jeremy joked, "Ryan held the seat for the past fifty years. Mary knew he couldn't go on forever. Mary told me she'd been contributing big bucks to both parties on your behalf and when old Jim mentioned retirement, Mary came through with more money."

"On top of it, when Ryan's kids found out you were the son of Alice Jennings Foster, they got behind you. All of Ryan's kids remembered your mother from grade school and said they liked her."

"My mom went to her Junior Prom with one of Ryan's sons."

"It's kind of sad," said Jeremy. "He waited until people considered him a joke. Ryan did some good things during his career down in Washington, but by the time he left, I heard his aides had to lead him by the hand into the House, sit him down and prop him up. His enemies joked about his hair, saying it was prematurely orange. "

Tom quipped, "Timing. You have to know when it's time to leave. I hope both of us know when it's time to hang up our cleats."

"I'm glad I resigned by mail and didn't wait to do it at a public meeting."

"Me, too. This way it allows the board to vote on our replacements without regard to whom we might want. This way, it will be fair. We'll have no say in who gets our seats."

"That's the way it should be, but I wonder whom the board will choose."

"I hear one of the choices is Reverend Jonas Thompson," said Tom.

"And I hear the other is Alice Jennings Foster," grinned Jeremy.

The two friends looked at each other and erupted into howls of laughter."

People on the street laughed with them, not even knowing what was so funny.

The two friends continued down the street enjoying each other's company.

"This story would make a great screenplay," said Jeremy

"You're the writer, Jeremy."

"Let's do it," said Jeremy

"Okay, we'll do it."

"The screenplay will be the best," encouraged Tom. "Our final collaboration."

Jeremey looked at Tom sadly and said, "Seriously?"

Tom realized what Jeremy was feeling. "I mean for a while."

Jeremy's face brightened and said, "You had me worried for a second."

"Jeremy, we will always be brothers, and we will always be there for each other."

Both men changed the subject before they became any more emotional. Jeremy continued, "It's a little premature, but I have the actors in mind to play most of the characters."

"Me, too."

"For Mary, I say we cast the actress nominated every year for something. She's perfect for Mary. She's the one who played a nun in the film about priest abuse."

"It's who I had in mind, exactly."

"Let's go down to Starbucks, the one on Main Street. We'll sit there until we have the whole cast for the film."

"Great idea, after all, wasn't Starbucks where our first collaboration began?

Tom and Jeremy each fist bumped and took off down the street.

THE END

AUTHORS' BIOGRAPHY

John J. Dunn is a former educator and school board member. John is a practicing attorney and writer.

He and his wife, Marylyn, live in New York and have two grown children.

Made in the USA
Columbia, SC
30 November 2018